Rau

Born in a village in Maharashtra's Satara district, N.S. Inamdar (1923–2002) was one of India's foremost Marathi novelists, with a writing career spanning over five decades. He is the author of sixteen historical novels and an autobiography.

Vikrant Pande has translated Ranjit Desai's *Raja Ravi Varma*, Milind Bokil's *Shala* and N.S. Inamdar's *Shahenshah*. He has worked for over twenty-five years with various multinational companies and is currently heading TeamLease Skills University at Vadodara.

RAU

THE GREAT LOVE STORY OF BAJIRAO MASTANI

N.S. INAMDAR

Translated by
Vikrant Pande

PAN

First published in English 2016 by Pan
an imprint of Pan Macmillan India
a division of Macmillan Publishers India Private Limited
Pan Macmillan India, 707, Kailash Building
26, K.G. Marg, New Delhi – 110 001
www.panmacmillan.co.in

Pan Macmillan, 20 New Wharf Road, London N1 9RR
Basingstoke and Oxford
Associated companies throughout the world
www.panmacmillan.com

ISBN 978-93-82616-80-1

First published in Marathi as *Raau* by Continental Prakashan, Pune, 1972

Copyright © Subhashchandra G. Arole, Avanti Subhashchandra Arole,
Aditya Subhashchandra Arole 1972, 2016
Translation copyright © Vikrant Pande and Subhashchandra G. Arole,
Avanti Subhashchandra Arole, Aditya Subhashchandra Arole 2016

All rights reserved. No part of this publication may be reproduced, stored in or introduced into a retrieval system, or transmitted, in any form, or by any means (electronic, mechanical, photocopying, recording or otherwise) without the prior written permission of the publisher. Any person who does any unauthorized act in relation to this publication may be liable to criminal prosecution and civil claims for damages.

1 3 5 7 9 8 6 4 2

This book is sold subject to the condition that it shall not, by way of trade or otherwise, be lent, re-sold, hired out, or otherwise circulated without the publisher's prior consent in any form of binding or cover other than that in which it is published and without a similar condition including this condition being imposed on the subsequent purchaser.

Typeset by R. Ajith Kumar, New Delhi
Printed and bound in India by
Replika Press Pvt. Ltd.

ONE

Shanivar wada was overflowing with guests. The haveli stood as a symbol of the power the Peshwa enjoyed in Pune. The celebrations continued for nearly a week. Each invitee, from Chhatrapati Shahu Maharaj down to the lowliest soldier in the cavalry, had come bearing gifts as a token of appreciation. The enemy camps, defeated in battle, offered a hand of friendship by sending in their clerks as representatives. The Nizam too had sent his personal secretary to ensure that he was well represented.

Meanwhile, Bajirao Peshwa and his younger brother, Chimaji Appa, were in Gujarat on a campaign against the Dabhades and were not present for the *vaastu shanti* ceremony of their newly built haveli. The Peshwa's son, Chiranjeev Nanasaheb, showered personal attention on all the guests.

Kashibai, Bajirao's wife, decked in an embroidered sari, with exquisite jewellery adding an allure to her fair complexion, hurried from one room to another playing the role of a perfect hostess. Her maid, Yesu, ever alert, rushed to fan her every time she noticed a drop of sweat trickle down her mistress' aquiline nose.

Returning from a darshan at the Ganesha temple in the afternoon, Kashibai decided to rest a little. She warned Yesu, 'Let there be no disturbance for a while. Don't allow anyone in. Except, of course,' she added, after a pause, 'Sasubai and Chiranjeev.'

Kashibai arched her eyebrows enquiringly on not getting the usual nod from Yesu.

'Is that understood?'

'Ji, Baisaheb ... there was something...'

Seeing Yesu hesitate, Kashibai asked, a little irritated, 'What is it?'

'May I say something?'

Kashibai did not answer. Her silence was an implicit approval for Yesu to continue.

Having got her mistress' attention, Yesu said, 'It has been four days since a lady, who claims to be from Saswad, waits to seek an appointment with you. If you permit, I shall show her in.'

'Who is she? Ask her to meet the office staff or let Chiranjeev see her. We have donated a lot. One more beneficiary won't hurt.'

'She does not seem to be here for alms. She insists on meeting you.'

'What did you say her name was?'

'Bhanumati. She says she is the wife of Gopalbhat Atre.'

'Bhanumati? Bhanu!'

Kashibai sat up with a start. The name evoked memories of years long gone by.

When she had come to Saswad as a newly-wedded young girl, Kashibai's mother-in-law had arranged for a few Brahman girls to be her playmates. Bhanu was one of those whom

Kashibai never forgot. Dark-skinned, short and stout, Bhanu was one who never respected authority and would often pick a fight with Kashibai. She wondered how Bhanu looked now.

It had been ages! Childhood had vanished and so had childhood friends, who now maintained a respectful distance. The haveli at Saswad was too small to contain the ever-growing esteem of the Peshwa. Annexing territories at a rapid pace, he had amassed wealth and power in a very short period of time. And she was, after all, Bajirao Peshwa's wife. The very thought made Kashibai glow with pride.

'Shall I send her in?' Yesu interrupted her thoughts.

Kashibai could not believe her eyes. Was she the same Bhanu who, pulling her skirt above her knees, would not hesitate to playfully drench Kashibai with water? Gone were the green bangles which adorned her arms right up to the elbows. She looked weak and bent with age, her face gaunt. She reminded Kashibai of a tree whose sap had dried. She had wrapped herself in the reddish-brown sari worn by widows and, despite the effort to cover, the shaven head was evident.

A shiver went down Kashibai's spine. She blurted out, 'Is that you, Bhanu?'

'Yes.'

'Look at your state! I had no idea...'

'It is better that way. In any case, this is not the time to talk of such things. You have been busy with the havan, feeding of the Brahmans and the chanting of the mantras. It is a proud moment for Shrimant to have built this fine haveli.'

Kashibai's alert ears picked up the sarcasm couched in her praise. When they were children, Bhanu had had a habit of laughing while teasing Kashibai. She now seemed to be teasing again while maintaining an outwardly civil appearance. Kashibai noticed Bhanu clutching a small wooden box wrapped in red cloth. Many ladies had insisted on handing over gifts personally to her. Maybe this childhood friend too had something to offer.

'I hope it was not difficult for you to recognize me,' Bhanu said, adjusting the cloth over her head.

'I was stumped for a brief moment. But your voice gave you away. It is just the same! You remember the days when we used to play in the haveli at Saswad?'

'I am grateful Baisaheb remembers the good old days.'

Kashibai smiled. 'How can I forget? Please sit down. Make yourself comfortable.'

Sitting on the floor at the edge of the carpet, Bhanu said, 'I have been waiting for the past four days to seek your audience. But who has the time to listen to a widow? I had to push my way through to meet you.'

'Is that so?' Kashibai asked. 'I need to instruct the office. This is not the right way to treat guests.'

'There is no need to trouble yourself for an ordinary widow like me. The Peshwa has moved to a royal palace now. I have been witnessing the glamour and respect this haveli attracts. Not to mention the sprawling gardens, elephants, stables filled with horses, hundreds of servants at your beck and call, and what have you! The Peshwa has been lucky. It is only people like me who...' She could not continue as a sob escaped her lips. She dabbed her eyes with the edge of her pallu.

Such scenes were common for Kashibai. Chiranjeev had been instructed to ensure no one returned empty-handed. She said, 'Bai, there is very little we can do against what fate has in store for us. I will instruct the office to...'

'Baisaheb, I have not come here to ask for anything,' Bhanu

interrupted, wiping her tears. 'In fact, I have come here to give you something.'

She placed the box on the carpet.

Out of habit, Kashibai stretched out her right hand to signify her acceptance.

'Wait!' Bhanu said. 'Do you not want to know what is inside?'

'I am happy to receive whatever you give with love and affection. I don't need to know what is in it beforehand.'

Bhanu said, 'I am sure the function was carried out in a grand manner. I can imagine the waters of the Ganga and Yamuna being sprinkled to purify everything. The grandeur of the Peshwas cannot be complete unless there is an accompanying pomp and show of elephants, horses and camels. It would thus be appropriate that you have a look at the contents of the box before accepting it.'

'As you wish; tell me.'

'The box contains ashes; those of my deceased husband.'

'What? Have you lost your mind? Bringing ashes on such an auspicious day?'

'The way the Peshwa is behaving, it won't be long before I go mad.'

'Are you joking with me?'

'Fate has played a joke on me. It is ironic that the person who was my childhood companion should have her husband committing...'

'Don't forget propriety, Bhanu,' Kashibai interrupted, her voice taking on an edge. 'The person you are referring to as my husband is the owner of this haveli and people call him Shrimant Peshwa. If you cannot maintain decorum, I will have to end this meeting right away.'

There was a stunned silence for a moment as both women assessed each other. Bhanumati then said, her head bent low, 'Please forgive me. I have transgressed. Please do accept my gift.'

'What has the Peshwa done to you? What joke are you talking of? I want to know what's compelling you to insult me on a day like this.'

'I am merely a Brahman's wife. We have neither power nor money. Who is there to listen to our woes?'

'Please continue...'

'Will you believe me if I tell you that my husband was killed because of the actions of the Peshwa?'

'I am surprised to hear this. I wasn't aware of it. The Atres are not our enemies. They are as close to us as the Purandares. I have not heard of the Peshwa being against the Atres.'

'One does not have to be an enemy to get killed.'

'Don't speak in circles. Please explain.'

'For ages, we have been the *vatandars* of the Saswad region but the Peshwa decided to side with the Purandares and, in the process, denied us our hereditary rights. One fine day, from landlords we became paupers. We were left with nothing.'

'I am not interested in official matters. I don't involve myself in politics.'

'But it is such politics that led to the death of my husband. He was unable to bear the insult and killed himself. I was widowed and left to fend for myself. The Peshwa is enjoying the heights of glory. Let these ashes be a reminder of the crimes committed. I am sure the curse of this hapless widow will not go to waste. I take your leave. Goodbye!'

Bhanu turned abruptly and left without looking back.

The small wooden box lay on the carpet untouched.

For a long time after Bhanu left, Kashibai sat with her chin resting on her palm, lost in thought.

She got up with a sigh when the servant came in to light the lamps. She said, pointing to the box, 'Take this away. And if Chiranjeev has performed his evening prayers, ask him to meet me.'

Kashibai's newly-wed daughter-in-law, Gopika, daughter of Bhikaji Naik Raste, came in first and, bending down, touched her feet. Kashibai laid her hand on Gopika's head and blessed her saying, *'Ayushmaan bhava.'*

The girl stood for a moment and then left without saying a word.

Chiranjeev Nanasaheb entered as soon as she left.

Chiranjeev's fair skin glowed in the light of the chandeliers. He was eleven years old but was already growing into a well-built youth with his father's shoulders and arms. His sharp nose was again a distinct reminder of his father, though he had his mother's face. Kashibai enjoyed looking at her son and comparing such features.

He wore a dhoti with an embroidered border. A gold chain adorned his chest. A satin *angavastram* completed the attire. Nanasaheb touched his mother's feet. She ruffled his hair affectionately and said, 'I hope you have looked into the pending official matters.'

'They are unending, thanks to Rau's campaign. There are hundreds of things to do. But I got your message and came immediately.'

Kashibai longed for his company. Ever since he had started showing interest in official duties, he spent time away from home at the Chhatrapati's court in Satara. Even back home in Pune, he would be involved in some duty or the other.

'Isn't the campaign against our own people this time?'

'Well, it depends on how you look at it: enemy or our own people.'

'It seems it has become your habit to use such diplomatic language,' Kashibai observed.

'I may have said that inadvertently. Everyone, including Shahu Maharaj, was confused. No one believed that our Senapati Dabhade would side with the Nizam. When things became clearer, the Chhatrapati had no choice but to allow us to attack our erstwhile ally. We can win over the Dabhades, but I am not sure of Umabai…'

Kashibai smiled. 'I am surprised that the Peshwa's son considers a woman a threat.'

'We do not doubt our capabilities. We have routed the Rohillas. Even the Rajputs were shown the door. The mighty Mughals have had to retreat many times as well, but this is different. We cannot be sure what this woman will do. She has vowed to take revenge.'

'I don't get to hear of these things. But I was told Umabai and her son have now taken up arms against us.'

'You will be surprised to hear the vow she has taken.'

'What is it?'

'She has vowed to fight till the end.'

It was the twilight hour. One could hear the changing of guards. There was a flurry of activity outside, penetrating the silence of the room.

Kashibai had heard such threats often. Despite that, a shiver ran down her spine. She was silent for a while. Chiranjeev, noticing his mother's discomfort, said, 'There is no need to worry. Tirtharoop is safe. My Kaka is there with him. We are sure to win. I have received a message from Kaka.'

'I hope Swami is fine.'

'He has been enquiring about the vaastu shanti ceremony.'

'Oh, I see.' Kashibai was happy to know that he had remembered her in the midst of a campaign.

'I have been asked to give a detailed reply on how we took care of the guests. Ambaji Pant Purandare too was surprised to find Rau so involved. Remember, when I got married last year, we had invited a group of dancers from across the Narmada region? They had enjoyed a lot of benevolence thanks to Rau. I have been asked to ensure they are taken care of this time too.'

'I am surprised he remembers all this.'

'Yes, that too when he is busy leading the campaign against the Badshah. By the way, Kaka has sent in his enquiries.'

'What does Bhauji say?'

'He says he has prayed to Lord Balaji to make the event a grand success.'

'What does he write about himself?'

'Does Kaka ever write anything about his own self? He rarely replies to my queries about his health.'

'I really admire your Kaka. His wife died in childbirth leaving behind an infant to be taken care of. Yet, all he can think of is to follow his elder brother like a shadow. Don't forget to send him my blessings.'

'I will. But what was the reason for which you wanted to speak to me so urgently?'

Chiranjeev looked at his mother. He had not had time in the last one year to sit with her and talk at leisure. Ever since his marriage last year, he had been busy in the court at Satara. Then, on returning to Pune, he had been entrusted with the work in the office and had rarely got a chance to meet her in private. He remembered his younger days when he could cajole and complain, and take liberties with her. He used to lovingly call her Tai.

Kashibai picked up a small silver box lying on a tripod. Taking a few cardamom pods from it, she put them in his palm and said, 'I want you to send Rau a little sacred ash from the temple's sanctum sanctorum. Ask him to tie it into his amulet and wear it in his armband. It will protect him from harm.'

Chiranjeev could not hide his smile. He said, 'Rau Swami will laugh at my suggestion. He will...'

'Let him say whatever he has to. You men have no understanding of the woman's mind.' Two large teardrops glided down Kashibai's cheeks.

Nanasaheb was disturbed seeing his mother in tears. He said, 'Tai! Tai! Don't cry. I had blurted out in jest. Of course I will write as you command. Please don't get upset.'

'Nana! What shall I say? I am so happy to hear you call me Tai. Why should I be angry at you? But I am saddened when I realize you don't understand our traumas. You were a child a few days back, hovering around me, calling me Tai and cajoling me for everything. But how fast you have grown! You are married and now you formally address me as Matushree and I call you Nanasaheb! But that is the law of nature. The mind understands but the heart is unwilling to accept. This timid girl is now addressed as Kashibai sahiba by everyone. I am lucky to have an obedient son and a dutiful brother-in-law. I should be happy. Anyway, let that be. I hope you will follow my instructions.'

'Your wish is my command. I will write to Rau Swami

personally and I will plead with him. But I don't want you to cry any more.'

Kashibai wiped her tears saying, 'I don't want to hold you back. You have a lot of pending work.'

Nanasaheb did not get up. He rubbed his palms and fiddled around not knowing how to broach the topic. He said, 'I know the turmoil Matushree is going through today.'

'How do you know?'

'I saw the lady who had come from Saswad to meet you.'

'How did you come to know of it?'

'It is my duty to know what happens here!'

Radhabai, Bajirao Peshwa's mother, arrived at the haveli a fortnight after the celebrations. Despite being in her sixties, she walked with a straight spine. The grey eyes added to the charm and beauty of her fair Chitpavan Brahman complexion.

Her palanquin stopped at the courtyard facing the main gate. Ignoring the helping hand of a maid, she stepped out to survey the newly built haveli. Her eyes had the look of a woman who was used to hearing tales of valour of her two sons, having lost her husband a decade ago.

Ambaji Pant stepped forward. Accepting his namaskar, she said, 'Pant, I don't see the outpost for the flag constructed yet.'

'We expect the flag to be hoisted soon; within a few weeks at the most.'

'That's good. I want Rau, when he returns from his campaign, to be able to see the flag even before he enters Pune.'

She stepped inside and moved towards her quarters. She bowed in obeisance at the temple at the entrance, accepting the holy water in her palm from the priest, Krishna Bhat Karve. Sitting down on a low stool, she said, 'Pant, I hope you took good care of Paramhans Brahmendra Swami of Dhawadshi.'

Ambaji Pant Purandare was responsible for the affairs of the treasury at Satara. He was aware of Radhabai's devotion to the Swami there.

'We followed all the instructions properly.'

'He has sent his blessings to Rau. I hope they have been conveyed.'

'Yes. Nanasaheb and I were personally involved to ensure that Swamiji received all the benevolence as per Rau's instructions.'

'What was the donation?'

'It was adequate and as per protocol. Matushree need not be worried.'

'Pant, please be specific.'

Ambaji was expecting that. It was difficult to stand in the line of fire of questioning from Matushree. He glanced in the direction of the office to see Nanasaheb busy with paperwork. He had no choice but to answer her.

He said, 'We presented jewels and silk dresses for the temple at Bhargavram, while Brahmendra Swami was given a beautifully embroidered silk shawl.'

'And what about the temple at Bhuleshwar?'

'We discussed the request made by Matushree. We…'

'So you haven't given anything yet?'

'It was decided that we would consult Shrimant on his return and then take further action.'

'Who decided this?'

'Chiranjeev Nanasaheb and I. Shrimant had given us the responsibility before leaving for his campaign.'

Radhabai did not respond. But her discomfort was evident.

Not wanting to say anything to Pant, she kept quiet. Since the death of her husband ten years ago, her wishes had always been fulfilled by her sons, even when it came to matters of the treasury. Quite evidently, things had changed. She raised the topic when Nanasaheb came to pay his regards.

'Chiranjeev, it seems you have taken up the task of managing the treasury these days,' she said as she blessed her grandson.

Nanasaheb stood with his back against a beautifully carved pillar. He said with his head bent low, 'Your wish is my command. Please pardon me if I have slipped anywhere inadvertently.'

'My wish may have been the command earlier but it seems Rau has entrusted his faith in you than me these days.'

Nanasaheb's voice was filled with anguish. 'I am but a mere child. If I have made a mistake, please guide me.'

'If that be the case, why do you need instructions from Rau when I had conveyed my wishes?'

'I suppose Matushree is talking of the donation to Brahmendra Swami.'

'Yes. After all blessings from such realized souls will only add to our wealth. Rajarshi Chhatrapati Maharaj himself considers it his good fortune to be at the feet of Swamiji. I had merely requested for a village to be donated to him. Does that require such consultations? Why do you need to deliberate so much over such a small request?'

'It is under the purview of the treasury…'

A small spark was enough for her to erupt in anger.

'I have been aware of the affairs of the treasury even before you were born. Don't teach me its functioning.'

Nanasaheb fell silent. Ambaji Pant came to his rescue.

'It is not Chiranjeev's fault. It was I who had suggested we wait for Rau Swami's return. You know he too has a lot of faith in Paramhans. I felt it would be a nice gesture if Rau himself could make the donation. He is busy with the campaign right now. Chiranjeev would not have delayed your wish otherwise.'

Radhabai knew Pant well enough to know he was protecting Chiranjeev. Pant had served the Peshwas since the beginning. She smiled and said, 'After all my suggestion too is for Rau's welfare, isn't it? I know he is busy right now. I am told Umabai herself is planning to enter the battlefield with her son. Isn't it quite natural that in such times I want the blessings of saints to protect my son?'

'I appreciate your sentiments, Matushree,' Pant said, a little relieved. 'I will ensure that the benevolence reaches the Bhuleshwar temple the moment the campaign is over. May I take the liberty to ask you something?'

'Please. You don't need my permission. I may have spoken harshly without meaning to. We have known each other for years now.'

The servants arranged for two low stools on which Nanasaheb and Ambaji sat down. Pant, fiddling with the edge of his angavastram, cleared his throat and said, 'I wanted to talk about Chimnaji Pant.'

'Appa? What about him?' Chimaji Appa was often called Chimnaji Appa.

'His wife passed away six months back leaving an infant behind. I suggest…'

It was a topic which was uppermost in Radhabai's mind. Chimaji Appa had been widowed at the young age of twenty-three. He had been trying to forget his sorrow by throwing himself into work and giving a helping hand to his elder brother in all matters of state. He would often talk of retiring. Matushree was worried.

'Are you suggesting he gets married again?' She tried to avoid showing her anxiety. 'I was planning to talk about it the moment they return from the campaign.'

'I hope Matushree is able to convince him. He has to find a way to forget his sorrows though I doubt he will agree to marry again.'

'Why do you say that?'

'You must be aware of what happened when they were about to leave for the campaign. When I recounted this to Shahu Maharaj, he was very upset and wanted me to inform you.'

'What are you talking of? I have no idea.'

Ambaji Pant did not reply immediately. It was the hour of dusk, the time to light the lamps. He did not feel it right to narrate something unpleasant at this hour. Turning to Nanasaheb, he said, 'I suggest you tell Matushree.'

Nanasaheb glanced at the idol of Narayan in the temple. It looked grim in the light of the lamps. He gazed at the idol for a while before saying, 'I suppose Matushree may be aware but let me recount. The day when Rau Swami was preparing to leave for the campaign, Kaka's mother-in-law came over with young Sadashiv Pant in her arms. She appealed to his duties as a father to stay back for the sake of the child. Instead, he said, "I am, after all, a servant of Shahu Maharaj. How can I stay back when the job demands my presence? It is my duty. And I would be most happy if my son or I were to sacrifice our lives for the same. That would be our redemption."'

'I can't believe it! But I know. He does not consider anything to be more important than serving the cause and helping his brother achieve it. Pant, as an elder, you need to take the responsibility to drill some sense into him.'

'I am at your service.'

Winter was gradually receding, signalling warm days ahead but the cold lingered in the gardens at Kothrud making the shade under the trees a pleasant place to relax.

A little distance from the Mrityunjay temple stood a small but elegant building which the Peshwas used for overnight stays whenever they visited that side of the town. It was currently occupied by the *kalavants*, the singers and entertainers who enjoyed the patronage of the current Peshwa.

A small fountain spluttered nearby, the wind turning the water into a fine spray. Basanti, the maid, sat at the edge of the fountain admiring the building. Her mistress, Baiji, would normally come out at this time and sit there humming to herself. But today was a busy day. The imam had announced the sighting of the moon the previous night and Ramzan Eid had been declared. The mini haveli was busy entertaining visitors.

Basanti glanced at the entrance of the haveli. The palanquin bearers were waiting patiently for Baiji to leave for the mosque to read her namaz.

A few poor people had gathered at the edge of the gardens in anticipation of the charity traditionally distributed on the occasion of Eid. The crowd parted giving way to a procession of a few servants who walked towards the haveli holding trays covered with cloth. Chanda, the jamdar, led the group sitting astride a horse.

Chanda dismounted near the fountain and touched his right hand three times to his forehead as he wished *adaab arz* to Basanti. A smile played on his lips. 'Eid Mubarak, Basanti! Eid Mubarak!'

'Mubarak! Eid Mubarak!' she replied. Looking at the trays carried by the servants, she asked, 'Jamdar, is that the *khairaat* for Baiji?'

'Khairaat? Does the Shrimant have time to distribute largesse when he is busy with the campaign? This festival is not even celebrated in the haveli.'

'Then what are the trays for? I asked as it is Eid today,' Basanti said, covering her face partially with her dupatta.

'Shrimant has sent a special gift for the singers; for Mastanibai.'

'Oh, you mean Baiji? So it *is* khairaat. After all, it is her festival today, the day of Eid. It seems she has not been forgotten despite Shrimant being busy in his campaigns or whatever. I hope you understand.'

'I am not a dunce to not understand, Basanti. Put these trays in her private quarters and relieve us. We have other important tasks at hand.'

'Oh, I see. I was not aware that despite the Shrimant being out of Pune, the jamdar at the haveli has enough tasks to keep him busy.' Basanti was enjoying teasing and flirting with Chanda.

Chanda too was enjoying the conversation. He glanced at her face, visible through the diaphanous dupatta. He was about to retort when a hoarse voice from the building interrupted their conversation. 'Basanti! Basanti! Where are you?'

It was Raghu, the cross-dresser. Seeing her sitting at the fountain, he skipped down the steps.

'So here you are, chatting with this jamadar. Baiji is searching for you all over the place.'

'It is *jamdar* and not jamadar. Chanda Jamdar.' Chanda stressed on the words for effect. 'You seem to have forgotten me.'

'He is a very distinguished official and has lots of other important jobs to do. Is that clear?' Basanti's voice lacked conviction as she continued with her charade. 'Help him to put the trays in Baiji's private quarters and relieve him at the earliest.'

'Jamdar, how can I afford to forget you? Come with me. I will guide you and your men.'

Chanda did not move. Instead, he asked his men to follow Raghu.

When they were out of earshot, Basanti said, 'Jamdar, you may wait here. Raghu will take care of the things. I have to excuse myself. Even a mere maid like me has things to do.'

She had barely taken a few steps when she stopped. She went back and plucking a white lotus from the fountain, she handed it to Chanda saying, 'It is the day of Eid. Please accept this as a gift from me. Eid Mubarak!' Then she turned abruptly and left before he could respond.

Chanda eyed her figure as she walked away from him. Touching his right palm to his forehead, he muttered, 'Eid Mubarak! Eid Mubarak!'

Chanda and his men left soon after.

After a while, Basanti ran down the steps and warned the palanquin bearers, 'Baiji is expected any moment. Hope you folks are ready.'

'I am coming down in a minute,' they heard a sweet voice from inside.

Within moments a slim, petite woman, covered from head to toe in a light blue satin cloak, walked down the steps. She wore shining red *mojadis* on her feet.

She had flicked back the gossamer veil before walking down the steps, but quickly covered her face as she got closer to the bearers waiting in attendance. Her large doe eyes observed the garden outside. The sounds of the conch and bells at the Mrityunjay temple in the garden announced that aarti was in progress. The golden spire of the temple gleamed in the evening sun.

The palanquin, swinging slightly, moved at a brisk pace towards the mosque. Basanti walked alongside, holding her mistress' mojadi sandals in her hand.

Meanwhile, Nanasaheb was busy writing to his father. 'Please don't worry about anything. All the functions went off as per plan. Today is Ramzan Eid. As per your instructions, your special gifts were sent across to Mastanibai at the haveli at Kothrud gardens.'

Radhabai's two daughters resided in Pune. The elder one, Bhiubai, was married to Abaji Naik of Baramati. He had an official residence at Pune. The younger, Anubai, was the wife of Vyankatrao Ghorpade of Ichalkaranji who was busy giving a helping hand with his cavalry in the campaign. Anubai preferred to spend time in Pune rather than at Ichalkaranji.

Radhabai liked to listen to the reading of the Bhagavata Purana each afternoon. She would often invite her daughters so that they could spend some time together.

Radhabai sat resting her back against large pillows while her daughters sat on either side. The reading was over and they were alone now.

'I have something to say,' Anubai said, adjusting her embroidered shawl on her shoulders.

Radhabai looked at her younger daughter. She resembled her elder brother a lot, both in looks as well as behaviour. She had the same enthusiasm and energy. No one would believe she was twenty. She looked like a teenager. These two children were the apple of Radhabai's eyes but she avoided giving them too much attention as it would hurt her other daughter. Bhiubai was almost twenty-five but had not yet been blessed with any children.

Anubai, seeing no response from her mother, said, 'If Matushree is not interested, I will keep quiet.'

'I know you can't hold back from speaking even if I were to tell you that I am not interested,' Radhabai teased her.

'Anu, don't you know Matushree is stressed these days?' Bhiubai came to her mother's rescue and held her hand affectionately.

'How am I to know? Would you care to elaborate?'

'Rau is on a campaign. That is enough to keep her worried all the time. After all, any campaign is fraught with dangers.'

'Rau is not alone. Appa is with him; and his sardars too. What is there to worry about?'

'One is always worried when near and dear ones are involved.'

'It is not for Matushree to worry alone. In case the Baramatkars don't know, let me remind you that the Ghorpades are there supporting Rau in person.'

Anubai did not realize that her words hurt her elder sister. Bhiubai felt humiliated and squeezed her mother's hand. She cried out, 'Matushreebai...'

Radhabai had to interrupt. She said, chastising her daughter, 'Anu! I am surprised you dared to insult your elder sister in my presence. I wonder how much you two fight when I am not around. Both of you are married to senior officials. You should know how to behave!'

'We maintain decorum as daughters-in-law,' Anu replied, ignoring her mother's reprimand. 'I don't see any need to do so in my mother's presence. Can't I take liberties with my Akka? She loves me dearly, after all!'

'Anu, it is not good to blow your own trumpet, boasting of your husband's participation in the campaign. Our elder son-in-law may not be fighting battles but you must know that armies don't run on empty stomachs. It is thanks to largesse provided by such landlords that the Peshwas are able to sustain their wars. We all have to be grateful to them.'

'That may be so. But Matushree, it is only thanks to sardars like ours that the sahukars are able to live. We provide patronage.'

Radhabai was amused by the friendly altercation between the two sisters. Then Anubai said, 'I have been delivered a letter by one of our messengers.'

'How is Rau?' Radhabai asked, a little excitedly.

'He is fine. He has selected a lovely white steed for his dear sister,' Anubai announced with pride in her voice.

'Oh, I see! What else does the letter state?'

'It is Rau's desire to see his sister astride this horse next time he leaves for a campaign…'

'Issh! What kind of desire is this? Do women go on campaigns? What do you have to say, Matushree?' Bhiubai glanced at her mother, not enamoured with the idea proposed by Rau.

'He must be pulling her leg,' Radhabai said. 'Haven't the Baramatkars received any letter?'

'No, instead Bhikaji came with a message.'

'Bhikaji?' Radhabai's voice rose sharply. She threw a quick glance at her daughters and then regained her composure.

The daughters had noticed the change in their mother's expression but did not react. Anubai was eager to say something but held back her words. Bhiubai, unable to contain her emotions, said, 'Matushree, now that we are discussing the subject, I wonder why Rau Swami sent Bhikaji when he knows we don't like him at all.'

Anubai, coming to her mother's defence, said, 'Don't you know Matushree is already under a lot of stress? Don't trouble her further.'

Radhabai waved her hand dismissing Anu's comment. 'Let it be, Anu. There is no point in telling Rau, but I will speak to Appa about this. If the Baramatkars don't like Bhikaji, I will ask Appa to post him elsewhere.'

Anubai interjected, 'I don't know whether the Baramatkars can take such a moral high ground.'

'It is not that sardars have not kept concubines for their pleasure. But I don't understand why Bhikaji, a child born out of such a relationship, should be given the high post of a *shiladar* by the Peshwa. He is a confidant. He delivers key messages and is part of their strategic discussions.'

Radhabai, unable to bear the arguments, stood up and moved towards the sanctum sanctorum of the small temple in her room. She stood facing the idol, tears flowing down her cheeks.

Both the sisters fell silent seeing their mother's reaction. Anubai put her hand on her mother's shoulder and said, 'Matushree, please pardon me. I should not have spoken.'

Bhiubai added, 'Matushreebai, please forget whatever we said.'

They insisted she move to the gardens outside. When they were seated near a bed of roses, Anubai asked, 'Are you still angry with us?'

Radhabai was silent for a while. She said, 'I am not angry

with you. I am angry with myself. If the man does not behave properly, it is the woman who has to take the blame. You are grown up now. I can speak freely. There is no point in hiding from you. Bhikaji is his child from the other...'

Anubai cupped her mother's mouth with her palm. She said, 'Please! You don't need to speak about this.'

Radhabai gently removed her daughter's hand and continued, 'I am telling you as this could happen to anyone. Our men are out on campaigns or shikar all the time. I remember it was during Rau's marriage; the elder Peshwa, Rau's father, had invited a lot of singers for the ceremony. She too was there. I was told she was a Rajput; later someone told me that her name was Mankunwar. In his last days, he spent most of his time with her. Bhikaji was born to her. In his dying moments, he handed over Bhikaji's responsibility to Rau. It is sad that he never mentioned to me...'

'Matushree!' Bhiubai began but checked herself.

Radhabai looked at her daughter. 'Please speak your mind. Don't hesitate.'

'Matushree, I remember Bhikaji's mother was present during Rau's marriage. A couple of years back, during Nanasaheb's wedding, Rau had invited a group of singers. I am told one of them is being hosted by Rau in the haveli near Kothrud gardens. I fear it may be the same story being repeated...'

'Don't be silly,' Radhabai chided her daughter. 'It must be just a coincidence. You are reading too much into it.'

No one spoke for a while.

It was evening and the golden rays of the dying sun illuminated the shrubs in the garden. Getting up, Radhabai said, 'It is time to light the lamps. Time and tide wait for none.

All we can do is to light the lamps and pray for the welfare of our loved ones.'

The Peshwa was busy fighting against the erstwhile commander, Dabhade, in Gujarat. The opponents matched each other in strength. Messengers would reach Pune daily with the latest news. Everyone waited with bated breath not knowing what the next news held in store.

It was a point of discussion in most of the households. All the youth were enrolled in the campaign and, quite naturally, everyone was concerned.

Nanasaheb and Ambaji Pant busied themselves in administrative matters, but could not take their ears away from the latest news.

The family members had assembled for the celebration of the birth of Lord Maruti. After the celebrations, Radhabai asked Kashibai to stay back for a while. Kashibai understood that her mother-in-law wanted to speak to her in private.

When they were alone, Radhabai said, 'Please sit. I need some advice from you on an important matter.'

Kashibai looked at her mother-in-law in surprise. She could not remember the last time she had been asked for advice. She wondered what the issue was.

'Rau has built this wonderful haveli. You are now the host and the proud owner. You should ensure you don't forget protocol,' Radhabai said, her voice a little harsh.

Kashibai was taken aback at such a direct affront. She was unable to recall any behaviour of hers which could have been construed as questionable. But she thought it wise to not react.

Radhabai continued, 'I may or may not be there tomorrow. My days are numbered. You have to carry the traditions forward. You were under my direct observation till this haveli was built. But I have been noticing a change in your behaviour ever since you moved in here.'

'Please let me know if I have erred,' Kashibai mumbled.

'There is a certain protocol a Peshwa's wife needs to follow; whom to speak to and whom not to.'

'I would be grateful if you can explain with some examples. Who else, other than you, will guide me?'

'Don't think you can trap me with such sweet words,' Radhabai erupted. 'Examples are of use when you don't know. Nana and you feel that there is no need for my advice any more, isn't it?'

Tears were threatening to flow down Kashibai's cheeks. She pursed her lips and stood there, her head bowed low. A few silent moments passed. Radhabai picked up a fan lying on a low stool and fanning herself said, 'I am told that one Bhanumati from Saswad met you a few days back. Is that true?'

Kashibai was relieved. So the matter was related to people meeting her without explicit permission from her mother-in-law. She said, letting out a deep sigh, 'Yes, it is true. The security had been a little lax during the ceremonies and she was able to reach me directly. I had not invited her but...'

'Isn't she a childhood friend of yours?'

'She was my playmate at Saswad as per your instructions then.'

'You were a child then. It is our duty as Peshwas to take care of the poor and help them monetarily, if need be. But you cannot allow someone to take advantage of them having been your childhood friend. You need to ensure you keep commoners at bay.'

'I made a mistake. Please pardon me. I will not allow this to happen again.'

Radhabai was not one to be satisfied with such apologies. She had taken up this matter to probe Kashibai's mental state. It was not this issue which was uppermost in her mind.

Kashibai stood there in her lovely green embroidered sari which matched the colour of the bangles on her arms. A necklace of large emeralds complemented the mangalsutra. Drops of sweat gathered at her forehead. Her delicate lips were dry.

Radhabai asked her next question as she trained her grey eyes on Kashibai. 'I am told you have given permission for an *abhishek* to be performed at the Mrityunjay temple at Kothrud. Is that true?'

'Yes, that is true. Please pardon me if I have made a mistake. The priest there had sent a formal request through our main priest, Krishna Bhat Karve.'

'No one needs permission to perform such a puja. I wonder why the priest had to send in a formal request.'

'That is because the person performing the puja is not a Hindu. I am told it is a Muslim lady wanting to pay her obeisance. That is the reason the priest asked for prior permission.'

'Did you give the permission?'

'Yes. I thought it was not right to refuse someone wanting to pray at the temple.'

'I don't understand the reason for the person wanting to conduct the abhishek. Did you not enquire?'

'Yes. I was told it was for the welfare of Rau Swami. It was to pray for his good health.'

'Are you not concerned for his well-being?'

'Is that a question to ask? Of course I am very much concerned.'

'Did you not find it odd that some Muslim lady is performing the puja, while you and I are doing nothing? Did you not bother to think that the welfare of the Peshwa should primarily be our concern and not that of a dancer who survives on the crumbs thrown by the Peshwa? As a matter of protocol, I used to ensure that all the temples carried out the puja for his welfare whenever he went on a campaign. But this time it is a fight between our own people. I had thus not given such orders. And here, without bothering to enquire, you have gone ahead and given permission for the abhishek; and that too to a Muslim woman!'

Radhabai put the fan down and picked up her rosary. She was silent for a while as her fingers moved the beads. The silence was uncomfortable. Kashibai was not convinced that she had done anything wrong in allowing someone to perform the puja. A few moments later, Radhabai put the rosary down after touching it reverently to her forehead. She said, 'I have revoked the permission given by you. Instead, the puja will be performed this afternoon under our instructions. We will be visiting the Mrityunjay temple this afternoon. I want you to come along. I have instructed Pant to arrange for your palanquin.'

Kashibai returned to her quarters after touching Radhabai's feet. Yesu was waiting in attendance. She said, 'The young lord was waiting to meet you. Shall I send for him?'

'No. I am busy right now. I will let you know when I'm free.'

Yesu was surprised to see Kashibai's reaction. Normally her mistress would be waiting for her son's visit eagerly. She was about to step out of the room when Kashibai added, 'Please send a message to Pant that I am not feeling well and that I will not be able to visit the temple this afternoon. He need not arrange for my palanquin.'

Nanasaheb went to his mother's quarters that afternoon. The maid, unsure of her mistress' reaction, sent in a request first and was pleasantly surprised when Kashibai received Nanasaheb eagerly. Her mental turmoil had quietened considerably.

Nanasaheb came into the room and, touching her feet, said, 'Tai, I had been waiting to meet you. What took you so long?'

His mother said, avoiding his gaze, 'I wasn't feeling well. I had decided to rest for a while.'

'I am surprised. The *vaidyaraj*, in his daily morning report, said he had checked your pulse this morning and that everything was fine.'

'Not all ailments can be detected by the vaidyaraj.'

'I hope you are fine now. Or shall I come later?'

'No, no,' Kashibai said. 'Your presence here is enough to ward off any ailments.'

'Is that the reason then for not allowing me in since morning?' Nana teased his mother.

'Oh, let that be. Tell me, why did you want to see me earlier?'

'It wasn't urgent but I was keen that I should be the first to tell you. I came to know that the permission you had given to perform the abhishek at the temple in Kothrud has been rescinded by the elders. It has created an embarrassment for us.'

'Oh, is that so?' Kashibai said, without showing any curiosity.

'It isn't very serious but it does not show us in good light.'

'I will not involve myself in any such decisions. That way there will be no trouble.'

'Frankly, I feel Matushree has made a mountain out of a molehill.'

'You should not talk about elders with disrespect.'

Nana looked at his mother who tried to avoid his gaze. He knew she was not being candid. He said, 'Tai, tell me what you really feel.'

'Who cares about my feelings?'

'Haven't I come to discuss with you?'

'To discuss how it was an embarrassment in the presence of the servants, is it?'

'Tai, I was given the task of managing the official duties in Rau's absence. Should I not look into them?'

'Then please let me know what *my* duties are.'

'How can I order you? Please scold me if I have made a mistake.'

'Nana, I am totally confused. What is your advice?'

'I was told that Matushree has asked you to attend the puja at the temple. When I heard that you have sent a message regretting your inability to attend, I rushed to meet you.'

'I don't feel like stepping out.'

'It won't be appropriate. And more importantly, the abhishek is being performed for the welfare of Rau Swami. If you don't attend, it might…'

A smile flickered across Kashibai's face. She asked, 'Nana, where is my daughter-in-law these days?'

Nanasaheb was surprised at the sudden change of topic. He blushed and said, 'I don't know. Bapuji Shripant may know. May I know the reason why you ask?'

'I wanted to ask Gopika something.'

'I am unable to follow you.'

'I want to ask her whether she has performed any abhishek for the welfare of my son!'

'Tai...'

'Nana, you men will never understand our emotions. What is the need to display something hidden deep in my heart? I pray for him each moment. I never felt I needed to do something specifically for his welfare. But there is no point in explaining this to you. You have to bother about protocol. Please send a message that I will be ready to leave for the puja at the designated hour.'

'Tai! You don't know how happy I am! I didn't expect you to change your mind so easily.'

'Nana, I have to look at it from all angles. I am a daughter-in-law and a mother-in-law at the same time. I don't want my daughter-in-law to use any of my actions as a precedent.'

Mother and son sat chatting with each other. When she stepped out of her quarters, a smile of contentment played on Kashibai's lips.

The messenger, astride a horse, stopped at the gates of the haveli. The horse was foaming at its nostrils and mouth, tired after a long and arduous journey. The messenger dismounted and, clutching the dak bag to his chest, walked towards the gate.

The guard at the gate asked, 'Whom do you have to meet?'

'I have to meet the young lord. Or else, Ambaji Pant. Where can I find them?'

'They are in the office. You may go there.'

The messenger reached the office to find clerks busy writing with their quill pens. They looked up.

'What is it?' Pant's voice boomed as the messenger stepped in, bowing in *mujra*.

'An urgent message, sir.'

The havildar handed over the bag to Pant. Seeing the royal seal, Pant touched the bag reverently to his forehead. He carefully removed the seal and then undid the silken knots to open the bag. He put his hand inside and took out the few pages of handwritten notes. The activity in the office had come to a standstill as everyone held their breath.

Pant scanned the pages. He was used to the official cursive writing and found it a little difficult to read the haphazard scrawl of the Peshwa. Soon his thick moustache quivered and he closed his eyes in contentment. Quite evidently, it was good news. He passed on the papers to Nanasaheb saying, 'It is appropriate you read it yourself.'

It did not take more than a few minutes for Nanasaheb to read the letter. He got up and bowed to the Ganesha idol placed in a corner of the office. He could not contain his happiness and turning to Pant said, 'Victory! We have won! Rau Swami has finally managed to rout the enemy. It is a great day for the Peshwa. Pant, please convey the good news to Matushree personally. I will inform Tai.' He turned to leave but paused to remove a ring from his finger. Throwing it in the direction of the messenger, he said, 'This is a gift from my side. You will get your due reward from the office later. Now, pick up a trumpet and go around the town announcing the victory. Let the town know that the enemy has been defeated and the Peshwa has won.'

The news spread like wildfire. The clerks were deputed to stand at the door of the haveli in a line and pass on gifts to the people celebrating in the streets. Boxes of sweets were distributed as per protocol to the sardars, sahukars and other important officials around the city.

Within half an hour, a procession left the haveli with the royal insignia as a representation of Bajirao Peshwa. Ambaji led the procession and distributed sweets to the people who thronged to celebrate.

In the battle which ensued near Dabhoi, Trimbakrao Dabhade and his three key sardars were killed. Not only did the Dabhades suffer personal loss, their entire army was routed while the Peshwa captured their elephants and other cavalry.

The defeat of the Dabhades had repercussions right up to the Nizam in Hyderabad. It changed the political landscape beyond the borders of the Narmada. In a short span of time, two of the key rebel generals had been brought to task by the Peshwa, thus enhancing the prestige and status of Chhatrapati Shahu across India.

Umabai Dabhade could not reconcile to the fact that the Peshwa had killed her son. She took charge of the army and vowed to avenge the loss. Not one to give up easily, she schemed of ways to attack the Peshwa's army on its way back from Gujarat.

The news reached Pune that the Peshwa was on his way home and that Chimaji Appa was expected to reach the city first.

The advance party reached the borders of Pune in no time, followed by the news that Appa was expected to arrive any moment. After a quick darshan at the Ganesha temple, he proceeded towards Shanivar wada.

Radhabai was waiting to receive her younger son in her quarters. She exclaimed, as he bent down to touch her feet, 'Appa! It has been ages since I last saw you! I hope everything is fine.'

Appa replied, 'I have your feet in sight now. What else do I need?'

Radhabai asked Appa to sit next to her. Nana entered at that moment and touched Appa's feet. He blessed him, 'Ayushmaan bhava! Nana, I could not recognize you for a moment. How tall you have grown! Isn't that so, Matushree?'

Radhabai smiled. 'You are seeing him after many months.'

Chimaji Appa rested his back against the pillows saying, 'That is true. I am returning after nearly seven months. I did not realize how time flies when one is on a campaign.'

'Do you realize how torturous it is for us to spend each day? You must be tired now. Give me a brief summary of the campaign. I will hear the details later.'

Chimaji was Nana's favourite uncle. He knew Chimaji was bone-tired. He said, 'Kaka must be tired after the long journey. Let him rest for a while. We can hear about the exploits at leisure.'

'Oh, no. Not at all,' Chimaji said, wiping his face with a towel. He was drenched with sweat. Radhabai looked at her younger son's handsome face. His normally fair face had tanned due to being out in the sun for months together on horseback. He was around twenty-four now. He had never been well built since childhood, being always on the leaner side. But she had never heard him complain of ill health. His young face showed signs of fatigue.

Chimaji said, 'Matushree, you must hear about what Rau did. He has been brilliant. The Nizam had entered the battle to support the Dabhades, but thanks to Rau's strategy, the Nizam's forces could not join our enemy. That ensured our victory.'

Radhabai interrupted, 'I have heard of your victories. I have not heard of the losses we have suffered.'

'We lost around fifty sardars. Dhamdhere was one of our main losses. Another fifty were injured.'

'You mean Narayanji Dhamdhere?'

'Yes. Rau felt the loss dearly. We never expected that.'

'I am told Umabai has taken charge now.'

'That is true. She has taken over as the commander now and has vowed to take revenge.'

'Keep one thing in mind, Appa, Umabai is not a lady who will forgive easily. Ask Rau to be careful. She is a woman possessed. You have disturbed a hornet's nest.'

'I shall convey your message,' Appa said and, after a while, he took his leave.

A servant was ready with his sandals. Putting them on, he walked towards his quarters. Suddenly, he stopped and told the servant at hand, 'Please ask Vahinisaheb if she is free to meet me. I would like to pay my regards.'

He stood in the passage, waiting with his back resting against a pillar. The servant returned within a few minutes. 'She is waiting for you. Please proceed.'

Yesu stood at the entrance and bent in mujra to greet Appa.

Kashibai was sitting on a swing, resting her back against thick pillows, when Appa entered and bent down to touch the floor with his hand. 'Bhauji, is that you? Look at your face!

You look so tired. I had been warning you not to go on this campaign. I can hardly recognize you.'

Gesturing to him to sit down, she continued, 'Please sit. You must be tired.'

'Why would I be tired? Rau was the one in command. I had no direct responsibilities.' Appa rested his elbow against a pillow. He said, 'Vahinisaheb, you have been apprised of the campaign on a regular basis, I hope. I had instructed Nana to ensure that.'

Kashibai smiled. 'I was not worried knowing you are there with Rau.'

'You are saying this to humour me.'

'No, I mean it.'

'If that be the case, why did you send sacred ashes for him to wear in his amulet? Wasn't my presence sufficient?'

'It is not a reflection of my lack of trust in you. It shows that my faith in my sindoor is not strong enough.'

'I am unable to follow you. But I know one thing for sure; your sindoor protects not only you but also lakhs of other women whose men repose their faith in Rau.'

'I hope Rau Swami is fine and keeping good health.'

'You need not worry. He is absolutely fine and will be here soon.'

Kashibai was enjoying the conversation with her brother-in-law as she sat on the swing, swaying gently. She clapped once and a maid arrived with some cold juice.

She said, as Appa enjoyed the sherbet, 'Appa, I observe you are concerned about everyone around you. Should you not spend time with your infant child? When you left he was just a month old. You have been out for nearly seven or eight months. He has started recognizing people now. His grandmother, your mother-in-law, has been taking care of him. Not only does she have to look after him but she also has to deal with her sorrow of having lost her daughter at such a young age. Please meet them before you go to your quarters.'

'But Vahinisaheb…' Appa started.

'No buts,' Kashibai interrupted. 'Sadashiv Pant's grandmother is waiting for you. You could not give her comfort before you left. Please go and meet her now. She will feel good.'

Appa stood up. Before leaving he said, 'Now you know why I am never worried. Why should I be when I have such caring people around me?'

The date for Bajirao's arrival in Pune had been fixed and a letter with the details reached Shanivar wada spurring uncle and nephew into action. The wada had been built according to the vaastu specifications laid down by the Peshwa and he would enter the haveli as per the auspicious day and time suggested by the almanac.

The Peshwas, after returning from any campaign or expedition, would first hold their durbar to honour the men in battle who had laid down their lives. Widows and children of such men would be given benefits from the state treasury. The Peshwas accorded this the highest priority. The temporary accommodation and the durbar for the ceremony were set up in Kothrud gardens.

That morning, Nana and Chimaji Appa, who had finally taken three days of well-deserved rest, marched out of their haveli on horseback along with a few select armed soldiers. Chimaji Appa's face had regained the lost colour and looked bright again.

The gardens of Kothrud, on the banks of the river Mutha, spread for nearly a mile. The water in the river had reduced considerably due to the hot summers, leaving huge pools spread across intermittently. Selected sardars had set up their camps along the borders of the gardens.

The soldiers were enjoying a siesta in the cool shade of the mango orchards which were in full blossom when, seeing Appa arrive, they hurriedly stood up and saluted.

The dense shade belied the hot summer. Appa spent some time inspecting the arrangements before going to the Mrityunjay temple. After washing his feet, he prayed at the sanctum sanctorum before entering the hall where thick dhurries had been laid out.

The temple priest arrived with a tray of fruits and a glass of milk. 'I hope Rau Swami will be pleased with the arrangements,' Nana said, looking at Appa.

'He trusts your aesthetic sense. That is why he left the arrangements here at the gardens to you,' Appa said, removing his turban. Loosening the knots of his *angarkha*, he rested his back against a bolster and said, 'I love the place you have selected for my brother's rest – the temple on one side and the beautiful river on the other. It will be a pleasing sight when he notices the tents erected on the slopes of the mountain on the opposite bank. I will tell him that Chiranjeev has done this all on his own.'

'Uncle, all the credit goes to you. I am but a novice.'

'Nana, when it comes to talking sweetly, you are no less than my sister-in-law,' Appa said, smiling indulgently at his nephew.

'That reminds me, I haven't made any arrangements for private accommodation. Matushreebai will stay back at the

Shanivar haveli but I expect Tai to come. I wonder why Rau did not mention anything regarding this.'

Appa smiled. 'Don't worry. Rau has given me all the instructions. I wonder whether, in the garb of enquiry, you were hinting at a private tent for your own self!'

Nana blushed and did not dare to look up. Appa was about to continue when a commotion outside interrupted their conversation. He asked, raising his voice, 'Who is it?'

The noises increased. Nana went out to see the guards holding a man who was shouting, 'Leave me! I want to complain to Shrimant personally. You may have won a lot of accolades in the battles but that gives you no right to harass me. I know Shrimant is here. I will present my case to him.'

Nana raised his hand indicating to the guards to release him. He said, 'Present him before Appa.' Walking into the hall, he said, 'Looks like some minor complaint. I have asked them to present the complainant here before you.'

Two guards pushed the man inside. Appa, looking at his effeminate body from head to toe, asked, 'Who are you?'

'Sarkar, I am Raghu, the dancer.'

'Dancer? What are you doing here?'

'We stay with Baiji in the haveli at the corner of the garden. I am employed with her.'

'Baiji?'

Raghu, willing to take on the guards a moment back, seemed lost for words now. Nana came to his rescue. 'There is a group of dancers stationed here. Their lead dancer is someone by the name of Mastani. Rau Swami has permitted them to stay here.'

'Why are the dancers staying so far away from the city?'

'They are Musalmaans from Bundelkhand and have a large troupe. It was more convenient to house them here.'

'I see! What does this dancer want?'

Raghu, licking his lips, said, 'Sarkar, your soldiers have taken away two of my mistress' pet deer by force.'

'Pet deer? Why do you keep pet deer?'

'It is my mistress' hobby to keep pet deer. I had brought them here so that they could drink water at the river when three or four soldiers stepped out of the bushes and grabbed them.'

'What did you do then?'

'Sarkar, look at me! Do you think I can challenge them? One of them held my hand tightly. My god! He was so strong!'

Appa could not hide his smile. The dancer seemed enamoured by the man's strength! Nana asked Raghu, 'Can you recognize these men?'

'They seemed to be Holkar's men.'

'Why do you say that?'

'Their leader seemed very pleased with the catch. The one with whiskers said, "We will present the pair to our Subedar. He has not enjoyed venison in a long time." And he…'

'Speak up! You need not be afraid,' Appa said, seeing him hesitate.

'And he said Shrimant will also enjoy the lavish spread. Sarkar, they are horrible men. They need to be punished. You need to pull their tongue out!'

'Enough!' Appa shouted. 'Our men will look into it. You may go now. Do you have anything else to say?'

'Nothing else. Please ask them to hurry or my mistress might die if she loses the deer.'

Appa closed his eyes, resting his head on a soft pillow.

Nana and Appa left the temple premises after sundown, their horses cantering their way towards the river.

The trumpets followed the bugles and pipes. Their sound rent the air and the people in Pune knew that Shrimant Bajirao Peshwa was approaching the city.

At Kothrud, Chimaji Appa, along with the moneylenders and the rich businessmen of Pune, stood in reception. It was a sight to behold. The dust raised by the marching horses shone in the rays of the setting sun creating a golden halo around the troops.

Bajirao Peshwa, astride a white steed, spurred the horse and galloped ahead with a few select sardars. He pulled the reins as he reached the cantonment. The horse neighed loudly as it lifted its forelimbs.

Bajirao patted the horse affectionately and jumped down. A syce immediately rushed forward to hold the reins and lead the animal away. The moment the Peshwa, wearing Gujarati-styled mojadis, landed on the ground, he was greeted with a round of mujras. He raised his right hand in acknowledgement and then hugged his brother, Chimaji Appa. Nana stepped forward to touch his feet.

Looking at Bajirao, it was evident he had been on a long march. The angarkha, churidar pyjamas, the turban – they all were dust-stained. Bajirao glanced at the cantonment for a moment and then moved towards his tent.

Trumpets sounded as soon as he stepped into his tent. A seating arrangement had been made ready. Nana helped his father untie the scabbard before taking a seat. A servant, standing nearby, received the sword and a small dagger, and stepped back.

The Peshwa sat down folding his knees. The others followed suit while the six sardars, who had accompanied the Peshwa, remained standing.

'Appa, what's the news from Satara?' Bajirao asked, looking at his brother.

'Chhatrapati Maharaj has personally gone to Talegaon to console Umabai.'

'I understand. She has lost her son. But I was helpless, being tied up trying to stem the rot created by traitors like Dabhade,' Bajirao said.

'Dabhade was an old servant and a trusted commander. I am told the Maharaj was hurt that he died in battle,' Appa said.

Bajirao raised an enquiring eyebrow. The forehead creased for a brief moment and the words erupted, 'He should have thought hard before jumping into battle. Once you jump into the fray, you have to play by the rules. You cannot hide behind your rank. I had no option.'

The Peshwa's trusted lieutenants – Malhar Rao Holkar, Ranoji Shinde, Aavji Kavde, Pilaji Jadhavrao, Baji Bhimrao Rethrekar and Vyankatrao Ghorpade – stood behind him. Malhar Rao Holkar said, 'It seems Appaji Swami is not aware of the incidents since his return to Pune. If I may...?'

Bajirao's face relaxed hearing Malhar Rao. He said, 'Sure! Please go ahead.'

'Appa would be aware that we had managed to keep Nizam Ali at bay while confronting Dabhade. When you returned to Pune, we too were under the impression that the Nizam would not come in the way, but the Nizam's men took us unawares in the night. Ranoji and his men fought bravely and repulsed the attack. While we lost a lot of our men, we had clear proof of Dabhade's treachery.'

'And such men are called commanders of the state!' Bajirao's voice boomed. 'I had to put to task Chandrasen Jadhav too in a similar manner earlier. Forgetting the loyalties of their ancestors, these traitors joined the enemy camp. I hope the treatment meted out to the Dabhades will wake up the people sitting in Satara.'

'I don't know when our men will learn,' Appa said, 'but one thing is clear, the Nizam will think twice before confronting us again. He was hoping to defeat us thinking he had the support of the Maharaj at Kolhapur. But the Maharaj broke his pact with his brother and the territory up to Varna is now lost to the Nizam. We will have to take him to task one day. Hopefully, we won't have to worry about someone from this side supporting him.'

Rau looked at his son sitting next to him. Seeing his youthful face, he was reminded of his own days. He was the spitting image of what he was a mere twenty years back. Turning towards Baji Bhimrao Rethrekar, he said, 'Bajipant, I didn't ask Chiranjeev to accompany us this time thanks to your advice. But I am going to send Nana on a campaign next time. I won't listen to you or Matushreebai then.'

'I shall wait for that moment,' Nana said eagerly.

'But it is not that a person can contribute to the affairs of the state by going on a campaign alone,' Rethrekar insisted, bowing a little in respect. 'Nana is serving under Chhatrapati Maharaj at Satara. The Maharaj loves him dearly.'

'He is my son first,' Bajirao said, smiling. 'He needs to get used to such campaigns, getting exposed to the elements of nature. One doesn't become a hunter by fishing in a pond or killing meek deer in the woods.'

Everyone knew the Peshwa was referring to the hunting expeditions of the Maharaj. Seeing no one respond, Bajirao continued, 'Nana, consult the almanac to fix a time for the special durbar tomorrow. I have a lot of other important tasks once we finish the job of honouring the men in battle. I have to meet the Maharaj personally and debrief him about the campaign. We have to make future plans too. Let us conclude this meeting now. I am sure the sardars have work to do in their respective camps.'

The sardars saluted and left the tent one by one.

The durbar, in honour of those who had laid down their lives and had shown great courage in the battle, was held the next afternoon. Ambaji Pant provided a list of men whose next of kin would be honoured by the Peshwa.

It was evening by the time Bajirao returned to his tent. Candles in brass candelabras burned brightly. Bajirao, dressed in ceremonial attire, was being helped by his personal assistant to undress when a servant came in and announced, 'The royal palanquin from Pune is waiting for your instructions.'

Lost in thought, Bajirao asked, 'What did you say?'

'The royal palanquin awaits your instructions.'

'When did it arrive?'

'It has been nearly half an hour.'

'And you are telling me now?'

'Shrimant was in durbar then,' the assistant said.

'That's right; you could not have informed me then.'

Kashibai's tent had been set up next to the private quarters meant for Bajirao. A thin embroidered curtain separated the two. Yesu, Kashibai's maid, entered the tent and said saluting thrice, 'Baisaheb awaits you.'

'Please inform her that I will join her in a moment.'

Bajirao entered the square tent, brightly lit with lamps and decorated with beautifully painted curtains depicting scenes from the epics. A small seating arrangement facing eastwards had been prepared, while Kashibai, bedecked in jewels from head to toe with an embroidered shawl wrapped around her shoulders, stood in a corner. The maid held a tray in her hand. It was a traditional custom to welcome the husband home.

For a moment their eyes met. After that Kashibai kept looking at Bajirao's feet. She had been waiting to see them for the past seven months.

She did not dare to look into his eyes. For a few moments they both stood quietly. The room filled with an awkward silence when Kashibai said in a soft voice, 'I request you to please sit down.'

Bajirao sat down at the designated place and Kashibai, taking the tray from Yesu, put a tilak on his forehead. She threw a few grains of rice over his turban and then moved the tray around his face clockwise. The dangling nose piece added to the beauty of her aquiline nose. Bajirao looked at Kashibai as she moved the tray around. In a symbolic gesture, he removed a ring from one of his fingers and put it on the tray. Yesu took the tray and left the tent, leaving them alone.

Kashibai stood as Bajirao relaxed, pushing himself against a large pillow. Looking down, she said, 'I was planning to come here in the morning but...'

'Well?' Bajirao asked.

'I was told by Sasubai that it was not an auspicious time. I had to wait till late afternoon.'

Her words were music to Bajirao's ears. He said, teasing her, 'Did Matushreebai really say so or is it your way of exacting revenge for my late arrival?'

'Come on! Can I compete with you in these matters?'

'I know! I was feeling guilty for having delayed my arrival here.'

'I don't need an auspicious moment to see you but, then again, I cannot ignore certain mores. I have to follow them.'

'I am aware. I remember you sent me sacred ash from the temple when I was on the campaign.'

'I wonder if you missed me at all!'

'Why? What makes you say that?'

'You sent so many letters: instructions for Chiranjeev and such, but I don't remember a single personal message for me.' Kashibai had so far been looking at the carpet. Now she looked into his eyes.

Bajirao could sense both desperation and helplessness in those large vulnerable eyes. He knew he had no excuse. Trying to laugh it off, he said, 'I know how to get out of the enemy's clutches, but I surrender when it comes to your words. I surrender. I am speechless.'

Kashibai said, 'It is not a question of who wins or loses. I just said what came to my mind. Please forget it. But it reminds me of an incident when you were on a campaign to Bundelkhand a few years back.'

'What about it?'

'After defeating Muhammad Khan Bangash you had sent me a letter. Do you recall?'

'Yes, I do!'

'It is a letter I treasure. You had mentioned that I was the first one you thought of after defeating the powerful enemy.' Letting out a deep sigh, she continued, 'But Chiranjeev tells me this campaign was different.'

'That is true. That was a fight against the enemy but here we were fighting against our own.'

'I remember an amusing incident,' Kashibai said, looking into her husband's eyes. 'You had mentioned that the women of Bundelkhand are very attractive and that the men there take advantage of their beauty. There was a local saying of sorts...'

'Yes, I remember! Malhar Rao and Ranoji Shinde have mentioned it often. They say the Bundels give their daughters in marriage to trap their sons-in-law.'

'You had also mentioned we were lucky not to have a daughter.'

'I am surprised you remember my letter verbatim.'

'These memories help me to live.' Kashibai closed her eyes, lost in thought. Then she continued, 'You are out for months at a stretch. All I can do is to wait endlessly. The sun rises and sets, the stars in the sky shine and the moon showers its beams upon the gardens. The cool breeze of the dawn or the soothing westerly winds of the evening – neither are a balm for the soul. I move from one day to the next on the carriage of memories.'

'Wah! I did not know you could speak in poetry!' Bajirao said.

It was long past dinner time, but the servants did not dare to interrupt their conversation. Hours went by...

The auspicious day for moving into the Shanivar haveli was still a fortnight away. The Peshwa began his other duties from the temporary quarters set up in the gardens at Kothrud. The office would begin in the afternoon and continue till late hours of the night.

Nana was to leave for Satara as the Chhatrapati had already sent a few reminders. Ambaji Pant Purandare, who would normally accompany Nana to Satara, was busy with the office work in Pune and sent his son Mahadoba Purandare instead.

Kashibai, in the meantime, had a visitor in the form of her brother, Krishnarao Joshi Chaskar. He was ushered in the moment he sent word of his arrival.

He had been on the campaign to Gujarat but had not returned to Pune. Instead, he had taken a detour to visit his village at Chas. Kashibai had been proud of the fact that her brother had accompanied the Peshwa on the campaign.

'Come in Krishnarao. Take a seat. I hear you have shown much valour in this campaign,' Kashibai said, welcoming her brother.

Krishnarao was a couple of years younger than Kashibai. Medium built, he had the fair skin of a typical Konkanastha Brahman. The shrewd penetrating eyes added to the intensity of his face. Folding his hands in namaskar he took his seat and asked, 'Who told you about my valour?'

'No one needs to tell me. It was an important campaign and you are, after all, my brother! Undoubtedly, you would have done a good job.'

'You are right, Tai! This was a different kind of campaign. I was with Shrimant all the time. He entrusted me with many an important task and I managed to complete each one of them successfully. I was in the battle, a naked sword in my hand, leading many assaults.'

'I am taunted about people from my family not supporting the affairs of the state but you have managed to wipe out the black spot of such allegations now. I am sure Shrimant too is happy, isn't he?'

'Tai, this is something I wanted to talk to you about.'

'Are you saying he is not pleased?'

'Tai, our Matushree did not allow me to stay home because she wanted me to let you know of the unfairness with which

I had been treated. Tai, the Peshwa honoured a lot of sardars and shiladars upon his return to Pune.'

'I am aware; and you too were.'

'Yes, but nowhere in comparison to what the others got.'

'Krishnarao!' Kashibai's voice rose in indignation. She would not tolerate a snide remark about her husband.

'Tai, if you will get upset, I would rather keep quiet. I will tell Matushree that you don't like being told the truth.'

'Krishnarao, don't speak in circles. I may be married to the Peshwa but that does not mean I will tolerate my family being treated unjustly. Tell me what happened.'

'What is there to tell? Most of the people were honoured with the gift of a village or large sums of money. Some others got a *jagir*. Do you know what I got?'

'Tell me...'

'A mere thousand rupias! Tai, that's the value of my contribution! An ordinary shiladar like Ranoji Shinde is gifted a village and a cowherd like Malhar Rao Holkar gets a jagir.' Krishnarao's voice was tinged with ridicule. 'I was thrown a lagniappe of a mere thousand rupias.'

Kashibai was silent. She was not aware of his work in the campaign nor she was aware of the reason behind the Peshwa's gesture, though, in her heart, she did feel her brother should have been treated with honour and dignity, at par with others. The thought that her husband may have insulted her brother did cross her mind. Seeing her silent, Krishnarao said, 'Tai, if you feel I erred in saying something wrong, please do tell me.'

'Krishnarao, I normally don't involve myself in official matters but I will surely speak to Shrimant about this. May I ask you something?'

'Yes, please.'

'I don't see any battle wounds on you.'

Kashibai's taunt was not lost on Krishnarao. He said, 'Tai, do you mean to say I would be considered brave only if I suffered from many wounds? Have you asked Shrimant where all he has been wounded?'

'Krishnarao!' Kashibai shouted, her voice taking on an edge. 'I am talking to you as your sister, but I will not tolerate any insults to Shrimant.'

Krishnarao was taken aback and shrank in fear. His shrewd and selfish eyes glanced around once and then he said beseechingly, 'Tai, I think you misunderstood me. I just wanted to say that wounds on the body need not be the only criterion to measure ones's valour on the battlefield. Tai, please don't take me otherwise.'

Controlling her emotions, Kashibai said, 'Krishnarao, I am proud of the Chaskar Joshis. Please rest assured that I will speak to Shrimant at an appropriate time.'

At that moment, the servants arrived carrying tumblers of milk. Krishnarao gulped down the milk in one go. Wiping his luxuriant moustache with his angavastram, he got up and took his leave. A smile of satisfaction played on his lips as he exited Kashibai's quarters. Kashibai too, having met her brother after a long time, felt happy.

The auspicious time to enter Shanivar haveli was set for the evening. The people in Pune lined up on the streets to see Bajirao Peshwa, astride a white steed and wearing a ceremonial dress, ride towards his haveli.

After the darshan at the Ganesha temple, he moved across the town to pray to various deities. The town had decorated itself for the joyous occasion with arched doorways made of leaves and rangoli decorations at the entrance of the houses. The trumpets began as soon as the Peshwa reached the haveli. He entered the main door amidst the din of various instruments.

After an hour of ceremonial durbar, where five selected sardars were honoured, the Peshwa went to Matushree's quarters to take her blessings before retiring to Kashibai's palace.

The next day, Chimaji Appa along with some of the key workmen who had built the haveli assembled in the main courtyard. They took Bajirao on a guided tour of the haveli. Chimaji Appa excitedly showed one chamber after another till they reached a closed door. Bajirao asked, 'What's behind this?'

Appa answered, 'It has been especially made for the lord of the haveli. We have named it Sheesh Mahal, the hall of mirrors.'

The huge hall was lit with candles burning in candelabras. The mirrors, placed at strategic locations, lit the entire hall with millions of images of the candles. Bajirao's expression was enough for the others to know that he had been suitably impressed.

'Wah! It looks as though it is Indra's mahal!'

'I was sure Rau would like it,' Appa said. 'We had brought in masons all the way from Jainagar in Rajasthan. Rau, you are yet to see the best part, though!'

'Is it?' Bajirao asked. 'What else do you have in store?'

Appa looked towards the west wing of the hall, where a statue stood near a bed. The nymphet, made of *panchadhatu*, was an object of beauty with her slim waist, voluptuous breasts and slender arms. Appa pointed at the statue and, on cue, it moved a few steps forward, rang a bell hanging on a stand and then stepped back. Before taking its original position it bent in a slight mujra. It was a sight to behold.

Bajirao, unable to contain his curiosity, touched the statue and exclaimed, 'Wah! It is unbelievable. It can be easily mistaken for a real woman. I am impressed.'

The architects were delighted to hear their hard work being appreciated by the Peshwa.

On the eastern side, beyond a courtyard, was Kashibai's palace. Appa led Bajirao to a point near the eastern wall of the hall where on the floor was a square piece of embroidered satin cloth. The area covered was two square feet.

'We have one more magic to show you.'

'What is it now?' Bajirao asked, his curiosity getting the better of him.

The servants, on an indication from Appa, removed the satin cloth to reveal a beautiful lotus carved on the marble floor.

'It is a lovely carving; but what about it?'

Appa, blushing a little, said, 'It is a delicate but very useful matter. The moment Rausaheb stands on the lotus, his image will be visible to Vahinisaheb in her mirror in her room. And...'

'I see, I see! I was not aware that my brother had a romantic side too,' Bajirao said as he moved out of the hall of mirrors. A few large halls followed by a private meeting room completed Bajirao's quarters.

Bajirao, assisted by Appa and his men, inspected the entire haveli before exiting from the western gate. The work was almost over. The men were working at a frantic pace to complete the remaining parts. Bajirao, walking along with Appa, said, 'The haveli has been built with a lot of attention to detail, but we should remember that it is the Peshwa's haveli.'

'I did not get your meaning,' Appa said.

'I mean we need to have a strong fortified wall around the haveli. One cannot be careless these days. The Nizam had attacked Pune a few years back, remember? We need to protect ourselves.'

'I am aware and we are planning for the same. It will be ready in another couple of years at the most,' Appa said.

By the time the Peshwa returned to his quarters, the sun was high up in the sky.

The sardars left to resume their respective duties to their appointed jagirs once the durbar was over. The Shanivar haveli went back to its regular routine. Both Bajirao Peshwa and Chimaji Appa would spend the whole day looking into matters of the state. Their day would end with a meeting in the private discussion room where spies from across India would report their observations.

It was late in the evening. Bajirao seemed tired, restless and eager to go to Kashibai's quarters when Chimaji Appa said, 'I wanted to talk to you about a few things but was not sure of how to put them across.'

Bajirao's tired eyes sparked for a brief moment. He said, 'Appa, you normally do not hesitate. What is the matter?'

'It is a little personal.'

'Personal? You mean regarding me?'

'Yes.'

'Go on then.'

'It is regarding the message you had sent to the Baramatkars through Bhikaji.'

'What about it? I thought it would be good if Bhiubai and

her in-laws were informed of our return and about the general state of affairs here.'

'The Baramatkars felt insulted. They have their own pride, now that the Peshwa's sister is married to their son. Apparently, they did not like the fact that your message was sent through Bhikaji, an illegitimate son...'

'I see,' Bajirao interrupted, sounding a little irritated. 'I have never considered Bhikaji as my father's illegitimate son. He is a brother to me.'

'But he is considered as one of low caste. It is insulting to send someone like him to represent you.'

'Do you think so, Appa?'

'What I think is irrelevant. There was a complaint from the Baramatkars and Matushreebai too did not like it. I thought it was best you knew about it.'

'Oh, I see! So the matter has already been discussed.'

Appa was silent. Bajirao continued, 'Appa, is it Bhikaji's fault that his mother was from a low caste?'

'It is not about whose fault it is. Society has some rules and if someone is insulted by breaking the rules, why do so? Secondly, it is also a question of the prestige accorded to the office of the Peshwa.'

'Appa, our prestige is not decided by such things.'

'Rau, we cannot look for logic here. We need to honour societal mores.'

'Appa, the Baramatkars are becoming far too big for their boots. I feel they are using Bhikaji as an excuse. Having lent money to the Peshwas, they are trying to exact their pound of flesh now.'

'That may be true but it is best to avoid sending Bhikaji to their place if they don't like it.'

'I agree. I will keep that in mind. They are trying to impress us with their wealth. We will live with it. Did you have anything else to say?'

'If Rau does not mind, I do have one more thing to discuss.'

Bajirao smiled. 'Appa, it is not a question of whether I mind. I don't like it that I am being blackmailed just because I am indebted to them. But we can't do much, can we? Anyway, what was it you wanted to say?'

'It is a delicate matter…'

'Is it? Then the sooner you say it, the better!' Bajirao said, nudging him.

'I was inspecting the arrangements at Kothrud the other day with Nana, when someone from the dancer's troupe came in with a complaint.'

'Dancer? Is she the same one who had come last year during Nana's marriage celebrations?'

'Yes, she is.'

'Mastani, isn't it?'

'Wah! I am impressed with your memory.'

Bajirao smiled to himself. 'I remember what is worth remembering. So what about the complaint?'

'Apparently some of Holkar's men forcibly snatched a pair of their pet deer. They made a reference to something which I did not like.'

'What did they refer to?'

'I am embarrassed to repeat what they said, Rau. He seemed to indicate that you ate what is not allowed as per the norms of a Brahman.'

Bajirao turned his face away. He was silent for a while. The light from the candles shone on his face, his lips pursed in concentration. Bajirao knew that Appa was telling the truth.

Hoping against hope, he continued, 'People may say all kinds of things, but should we not stop them from making such wild allegations?'

It was difficult for Bajirao to confront his brother. Guilt was writ large on his face. He argued, 'Appa, I am on campaigns day in and out. I am constantly in the company of all kinds of people, whether tribals, fishermen, Marathas or ryots. They are with me come rain or shine.'

'Don't I know?' Appa interrupted. 'But can we afford to forget our religion, our culture? We are Brahmans after all!'

'It is fine to practise religion within the four walls of this palace, Appa. But we need to turn a blind eye to some of these things.'

'Blind eye? Rau, people have blind faith in the Peshwa. He is revered for being a Peshwa as well as a true Brahman. If they gossip that...' Appa could not complete his sentence.

Bajirao was silent for a while.

'Appa, I will keep that in mind. I know how you feel and shall try my best. You may tell Matushreebai not to get unduly worried.' Getting up he muttered, 'Appa, should we not wonder at times about the fact that the same Brahman is also holding a sword in his hand?'

Without waiting for Appa's reply, he walked out of the room.

The news of the Peshwa's return prompted a number of merchants to make a beeline for Pune and Satara to display their wares. Merchants, selling a variety of items from guns, swords and other warfare-related things to expensive zari clothes, perfumes, gems and jewellery, set up their shops in the bazaars. Business was brisk.

One afternoon, Kashibai was informed that a jeweller, specially selected by Bajirao, had been sent for her. 'Shrimant is busy in the office but has requested you to have a look at the collection and select whatever you like.'

Kashibai stepped into the courtyard and sat on a swing hung there on silver chains. The jeweller sat down on the floor and began showing his collection. There were wooden boxes wrapped in white muslin cloth. Jewellery of gold, silver, pearls, precious stones – he had it all and in different styles, whether Karnataki, Deccani, Gujarati, Mughlai, Lakhnavi or Allahabadi. Each one was special and irresistible. Holding a gold necklace in his hand, he said, 'This is a piece especially for Baisaheb. Observe the way the jewels have been set – there are sapphires, diamonds, emeralds and garnets. It will look very nice on you.'

Kashibai sat on the swing wearing a beautifully embroidered silk sari, the pallu covering her head as usual. Seeing him speak to her directly, she adjusted the pallu out of habit and said, looking at the scribe who stood nearby, 'None of these are appealing. I would like to see something unique.'

'*Wahi hukum Peshwa sahib ne humko diya hai. Aajkal yeh Dilli mein khub pehente hain*,' the jeweller tried again.

'Maybe, but they do not appeal to me,' Kashibai said.

The jeweller was a little disappointed. He was unable to fathom Kashibai's taste. He showed her a variety of jewellery. Whether an exquisitely designed pearl necklace or a cummerbund made of precious stones, Kashibai would look at each one of them and push them aside without showing further interest. Seeing Kashibai reject each and every item, the scribe said, 'Shrimant had sent him hoping you would find something that you fancy. He will be disappointed to know that you did not like anything from the lot.'

The jeweller, taking advantage of the opening made by the scribe, added, 'I have something which Baisaheb will not refuse once she sees it.'

'Show me,' Kashibai said, without showing much curiosity.

The jeweller pushed everything aside and gently opened a small box made of sandalwood to reveal a large ring. Nine different jewels were set on the periphery of a gold coin, the size of a *hon*, while a beautiful image of Goddess Lakshmi was carved in the centre. The clerk, taking the box from the jeweller, passed it on to Kashibai. The jeweller lost no time in singing paeans. 'It is a one-of-a-kind ring, Baisaheb. Each of the nine gems are rare and it took years to find them. There are many who may want to possess it, but my intention is to give it to someone who has the credentials to wear it. The ring will bring the wearer immense luck and will get him whatever he desires.'

Kashibai did not react to his praise. The jeweller continued, 'Baisaheb may not believe me but these are not my words. I had shown this to one of the most famous astrologers in Kashi. I came all the way here as I believe the rightful owner is here. Whatever you say, I am going to leave this here.'

Kashibai smiled indulgently picking up the ring. She looked at it carefully. The image of Lakshmi, the setting of the precious stones – it was a very impressive ring indeed. She was happy she had found something unique. Looking at the scribe, she said, 'It would look good on Shrimant, wouldn't it?'

He replied bending his head, 'What a question to ask, Baisaheb? Of course, it will look lovely!'

'If that be so, then keep this ring aside. And you may inform Shrimant that I am done with my purchases.'

The scribe was taken aback. Kashibai had not bought anything for herself. Seeing his reaction, Kashibai said, 'I have bought what I wanted to. Don't worry. You may escort the jeweller out now.'

The jeweller picked up his wares, a little disappointed.

That night, when Bajirao came into Kashibai's quarters, he said, 'I had sent the jeweller with a lot of hope, but it seems you did not buy anything for yourself.'

'There was nothing worth buying.'

'Oh, I see! You mean there was nothing which caught your fancy? When he showed me his collection I was quite amazed by the beauty of it. The pieces seemed made for queens and you say you did not like any of them?'

'I am not saying that he did not have anything beautiful,' Kashibai said, smiling. 'What I mean is I did not find them exceptional.'

'What, according to you, is the most exquisite jewel then?' Bajirao asked, raising an eyebrow.

Kashibai blushed pink. Looking at her toes, she said, 'My most precious jewel is right here. There is nothing more precious than that.'

Bajirao laughed.

'No doubt women are so naïve. I find a jeweller and all you do is send him back, thanks to your romantic ideas!'

Kashibai joined in his laughter and then picked up the sandalwood box kept on a silver tray. She took out the *navagraha* ring. 'I did not send him back empty-handed after all. This is what I bought,' she said, stretching her hand forward.

'The clerk mentioned it to me. It is the navagraha ring, isn't it?'

'May I ask Shrimant to show me his hand?'

'What! It is surely a lucky day for me!' Bajirao gave Kashibai his right hand.

Kashibai slipped the ring in, her fingers quivering with excitement. She continued to hold his hand and said, 'There! What an auspicious ring it is! I would not have any worries as long as you continue to wear it. I need nothing, least of all any jewellery for myself.'

Bajirao said, looking at her face, 'I know now that no jewellery can enhance the elegance of this exquisite jewel!'

One afternoon, Bajirao entered his private quarters for a siesta after lunch, with Kashibai following a few steps behind. The maid brought a tray of betel leaves, as it was the tradition to have a paan after meals. Bajirao, resting against a set of thick bolsters, leaned forward to pick up the paan from the tray when Kashibai said, 'Wait! I shall serve you myself.'

'Wah! It is my privilege to be served by you today,' Bajirao said, smiling.

Kashibai blushed. 'You speak as if I don't serve you on most days.'

'I wanted to ask you something,' Kashibai continued.

Bajirao looked at her questioningly.

'You are on campaigns all the time. Who serves you paan after your meals?'

'Paan?' Bajirao raised his eyebrows in surprise. A mischievous smile then flickered across his face and he said, 'Oh! There is no dearth of young, lovely hands to serve me there.'

'How would I know?' Kashibai said, her cheeks flushing with anger.

'But I must tell you, paan served by any delicate hand tastes equally good.'

Kashibai, wiping the beads of sweat off her forehead, muttered, 'Oh, I see!'

Bajirao was in a playful mood. He was enjoying the paan. He said, 'Did I tell you about the interesting incident at Nizam Ali's camp?'

'No. What about it?'

'He had taken me to his zenankhana so that his wives could have a look at me. They showered a bucket of pearls on me. Did you hear about this?'

'Yes, I did. Those women must be crazy. How can they demand a man to be brought into the zenankhana?' Kashibai asked, looking into Bajirao's eyes.

'I too don't understand. But Nizam Ali was insistent. He said his begums were very keen and that they had heard a lot about me and my looks. Tell me, am I not handsome?'

Kashibai glanced at her husband's face for a moment and said, 'I can't praise your looks here!'

'What is wrong in the request made by those begums then? And one more thing: you asked me who serves me paan after my meals. But you didn't ask who serves me the meals.'

'Why don't you tell me then?'

'You know my favourite horse – the white one. I am served meals sitting on his back.'

'What? Are you saying you eat your meals on horseback? Don't pull my leg now,' Kashibai said.

'I am not pulling your leg, but I am surely surprised at your innocence. Do you really believe that I am served my meals sitting comfortably and then served paan, followed by a siesta?'

'How will I know? You never tell me about these things.'

'I don't tell you about things which will make you more worried. But let me tell you, had you asked whether I get to eat or not, it would have been a more relevant question than asking who serves me paan.'

Kashibai let out a deep sigh. 'So you were teasing me when you said some lovely hands feed you.'

Bajirao laughed. 'You really believed me? The only things that surround me on campaigns are my men, the cannons, the guns and what not. Where is the question of a maiden serving me? Do you understand now my eagerness to be served the moment I am back home?'

'Issh! Don't tease me now.'

Kashibai glanced at the door to see Yesu standing guard. There was no one within earshot. She said, 'I have been wanting to speak to you regarding my brother.'

'Krishnarao? What about him?'

'He met me a few days back and was upset about the way he had been treated at your durbar.'

'How should I have treated him?'

'What can I say? All I know is that he is your brother-in-law and much younger too. You can give him a little extra out of affection, can't you?'

Bajirao sat up. He adjusted his silk dhoti as he straightened his legs. Kashibai, having blurted out about her brother, felt a little awkward. She was unsure, having opened the topic for discussion. Bajirao said, 'I agree Krishnarao is my brother-in-law, but the durbar has its own rules. There is a protocol to be followed. I cannot treat him differently from others just because he is related to me. I can't upset the other sardars by being partial. But...'

'It is fine then,' Kashibai interrupted. She realized she had erred in putting forth her brother's case.

'But I am in a great mood today,' Bajirao continued. 'I will grant your request and give a special gift to Krishnarao. But mind you, the gift will be a personal one and not from the state treasury. Is that fine? Now, come on! Look at me!'

Kashibai smiled. She glanced up and looked into Bajirao's eyes as he got off the bed. Picking up a paan from the tray, he said, 'It is my turn to give you a paan now.'

Kashibai accepted the same with trembling fingers. Her wish had been fulfilled and happiness was writ large on her face.

Kashibai was on her way to the temple in her closed palanquin and reached Jogeshwari at her usual time. After her prayers, she was about to sit in her palanquin when a woman came running and touched Kashibai's feet saying, 'Baisaheb, I have a complaint.' It was Basanti.

'What is it about?' Kashibai asked, raising her voice a little to show her irritation.

'My mistress had sent her complaint to the young sarkar but nothing has come of it. Our mistress is mighty upset.'

'She complained to Appa, is it? Send your request to the haveli and Shrimant Peshwa will look into it. I don't interfere in matters of administration.'

Kashibai was about to step into the palanquin when Basanti said, 'Baisaheb, we have tried this too. We sent a request to Shrimant but were shooed away from the gate itself. That is why I have come to meet you.'

'Is that so? What is the name of your mistress?' Kashibai asked.

'Mastani. She is a dancer. A singer and dancer. We are staying in the gardens at Kothrud.'

'Mastani, is it? Anyway, whatever be it, I will pass on your message,' Kashibai said. Then turning to the clerk standing close by, she said, 'Please note this down and pass on the message to the Peshwa. And don't let anyone stop her. I wish that she gets justice.'

The clerk nodded.

That night when they were resting in their quarters, Kashibai recounted the episode of that morning. She said, 'Seems to be a helpless woman. I hope you will give her justice.'

Bajirao, his eyes heavy with sleep, nodded, 'I will look into it.'

Chimaji Appa went to meet the Chhatrapati at Satara while Bajirao moved his accommodation to the gardens near the base of the hills where there was a Ganesha temple. A makeshift durbar was set up in the huge hall inside the periphery of the temple.

The next morning, a large crowd had assembled to present their problems. Bajirao would listen to each one of them carefully and give his decision, which would be noted by Ambaji Pant Purandare sitting next to him. The orders would be passed on immediately. Looking at the list of complainants, Bajirao asked, 'What do these baijis want?'

He looked up to see Mastani standing with her head bowed. A pink dupatta hid half her face, while she held one end of it with two delicate fingers covering her mouth. For a moment, the slim figure of Mastani attracted Bajirao's attention. The way she stood spoke a lot about her upbringing. He noticed how shyly she held the dupatta. Arrested by her eyes for a brief moment, he looked down at the papers again and asked, 'What is your complaint?'

'Ala Hazrat, we have made our request earlier but no

action has been taken so far. We need your personal intervention.'

Bajirao asked, looking at her, 'What exactly is your complaint?'

Mastani was about to say something when Pant interrupted saying, 'She and her troupe had danced at Nana's wedding and Shrimant may recall having given her permission to stay at Kothrud gardens. She was asked to stay back as we had plans to use her troupe for future performances. Her complaint is that two of her deer have been taken away by Holkar's men. She wants to get them back.'

'Have you not got them?' Bajirao asked. The question was directed at Ambaji Pant while he continued to admire her curvaceous figure. When Bajirao's eyes met hers again, the two fingers holding the dupatta parted for a brief moment to join the other fingers as she bent a little in salaam.

Ambaji was busy looking into the papers. He said, 'We had noted the complaint, but then we were busy with matters of the cantonment and the issue was not taken up.'

'Have you asked Malhar Rao Holkar?'

'No. It seemed an ordinary matter and we did not want to rake the issue.'

'Anyway! You are unlikely to find your deer now but we will compensate you adequately from the personal treasury meant for shikar. Malhar Rao Holkar and we are family. Pant, please do the needful.'

'I will,' Pant said, nodding his head. 'The orders will be followed but...' He stopped mid-sentence.

'What is it? Do you have any objection?'

'No, no. The decision is absolutely fine,' Pant said hurriedly. 'But it would not be correct to compensate her from your personal treasury.'

Mastani spoke before Bajirao could reply. 'Not that the deer were very expensive, but they were dear to me. They would sit next to me whenever I sang.'

'Oh! So you sing too!'

Mastani did not reply but she looked up to meet Bajirao's eyes. The silent exchange conveyed a lot.

Pant said, 'Shrimant would remember she sang during Nana's wedding celebrations.'

'I may have heard but I was far too busy then to remember. But we are free now,' he said.

'I have a wish,' he continued.

'As you command,' said Pant.

'I was not talking to you,' Bajirao said, as he continued to look at Mastani. Pointing a finger in her direction, he said, 'I am talking to Mastani.'

'Ala Hazrat, your wish is my command.' The delicate lips parted as she spoke. Her mellifluous voice was music to Bajirao's ears. He said, 'Mastani, I wish to hear you sing. I am sure if animals are enthralled by your singing, we too shall be.'

'Whenever you command, my Lord, I shall make myself available.'

'Pant,' said Bajirao turning towards Ambaji, 'today is Sankashthi, an auspicious day. We will be having our meal late this evening. We would like to listen to Mastani's song here in the temple, this evening.'

'It would be an honour for me to sing, huzoor. May I say something?'

'Ask what you want. Are you expecting a gift?'

'Not at all! Your presence is the best gift I can get. It is regarding something else.'

'Go on.'

'We are staying in the gardens at Kothrud. The arrangements there are not very comfortable. The shiladar and his troops are camped there, making it difficult for us. We do not feel safe. We request you to look into the matter.'

'Pant, please ensure you put adequate guards outside Mastani's quarters. Let Chanda Jamdar look into it and warn him that I don't want any more complaints in this regard.' Turning towards Mastani, he added, 'Anything else?'

Mastani bent low in salaam and said, 'Nothing else, huzoor. I got what I wanted. What more can I ask for?'

She took a few steps taking care not to show her back and then withdrew from the hall.

The moment Mastani left, Pant asked, 'If I may say something, Shrimant.'

Bajirao was still looking at the door through which Mastani had left and it took a few moments for him to realize that Pant was talking to him.

'Were you saying something?'

'Nothing important, but I remember you telling me that the singers should be asked to sing only on specific occasions.'

'Did I?' Bajirao asked, raising his eyebrows quizzically. He then added, 'Please get the arrangements done without further ado. I shall explain to Chimaji Appa in case he objects. You sit in the office the whole day, but we are out there in the field fighting battles. You won't understand our state of mind.'

Bajirao stood up and left leaving Ambaji to wind up. He muttered as he collected the papers, 'It is true. I don't understand anything at all.' Turning to the clerk he said, 'We have to despatch an urgent letter. Get the quill and ink.'

'Whom do we address it to?' the clerk asked.

Ambaji glanced at the door through which Bajirao had

exited and said, 'We need to send an urgent letter to Chimaji Appa, lest he shows his ire later.'

The clerk merely nodded, not having understood Ambaji's comment.

The evening had become pleasant with the sudden gathering of clouds that afternoon followed by easterly winds which had brought the rains along.

The hall looked beautiful with various flower decorations. A bright red satin carpet over a white sheet added to its allure. The arrangement for the Peshwa and others was made separately. A mild but intoxicating smell of henna pervaded the place.

At the appointed hour, Mastani and her troupe entered. They were accompanied by Raghu the cross-dresser, Babu Gurav and a musician on the sarangi. Basanti, the ever-alert maid, stood behind her mistress.

Mastani stood on the carpet wearing a lovely white salwar which contrasted with her pink kurta. The diamonds on her kurta, set in a square pattern, sparkled in the light of the lamps. She had casually draped a yellow, transparent dupatta, with which she had covered half her face. Her hands were beautifully decorated with henna and her feet shone with red lac paint. A pearl necklace added to the beauty of her slender neck while matching earrings dangled from her lobes. She looked stunning as she stood with her slender fingers touching her red lips. She observed the audience with her almond-shaped eyes.

At that moment, the guard announced the arrival of Shrimant Peshwa. Mastani looked down at the carpet and pushed her dupatta further towards her nose.

Mastani's heart was pounding nervously and her chest heaved with tension. The dupatta slipped off her voluptuous breasts without her knowledge. Bajirao entered with Vyankatrao Ghorpade and Baji Bhivrao Rethrekar. As soon as Bajirao sat down, the others followed suit. Kunwar came in hurriedly with a tray of jasmine flowers strung together like a wrist band. He offered one to Bajirao who wrapped it around his wrist and then the tray was passed around to others.

Mastani, standing alone on the carpet, was an arresting figure with her arched eyebrows and a sharp nose accentuating her pink cheeks. A singular thought raced through Bajirao's mind – what a beauty! Casually, he gestured to her to sit.

Bowing thrice in an elaborate mujra, Mastani sat down on her knees as Bajirao inhaled the sweet perfume emanating from the jasmine flowers and settled in his seat to enjoy the performance. All present were eager to see Mastani perform.

Bajirao asked, 'I don't see Ambaji Pant Purandare here?' Bajirao smiled a knowing smile when someone informed him that he was not well and had excused himself. He nodded to Mastani to begin singing.

The sarangi player tuned his instrument while the percussionist checked the tabla. Both waited for Mastani's cue to begin.

Briefly touching her forehead with her left hand in salaam, Mastani closed her eyes and began...

> *'It rains all the while through my eyes*
> *My eyes, they rain all the time...'*

The first few lines touched a chord and Bajirao exclaimed in appreciation, 'Wah!'

Accepting the compliment, Mastani looked at Bajirao as she saluted and continued,

> '*My eyes, they rain all the time*
> *Till I see him in mine...*'

The audience was enthralled as Mastani's melodious voice reached the higher octaves. Bajirao was enjoying the performance. The notes fell like the soft, enchanting petals of the parijat flower. The lyrics and the tune mixed effortlessly creating magic while Mastani's dancing eyebrows and her expressive eyes mesmerized those in attendance.

When Mastani stressed on the word 'eyes', everyone present could not help but notice the way her eyes danced to the emotions.

Bajirao was clearly an avid lover of music and his 'wah wah' was timed perfectly, encouraging Mastani. The audience too followed suit. At the end of the performance, accepting the applause, Mastani touched her palm to her forehead once more. Basanti brought her a small tray with a few cloves and pods of cardamom. Picking up a clove, Mastani prepared for her next song.

The heady feeling of the first performance was yet to soak in completely.

Bajirao, looking at Ghorpade, asked, 'Have you heard anything like this before?'

Shaking his head, Ghorpade said, 'We have heard a lot in Gujarat and Rajasthan but nothing to match this.'

'Mastani, we are really pleased. Let us hear one more!'

'My pleasure,' Mastani replied and nodded at her accompanists.

The performance continued, one melody after another, and the hall reverberated with 'wah wah' and requests for encore.

Bajirao continued to sit in his place after Mastani had finished her performance and left, bending thrice in salaam. Rethrekar, noticing his silence, commented, 'It is a rare find, Baji Pant! Where do we get to hear such melody?'

The clear moon on the fourteenth day of the month shone in a cloudless sky as Shrimant Peshwa walked back to his chambers, lost in thought.

Bajirao was to attend the royal court at Satara. Not knowing when he would get an audience with the Chhatrapati and the number of days he would have to camp before returning to Pune, he issued instructions to Ambaji Pant to ensure all necessary work was carried out at the earliest.

One afternoon, Bajirao was about to leave for his siesta when Ambaji Pant said, 'We have got the accounts of the Gujarat campaign finalized. Would you like to see them?'

'If they are ready, let us have a look. Give me a quick summary.'

Ambaji took out a sheet for Bajirao to study. He quickly scanned it before asking, 'I hope everything is in order?'

'I have checked it myself. Everything is fine. This is the final amount,' Pant said, pointing to the figure at the bottom.

'Three lakhs! That means we have a loan of that amount, is it?'

'That is right. We sent all the proceeds from the collections to the Dabhades at Talegaon. There was hardly any cash collected. Rest were expenses including those in honour of the sardars. The final outcome is a debt of three lakhs.'

'Pant, what is the total debt we have as of now?'

Ambaji Pant did a quick calculation after scanning a few other papers and answered, 'A little over thirty lakhs.'

'Thirty lakhs!' Bajirao repeated in surprise and awe. 'Ten-odd years ago we ascended to the post of Peshwa. My departed father and the Maharaj were quite confident then, having secured the promise of Swaraj from the Delhi durbar, that we would be able to garner a lot of revenue. But it seems, despite many a successful campaign, all that we have managed is an ever-growing mountain of debt. Ambaji Pant, what do you advise?'

'I feel we should insist on implementing our title of Sardeshmukh, the right to earn a tenth of the revenue in the south, from the Nizam. I feel the Nizam cares two hoots about the firman from Delhi and considers it as worthless as the paper on which it is written.'

'Remember, we had made the Nizam bite the dust two years back at Palkhed. We need to ensure that we get the collections as planned. I recall we had sent our clerks and sardars to all important towns. What was the outcome?'

'The Nizam played a trick on us. While pretending to give orders and help us, he managed to divert the revenue to his treasury. Had Appa not looted Malwa and you not got the huge cache from Bundelkhand, we would not have been able to run the day-to-day affairs of the state.'

Bajirao paused for a moment to think and then said, 'Send strict instructions to all the clerks that they are to collect the revenue due to us at any cost. If need be, send our troops, burn, pillage, do whatever it takes! Let the Nizam know, if push comes to shove, we will not hesitate to attack his territories.'

'May I suggest something?'

'Please do, Pant.'

'I fear we will not collect anything and instead take up arms against the Nizam.'

'That is even better! It has to happen some day. Unless we make the Deccan free of the Nizam's rule, we can never breathe easy. I think the time has come to teach him a lesson.'

'Shrimant, it would mean taking additional debt while we prepare for the battle. The moneylenders are already clamouring for their earlier loan. I wonder how we can ask them for more!'

Bajirao was aware of the situation. When he returned from his campaign, most of the moneylenders had sought an audience with him and had hinted, directly or indirectly, for their money to be returned. Despite the success of the campaign, he had returned poorer. The thought disturbed Bajirao.

Ambaji Pant continued, 'We can somehow manage all the moneylenders except Babuji Naik Baramatkar. He is quite insistent and I had to, the other day, listen to his rant. I somehow managed to excuse myself after making all kinds of promises. If he withdraws his support, we will be in trouble.'

'Pant, he is my sister's father-in-law. Should he not exhibit patience?'

'May I say something at the risk of sounding blunt?'

'Please.'

'His arrogance stems from the fact that your sister is married to his son. He knows he cannot be touched.'

Bajirao studied the papers once more. After a while, Ambaji Pant said, 'I have a suggestion.'

'Anything which helps us get funds is welcome.'

'I suggest you meet the Nizam and start a dialogue of friendship. While you engage him, we will instruct our men to ruthlessly take what is due to us. Let them use force, burn, pillage, the way you said. While the Nizam is under the false impression that you are extending an olive branch, he will not raise a storm. In the meantime, our coffers would be refilled and we can then decide the next course of action.'

'Sounds good. Let me think over it.'

After his meal, Bajirao was relaxing in his room when Kunwar came in to announce that Matushree was expecting him.

'Where is she?'

'Just finishing her prayers.'

Bajirao went to his mother's room. She asked, 'Now that the campaign is over, I want to discuss something with you. Rau, what are you planning for Appa?'

'The moment the rains are over, he will be marching over to Konkan after Vijayadashmi.'

'I am not talking of your campaigns, Rau! Appa has a motherless child. Do you realize that?'

'Are you suggesting he get married?'

'Yes! He is constantly out leaving an infant son behind. Who is to take care of the child? His wife's mother is managing somehow but don't you think Appa should get married?'

'I understand, Matushree,' Bajirao concurred. 'Do you have someone in mind?'

'Once decided, we can find someone quite easily. Rau, you need to make Appa understand. He has not even seen twenty-five winters. I dread to think of him being out all the time.'

'I will convince him. Leave that to me.'

'Despite having a beautiful wife back home, men have a tendency to go astray. And in Appa's case, he is all alone. What stops him from straying from his path? And one more thing...'

'Yes, Matushree?'

'Naro Bhikaji of Colaba has an eight-year-old daughter. I feel we should get Appa married to her. Bhikaji would not refuse our request. Diwali is a good time for the marriage. I hope you can get the arrangements done by then. I want a grand affair. We should invite the Chhatrapati, who loves Appa dearly. We need to invite all the sardars and treat them as protocol demands.'

Seeing Bajirao lost in thought, Radhabai quickly surmised there was something else troubling him. She asked, 'Rau, you have some concerns. Won't you tell me?'

'Matushree, these are not insurmountable problems. Leave them to me; you need not worry.'

'Rau, don't you trust me? I can suggest something only if you confide in me.'

Bajirao said, 'I agree we need to get Appa married but I suggest we don't announce it right away. A huge house needs a sound foundation. We need to spend appropriately, keeping the Peshwa prestige in mind. I shall see that we follow all protocol.'

Mother and son continued to chat for a long time. Radhabai was well versed in all matters of administration and asked a lot of questions. She said, wrapping up, 'Once Appa is married, I will be free to go on my pilgrimage.'

'We shall see,' Bajirao said, trying to dodge the topic.

'I am not talking of leaving right now! By the way, I don't see Bhikaji these days. Where is he?'

'I have sent him to Sagar. Did you want to speak to him?'

'No. I just wanted to know where he was. I am sure he has gone for work.'

Radhabai chose not to probe further.

That afternoon Kunwar informed Bajirao that Kashibai would not be coming for the darshan at the temple as her leg was aching.

Bajirao reached her quarters to enquire and found her playing a game of chess with her maid Yesu, who hurriedly got up and left.

'I am sorry your maid had to leave halfway through the game. I came in as I was told you were not feeling well and have cancelled your visit to the temple.'

'That is right. My leg is hurting. All this getting in and out of the palanquin is too much.'

Bajirao sat on a low stool and looking at the chessboard said, 'Oh! It seems you have got a new set of pieces. Where did they come from?'

'Pilaji Rao got them from Khambat especially for me. What brings you here, by the way?'

'Nothing really. I came in to enquire about your health.'

'Now that you are here, how about a game of chess?'

'I will, provided you don't go away leaving the game halfway through. You always find an excuse and go away, especially when I am about to leave.'

'I won't, I promise you.'

Rau was satisfied. Kashibai laid the pieces and a game began. After a while, Bajirao said, 'I have a task for you.'

'Please tell me. I shall do whatever I can.'

'I want you to decide when and what reward should be given to the performers. The clerks are there to help, but you must take the final decision. Whenever I get a list, I shall mark the names of the craftsmen, musicians, dancers and singers but you should take care that they are suitably rewarded.'

'What made you think of this today?'

'Had I given you this task earlier, the complaint about the singer would not have reached me, isn't it? If you look into the matters, things will be taken care of smoothly.'

Bajirao looked at Kashibai's face but she did not react.

Bajirao fumed with anger, his eyes bloodshot, as he read the letter which had been offered by Ambaji Pant. He said, 'Pant! Do you see the temerity of Udaji Pawar? I made him a sardar and appointed him at Dhar. Look at what he has done!'

Everyone in the office was silent, as they did not dare to speak. Rau's temper was well known.

Pant tried to defuse the situation. 'I am sure it is Udaji's mischief. I would request Shrimant to ignore it.'

'Mischief? You call this mischief, Pant?' Bajirao thundered, his voice rising with each word. 'Earlier, he joined the Dabhades in the campaign against us. That was his first mistake. I didn't say anything. And now, he is looting our own territories and fighting with our sardars. You call such acts mischief?'

'If you order, I shall send him a letter of warning.'

'It is beyond warning now. We need to do something so that such fellows remain under our control and fear us. Otherwise, there is no difference between the Marathas and ordinary plunderers. Send a note to Pilaji Jadhav. Are his scribes here?'

Pilaji's clerks stepped forward and saluted. Bajirao said, 'Inform Pilaji to send two batteries of his soldiers to Malwa. They should capture Udaji, bind him in chains and drag him here. Inform me after the task is done.'

Udaji Pawar was a senior official and had personal relations with Chhatrapati Maharaj. No one had expected such harsh orders. Pant tried to intervene. He said, 'Isn't the punishment a tad too harsh? His reputation will be ruined. Chhatrapati Swami too may feel bad.'

'I normally respect your advice, Pant, but in this case I am not going to listen. Pawar has insulted the empire and I will not tolerate that. Please take action on the orders immediately.'

No one had the courage to intervene again. Ambaji Pant started writing the orders. At that moment, another clerk came in with a letter. Bajirao scanned the letter and then, handing it over to Pant, asked, 'Is this true?'

Pant glanced through the letter quickly and said, 'Yes, it is.'

'I will look into it later. Meet me in my private chambers once this task is done.'

Bajirao got up for his meal where he was joined by Babuji Naik Baramatkar's son and Bhiubai's husband, Abaji Naik Baramatkar. His other brother-in-law, Vyankatrao Ghorpade, too was present. The news that the Peshwa had ordered Udaji Pawar to be tied in chains had spread leading to a silent, humourless lunch. Bajirao too did not engage in much conversation.

At the end of the meal, Bajirao said, 'Abaji Naik, can you come into my private chambers? I want to discuss something.'

As soon as they sat down, Bajirao said, 'Abaji, you are my brother-in-law and I treat you with all due respect. But I find that you have taken advantage of my goodness and stabbed me in the back. I never expected that.'

Abaji was enjoying a paan, thinking that the discussion would be something casual. He sat up hearing Bajirao's allegation. 'What? I have been treacherous? What makes you say that?'

'Let me show you some proof,' Bajirao said, throwing the letter at Abaji. One look at the letter and Abaji's face fell. He quickly tried to collect himself and said, his voice taking on an edge, 'What is wrong with that? I fought in Gujarat along with you. As part of the loot, we kept one elephant with us. What is so wrong about it?'

'Abaji! Whatever we get in the campaign as loot needs to be deposited with the royal treasury first. Don't you know these basic rules?'

'These rules apply to your ordinary sardars or people like Ranoji Shinde. We are not just sardars but also well-respected sahukars, the ones whom the Peshwas are indebted to. Why make a fuss over a single elephant? And that too accusing me of back-stabbing you!'

Bajirao tried controlling his anger. He shouted, 'Abaji Naik, I thought you would readily accept your mistake and return the elephant to the treasury. But you seem to be taking undue advantage of your familial relationship with the Peshwa. This will not be tolerated.'

Abaji was not one to cow down. He said, arrogance dripping in his voice, 'I have earned the elephant in a battle. As a matter of pride and a symbol of our victory, the elephant will remain in the haveli of Sahukar Naik Baramatkars.'

'Lest you forget, it is the Peshwa who decides what is right and what is wrong. You may leave now.'

Bajirao walked out of the room before Abaji could get up.

That evening, before Abaji Naik realized, his haveli was surrounded by the Peshwa's soldiers.

It was past midnight. Bajirao Peshwa paced in the deliberations room, his hands clasped behind his back. A heap of pages lay in a corner while Ambaji Pant stood waiting for his master to speak. Unable to wait any longer, he said, 'Shrimant, I urge you to listen to me. I have been in the service of the Peshwas since the time of Nanasaheb. My advice is in the interest of the state.'

Bajirao stopped pacing and said, 'I have been deliberating over what you said. Our emissaries are spread across Hindustan, right from Gandhar in the west to Kamrup in the east and they keep me abreast of all that is happening across the country. I know what is happening in Delhi and sometimes feel like rushing to Indraprastha but then practical realities make me stop. How long can I sit twiddling my thumbs?'

'Shrimant, ever since we taught Muhammad Bangash a lesson, the Marathas have established their supremacy over Rohilkhand and the Doab province. No doubt the Rajputs, Jats and some of the Mughal troops look to us with hope. It is for the same reason Sawai Jaisingh of Jaipur has sent his emissary. I suggest you meet him.'

Ambaji had been repeating his request ever since they stepped into the private deliberations room.

'Pant, I don't trust these Rajputs. You know the way Sawai Jaisingh's forefathers treated the Marathas. It is his family that caused a lot of trouble, siding with the Mughals, while the elder Maharaj was toiling day and night to establish the Maratha empire.'

'Those are things of the past, Shrimant! We need to take advantage of the new order. What is the point in raking up old issues?'

'Times change and so do people, but I will believe that when I see them. I don't trust the Rajputs who, while needling us against the Mughals, kowtow to the Delhi durbar. I suspect they would be happy to see us routed so that they can themselves sit on the throne at Delhi.'

'That may have been their ambition, I agree,' Pant concurred, 'but they are in no position to do so on their own. Today, the only true power in entire Hindustan is that of the Marathas. That is the reason they have come to us. Please hear them once and then take your decision.'

Bajirao was finally convinced of Ambaji's logic and agreed to meet the Rajput emissary. Ambaji stepped out and brought in the emissary who had been eagerly waiting outside.

Sawai Jaisingh's emissary was a tall and fair man, sporting a bushy moustache in the Rajput style and a traditional turban. He wore a loose kurta over a pair of churidar pyjamas. He bowed thrice in the Mughal style as soon as he stepped into the room.

Bajirao, without wasting time on formalities, got to the point. 'Emissary! I have heard everything from Pant. I am told that Sawaiji wants me to attack Delhi and that this is an opportune time to do so. My question is, what support will the Rajputs offer us?'

The emissary was overwhelmed seeing Bajirao's imposing personality and his penetrating eyes. But he was an emissary, well versed in politics and not one to get rattled. He said, 'When the Maratha forces cross the Chambal and enter the Doab province after crossing the Ganga and Jamuna, the Rajput forces will be there to support you.'

Bajirao's forehead creased in irritation. He said bluntly, 'I am not interested in your politically correct and ambiguous statements. Please state clearly what support your kings from Udaipur, Jaipur and Jodhpur are willing to offer: whether in the form of troops, money, weapons and armoury or whatever else.'

The emissary was not one to give in easily. He answered, 'Sawaiji has sent me with the explicit purpose of meeting you. The Mughal atrocities have weakened Hindu dharma and most of our pilgrimage spots are under their control. To free such places from their tyranny and get the flag of sanatan dharma fluttering on Indraprastha is the sole intention of Sawaiji and we shall provide all the support it takes to achieve this objective, whether such support requires troops, arms or money. Shrimant may state what he has in mind.'

Bajirao was not one to be swayed by such words. He said, 'It is fine then. I shall ask for your help when we reach north. We shall need a crore of rupees once we cross the Narmada. We will require another five crores till we reach Delhi. Is that agreeable to you?'

The emissary had never expected Bajirao to explicitly state the amount. He was taken aback but the seasoned man did not allow his emotions to show on his face. He said, 'The amount is a little high but I shall nevertheless convey your wishes to my master. Shall I let him know that the Maratha troops will cross over after the monsoon?'

Bajirao was impressed with the emissary's courage to get an definite plan of action from him. He said, 'Please tell your master that Bajirao is a Peshwa and not the ruler of the Maratha empire. We act on orders from the Chhatrapati alone. We will take his blessings to march to Delhi once Sawai accepts our demands.'

'I shall convey your message and return within a fortnight with my master's reply.'

After the emissary had been escorted out, Bajirao said, 'We will soon know whether the Rajputs honour their promises, as they are famously known for. I will be going to Satara soon and shall have a word with the Chhatrapati. In the meantime, send a confidential message to all our representatives and ensure that we get up-to-date information on everything happening there. Half the victory lies in getting the right information on time.'

It had been three days since Bhiubai had set up camp in Radhabai's quarters. Despite Radhabai's best efforts, her daughter was unwilling to give in. She had only one question: 'Why should we allow Rau to have his way? He may be a Peshwa but it is a matter of just one elephant. It does not do our reputation any good by having his soldiers surround our haveli. It is too much!'

Radhabai tried cajoling her daughter. She said, 'Bhiubai, I have a lot of affection for our son-in-law and understand his prestige and position in society. You know I have a bias towards him compared to our younger son-in-law but then…'

Bhiubai interrupted her mother saying, 'Matushree! You claim to love him but Rau goes about putting him under house arrest. And yet, you keep quiet. What do I make of it? You need to take a call now.'

'There are rules to be followed in administration, don't you agree? My son-in-law did not follow the procedures and hence…'

Bhiubai lost her temper. 'What procedures are you talking of? Just that he kept an elephant which he captured in the war? That's all! Don't we have that liberty either?'

'Who says you don't? I am told my son-in-law spoke rudely. Rau is your brother but also a Peshwa. He cannot tolerate any insubordination or an insult to the title. I cannot interfere in his decisions.'

Bhiubai sat in a huff hearing her mother's final word. Radhabai felt guilty at having snubbed her daughter. She had a soft corner for Bhiubai as she had not conceived a child yet. The very thought troubled Radhabai. At the same time, she knew that it was wise to not undermine the position of Rau by interfering in his administrative decisions. She said, 'Bhiubai, it is fine if my son-in-law keeps the elephant as a trophy but would it not be appropriate that he deposit an equivalent amount in the treasury?'

'Rau could have easily suggested that. The Baramatkars have enough money to bother about paying for one elephant.'

It was an indirect snub which hurt Radhabai. She said, 'You don't need to say such things. There is no need to point out who has money and who has not. The Peshwa did what was right and just. Nevertheless, I am sure we can find a way out.'

'That is what I am here for! Why don't you get the guards removed? Find a way so that the problem is resolved but the elephant remains at the haveli.'

'Let me see what I can do,' Radhabai said and then asked the guard standing outside to send for Ambaji Purandare.

Ambaji Pant came in and stood respectfully in a corner. He was aware of the pleas made by Bhiubai to her mother over the last few days. But being a servant, he stood as if he had not a clue and was waiting for orders.

'Pant,' Radhabai began, 'is Abaji Naik's haveli still being guarded?'

'Yes, it is. I was against it but Shrimant had issued strict orders. I was helpless.'

'Is there a way out, without Naik having to return the elephant?'

'If Naik agrees to pay the cost of the elephant, we can work that out.'

Matushree asked, 'What would be the cost?'

Bhiubai interrupted. 'It would not look nice if we ask my in-laws to pay for the elephant.'

'Bhiubai! Haven't you left it to me now? Let me handle it my way.'

Turning to Pant, Radhabai repeated, 'What would be the cost?'

'I haven't seen the elephant but on an average it would be around two thousand rupias or so.'

'Pant, take around two and a half thousand from my personal expense account and deposit the same in the treasury. Send the receipt to Abaji Naik and get the guards removed.'

'I need to take Shrimant's permission for this. I am not sure if he will agree to the way suggested by you. I don't want to face his ire.'

'You don't worry. I will take care of it. Now, get this done urgently.'

Pant was not at all happy with the prospect of this task. Seeing him hesitate, Radhabai asked, 'What now?'

'I have never taken such a step. I haven't done something where the mind is willing but the heart is not. Anyway, I will look into it.'

He took his leave and then, after lunch, went to meet the Peshwa. He said, 'I was wanting to say something. May I?'

Bajirao looked at Pant.

Pant continued, 'I am not keeping well these days. My elder son, Mahadoba, is grown up now and can manage the work of the office quite well. I would like to be relieved and take retirement. I wish to go on a pilgrimage once I am relieved of my duties.'

Bajirao raised his eyebrows questioningly. 'What is the matter? It was just a few days ago that you were urging me to march on to Delhi and now you want to retire? The Purandares play a role equal to the Peshwa when it comes to administrative matters. Should I be telling you that people like you should work till their last drop of blood or till their last breath?'

Pant had no answer. He stood dumbfounded and was a little relieved when Bajirao excused himself leaving him alone.

Kashibai was in her quarters when Yesu came in. Not sure of how she should start the conversation she had come for, she indulged in arranging the things in the room. Noticing her, Kashibai asked, 'Where is Shrimant, Yesu?'

'He has gone horse riding towards Parvati maidan this morning.'

'Oh, is that so?'

Seeing Kashibai silent, Yesu took the opportunity and said, 'Baisaheb, I want to say something.'

'What is it about?'

'That Chanda Jamdar has been given the task of managing the guards at the Kothrud haveli. He struts around like an important official. Yesterday, the maid, Basanti, had come complaining to Ambaji Pant in the office regarding him.'

'Basanti? Isn't she the same woman we met in the bazaar the other day?'

'Yes, she is the handmaiden of a singer. She complained to Ambaji Pant that Chanda flirts with her all the time. He asks her to sing that song.'

'What song?'

'The one which Mastani sang for Shrimant a few days back.'

Kashibai shook her head saying, 'Aren't you making a mountain out of a molehill? I will speak to Swami and get it sorted out.'

'I did not mean to complain. I thought I would bring this to your notice. I will take back my words, if you are offended.'

Kashibai did not respond but Yesu had triggered a stream of thoughts. She asked, 'What song was it, Yesu; not that I understand their Yavani language.'

> *'My eyes, they rain all the time*
> *Till I see him in mine...*

'You know, Baisaheb, it is about a woman pining for her lover. She says the rainy season may come once in a year but her eyes are constantly raining tears.'

Kashibai looked out of the window as the sky turned dark with approaching clouds. She said to herself, 'It seems the rains will start soon.'

Yesu, not realizing that her mistress was speaking to herself, said, 'That's right. The rains are almost here. Maybe that is the reason Shrimant decided to go for a horse ride before it starts pouring.'

Kashibai pulled the satin curtains across the windows. The black clouds disappeared from her view.

A part of the area at the base of Parvati hill had been cleared of the bushes and levelled flat for the Peshwa to inspect the horses assembled there by various traders for sale.

Bajirao, accompanied by Bhivrao Rethrekar, entered the ground. Bhivrao was a close confidant and adviser of Bajirao, their familes well known to each other since Bajirao's father's time. Bajirao would take his advice for various things. Looking at the horses, he said, 'Bajipant, it seems there are a lot of traders waiting for us.'

Rethrekar, observing the line of horses on display, said, 'Of course! Where else would they find a buyer who knows the fine art of selecting the best horses? This is public knowledge now.'

Bajirao moved along the lines observing the horses. The moment he reached a trader, the trader would bend low in salaam and wait for him to say something. Each trader would list the traits and special characteristics of the horses he had on display. The traits were exotically called Panchakalyani, Jay Mangal, Kamalkanth, Devamani and such. Bajirao's eyes stopped at a black horse. Sensing the Peshwa's interest, the trader stepped forward with the horse. The men from Bajirao's stables did a thorough inspection. Bapuji Shripat, the chief of the stables, gave his verdict, 'Shrimant, it is a good Panchakalyani horse.'

'What would be his age?'

'Just two years, sarkar,' the trader answered.

An imperceptible nod was enough for the trader to know that the horse had been sold. He immediately handed over the reins to the stablehands.

Bajirao and Rethrekar continued their inspection. The ones selected were taken charge of by the stablehands, while the clerks were busy noting down the details of the deal.

It was getting hot. At that moment, Bajirao noticed a white steed. Pointing at him, he asked, 'Bajipant, what do you think?'

Bajipant inspected the horse and said, 'He is a fine-looking horse; one that would add glamour to your collection. If you agree, I will ask them to take it to the stables.'

Bajirao did not answer immediately. Instead, he called the trader and asked, 'Any flaws?'

'Flaws? None, sarkar, but he is a little hot-headed.'

'What do you mean?'

'He does not like ordinary men to ride him.'

'Let me check,' Bajirao said and asked the men to saddle the horse.

Rethrekar warned, 'I suggest I take a ride first. I would not advise you to mount this beast without checking him out first.'

'He looks like a fine horse and I like him. Such beauty is wont to have a little attitude, isn't it?'

Bajirao jumped down from his horse in a single smooth movement. Holding the whip in his right hand, he fixed his leg into the stirrup and was about to mount when the horse neighed loudly raising his forelegs, but Bajirao managed to push himself on to the horse's back and hold the reins. The syce ran to control the horse but Bajirao, indicating with his right hand to stop, patted the horse on his thighs. The horse immediately put his legs down and, in the next moment, started galloping. Bajirao, holding the reins in his hands, held the horse tightly with his thighs pressing against it. Tackling bushes and other obstacles along the way, the horse galloped, unmindful of the rider.

Within moments, they had crossed the flat maidan and reached the banks of the river. The horse rushed across the sandy bank and on to the dry riverbed. At one place, there was a small pool, around eight feet wide. He jumped the pool in a smooth flying arc and crossed over to the other bank.

It was a rough terrain with small bushes and trees. The horse continued his run through the bushes and reduced his speed after a while, tired of the sprint. Bajirao was impressed with the way the horse had galloped through the obstacles. On spotting a group of men and women, he pulled the reins to stop the horse. The horse neighed loudly, raising his forelegs again before halting.

One man from the group, curiously watching the horse and the rider, suddenly recognized Bajirao and exclaimed, 'Isn't that Shrimant himself? What is he doing here all alone?'

The horse was dripping with sweat. Bajirao relaxed his grip seeing that the horse stood still. Wiping his face with the dangling edge of his turban, he asked, 'Who are you and what brings you here?'

One of the maids came running forward. It was Basanti. She said, bending low in salaam, 'Shrimant, your horse is tired. May I escort you to where Baiji is waiting?'

'Baiji?' Bajirao asked.

'Mastanibai! You heard her sing the other day, do you recall?'

'Oh, I see!' Bajirao exclaimed. Pointing at the group with his whip, he asked, 'What are these people doing here?'

'Today is the day of Bakr Eid. Baiji has come to distribute largesse.'

Bajirao turned his horse to follow Basanti. The group, assembled to receive the dole, made way. Bajirao's eyes met Mastani's as she sat on a raised platform. She hurriedly got up and saluted. She asked Basanti, who stood near her, 'How is it that Shrimant is here?'

'I have no idea, Baiji!'

Bajirao, noticing their whispering asked, 'I had allowed you to stay in the gardens at Kothrud. How come you are distributing your dole here in the jungle instead?'

For a moment Mastani looked at Bajirao. Then looking down, she said, 'There is a Mahadev temple close to our quarters. We did not want to despoil the temple with our dole,' and saying so, she pointed towards a table where the meat was kept ready for distribution amongst the poor. She said, 'Our charity is of the kind you would not want us to do near your temple. That is why we chose this faraway place.'

Bajirao, having understood the situation, joked, 'So would I be a likely beneficiary today?'

Mastani did not dare to look up. She turned to her maid and said, 'Sarkar is a Brahman. Our charity would not suit him, but if sarkar insists, he may come to our house and I shall try my best to make it acceptable.'

Basanti looked at Bajirao expectantly. He said, 'I am tired of riding the horse since morning and I am thirsty. I will go towards the temple and ask one of the priests there for some water.' Bajirao turned his horse towards the temple at Kothrud gardens and galloped away.

Chanda Jamdar came running when he saw Bajirao reach the temple. He held the reins for him to get down. After a quick mujra, he muttered, 'I was not aware ... Shrimant came unannounced...'

Bajirao jumped down and then, stretching himself, said, 'Get me some water. I will have a darshan at the temple while you send someone to the haveli and let them know that I am here. And send the message to Parvati maidan too. They would be waiting for me.'

The priests, on seeing Bajirao, hurriedly came out. One of them handed over a tumbler of water to Bajirao. He drank to his heart's content and then splashed water on his face. Entering the sanctum sanctorum, he prayed before going to the large hall in the courtyard. The priest was nervous since he did not know the reason for Bajirao's unannounced visit.

As Bajirao came out of the temple, he heard horses and saw Basanti and Mastani riding towards him. Bajirao stood on the steps watching them. Mastani, turning the horse skilfully as it reached the base of the steps, jumped down with grace. Bajirao was reminded of a delicate flower landing softly on the ground.

She said, 'Huzoor, it is the day of our festival. It is Allah's blessings that you have honoured us by coming to our lowly abode. I would be most disappointed if I don't get a chance to serve you; even Allah would not like it.'

'Is that so?' Bajirao said, unable to take his eyes off her face. 'What do you propose?'

'Shrimant may rest here awhile. I shall try my best within my means,' said Mastani, her heart beating loudly in her chest. Her pink cheeks had taken on a deeper shade and there was a mixture of excitement and fear in her eyes.

'Fine. Arrange for a mat below the tree there. I shall rest for a while.'

Mastani was pleased. Bajirao was resting when a Brahman came along with milk in a silver tumbler. Mastani followed him. She said, saluting thrice, 'Huzoor, the food we have prepared may not be appropriate for you. You are a Brahman and hence I have brought a tumbler of milk for you. Please accept it.'

Bajirao did not stretch his hand forward to take the tumbler. His eyes bore into Mastani's face, the near-transparent dupatta adding to the allure of her fair skin. Each part of her body from her delicate feet to her curvaceous figure, narrow waist, shapely breasts, a pointed chin and arched eyebrows arrested Bajirao's attention. He looked at her with a sense of dissatisfaction, unable to drink in enough of her beauty.

Mastani indicated with her eyes to the Brahman to offer the tumbler once again to Bajirao. Seeing the subtle dance of her eyebrows, Bajirao could not resist and exclaimed, 'Wah!'

Mastani's beauty had transfixed Bajirao. She blushed feeling the intense scrutiny of his eyes but did not dare to look up as she took the tumbler from the Brahman and offered it to Bajirao.

Bajirao accepted the tumbler and put it to his lips. Mastani whispered softly under her breath, 'May Allah take care of him.'

Bajirao did not hear her words. At that moment, voices could be heard from the other end of the garden and soon the search party looking for Bajirao arrived.

Kashibai had left a day early. The Peshwa family tradition demanded that they stop at the temple of Kurkumbh Devi for a darshan en route to Satara. Kurkumbh was the family deity of the Peshwas. Kashibai would insist that Bajirao take the goddess' blessings before leaving or returning from any campaign.

The caravan for the palanquin consisted of Ambaji Purandare leading it with a cavalry of fifty. It was evening by the time they had navigated the winding roads of Patas to reach the Kurkumbh temple.

The temple was situated atop a hill. Ambaji Pant, noticing that it was getting dark, said, 'Baisaheb, please continue to sit in the palanquin. Your leg is troubling you and the climb will make it worse.'

Kashibai said, getting down from the palanquin and wrapping a shawl around her shoulders, 'We have always walked up the hill whenever we have come here. If the Lord so desires, I am sure we will manage.'

Everyone dismounted and started climbing up the hill. A few soldiers held burning torches at intervals along the path. Halfway up, she stopped to catch her breath when Pant requested once again, 'I wish you would sit in the palanquin. It is right behind us.'

Kashibai smiled and, shaking her head, continued to climb

up. After an hour, they reached the temple. Kashibai paid obeisance from the outer hall itself. Another hall had been converted into a temporary resting place for Kashibai. The temple had become popular when people around came to know that it was the family deity of the Peshwa family. The village at the base of the hill thus attracted crowds. Kashibai rested for a while in the verandah adjacent to the hall. In the far distance, she could see burning torches being carried as men went about their work.

A rider reached at noon the next day to announce that Shrimant Peshwa was expected shortly. Kashibai, sitting in the verandah, could see the meandering roads from Patas leading to the temple. Soon, a group of fifty-odd soldiers on horseback were visible.

The sun was moving towards the western horizon when the horses, kicking dust, reached the village near the temple of Kurkumbh. Kashibai spotted Bajirao as the horses, climbing up a steep slope, reached the flat ground from where the steps began. Jumping down from the horse, Bajirao flung the reins to a syce in attendance and walked towards the steps. He touched the first step with his right hand and then touched his forehead reverently before he began climbing up, two or three steps at a time. Kashibai winced at the memory of her painful climb the previous night when each step had been a challenge for her, while her husband was now merrily running up the steps after having travelled nearly twenty miles. Her own inability and apparent handicap irritated her.

Soon, the servants came running to announce that Bajirao had reached the main door and was expected any moment. Kashibai left the verandah where she had been sitting and went into the hall.

Horns and trumpets announced Bajirao's entry into the courtyard. Removing his shoes at the entrance, which one of the servants picked up immediately, he walked towards the temple. Another servant came rushing in with a jug of water. Bajirao splashed some water on his face. Then turning towards the temple, he folded his hands in namaskar from a distance before going to the temporary quarters prepared for him.

The priests waited patiently for their royal guests. Soon, Bajirao and Kashibai came in. They prayed together while Kashibai offered a necklace of gold coins to the goddess. After accepting the holy water, they stepped into the courtyard.

A special seating arrangement had been made for the couple. Having finished their meal, they sat in the open courtyard in the pleasant breeze. It was a relaxing evening with small talk amongst those present. Bajirao asked, looking at Kashibai, 'Ambaji Pant informs me that you insisted on climbing up despite your leg troubling you. Why the adamance?'

'It did not feel right to come up in a palanquin to offer my prayers to the goddess.'

'It is not about showing off your power or prestige. You should take care of your health,' Bajirao said, concerned.

Kashibai sat resting her back against a thick bolster. Her arms sported the green bangles which the priest had given as his offering to her. She had wrapped a shawl around herself. On the other hand, Bajirao merely wore a thin silk kurta. The gems of his nine-gem ring sparkled in the moonlight.

Bajirao asked, 'How is your leg now?'

'There is a little pain, but nothing to worry about.'

'Ambaji told me that you had to stop midway as it was hurting too much.'

Kashibai said, blushing a little, 'I am not like Shrimant who can run up the steps without stopping even once. It was good that I came up earlier, else it would have been an embarrassing sight, with me struggling far behind you!'

Bajirao smiled at the thought and said, 'That is why I had arranged for the palanquin. Else, I would have sent your favourite horse.'

'Horse!' Kashibai said, putting her finger to her lips in surprise. 'Were you expecting me to ride a horse?'

'Why? What objection do you have? It is not that you cannot ride a horse. You used to boast of the way you would gallop when you were at your mother's place.'

'That was long back, when I was young! I cannot do those things now. How odd it would look if a man and a woman were to be seen galloping together!'

'I never thought of it, actually. I just do what I feel like.'

It was a lovely evening as the moon rose in the sky. The breeze was pleasant, bringing in the sweet fragrance of flowers. Resting against a bolster, Bajirao closed his eyes and was soon asleep.

Kashibai hadn't noticed and said, 'That reminds me...' Then, seeing that Bajirao had slept off, she took off her shawl, draped it on him and quietly walked back to her room.

Bajirao had taken up residence in Nyaya Bhawan at Satara as they waited for the Chhatrapati's audience at the royal palace. Chimaji Appa, Nana, Ambaji Pant and Mahadoba Purandare along with Bajirao chose an auspicious day to pay their respects to the Maharaj. Servants carrying trays covered with a bright cloth walked behind them.

Chhatrapati Maharaj sat in the durbar hall with his sardars

and other officials in attendance. Two servants, holding a large fan, stood behind, waving it gently. The Chhatrapati, a dusky complexioned sixty-year-old maharaja, sported long white hair that reached his shoulders. His luxuriant moustache too was white. One look at his serene face and it would become clear that the Chhatrapati bore no ill thoughts against anyone. He was a man with a pure heart.

Bajirao entered the hall and bent low in mujra. The Maharaj blessed him and asked him to stand near him. Bajirao indicated to his men to present the trays. Seeing a collection of exquisite clothes, gems, jewellery and handicrafts from all over India brought a smile to the Chhatrapati's face.

Those in attendance at the court that day enjoyed, for nearly an hour, a dance performance in honour of the Peshwa's arrival. After the dance, the Chhatrapati took an update of the Peshwa's activities and thanked him for the lovely gifts. He suggested that Bajirao stay back in Satara till the end of the rainy season and enjoy his hospitality. As the servant got the tray with paan, it was an indication that the meeting was over. The Chhatrapati asked Bajirao to follow him into his private chambers along with Chimaji Appa.

Sitting on a satin carpet on the floor, he asked Bajirao and Chimaji to take their seats on a cotton dhurrie laid nearby. Bending in mujra, they both sat down and waited for the Chhatrapati to speak. A vetiver screen separated the ladies' sitting space where the Chhatrapati's favourite queen, Virubai, sat. The Chhatrapati began, his voice a little serious, 'Rau, I am both happy and sad to know that we have won against the Dabhades. It would have been far better had we managed to avoid the conflict altogether.'

Bajirao interrupted before the Chhatrapati could continue,

'Dabhade's resistance was not much. I have come here to discuss a large political plan. We can talk about Dabhade some other day.'

'I have been briefed by Chimnaji Pandit,' Shahu Maharaj said. 'I know you are tempted to march northwards. But you must remember one thing: I had made a promise to Aurangzeb Badshah when he released me.'

Shahu Maharaj paused as he closed his eyes and seemed lost in the past. After a while, he said, 'I had taken a vow holding the tail of a cow in my hand that I would never allow the Marathas to challenge the Mughal throne. Rau, you must remember this. I always say "don't destroy the old and don't grab something new".'

Bajirao's forehead creased in irritation and for a moment he forgot that he was in the Chhatrapati's audience as he muttered, 'What is the value of a promise made to infidels? They are a bunch of crooks. I don't think Your Highness should bother about promises you made back then. Politics demands that we do what is good for us.'

'Rau, political pressures may demand so, but I cannot afford to have the word go around that there is no value to the Chhatrapati's promises.'

'I understand your sentiments but before Your Highness reminds me of the promise made to the Mughal Emperor, I would like to remind you of another vow taken much earlier.'

'What is it you are talking of?'

'I have heard from my elders about the vow the elder Maharaj had taken at Raigadh on the day of his coronation.'

The Chhatrapati was silent, encouraging Bajirao to continue. 'Taking the waters of all the sacred rivers in his palm, the elder Maharaj had taken an oath to release Hindustan from the grip of the Musalmaans and that he would see the flag of Hindavi Swaraj fluttering in all its glory at each and every pilgrimage place. Didn't Your Highness appoint us as the Peshwa precisely to fulfil this dream? We are bound by our duties. What else is the use of such high-sounding titles if not for making those dreams come true?'

Bajirao's voice quivered with emotion. Chhatrapati Shahu, calm and composed as always, heard him patiently. Appa intervened, 'Please listen to what Swami has to say, Rau. He is not against the temples being freed from the clutches of the Musalmaans. We can still achieve that while keeping our relations with the Mughal Badshah intact.'

The Chhatrapati said, 'I agree with Chimaji Appa.'

Bajirao was getting more irritated but an imperceptible nod from Appa, to avoid a confrontation, stopped him from reacting. Appa said, 'We can continue to expand our borders without needling the Mughal Emperor. We can use the powers given to us to collect taxes. I request the Maharaj to allow us to do this.'

'Rau, I suggest you stay back for a while, till the rains abate a little. Let us sit together, you and me, along with our other ministers and take an informed decision. Thereafter, I shall issue the necessary orders. And while you are here, please do drop in to meet me once in a while.'

It was an indication to get up. Bajirao and Appa picked up their paans from the tray. A servant came in carrying the Chhatrapati's sandals. Appa took the sandals from the servant and placed them reverently on the floor before the Chhatrapati. Slipping his feet into them, the Chhatrapati said, 'Rau, do you see how Appa takes care of me? It is not without reason that I address him as Pandit.'

When Kashibai reached Satara, the rains had set in completely. The Yavateshwar hill was covered with dense clouds hiding the Mangalamata temple atop it. The quarters where Bajirao was stationed had a sloping tiled roof and the raindrops falling on it made a loud continuous clatter.

Bajirao, on receiving a message from the Maharaj, reached the royal palace to find him busy chatting with some traders who had come to display their best breeds of dogs and exotic birds. The Maharaj was a lover of animals and enjoyed seeing the well-trained dogs carry out commands.

Seeing Bajirao, he dismissed the gathering. He asked Bajirao to sit near him and said, 'Rau, I wanted your advice hence I sent for you. But you need not have rushed. It was nothing urgent.'

'What can I do for you, Swami?'

'Well, there was an interesting case on which I had to give a decision. I wasn't sure hence I thought I would discuss it with you.'

'I am sure you would have taken a wise decision. What can a mere Peshwa advise you, Maharaj?'

'No, Bajirao. Sometimes one may tend to take a decision in a hurry just to get over the issue. It may not always be right.'

'I may be able to give my views if you share the details.'

'It so happened that Yashwant Rao Prabhu, one of my respected sardars, had got a maid as a gift from me. Unfortunately, in a rush of lust, he forced himself on her one day. When he found out that she was pregnant he put her in chains. When the news reached me, I debarred him from the court for a month.'

'What? Are you saying he got away with such a mild reprimand for the kind of crime he committed? Please don't mind my impertinence but the royal durbar has dealt with such matters quite differently earlier.'

'I know, I know. I have heard and also read in many court papers of the elder Maharaj giving orders to cut off the limbs or break the bones of such offenders but I feel that one should be given a chance to reform.'

'I suppose Maharaj's decision is right then!'

The Chhatrapati did not react but looked at Shrimant Bajirao, knowing that his Peshwa was not in agreement but was just being polite. He said, 'Rau, I have heard a few complaints about you lately.'

'Is it with regard to the dispensation of justice?' Bajirao asked, a little surprised. 'If you point out a particular instance, I shall try and remedy my actions.'

'Rau, sometimes power can corrupt and lead to arrogance. In a heady state of unlimited power, each decision can seem right.'

'I urge you to point out my mistake. I know I have your blessings and I would like to use your guidance to improve myself. Please tell me, Maharaj.'

'Rau, you know the decisions which I may have objected to hence I will not elaborate here. I may accept whatever decisions you take as my love for you makes me blind at times. But remember: many decisions seem fine till you and I are around. Later, they would look unacceptable to many.'

Bajirao was lost in thought. He wondered which incident the Maharaj was referring to. He knew that with age the Chhatrapati had become a little more tolerant. But the Peshwa could not afford to be lax and had to deal with a firm hand. Taking leave he said, 'I shall keep your advice in mind.'

That evening while sitting with his brother, he shared the conversation he had had with the Chhatrapati. 'I am still at a loss to understand what the Maharaj was referring to,' Bajirao said, wondering about the root of the conversation.

Appa, going through the notes sent by the spies, said, 'I just got news from Pune that Babuji Naik Baramatkar has sent a formal complaint against the Peshwa.'

'Oh! So that's what it is!' Bajirao said with a knowing smile.

It rained the whole of July. The skies cleared a little after nearly a month of rains.

Chiranjeev came in early one morning to meet his mother. Kashibai observed that he was beaming when he said, after touching her feet, 'Matushree, it's a lovely day, isn't it? Bright and sunny!'

'Yes, it is Shravan now. The rains will stop soon. So what's the good news?'

'I was sitting with Rau and Kaka last evening. Rau was trying to convince Appa to remarry. Rau was quite firm and did not give Appa much chance to protest. Appa finally relented!'

'Are you saying he agreed?'

'Not just that! Rau told him about the girl he has selected and that the marriage would take place in Pune the moment the rains stop. Appa had no option but to agree!'

'That is great! I am going to scold him now.'

'Scold? But why?'

'His father-in-law and I have been pestering him for a long time now, but he always had an excuse about his fate or something else. But look at the way he agreed when his elder brother forced him!'

'Can Appa ever say no to Rau?' Nana said.

'And by the way,' Nana continued, 'I have been asked to give you a message.'

'Regarding what?'

'Rau needs your advice.'

'My advice? Since when did he want that? He could have as well ordered.'

'It is regarding the Janmashtami celebrations. He wants to invite some of the singers from Pune for the function. He told me that he has given the responsibility of those singers to you hence your advice is required. Shall I invite them?'

'Who am I to say no? I will attend the kirtan, that's all. I am not going to be a part of the rest of the celebrations.'

'Rau told me that he would do whatever you decide. What shall I tell him?'

'Tell him that his wish is my command. I will be happy with whatever he decides.'

Nana took his leave.

That evening Bajirao despatched his messengers to Pune. The invitation to Mastani and her troupe to perform on the day of Janmashtami at Satara was received at Kothrud gardens.

The preparations for the festival began in full swing. A haveli had been built recently at Mahuli, on the banks of the Krishna, and the Peshwa issued orders for the performers from Pune to be stationed there.

At the haveli where the Peshwa was staying, the preparations for the kirtan were being supervised by Nana and Chimaji Appa. For two nights, the servants worked tirelessly. Carpets, coloured chandeliers and flowers created a wonderful ambience. An open courtyard for the kirtan was being prepared with seating arrangement for the royals on one side, while the ladies would sit behind a vetiver screen.

Knowing that there were enough people waiting to find faults, Chimaji Appa took special care to look into each detail.

Kashibai's left leg was troubling her again and she was unable to sit for too long. She was forced to stay back that evening at her residence, the pain in her leg being unbearable.

The sardars and their families started arriving and they were ushered to their respective seating places, as per protocol and hierarchy. Bajirao Peshwa stood at the entrance to receive the Chhatrapati, who arrived last, followed by his queens. After bending up to his waist in an elaborate mujra, the Peshwa guided the Chhatrapati to his seat. A low silver stool was placed on the carpet for him to rest his feet.

The kirtankar began by telling the tale of the birth of Lord Krishna. A small cradle, hanging with four golden chains covered with flowers, stood in a corner. In the cradle, on a silver tray was a lovely golden idol of baby Krishna.

The kirtankar sang in a melodious voice engaging the audience as he told the story of the birth of the Lord on a stormy night inside Kansa's jail, how the jail doors had opened automatically, and the way Vasudev crossed the river in the midst of floods and how the waters of the river in spate, on touching baby Krishna's feet, receded, allowing Vasudev to cross over and finally leave Krishna at the door of Yashoda's house. The kirtan ended with the singer ringing the bell to herald the birth of the Lord.

Shahu Maharaj stood up and everyone followed suit. The crowd cheered as they shouted the name of the Lord. The Chhatrapati gave a traditional tug to the cradle where the

Lord's idol was placed. It was the end of the kirtan session. Prasad was distributed and everyone dispersed.

Chimaji Appa escorted the Chhatrapati to the royal palace. Bajirao, along with a few select sardars, proceeded towards the haveli at Mahuli where the troupe waited for their royal guests.

Mastani stood up. Her kohl-lined eyes looked riveting, while a small black dot near the chin added to the beauty of her pink cheeks. The elaborate hairdo barely managed to hold the satin cap, stuck at an angle. She had casually thrown a rich purple dupatta over her shoulders. The silver anklets, ready for the dance, could be seen below her white salwar.

Mastani touched her hand to her forehead and walked over to the dance area, her anklets tinkling. Bajirao was mesmerized seeing her transform from the shy, reticent woman he had seen the other day to one who walked with the confidence and grace of a performer who knew her art. She turned to look at those present before her gaze rested on Bajirao.

At a cue from Bajirao, Mastani lifted her left leg and put it gracefully down on the carpet. The anklets tinkled. The grace with which she had taken the simple step made Bajirao inadvertently blurt out, 'Wah!'

Mastani's dance engrossed those in the hall as they watched her delicate fingers express the emotions, while her eyebrows danced in tandem. The feet, matching the beats of the percussion, created magic.

For an hour or so, Mastani danced, leaving the men desirous for more! The encores had been continuous. She would stop in between suddenly to look at Bajirao, who would nod his head in appreciation. She would then begin her dance as abruptly as she had stopped, leaving everyone stunned. Her coquettish gestures had the viewers spellbound. After an elaborate performance of nearly two hours, she stopped.

The servants arrived with gift-laden trays. Bajirao touched the trays as a gesture of his blessings before they were accepted by Mastani. She saluted once more and walked backwards till she exited. The anklets tinkled in rhythm as she walked away. The magic, created by the playful combination of the music and her dance, hung in the air long after the performance had ended.

Bajirao had stepped out of the hall when he received a message that Kashibai had sent for him. He rushed towards his quarters to find Yesu waiting for him outside. She said, 'Baisaheb dozed off while waiting for you. Shall I wake her up?'

Bajirao did not answer. He glanced at Kashibai sleeping soundly and asked, 'How is her leg now?'

'A little better,' Yesu said. 'The balm which the vaidyaraj prepared seems to have had some effect. I think she fell asleep when the pain subsided.'

Bajirao picked up a tumbler of milk lying near the bed and drank it in one gulp. He put the tumbler down on the table, banging it by mistake. Afraid that the sound may have woken up Kashibai, he turned around hurriedly but was relieved to find her still in deep sleep.

Bajirao stepped out into the night when the clock struck ten. Sleep eluded him. The sound of the anklets continued to ring in his ears and had been a constant companion ever since he had left the hall. Unable to control his emotions and confused a little at the intensity with which they raced through him, he paced the verandah for a while. The anklets continued to tinkle in his mind.

In a sudden decisive moment, he slipped on his shoes and,

throwing a shawl over his shoulders and a casual turban on his head, he walked out of his quarters. Kunwar, who was sitting and dozing near the door, stood up hurriedly but Bajirao gestured with a finger on his lips for him to keep quiet. Both of them stepped into the courtyard and moved towards the stables. Bajirao's favourite horse recognized his master's footsteps and dug his hooves into the ground in anticipation of a ride. Two syces slept nearby. Taking care not to wake them up, Kunwar gently guided the horse out of the stable. He selected another horse for himself and they both galloped towards Mahuli in the pitch-black night. Kunwar, having no clue of what his master was up to, simply followed Bajirao's horse. Suddenly, the sound of the raging waters of the river Krishna alerted Kunwar as they reached the banks.

Bajirao pulled the reins to stop the horse and said, 'Look around; the boatman should be sleeping somewhere nearby.'

Bajirao's eyes were fixed on the haveli on the other bank. Kunwar returned shortly, his voice trembling, 'The boatman has refused to take anyone across. Do I have the permission to tell him your name?'

'There is no need for that. Just hand this over to him,' and saying so, Bajirao took off the navagraha ring he was wearing.

Kunwar could not believe his eyes when he saw the ring in the mild light of a torch burning nearby. For a moment, he turned to look at Bajirao and then, better sense prevailed and he went to renegotiate with the boatman.

The negotiations done, Bajirao and Kunwar tied their horses to a tree nearby and got into the boat. As soon as they reached the bank, Bajirao instructed Kunwar, 'A certain Chanda Jamdar will be on guard. Tell him I am here and ask him to inform Mastani.'

Bajirao did not wait for Kunwar to return. The doors were open when they reached the top of the steps. Mastani, standing behind a curtain, was busy removing one piece of jewellery after another. Her silhouetted image could be seen against the curtain. Without any warning, Bajirao pushed the curtain aside and faced Mastani.

He caught her completely unawares. The jewellery she was holding fell down from her limp hand. Too stunned to even reach for her dupatta which lay on the ground, she gasped, 'Is that you, my lord?'

Bajirao glanced at the handmaiden who left quickly. Mastani's pink lips quivered. She said, 'It is so late in the night ... the river is in spate and ... you ... how did you ... why?'

She blushed ... she knew, yet she had dared to ask.

Two candles burned brightly on a stand nearby. Bajirao said, 'Mastani! I was helpless. The sound of your anklets led me here.'

'Yah Allah! At this hour? What will people think?'

Bajirao did not answer. Instead, he placed his palm on the candles, dousing the flames. The room was enveloped in darkness and the next moment, Mastani felt Bajirao's hand around her waist.

TWO

Appa's marriage took place in September, when the rains ended. Radhabai named her daughter-in-law Annapoorna. Immediately after marriage, Appa left for Konkan on another campaign.

Radhabai had invited many ladies including Kashibai's mother, Shiubai, for a festival. Nana's bride, Gopika, too was present. Gopika, a couple of years older than Annapoorna, had just turned ten. She and Annapoorna spent most of their time together, having found in each other a playmate, amongst the elders all around.

Radhabai would usually spend her mornings in prayer. She would engage the two young brides by asking them to memorize a few abhangs which she would sometimes ask them to sing in the evenings. Gopika was not happy with the knowledge that the younger Annapoorna was in fact her 'mother-in-law' and that she was the family's 'daughter-in-law'.

'Who is Shrimant?' Gopika asked one day. Annapoorna had heard that Bajirao would come to the puja room to take the holy water in the evenings. Curious to see him, they decided to linger in the room on the pretext of making garlands.

Bajirao walked in as usual and, after taking the holy water in his cupped palms, he left. He barely noticed the two young girls sitting in a corner, nervously glancing in his direction. Radhabai, upon spotting them, reprimanded, 'Don't you have any manners? You know very well this is the time for the elders to come for the puja. Now go and do your homework. Have you finished memorizing the abhangs I asked you to?'

They scampered back to their room. Gopika asked, 'So, is that whom everyone calls Shrimant?'

'Yes. That is right,' Annapoorna replied. 'I am told that I may be "mother-in-law" to you in a way, but you are elder to me in hierarchy. How is that so?'

'It has to be, isn't it? My husband, Shrimant's son, will be the Peshwa one day and my father said your husband would have to work under him. That makes me your senior, does it not?'

Thus their innocent talk continued.

Things were heating up. Bajirao's forces were creating havoc in the Gujarat, Malwa and Bundelkhand regions with the help of sardars like Shinde, Holkar and Abaji Kavde who went about collecting the revenues due to the Marathas, oftentimes by using force. The Mughal Badshah conferred with his key officials – Vazir Kamruddin Khan, Mir Bakshi Khan and others – to understand the impact of the Maratha raids. They were worried that Bajirao may choose to march upon Delhi one fine day. The Marathas were a force everyone across Hindustan seemed to be worried about.

Bajirao was busy going through the official papers when a messenger came in from Satara. Bajirao touched the satin bag to his forehead respectfully before asking Ambaji Pant to read the message aloud. Bajirao continued standing till Ambaji read the letter and then sat down. He said, 'Pant, Maharaj has asked me to meet the Nizam. He would not, under normal circumstances, ask me to do this. I don't know the reason for his orders.'

'Shrimant's aggressive revenue collection drive has made the Nizam nervous,' Pant explained. 'The Nizam considers the Deccan as his Subah and tries to create as many hurdles for us as possible when we go on our collection drive. The Chhatrapati believes a meeting with the Nizam could clear the bad blood.'

Bajirao did not like Ambaji's assessment of the Maharaj's orders and took some time to respond as he twirled his moustache and examined his reflection in the silver tray in which the letter was kept. He said, raising his voice a little for effect, 'Pant, you know my style. I prefer to meet the enemy on the battlefield. If the enemy wishes to meet us,' he said, using the plurative 'us' deliberately, 'they need to come with their hands folded and heads down. Send this as my reply.'

'Shrimant, I request you to consider what the Maharaj would feel if he were to receive this...'

'Then write to him: what exactly am I supposed to discuss when I meet the Nizam? We have been having our regular correspondence with the Nizam through our emissaries. What purpose does a meeting serve? Let the Chhatrapati know I believe it is a sheer waste of time.'

'I shall do as you command. Would Shrimant look at one of the lines in Maharaj's letter a little carefully?'

'Read it out to me,' Bajirao commanded.

'It seems the Nizam wants the meeting to take place at Rui Rameshwar on the banks of the river Manjra.'

'What do you make of it?'

'In the normal course of events, the Nizam would have

asked for a meeting in Aurangabad but we need to find out why he has chosen to meet in a deserted and far-off place like the one mentioned.'

Bajirao said, contemplating for a moment, 'Do so. After having routed the Nizam's forces at Palkhed, it is an insult for me to extend an olive branch. I know the Nizam's tactics. The moment we increased our efforts for tax collection he has gone running to the Maharaj for help. Anyway, if he wishes to get beaten in political discussions after having tasted defeat in war, I am game. But let the Maharaj know my views.'

'I shall do as you command,' Pant said.

'And one more thing – send a letter to Nizam Ali. Ask him to let us know in advance the points on which he wants to have a discussion. We shall reply suitably.'

Pant nodded.

After a week, Bajirao received another message from the Chhatrapati. The orders were clear – the Peshwa must go and meet the Nizam.

The news of the meeting, on orders from the Maharaj, spread like wildfire.

One morning, Kashibai's mother, Shiubai, came riding a horse with just two servants accompanying her. She asked, as soon as she dismounted, 'Is what I heard true?'

'Matushree, what made you ride all alone from Chas on horseback? Please rest awhile. We can talk later.'

'Tell me first, is it true?'

Kashibai did not answer but led her mother to the sitting room. She handed her a tumbler of water but brushing it aside, Shiubai repeated her question.

'What are you talking of, Matushree?' Kashibai asked.

'Are you saying you don't know despite staying here in this haveli? I heard of it in Chas and have lost my sleep since then. And I am shocked to see that things seem absolutely normal here! What kind of behaviour is this?'

'Matushree, will you tell me what it is about?'

'Bajirao is going to meet the Nizam on the orders of the Maharaj. Now, is that true?'

'It is,' Kashibai said, avoiding her mother's gaze.

'You seem to be quite fine with it, it seems.'

'I don't understand these political affairs. Nor do I try to interfere.'

'It is not politics. It is a calamity. Where is Shrimant? Call for him right away.'

Bajirao came the moment he got Shiubai's request for a meeting. He was a little surprised to hear that she had come unannounced. Shiubai stood up when Bajirao entered and sat down only after he took a seat. She erupted without waiting for Bajirao to speak. 'I heard that you are going to meet the Nizam. That is why I rushed here.'

'You heard right. They are the Maharaj's orders,' Bajirao said, without sounding upset.

'And I believe you agreed easily?'

'If Matushree wants to convey something, she may speak without hesitation.'

'Let me tell you something. I have heard it from a very informed source, so don't dismiss it,' Shiubai began. 'You are being sent to meet your end!'

'What! Why would the Chhatrapati want that? I am his servant after all.'

'That is what you think, but the Chhatrapati fears you are

getting too big for your shoes and that one day he may lose his throne. He wants you to be removed. So does the Nizam. It will be like killing two birds with one stone! Shrimant, do you realize that?'

For a moment Bajirao was stunned, but he recovered quickly and said, 'I find all this utter nonsense! I don't believe it.'

'I have written proof of the Nizam having promised to pay a sum of two crores if you are eliminated.'

'Two crores! Huh! I am sure it is just a rumour. I know the Maharaj is not happy with some of my decisions but that does not mean he is going to finish me off!'

'Anyway, my duty was to warn you. Now, it is up to you to do what you feel like,' Shiubai said, a little peeved.

'Don't get upset, Matushree. I know you mean well. Chhatrapati Shahu is at the same time a descendant of the elder Maharaj, and one thing is for sure: treachery is not in their blood. I know there will never be anyone born in that family who would think of eliminating a loyal servant with the help of an enemy. Trust me, you are getting upset unnecessarily.'

'It is possible the Maharaj himself may not do anything, but I am quite sure that the Deshashtha Brahmans are very jealous and are not able to tolerate the rise in the power and prestige of Konkanastha Brahmans like the Peshwa.'

'Now that you have voiced your concern, I shall surely take action and find out who is behind all this. Rest assured.'

Saying so, Bajirao abruptly left the room. Shiubai and her daughter continued talking for a long time on the subject.

With the orders from Satara explicitly asking Bajirao to meet the Nizam, the preparations for the impending meeting began.

While his key officials were busy in the north, Bajirao had a few confidants who were still around. He called for them to discuss his plans.

Paramhans Baba of Dhawadshi heard of Bajirao's plan to meet the Nizam and sent a strong message through his disciple asking him not to go ahead. As a courtesy to the religious leader, Bajirao replied diplomatically without agreeing to his wishes. Bajirao had deputed Ambaji Pant to work out the logistics of the proposed meeting.

One morning, as Bajirao sat in his office studying some papers, Kunwar came in to inform him that Kashibai had not eaten for three days. Bajirao got up immediately and on his way to Kashibai's quarters, ordered a tumbler of milk from the kitchen. Hearing footsteps, Kashibai turned to see Bajirao standing near her bed. She stood up and went near the window, her back towards him.

Bajirao asked, his voice full of concern, 'I was told that you have not eaten anything for the past three days. Is that true?'

Kashibai's tears began to flow again. Her eyes were swollen from constant crying and her cheeks were red. Lifting her chin gently, Bajirao said, 'Stop these tears now! The Peshwa is not used to seeing tears in their haveli.'

Kashibai's tears continued. Bajirao wiped her tears with a satin handkerchief and asked, 'Why trouble oneself so much?'

Kashibai replied in between her sobs, 'That is because someone else does things which gives one a lot of trouble. Why doesn't he stop? Why this adamance?'

'So you are referring to our plans to meet the Nizam, it seems,' Bajirao said. 'That is irking you, isn't it?'

Kashibai nodded.

'Is it in my hands? Chhatrapati Maharaj has personally ordered it. Should I refuse?'

'You can tell this to an ignoramus. Don't I know how much the Chhatrapati listens to you? Can't you convince him?'

Bajirao patted Kashibai's shoulders and said, 'I came in to enquire about you. If you are going to continue to cry, how do I talk to you?'

Kashibai wiped her tears with the edge of her pallu. Bajirao sat on the bed. Then Kashibai said, 'I have stopped crying. Now tell me!'

'It is ironic! I have gone on so many campaigns where the threat was real but no one stopped me then! Why make a mountain out of a molehill now?'

'It is different to go into a war against an enemy but quite another to meet a treacherous enemy all alone. How can you be so sure?'

Bajirao smiled. 'You make me smile. You are forgetting that the Nizam too would be alone and, in fact, he would be more worried than me!'

'You are just trying to convince me, I know. Can't you not go?'

'Yes, but on one condition.'

Kashibai was excited. She said, 'What condition?'

'Will you be able to tolerate the insult when I become a laughing stock? Everyone will say I got scared of the Nizam.'

'And to top it all,' continued Bajirao, 'he is a mere two pence Nizam! If I refuse to meet him, we stand to lose our prestige. Today, all of Hindustan shivers when they hear of the Peshwa, such is our might. To cow down at the prospect of facing the Nizam is worse than losing in a battle.'

'What can I say now?' Kashibai said with a deep sigh.

'You need not say anything,' Bajirao said, holding her chin. 'These lovely lips are not meant to discuss politics. They are for something else!'

Kashibai took Bajirao's hand and said, 'You have a way with words and know how to change my mind. You can't understand a woman's heart. And if you could, you would not treat it so casually.'

Bajirao smiled. 'If I did not care, would I have come rushing when I heard that you have not eaten for three days? Now, drink this milk! I want a beaming face to bid me adieu when I leave and not a crying, teary-eyed one.'

'I knew you would change the topic. Anyway, now that you have made up your mind, please take your brother along, and Shinde, Holkar and the others too.'

Bajirao laughed. 'That means you still do not trust me. If the Shindes and Holkars have to take care of me, what kind of a Peshwa am I?'

'Don't tease me now. Why can't you take them along?' Kashibai asked anxiously.

'Well, they are in the north. Don't worry; I will be safe and will return soon. Can I see your smiling face now?'

Kashibai tried to smile but all she could manage was more tears. Bajirao put the tumbler of milk to her lips. She somehow drank a little. As Bajirao was about to leave, Kashibai said, 'One more thing!'

Bajirao turned and asked, 'What is it?'

'I wish you to wear the navagraha ring I gave you. It is dear to me and I believe it will protect you from danger.'

Bajirao was taken aback at the mention of the ring. Kashibai said, seeing him not wearing it, 'It might be in the royal treasury. Please do take it before you go.'

Bajirao left the room lost in thought.

He tossed and turned in his bed, sleep eluding him. He recalled the anguish and the concern Kashibai had on his impending meeting with the Nizam. He had given the ring away that night in a moment of desperation. What was he to do now?

The next morning he asked Kunwar, when he came in to clean his room, 'Kunwar, you remember last year, on that Janmashtami night, we had crossed the river?'

'Yes, huzoor, I remember vividly,' Kunwar said, avoiding Bajirao's gaze.

'I had given a ring for the boatman to ferry us across. What happened to it?'

'The boatman took it.'

'Oh, I see!' Bajirao said, letting out a deep sigh. He had, for a moment, hoped for the better.

Kunwar, hesitating to say something, hovered around. He did not know how to broach the topic. He said, after a while, 'Huzoor, what made you remember that ring today?'

'What is the point anyway? I wish I could get it back.'

'Huzoor, it is in the royal treasury as we speak.'

'What! The royal treasury? How did it get there?' Bajirao asked, unable to believe his ears.

'Shrimant, please pardon me for telling the truth.'

'Please go on,' Bajirao urged, eager to know.

'It so happened, huzoor, when the next day the poor boatman started boasting of having received a precious ring, one of the guards posted at the riverside suspected him of having stolen it. On being whipped, he blurted out that he was given the ring by someone to cross the river.'

'Are you saying they all know now that it was I who had used the boat that night?'

'No, huzoor. They don't. The guard showed the ring to Appa who kept it with him and dismissed him.'

Licking his lips nervously, Kunwar continued. 'Appa called for me. I had no choice but to tell the truth when Appa threatened me with dire consequences.'

Bajirao asked, 'What happened then?'

'Appa, after hearing the entire episode, said, "I am keeping the ring with me but the news of Shrimant having gone to Mahuli should not be known to anyone."'

'Other than Appa, who else is aware of this?'

'Ambaji Pant.'

'Call him right now.'

Kunwar, happy to be done with the interrogation, left hurriedly. Pant came in and asked, 'Shrimant called for me?'

'Pant, I want to talk about something important. Please take a seat.'

Pant sat down on the carpet, a little nervous. Bajirao instructed Kunwar not to allow anyone in.

He said, turning to Pant, 'I am told that my navagraha ring is in the royal treasury. Did you know that?'

Ambaji's white whiskers quivered a little. He said, 'Yes, I am aware.'

'Why did you not tell me then?'

'Appa had explicitly asked me not to tell anyone.'

'Is it not your duty to inform me of whatever happens in this haveli?'

'Yes, Shrimant. But the issue at hand was a little delicate hence...'

'What is delicate about it?'

'It is a ring which is very dear to Kashibai sahiba. But the conditions in which you gave the ring to the boatman were different and hence...'

'So you hid everything from me, is it?'

'I did not hide anything but that night, whatever happened...'

'What happened? I met Mastani, that's all! Is that blasphemous?'

'No, but...' Ambaji did not continue.

'Tell me! Mastani is a dancer in our court, I was attracted to her and hence went to meet her. What is so unreasonable about it?'

'Shrimant, I am a mere servant of yours. It won't be appropriate for me to answer.'

'I would not like it if you keep quiet. Please speak your mind, Pant. What I did, was it inappropriate?'

'Shrimant, there is nothing wrong in you meeting the dancer. Many top officials and sardars visit such people to entertain themselves. It is even considered a matter of manly pride. What I found inappropriate was the fact that a gift given by someone who loves you so dearly was casually given away to a poor boatman. I wish you had thought of Kashibai sahiba's feelings before doing so.'

Ambaji's forehead was dotted with sweat. He had spoken his mind in one go. Bajirao said, 'The Purandares have served the Peshwas for a long time. Don't you know me well enough?'

'It is wise to be cautious, Shrimant. One never knows what one may do inadvertently.'

'You know, as a mere lad of nineteen, when the Chhatrapati

had handed me the job of the Peshwa, did I think twice? Ever since, I have been leading a life on the edge. There is no logic in love and war, Pant. Your advice to be cautious is of no use in these two cases!'

'What is there for me to speak then?'

'No, I am not denying my mistake. I should not have casually given away the ring so lovingly gifted to me by Kashibai. It was a blunder. Pant, I am not happy that my servants are not maintaining decorum, though.'

Bajirao had raised his voice inadvertently. Realizing that his master was upset, Pant said beseechingly, 'I beg your pardon, my lord.'

'Let this be the last warning! I don't want you to hide anything from me. If you do, I would have to ignore your age when I take action.'

Pant was taken aback. He tried, 'But, Shrimant...'

'I have nothing else to say. You may go now. There is a lot of work pending in the office.'

Ambaji Pant, with his head bowed, saluted and walked out of the room without saying a word.

The festival of Diwali was around the corner but everyone in the Peshwa haveli looked crestfallen. On the one hand, the Maharaj had issued summons for Bajirao to meet the Nizam and, to add to their woes, he had also ordered that the construction of the fortified wall being built around the Peshwa haveli be stopped. Paramhans Baba continued, through various letters, to urge Bajirao not to meet the Nizam. But Bajirao knew that the web his conspirators had woven in the court at Satara was too strong to be broken. He had no option but to follow the Maharaj's orders. He had decided to go ahead, and be prepared for the worst.

His decision further depressed everyone at home. The day of Diwali arrived and the new year was celebrated, albeit with a sad heart by everyone present. Bajirao had kept the Nizam engaged through letters, while all the spies and emissaries were asked to keep extra vigil and an alert ear to the ground to detect the slightest hint of treachery.

On the day of Pratipada, Bajirao visited Radhabai to take her blessings. Instead of returning to the haveli, he rode on his favourite horse towards the gardens at Kothrud. A few soldiers followed him.

It was a beautifully lit haveli which greeted Bajirao when he entered the gardens. The town house, where Mastani and her troupe were stationed, was blazing with lamps and festooned with flower garlands. The servants were busy bursting crackers in the lawns. As soon as he dismounted, a servant ran to receive him. The message of his arrival had already reached Mastani.

Entering the hall, he saw a lovely sitting arrangement ready for him. Mastani entered and said, 'Huzoor had sent these clothes and jewellery with a lot of affection. How am I looking?'

Bajirao was dumbstruck. Wearing a dark green silk sari, Mastani looked regal, like someone from an aristocratic family. She had tied her hair into plaits with thin flower garlands intertwined. Her earrings, necklace and the way she had draped the sari over her head – she looked as if she had stepped out of a royal household. The armlets, tied at the end of the sleeves of her blouse, enhanced the slim beauty of her arms.

Mastani blushed sensing Bajirao's intense scrutiny. She

adjusted the sari over her head and said, 'It is the start of the new year. I thought you would like this.'

Bajirao finally found his voice. He said, 'My God! You look like an apsara who has descended from the heavens.'

'Thank you,' Mastani said, and then clapped once. A few servants arrived with trays. Placing them next to Bajirao, she said, 'I have prepared some special sweets for you. Please have them.'

'Sure, sure!' Bajirao said, pleased, as he rested his back against a bolster. 'But on one condition, you need to give me company.'

'No, no! I am a mere maid of yours. Watching you eat is good enough for me.'

Bajirao noticed a flash of sadness in Mastani's eyes. Her eyes had revealed what the lips were trying to hide. Mastani could not believe that someone like the Peshwa, with his handsome looks and stature, could be her guest. She felt small, facing a colossus. She was a mere courtesan. What right did she have over him? A stab of woe pierced her heart. Bajirao perceived her hesitation.

'It is all right; I shall not force you. But do sit down.'

'I don't have permission to sit while you are eating,' she said.

'I am giving you permission.'

'You may but my heart does not allow me to. I am fine the way I am. Please tell me if you like the sweets.'

Bajirao picked up a piece of sweatmeat and looked at Mastani before putting it in his mouth. His eyes had challenged her. Her mere presence had intoxicated him. The one who stood before him was not an ordinary courtesan, one who merely entertained with her singing and dancing. The pull she created was magical. She had surrendered completely to him. And in response, Bajirao had made a space for her in his heart. He understood the full meaning of the sad look in her eyes that had flashed a few moments back. His mind was now in turmoil. He put the piece of sweetmeat back on the plate and stood up.

'Is something wrong? What has happened?' Mastani asked, a sudden fear gripping her.

'One thing is missing,' Bajirao said. His eyes looked around, searching for something. He said, 'On this day, in this attire, there is one thing missing.'

'Please command and we shall get it.'

'I have to get it myself,' Bajirao said. He called for Basanti and whispered in her ear. Shortly, Basanti returned with a silver tray on which was a small box containing sindoor. Mastani looked curiously at the box but soon realized the import when Bajirao took a pinch of sindoor in his fingers. 'No! This is not possible!'

'It is my wish, Mastani. Today is an auspicious day. Are you going to refuse?' Bajirao almost pleaded.

'Huzoor, I am a mere dancer, a lowly woman, an entertainer. I can't even equate myself with your shoes. My place is at your feet. Let me remain there, please,' Mastani entreated. 'I would consider my life fulfilled whenever I get even a moment with you. I will not be able to withstand the burning fire of passion. Please don't kill me.'

Bajirao looked at Mastani affectionately. 'Even the fire loses its power when it sees you. My dear, I have survived the fire when I took you in my arms the first time. Let there be the cool touch of a pleasant moon now.'

'My body isn't precious enough for huzoor to get burnt in the fire.'

'Mastani, it needs the eyes of Bajirao to understand the value of what you are. Now, don't entangle me in words any further. Isn't my wish yours too?'

'As you desire,' Mastani said shyly. 'I had surrendered whatever I had at your feet a long time back.'

Bajirao took the sindoor and placed it in the parting of her hair, in the tradition of a Hindu husband applying it on his wife's head on their wedding day. Stepping back a few steps, he looked at her face with satisfaction. 'That completes the attire now! It is perfect!'

Bajirao held her hands as he sat down. Mastani dared not look up, her cheeks blushing red with shyness. With a quick glance and a subtle yet effective dance of her eyebrows, she asked Bajirao to partake the sweets. As Bajirao enjoyed the sweets, his eyes observed her beauty – from the delicate yet inviting *nath*, the traditional nose ring, to the silver anklets. Handing him a tumbler of sherbet, she asked, 'I hear of some bad things. Are they true?'

Bajirao was used to such indirect questions. He nodded. 'That is right. I am going to meet the Nizam, but what is bad about it?'

'What can be worse?'

'You fear for my life, do you?'

'Chhee! I trust your abilities. But I am told Khan is a treacherous man and hence the heart fears whereas the mind consoles.'

'What do you suggest? Should I go?'

'Chhee! Who am I to advise you? Can I ask the eagle which flies high in the sky to fear the lightning and hide in the crevices of the rock? You may go without hesitation but I have one request. The month of Ramzan is about to begin. I will be fasting each day and praying to Allah to take care of you. My wish is that you return on the day of Eid and allow me to serve you. Would you agree to this humble wish of mine?'

'Of course! There is a lot of time for Eid yet. I would have met the Nizam by then.'

Mastani ordered for the tray of paan and Bajirao returned to Pune late at night. As he rode back, Bajirao turned a few times to glance at Mastani's haveli, still burning bright with the light of the lamps.

Winter was setting in. All the sardars who were to accompany Bajirao had already arrived in Pune and were waiting for the day of departure. The cavalry, foot soldiers and the elephant with a howdah were ready to leave. For such an occasion, it was necessary that the elephant accompanied the caravan. After all, it was a matter of showing off one's stature!

Bajirao first met Kashibai to take her leave. She put a blob of curd in Bajirao's palm as a traditional mark of farewell while trying to stop the tears which continued to flow. Bajirao proceeded to take Radhabai's blessings and then, after praying at the temple, jumped on to his horse and galloped out of the gate, without looking back even once.

The caravan moved towards Rui Rameshwar, the rendezvous point, and, within a fortnight, they reached the banks of the river Manjra. The Nizam's camp was visible on the other bank – an ocean of tents and shamianas spreading over nearly five miles of land. It seemed endless. Hundreds of flags sporting the emblem of moon and stars fluttered in the wind. Bajirao's camp, in contrast, was a much smaller affair. The emissaries began their visits with various messages flying back and forth.

On the third day, Ambaji Pant announced the arrival of the emissary from the Nizam's camp. He was accompanied by fifty soldiers, each one of them with a scabbard tied at his waist. As soon as the emissary entered Bajirao's tent, he bent low and saluted thrice. In response, Bajirao simply nodded his head and asked him to sit. The emissary spoke in Farsi, 'Nawab sahab is very pleased that you have agreed to meet him here. He sent his regards.' The long flowing beard of the emissary shook as he spoke haltingly.

'We too are glad to meet him. He may have forgotten, though, our earlier meeting,' Bajirao said.

'I don't understand, huzoor.'

'We had seen each other, albeit for a brief while, when our troops had clashed at Palkhed. He may not remember that, I suppose.'

Bajirao had deliberately reminded the emissary of the painful episode which clearly rankled, as was evident from his face. The fact that the Nizam had to run away from the battle was known to all. The emissary, tactfully avoiding further discussion on the topic, said, 'There must have been many instances of the Peshwa meeting our Nawab ever since he has been giving the Subedari of the Deccan. Nevertheless, he is happy to meet you once again.'

Bajirao came to the point. 'Let us fix the date for the meeting, now that we both are here.'

'It is precisely for that purpose I have come,' the emissary said, nodding.

'So what do you propose?'

'You have travelled a long distance. We propose you rest for a fortnight and then we fix up a suitable date.'

'We are not used to sitting idle and twiddling our thumbs,' Bajirao said, irritated at the delaying tactics being used by the emissary.

'I did not mean to suggest that. The proposed rest will do you good. We have a group of dancers and singers especially summoned from Lucknow. They will be here this evening. We suggest you enjoy their company for a while.'

Ambaji Pant was carefully listening to the conversation. He said, 'Shrimant cannot waste time on idle activities. We are here on the express orders of the Chhatrapati. Please ask the Nawab to fix up a date soon.'

Bajirao smiled and interjected, 'Pant, I too am in a hurry to return but let us see what the Nawab has in store for us. They say the dancers are from Lucknow and are experts in their field. Let us see.'

Ambaji Pant kept quiet. Bajirao continued, looking at the Nawab's emissary, 'Would you please clarify a doubt?'

'Huzoor, I will try my best.'

'Nawab sahab claims he is here to extend a hand of friendship. We came in with merely five thousand troops, but I find that your cantonment has almost forty or fifty thousand soldiers. For what does he need such a large contingent?'

'Your doubt is most valid, huzoor,' the emissary said. He had a habit of caressing his beard as he spoke. He said, 'Your troops, I presume, are busy with campaigns all over, while our Nawab believes in peace. We have a task of looking after just six Subahs in the Deccan. The entire army is thus at the disposal of the Nawab.'

'Are you saying the Nawab roams around the Deccan with the entire contingent in tow? Whatever his style may be, please ensure that on the day of our meeting, the entire camp moves back at least fifty miles.'

'*Tauba, tauba*! Doesn't Shrimant trust our Nawab?'

'It is not a question of trust. Nawab sahab is a friend and could have resolved matters easily by simply sending an emissary to Pune. I find it amusing that he talks of friendship and yet comes to meet with his entire army. Trust has to be mutual. You have fifteen days to move the camp back. If we don't find that happening, we will be forced to return without the proposed meeting. I suppose I don't need to tell you what happens then. My sardars, busy in the north, would be forced to turn their attention to the south!'

Bajirao's voice had taken on an edge. The emissary tried his best to pacify and mentioned the nautch girls from Lucknow a few times to deflect the issue, but Bajirao was determined and did not allow the discussion to deviate from the main point. Then, a clerk sitting next to Bajirao, handed a letter written in Farsi to him.

Bajirao glanced at the letter once and said, 'I am told that your people have despoiled the Baijnath temple at Parli. We would expect that such activities are stopped before the date of our meeting. Ask Nizam sahab to keep his donation for the temple ready. After our meeting, we shall send that across to the temple. Let the people know that our meeting was successful and that the Nizam has sent his offerings to the Lord at Parli.'

The emissary did not respond as he caressed his beard lost in thought. He got up to take leave when Bajirao said, 'One more thing!'

The emissary's forehead creased. He had already been subjected to a lot of torture for the past three hours. He wondered what more conditions he was to agree to. He stood, without showing any eagerness, as he waited for Bajirao to speak.

'Next time, please come with a few servants and no more! You are here for a friendship treaty and it is our duty to protect you. I hope that is clear.'

'Ji, huzoor,' the emissary mumbled and saluting quickly, exited the tent.

Within three days, a flurry of activities was visible in the Nizam's camp and soon enough the troops, as promised, started moving away. It was December and the days were getting shorter. The sandy banks of the Manjra were freezing at night.

The day of the meeting arrived. Bajirao, along with his key sardars, Ambaji Pant and a select group of a thousand cavalry decided to cross the Manjra. Shrimant Peshwa sat in the howdah on a richly decorated elephant. He was attired in the traditional Maratha style, his turban embellished with pearls, a curved knife at the waist and a sword with a golden handle engraved with gems resting on his thigh.

The elephant rose to the sound of trumpets and started walking towards the riverbank. Five soldiers, atop camels, carrying the Maratha flag and holding a rifle each, followed. Ambaji sat in a seat behind the howdah on the elephant's back. The royal procession was led by the sardar Somvanshi who rode a horse. The rest of the cavalry followed the elephant.

A huge shamiana had been erected by the Nizam for the

proposed meeting. The royal Nizamshahi flag fluttered, while a few horsemen stood guard outside. Nizam Ali, sitting on an elephant, waited to receive his royal guest.

Bajirao's elephant stopped a few hundred yards from the shamiana. The silver bells attached to the chains around the elephant's neck tinkled as the mahout commanded the elephant to gently sit down. A ladder was quickly placed and Bajirao, his hand on the hilt of his sword, stepped down.

Bajirao looked at the old Nizam dressed in regal clothes. His white luxuriant moustache stood out against his dark skin. The Nizam looked at Bajirao with a mixture of fear and caution. He saw Bajirao walk towards him with four of his sardars and stretched out his arms in welcome. They embraced and enquired about each other's health. The Nizam then, holding Bajirao's hand, led him into the shamiana where a special seating arrangement had been made for the royals. The others were asked to occupy knee-high seats on one side. Flower garlands, hung on the sides of the shamiana at regular intervals, spread a mild fragrance which was soothing.

As soon as Bajirao and the Nizam took their seats, the others followed suit after elaborate mujras. On cue, the servants came in with trays of gifts. Bajirao smiled and accepted the same with a nod of his head. The Nizam had gifted Bajirao, as a token of his first meeting, a pair of huge pearls, each the size of a marble, seven expensive sets of clothes, two horses and an elephant.

After the gifting ceremony, the chief of the dance school entered and requested permission to begin the performance. A group of fifty dancers came in and stood on a carpet in the centre of the shamiana. After the performance ended, the Nizam asked, taking a deep breath from the garland wrapped around his wrist, 'I hope Peshwa sahab enjoyed the dance.'

'It was excellent,' Bajirao said. 'It was in line with the expectation from someone like Nizam sahab, following the Badshahi tradition. No doubt your artistes are of a fine calibre.'

After such formalities, the Nizam requested Bajirao to follow him into a smaller tent attached to the shamiana. The other sardars accompanying Bajirao followed as well. Once they were seated, Bajirao opened the discussion by saying, 'I would like to hear your concerns and try and understand why they could not be resolved by mere correspondence.'

The Nizam glanced at the guards standing inside and with a wave of his hand dismissed them. He said, 'I was keen to meet you in person. I am sure there is nothing wrong in that!'

'Not at all! Please don't misunderstand me. Our earlier meeting was not under very friendly circumstances. Hence, I was a little reluctant.'

'On the one hand, you say it was not friendly and on the other, you seem to be scared. Am I to assume that Peshwa sahab is worried?'

'What makes you think that we are scared?'

'You asked my forces to be withdrawn. What else could be the reason?'

'Oh that! These are not good times, Nizam sahab. I did not want your forces to suffer.'

'I don't understand.'

'Let me explain: if, in the unfortunate situation wherein a treacherous act is conducted, my sardars, returning from the north, would not hesitate to finish your entire cantonment in retaliation. That would be tragic, wouldn't it?'

'Shrimant, I had heard of your cunning nature but I can see that now! I hope you do believe that we are here for friendship and don't harbour any ill feelings.'

'I was going by my past experience where the definition of friendship and enmity seemed a little confusing.'

'I would be happy if you could clarify.'

'It has happened not once but often. I was told that you had complained to the Chhatrapati about me. You tried bribing my commanders. You also tried to create differences between me and my key ministers attached to the Chhatrapati. Now do you call these acts of friendship?'

Nizam Ali did not respond immediately. He had not expected Bajirao to be so blunt and to the point. He said, with a smile on his face, 'Shall I say something, if you don't mind? It was not I who had approached the people you are talking of. They had come to us with complaints against you. They were, in fact, forcing me to take action. I was disappointed and surprised to know that the Marathas are hungry for false prestige. Bajirao sahab, I feel hurt that you are accusing me of having created a dispute amongst your men.'

Bajirao was silent for a while. He said, 'It is not a trait you find amongst the Marathas alone. It is seen in the Mughal sardars too.'

'Can you name someone?'

'Yes, I am talking of you!'

'What?'

'Let me clarify: you took charge of the Deccan as the Subedar under Mughal rule and now you want to establish your own empire. Isn't that treachery to the Mughal throne?'

'Bajirao sahab, I did not join hands with the enemy.'

'You seem to be forgetting that when the Badshah had sent his forces you had taken the help of the Marathas. I don't need to remind you who killed the Badshah's *mansabdar*.'

The Nizam was silent for a while. Seeing a stalemate,

Ambaji Pant intervened, 'Nawab sahab, these are things of the past. Why discuss them now? Let us talk of the future.'

The Nizam readily agreed and, nodding his head, said, 'Yes, I manage the Deccan as a Subedar and I am not happy that the Marathas are recovering their share of the tax from my territory.'

Bajirao interrupted, 'Wasn't that the agreement after Palkhed?'

'I agree, but I need a promise from you. I hope you are not planning to take over the Subah itself under the pretext of collecting tax?'

'No, Nawab sahab. Such a thought never crossed my mind.'

'It might, today or tomorrow!'

'Let us not speculate about what could happen.'

'I am not asking you to predict the future but I know one thing for sure – you are keen to march northwards and destroy the Mughal empire.'

'You are spot on! It was a dream the elder Maharaj had of liberating Hindustan from the Mughals. I am his servant, after all, and the Marathas won't stop till they reach their goal. There is nothing to be ashamed of here.'

Nizam was worried seeing such a confident comment from the Peshwa. He said, 'I am not going to interfere in whatever you do north of the Narmada.'

'What do we get in return?' Ambaji asked.

'We will allow you to collect your tax. But you must not disturb the peace.'

After some other small talk, the first of the discussions ended.

The stay on the banks of the Manjra extended for another month. A series of discussions, list of treaties, agreements and other documents went back and forth from one camp to the other. After a lot of persuasion, threat, cajoling and other tricks, the Peshwa managed to convince the Nawab on most of the terms. Chandi and Chandawar were part of Shivaji Maharaj's territory earlier. Bajirao managed to get them back after a lot of persuasion. It was an important win. They also got a revenue share of nearly fifty lakhs from the Khandesh, Aurangabad and Bijapur territories. These agreements were not in writing but Bajirao managed to convince the Nizam to place his hand on the holy Quran and take a vow to fulfil the promises made. The Nizam in return bought peace in his Subah.

After a royal feast hosted by the Nizam, Bajirao and his troops returned. He was smiling at the ease with which he had managed to get all his demands met and yet left the prospect of capturing the Deccan open.

All durbars, from Delhi in the north to Karnatak in the south, were eager to know the outcome of the meeting between the Nizam and Bajirao Peshwa. Bajirao's return to Pune after having grabbed a revenue share of fifty lakhs signalled an important victory. The recovery of the territories of Chandi and Chandawar added to Shahu Maharaj's happiness. Bajirao was given a royal welcome in Satara which included the firing of five cannons apart from the usual trumpets celebrating the arrival.

The entire city of Pune immersed itself in celebrations as if Bajirao had returned after winning an important war.

The festival of Holi was a few days away. Shanivar wada was hosting Bajirao's friends for the festival. A large tank had been filled with water. The office had been given a holiday of five days. It was after many years that the Peshwa was in town for Holi.

Yesu came running into Kashibai's room. Kashibai realized that there was something important she wanted to convey. Yesu said, 'Do you know what happened today? Annapoornabai saw our young master, Nanasaheb, throwing colour on Gopikabai. She then asked Nanasaheb to also throw colour on her. She too wanted to play. Matushree heard that and gave her a tight slap across her cheek, asking her to mind her manners.'

'It is appropriate in a way, Yesu. Annapoorna does not know that her husband Appa is away and that she should behave with propriety. She cannot be asking Nana to throw colour on her. Poor child! She is too young to know all this, you know.'

At that moment, Nana walked in. He asked, 'There is a dance programme later and Rau Swami has asked me to take your permission to call some of the dancers.'

'Who are you planning to call?'

'Mastani.'

'Fine,' Kashibai said, without looking at her son. 'I have no idea about these things.'

Nana was surprised at his mother's reaction. He said, 'I don't get you.'

'What can I say? You are grown up now and have to start looking into these matters.'

Nana could not understand his mother's words but realized that there was something amiss.

The celebrations with colours were over but Mastani's dance programme did not take place as expected.

Ambaji Pant Purandare was an old servant of the Peshwas having served under Bajirao's father. The day after Holi, he came into Bajirao's room. Seeing him, Bajirao asked, 'The Holi celebrations went off quite well, I suppose?'

'Yes. The people at Pune found you here after a long time. After all, you are never around, always out on some campaign or the other. They really enjoyed the fact that you were present.'

Ambaji Pant waited for a moment and cleared his throat dramatically. Bajirao guessed that he had not come to discuss the Holi celebrations. 'You wanted to say something?'

'I feel I should take retirement now. I would like to be relieved of my duties.'

'You have mentioned that earlier too. What is the reason now?'

'Matushree has expressed her desire to go on a pilgrimage and wants me to accompany her. I too am keen to join.'

'I know Matushree has been asking me but I have somehow not been able to decide.'

'What is there to decide? She wants to go, why not allow her?'

'It is not that simple. The places she wants to visit – Kashi, Gaya, Prayag – they are all under the rule of Muhammad Bangash. We routed the Rohillas soundly and they will be waiting to take revenge. It is dangerous for Matushree to be visiting places that are under their control. It is not safe. 'I explained this to Matushree but she is adamant. On top of it, she will not be going alone. There will be other family members and we will have to take care of all these people. It is a huge responsibility, Pant.'

'I agree. But she is determined. I request Shrimant to have a word with her, though I doubt if she will relent.'

'Let me try again. If she does not change her mind, I will have to send a large contingent with her but that creates another set of probable problems to deal with. Anyway, let us see what we decide.'

Ambaji, after a moment's hesitation, said, 'I am told Mastani did not dance during the celebrations.'

Bajirao turned to look at Ambaji, a little surprised at the mention of Mastani. He said, 'Yes. I did not want her to dance.'

'Everyone was disappointed. They were looking forward to it.'

'Henceforth, Mastani will not be singing or dancing in public.'

Pant knew of the changes in Bajirao's behaviour over the last few months. He had ignored it assuming it to be a minor infatuation. But clearly, things had progressed beyond what he had assumed. He said, choosing his words carefully, 'It seems she is under your special care now.'

'You may say that. But she is not going to sing or dance any more.'

Bajirao's firm decision rattled Pant. He had not expected Bajirao to accept his relationship so openly. Seeing Ambaji's confusion, Bajirao asked, 'May I ask why you are so curious?'

'You had met this Musalmaan girl in Bundelkhand and asked her to entertain the guests at the durbar with her dancing and singing. Now that Shrimant has decided to give her a special status, I suppose we will have to look after her. She would have to be made aware of all the protocols too.'

'You may do whatever it takes. I believe you can manage it.'

Pant was quiet. He knew that it was a delicate matter and he wanted to tread carefully lest he say something which may offend Bajirao.

Bajirao realized Pant's dilemma and said, 'Oh! I get it. That's why you raised the topic of Matushree's pilgrimage. I was wondering why you did not speak of Mastani earlier.'

'No, no! It is just a coincidence that I thought of Mastani and hence broached the topic. That is all!'

Bajirao said, 'Pant, I feel a lot of people are not as open with me as they used to be earlier. It might not be true, but somehow I feel so!'

Pant chose not to respond.

The festival of Muharram arrived. Ambaji took the opportunity to send a senior clerk to Kothrud gardens with a message for Mastani. Chanda Jamdar received the old man and escorted him into the living room, where Mastani sat behind a gossamer screen.

Chanda offered a tumbler of sherbet to the old clerk who said, 'I cannot take this, whatever it is. Take it away.'

'It is the festival of Muharram today. You are our guest. Won't you have it?'

The clerk said, raising his voice for effect, 'I do not believe in partaking anything offered by a Musalmaan. I am a Brahman, don't you know that?'

'Well, I do, but Shrimant himself does not mind, hence I offered it to you. Anway, if you don't want it, we will not force you.'

Mastani, listening to the conversation from behind the screen, said, 'Don't force him, Jamdar. Ask him the purpose of his visit.'

The clerk cleared his throat nervously and began. 'Pant has sent me with a message for you stating that you are henceforth Shrimant's mistress.'

'What does that mean?' The voice from behind the curtain was sharp.

'It means you will serve Shrimant and no one else.'

'Of course, you don't need to explain that. Please elaborate on the reason for your visit.'

'There are a few things which need to be followed for such people. I have been asked to give you the details and advise you accordingly.'

'I am all ears. Please continue.'

The clerk took out a sheet of paper from a satin bag and said, 'I am told I should read out each rule one by one.'

'Rules? What are they about?' Mastani asked.

'How such persons should deal with others,' the clerk replied. He continued, knowing that he was delaying unnecessarily, 'You should not enter Shrimant's private quarters unless called for.'

Not getting a response he read the rule again.

'I am listening. Please don't stop,' Mastani said.

'You should follow decorum when visiting Shrimant and should not sit till Kashibai sahiba or other ladies ask you to do so. You should not eat paan in the presence of Kashibai sahiba.'

'What if Shrimant offers me one?'

'The rule says not to eat it in the presence of Kashibai sahiba. It does not talk of what to do when it's offered by Shrimant.'

'Fine with me,' Mastani said. 'What else?'

'Kashibai sahiba, Matushree and Chotibai sahiba should be referred to as Baisahiba only.'

'And you?' Mastani asked, pulling his leg.

'Why would you call me anything? Please listen to the rules regarding Shrimant's family and do not interrupt me.'

'Carry on, please.'

'Shrimant's son is Nanasaheb and his brother Appasaheb. They should be referred to as sarkar. Lastly, don't use the spittoon in Shrimant's haveli.'

'Anything else?'

'One important rule: henceforth, you should not wear your Musalmaan attire and drop all the customs and mores followed in your religion.'

'I am unable to follow. Please explain.'

The clerk was used to writing and speaking what was dictated to him. Interpreting things was not his job. He fumbled before saying, 'I read out what was written. You may interpret the way you deem fit.'

The clerk was anxious. He was talking to someone who he knew was very close to Bajirao and he was worried that he may be reprimanded for any slip-ups. He wiped his sweaty face nervously and said, 'There are a few more but I am sure you can read them yourself. I will leave this letter here and inform Pant that you have been briefed.'

'Don't worry. Please tell him that I will look into it. But, before you go, I have one request,' Mastani said.

'Have you shown these to Shrimant before reading them out to me?' Mastani continued without waiting for the clerk to respond.

'I don't know. I was given this task by Pant and have followed his orders.'

Mastani let out a deep sigh. She was enjoying teasing the poor clerk, but now she felt depressed. She said, 'Tell Pant I have understood the rules and shall follow them as mentioned. But tell him he forgot to write one important rule.'

'Which is?'

'I know how to address Kashibai sahiba and the others, but what about Peshwa sarkar himself? What do I call him?'

'What's there to ask? Everyone calls him Shrimant. You too should do that,' the clerk answered immediately and then, realizing that he may be treading on thin ice, bit his tongue in shame. He kept quiet, lest he blurt out something more inadvertently.

Mastani ended the discussion by asking Basanti to get a tray of paan for the clerk. He gladly accepted one and left without further delay.

That evening, Mastani told Basanti, 'Please go to Shanivar wada and ask for Shrimant. Tell him I desire to meet him.'

Basanti reached the haveli to find that Shrimant Bajirao had left for Satara on some urgent work.

Kashibai had finished her tulsi puja and was getting ready when Yesu came in saying, 'Matushree has sent a message that you may visit her as soon as you finish your morning chores.'

Kashibai said, while adding the finishing touches to her make-up, as she looked in the mirror, 'Please convey the message that I shall be there immediately.'

Within a few minutes, Kashibai entered Radhabai's quarters to see her teaching young Gopika and Annapoorna devotional songs and couplets. Seeing Kashibai enter, she instructed the girls, 'Now, you two go and meet the priest, Krishna Bhat. Recite whatever I have taught you. I shall call for you later.'

When they left, she asked Kashibai to sit down and said, 'Your daughter-in-law, Gopika, is a bright child. She memorizes whatever I teach her very quickly.'

Kashibai was happy to hear that. Radhabai asked, 'Have you finished your morning chores?'

'Yes.'

'I have called you here to discuss something personal and important. I want your advice.'

Radhabai did not elaborate. She was quiet for a moment as she looked at Kashibai. She had seen her as a young girl when she had come into the Peshwa household. But soon, after Bajirao became the Peshwa, Kashibai had transformed from a gawky teenager into an aristocratic woman who knew the power of her husband's command. She had taken charge of Shanivar wada and was now in full control of the household. It had been a remarkable change. But she sat in the same humble posture in the presence of her mother-in-law as she did when she had first come into the house.

Radhabai said, turning to the matters at hand, 'I wish to go on a pilgrimage. Ambaji Pant is willing to accompany me and I will speak to Rau at an appropriate time. What do you have to say about it?'

Kashibai looked at her mother-in-law, a little surprised. She was not a lady who took advice from anyone, especially her daughter-in-law. She said, 'What is the hurry? You can always go later. Are you getting bored here?'

'Why should I be bored? Now the new daughter-in-law has arrived and very soon the household will have a great-grandchild. It is high time I turned my mind to things religious. Anyway, I called you for another reason.'

'Please tell me,' Kashibai said.

'You remember Rau had gone on a campaign against the Dabhades in Gujarat?'

'Yes, I do! My eyes had got tired of waiting for him.'

Radhabai said, 'Such things are often the cause of a woman's downfall. Keep that in mind.'

'Did I say something wrong?' Kashibai asked.

'Listen to me now. You will recall that I had refused a Musalmaan woman's request to perform abhishek at the temple.'

Kashibai rememebered that very well. She had found it odd then that her mother-in-law had taken such strong objection and put her foot down in not allowing a Musalmaan woman to pray for the safe return of Rau Swami. She said, 'I do remember but I wonder why you are referring to it now.'

'That same dancer, who wanted to pray for Rau's health, has his special favours now. Is that true? Is she his mistress?'

Radhabai's words were tearing into Kashibai's heart. She had heard of it but was not sure and now her mother-in-law was asking her pointedly. Tears rolled down her cheeks.

Looking at her daughter-in-law, Radhabai said, 'That's the problem, dear! These eyes are being used for just two purposes: one, to lie in wait for the one who has gone away, and second, to relieve one's burden by letting the tears flow. A woman should know how to use her eyes for much better things. When will you learn?'

Wiping her tears, Kashibai looked up. Radhabai continued, 'I am saying this as Rau's mother. If you learn how to use your eyes, you don't need to use your tongue. The eyes can speak a language far more powerful.'

Seeing Kashibai silent, Radhabai asked, 'Are you getting me?'

Kashibai said hesitatingly, 'I know she is his mistress now. What am I supposed to do?'

'You can do a lot, if you put your mind to it,' Radhabai said, a little frustrated at Kashibai's meek reaction.

She continued, 'There are some battles that you fight with intelligence, cunning and stealth. You too have to fight a battle which is your own, and without anyone's support. I know Rau since his birth; he has always had a rebellious streak in him. I am his mother after all. And I lived with his father for a full thirty years. Rau has tasted success ever since he became Peshwa and does not know the meaning of defeat. That makes him arrogant. Now that I will leave for my pilgrimage, you need to take complete charge. Having said that, I do believe Rau will not take any drastic step and behave inappropriately.'

Kashibai felt a little relieved. Things probably were not as bad as she had feared.

Rau, in the meantime, left for Konkan from Satara and was engaged with Siddhi Johar, the Abyssinian general, at Janjira. There were many skirmishes. Raigadh was captured and inducted into the Maratha fold increasing the pressure on Siddhi, but unfortunately the arrival of the monsoons delayed further action and Bajirao was forced to return to Pune.

Chimaji Appa too had returned from a very successful tax collection campaign in the north, having collected huge amounts in the Bundelkhand, Rajasthan and Malwa regions. Hundreds of camels bearing the collections were on their way to Pune.

Bajirao enquired about Appa's health to find that he was unwell. Rushing to his quarters, Bajirao found Appa sitting with his back resting against two pillows while Ambaji Pant read out some letters. A few medicine bottles could be seen on a tripod while a vaidyaraj stood in attendance. Appa's cough was getting worse by the day. Bajirao said, 'Appa, you have just returned from an extensive campaign and collected a lot of wealth, but you seem to be destroying your own wealth – your health!'

Appa was about to speak when a terrible bout of coughing racked his chest. The vaidyaraj rushed to give him a liquid medicine. Appa sipped it and said, after recovering his breath, 'Nothing's wrong with me. Just a mild cough which will go away.'

Bajirao looked at the papers in Ambaji Pant's hand and said, 'Why are you troubling him with administrative matters now? He can always look at them later.'

'I have been telling him the same thing but he just does not listen.'

Appa, rubbing his chest with his palm, said, 'It was I who called for him. There is a mountain of work to be completed. You were out at Janjira, while I was in the north. Who is to look into the matters here then?'

Bajirao was aware that Appa had gone to Satara after returning from the north. He was surprised to not find any message from the Maharaj regarding his successful campaign in the Konkan. Ambaji Pant read his mind and said, 'Shrimant carried out a successful campaign but unfortunately Chhatrapati Maharaj did not speak a word about it. Appa Swami felt hurt.'

Chimaji Appa's forehead creased in irritation recalling his visit to Satara. Bajirao said, 'Appa, the politics in Satara seem to be getting murkier by the day. I don't fear the enemy out in the open, but it is the enemy in disguise that I find very dangerous.'

Appa said, 'Rau, I was out for nearly ten months and when I presented the collections to the Chhatrapati, he seemed unhappy. I met Virubai to understand the reason for the Maharaj's displeasure to find that it was because you had apparently left for Konkan without meeting her. Virubai's displeasure became the Chhatrapati's!'

Appa's voice was bitter.

Bajirao said, 'I was in a hurry. The Chhatrapati knows that.'

'I found out the real reason for Virubai's anger. She had asked you to send twenty maids from Pune. She said Shrimant did not heed her request and she commented, "Is there a dearth of maids in Pune, for Shrimant not being able to fulfil my request despite repeated reminders?" She was quite irritated.'

Bajirao laughed out loud. 'I know she had reminded me but I was so engrossed in things at hand that I simply forgot. Anyway, if women start influencing administrative work, this is what happens. You presented a mountain of wealth to the Chhatrapati. Wasn't he pleased seeing that?'

'I feel ashamed to even tell you, Rau,' Appa said in a sad voice. 'He was annoyed because I did not get the musk deer which he had asked for! And he accused me of not working for him but for the prestige of the Peshwa. I was dumbstruck. For all the risks we take, the sacrifices we make, is that what we get? When the Chhatrapati himself makes such comments, I feel like giving all this up.'

Bajirao had a habit of ignoring these accusations for he knew that the Chhatrapati was being influenced by people who were jealous of the Peshwa's success. He said, 'Appa, don't take it to heart. Our job is to do our duty loyally and not bother about such innuendos.'

Bajirao got up when Appa said, 'Rau, you don't get involved in the administrative work. I will take care of the Konkan and also the English and Portuguese, who have captured a large part of the coast. You should focus on the north and put Sawai Jaisingh in his place.'

Bajirao knew his brother had not told him all that had transpired in Satara. He said, 'I am here for the next forty-five days. I shall be leaving after Diwali now. Till then, I suppose, I shall look into matters of the state.'

Appa's health recovered much before Diwali and he was able to get back to the office work. His son, Sadashiv Pant, was now four years old. The motherless child would spend most of his time in the company of his grandmother.

Bajirao came to take his mother's blessings to find the young Sadashiv dressed in a kurta and sporting a turban. He had a small toy sword tied to his waist. The doting grandmother ruffled his hair saying, 'Like father, like son. He says he is ready to go into battle.'

'Oh, is that so!' Bajirao said. 'Which one would you prefer – the one in Konkan against the firangis or in the north against the Badshah?'

Sadashiv observed his uncle wearing earrings and said, pointing at them, 'Whichever earns me these.'

Bajirao laughed at the child's wit. Radhabai said, 'He is learning fast. He has already memorized the Ramraksha and other shlokas. Now he wants to learn martial arts. He seems to be taking after his father.'

Bajirao got up to leave when Radhabai said, 'I believe you had called Kashibai to Satara.'

Bajirao nodded and said nothing. Radhabai continued, 'Unfortunately you stayed in Satara for a short while and returned to Pune. It is difficult for her to do these trips, you know. Don't trouble her unnecessarily. She is not keeping well.'

Bajirao, referring to the pain in her leg, said, 'I was told by the vaidyaraj that the medicine is working well and that her pain has subsided a lot.'

'I am not talking of that,' Radhabai said. 'You are soon going to be blessed with another son.'

Bajirao was taken by surprise. Quite obviously, he did not expect Radhabai to break the news. Embarrassed and not knowing what to say further, he mumbled, 'There is a lot of work pending in the office. I will take your leave.'

Shrimant Peshwa was irritated at having to leave the campaign at Janjira halfway. When the Portuguese emissary came in to have a discussion, Bajirao did not try and cover up his irritation. The emissary, Sanzgiri, was well versed in local languages and had come to find out Bajirao's plans regarding Konkan and also to ascertain the actual strength of the Marathas.

Protocol required that a gift be given before starting discussions. Hence, Sanzgiri presented a small satin bag containing a powerful pair of binoculars for the Peshwa. Bajirao asked, looking at Ambaji, 'So is this the bribe the Portuguese are offering?'

Sanzgiri was miffed at the gift being referred to as a bribe and said, 'The Portuguese governor has sent a gift to the Peshwa with love.'

Bajirao, not to be swayed by sweet words, said, 'We call it a bribe. I wonder why the governor remembers me now. It seems our action in the Konkan has awakened him.'

Ambaji, realizing that the discussions had started on a sour note, tried to pacify Bajirao saying, 'Firangi sahab has sent a very interesting item.'

The emissary, taking the cue, was quick to respond.

Placing the binoculars on the table, he said, 'This is a powerful instrument by which you can see in the far distance. In fact, you can see the stars in the daytime.'

Bajirao's anger was uncontrollable. He said, giving the pair of binoculars a contemptuous look, 'Keep them away.'

Sanzgiri came to the point without further ado. 'I entreat you to release our boats which are being held by you.'

Bajirao replied, 'We are not in the habit of returning ships which we capture during war.'

'We are not your enemies, sarkar. We believe there has been a terrible mistake.'

'While we were engaged in battle, we found that your ships were carrying ammunition for the enemy. Now what do I make of it? It won't take us much time to tie your governor to the mouth of the cannon and light the fuse.'

Bajirao's words sounded like cannonballs to the emissary. There was pin-drop silence as no one dared to speak. Sanzgiri tried again. 'I agree we were carrying ammunition but that was demanded by Siddhi. We were simply ferrying it. If the Marathas had asked for it, we would have gladly given it to them.'

'The habshis, Siddhi's Abyssinian troops, were targeting our troops. And they were firing cannons and ammunition supplied by you. How does that make the firangis our friends?'

Sanzgiri was well versed in the art of diplomacy. He said, 'We are mere traders, huzoor, just like the English. A trader is only interested in supplying what is asked for.'

'I don't have time to discuss your definitions. Those who help our enemies are considered as our enemy too. Your ships were helping our enemy, period. We plan to sink your ships.'

'Do I then interpret that the Marathas have now declared a war against the firangis?'

Sanzgiri's question was a threat cloaked as an innocuous question. Bajirao said, raising his voice, 'If your governor is itching for a war, so be it. Let him know there will be no one to welcome him in Vasai or wherever he wishes to go. There will be Marathas all over.'

Sanzgiri's throat went dry. He said, 'We have done nothing to be labelled as an enemy. On the contrary, we gave you a gift...'

Bajirao cut him short saying, 'Shut up! I don't understand your language of politics. If the Portuguese try to help our enemy once again, we will make you see stars in the daytime, without the need for a pair of binoculars!'

The Portuguese emissary realized it was wise to not argue with the Peshwa any more. He stood with his head bowed, looking down at the floor.

Bajirao ordered, 'Ambaji, ask the firangi emissary to take his leave. Our meeting is over.'

Shrimant Peshwa was busy till Diwali in the office, planning various campaigns and appointing sardars for the same. The moneylenders had given their support for the campaigns. Tired of continuous work, Bajirao decided to rest in the gardens at Kothrud for three days. He loved riding up the hillock on his horse in the early hours of the morning while Mastani, wearing a man's dress, would accompany him on another horse.

One morning, not finding Mastani waiting as usual, he asked Basanti, 'I don't see Mastani around.'

'Baiji is not well. She has asked you to go alone.'

Bajirao was surprised. He shrugged and spurred the horse. After riding till noon, he returned tired to the haveli. He turned the horse towards Mastani's quarters remembering to enquire about her health.

Mastani came down to meet Bajirao. Seeing her, he asked, 'Why did you not ride with me this morning?'

'I was not well,' Mastani said, avoiding his eyes.

'You seemed quite fine last night.'

Mastani did not answer and Bajirao realized she was avoiding him. He asked, 'Has the hakim given you any medicine?'

'Yes, he has.'

'I will ask him his diagnosis.'

'No! Please don't ask him,' Mastani pleaded, taking Bajirao by surprise. He was a little amused at her strange reaction.

He noticed that she seemed nervous. Hugging her tightly, he asked, 'When I see you like this I am worried. Tell me, is everything all right?'

Mastani rushed away to her inner quarters. At that moment Basanti walked in. Bajirao asked her, 'What is wrong with your Baiji? I want to speak to the hakim. Call him.'

'There is no need for the hakim to be called,' Basanti explained. 'Baiji is having some problems, you see,' she said, touching her stomach gently and blushing as she spoke.

The truth dawned on Bajirao and he rushed to Mastani's room. Upon entering, he found her sitting on her bed, resting against two large pillows. The moment she saw him, she covered her face with her palms. Bajirao gently removed her hands, saying, 'I know now. It is not illness, it is wonderful news!'

Mastani refused to look up. Bajirao turned her face towards him gently as she blushed red. 'Now, look at me! My child is growing in your womb. What can give me more happiness?'

Bajirao's happiness made Mastani ecstatic. Memories of the beautiful and sensual nights spent in the company of the dashing, handsome Peshwa rushed through her mind. She did not realize when her dupatta slipped down exposing her shapely figure. Her lips quivered and she heard his voice, 'My darling! My dear Mastani!'

Mastani, lost in the haze of happiness, murmured, 'Rau!'

Bajirao, elated at the way she had addressed him, said, 'Rau! Yes! That is what I am. Mastani's Rau. Say my name once more.'

The words floated in the air like a delicate fragrance, 'Rau! Mastani's Rau! Rau!'

The formal address of Shrimant, Swami, sarkar ... they all dissolved in that one beautiful moment leaving just Rau. On coming back to reality, Mastani rested her head on Bajirao's shoulder while tears flowed down her cheeks. Bajirao patted her back gently saying, 'What happened now? One moment ago you were so happy. What are the tears for?'

Wiping the tears with the back of her hand, Mastani said, 'Whether in sorrow or joy, we women know how to cry. Rau, these are tears of fear!'

'Fear? What should Mastani fear when she is with Bajirao?'

'I am nobody. The world knows me as a mere singer and dancer. The thought that I have to carry the son of the mighty Peshwa makes me scared.'

Bajirao played with Mastani's long curls for a while. He said, 'Now, stop crying. I am with you.'

'That is the reason for my fear. I have a storm in my life in the form of the Peshwa and I fear that my life, a mere dry leaf, will be sucked up and flung far away in this storm.'

'Don't be silly! Since the day I accepted you, my arms have been around you all the time. Have you forgotten the night at Mahuli on Janmashtami?'

'I won't forget that till my dying moment.'

'I had promised you that I wouldn't let you go as long as I was alive.'

'I know, and that is what keeps me alive.'

'Then wipe these tears away,' Bajirao said, handing her her dupatta which was lying on the bed.

Mastani suddenly became conscious and quickly wrapped the dupatta around her shoulders. Resting her head against Bajirao's chest, she said, 'I have nothing to fear as long as I have Rau Swami's support. Your love is growing inside my womb. I will proudly take care of him. He will be the reason for me to live. But I have one thing to say…'

'What is it?'

'The month of Ramzan is about to begin. I have my fasts…'

'No more fasts! You have to take care of the child now. Your name may be Mastani but you are mine. Your religion and mine – they are the same; you have to follow what I say.'

'I will do as you say. But please stay back and have your meal here. You must be tired after the ride.'

Bajirao agreed, saying, 'I will! Let the kitchen be informed that I shall have my meal after an hour. Let them prepare whatever they make for you.'

'How can I do that? You are a Brahman. Don't despoil your religion for me. Have you forgotten what you told me just now?'

'No, I haven't, but when two hearts meet these things are trivial. There is just one thing that I believe now.'

'And that is?'

'Rau and Mastani – they are inseparable!'

Sleep eluded Radhabai as she tossed and turned in her bed. She tried repeating the Vyankatesh stotra for a while, but the storm of thoughts swirling through her head did not abate. Getting up, she looked out of the window to find the lamp burning in the office. She wondered who might be up at such a late hour. The maid outside was dozing. She woke her up and asked her to check. The maid returned, rubbing her eyes, and reported that it was Chimaji Appa. Radhabai asked the maid to let Chimaji Appa know that she was waiting for him and that he should pay her a visit when his work was done.

Soon, Chimaji came into Radhabai's room. Radhabai said, 'I did not wish to disturb you. Hope I didn't interrupt. What made you stay up so late?'

'Nothing can be more important than meeting you. The office work will never end. Anyway, what makes you stay awake so late?'

'I asked you the same question.'

'The administrative work is getting difficult these days. I have to look at all the correspondence from our spies and our emissaries.'

'And what about the matters at home? How are you tackling them?'

'I am unable to understand you, Matushree. If you elaborate, I will be obliged,' Appa said, realizing that his mother was referring to some domestic problem.

Radhabai said, 'Appa, the matter is a little delicate. You know,' she said, lowering her voice, 'I am talking of Rau's behaviour.'

Appa was alert. There were many things he had heard of Rau but he did not want to talk about them. He said, 'I have heard a few things. What about his behaviour?'

'I heard from the chief priest this morning. It really surprised me.'

'What did he say?'

'I had assumed that his relations with the Musalmaan lady was a mere infatuation but I am told he spends a lot of time at Kothrud these days.'

'I too have heard that.'

'What have you done about it?'

'Matushree, he is my elder brother and like a father to me. I can hint at best. What else can I do?'

'Krishna Bhat tells me that Rau stayed back at Kothrud for three days and that he ate meat along with that Musalmaan lady.'

The lamp burned in a corner of the room. It was late in the night and the only sound that could be heard was of the crickets in the garden outside. Radhabai continued, her voice full of anguish, 'It is not that people have not kept mistresses earlier, but they don't forget their religion in that process. Appa, you must do something.'

Appa let out a deep sigh and said, 'I too heard of this. Earlier, he had eaten meat when on shikar a couple of times but never in public. I never expected him to do so, staying here in Pune.'

Radhabai looked at her younger son, his face a little pale due to his recent illness. She said, 'We need to act. He holds the post of Peshwa and if the news of his behaviour were to reach Chhatrapati Maharaj, it would be disastrous. Rau may not think of the consequences but we need to. Ever since the death of Dabhade, the Brahmans are not getting the donations due to them in the month of Shravan. Now, such news would be the ammunition they badly need. It would create havoc. Let's act carefully.'

'I can think of a way,' Appa said.

'Do whatever it takes, Appa, but Rau needs to mend his ways.'

'I will take my sister-in-law's help.'

'Kashibai? What do you plan to do?'

'Let her accompany Rau on his campaigns. I know you had asked her not to, given her pregnancy. But if she is with him, she can force him to visit the Narmada where she wishes to build a temple. It would serve two purposes: her wish would be fulfilled and, in the process, Rau will have to take a holy dip. Then, we can ask Krishna Bhat to take care of the religious purification rites.'

'It is worth trying. Appa, I am really disappointed with Rau's behaviour. No one in the family has behaved like this. Only his wife can save him now.' The anguish in Radhabai's voice was evident.

They chatted for a long time that night. Radhabai felt better having confided in her son.

As per the agreement with the Nizam, the Peshwa was permitted to collect rent from the territories of Khandesh, Aurangabad and Bijapur, but the Nizam would find a thousand reasons and stall their efforts. Bajirao was aware that the only way he could get his dues would be to take up arms and force the Nizam to pay. They decided to make a surprise attack on Khandesh and collect more than what the three Subahs would have given together. Bajirao and Appa worked out the details.

The plan was to attack Khandesh while the Nizam was busy in Karnatak. In the event of his return to Khandesh, Pilaji Jadhavrao and his men would engage the Nizam's troops on the banks of the Godavari. Bajirao decided to leave within a week.

That night, when he returned to his private chambers, Kashibai asked him, 'Are you planning to go to Khandesh?'

Bajirao smiled. He normally never discussed matters of the state unless they were critical. He said, 'I did not mean to hide anything but I thought it was not important enough to tell you.'

Bajirao removed his turban and stretched his legs. Tired with the deliberations going on the whole day, he was keen to rest. He said, putting a few pieces of cardamom in his mouth, 'You are not as innocent as I assumed. You too are keeping secrets from me.'

'Keeping secrets? Now what did I hide from you?'

Kashibai's face was glowing in the light of the lamps. Bajirao said, sitting on the bed, 'I am told Nana is soon going to have a brother. Did you tell me that?'

Kashibai blushed and avoiding his gaze said, 'Is it something a wife is supposed to tell her swami? You would have found that out soon enough.'

'Most secrets are revealed sometime or the other. That is not the point. Knowing them on time is the beauty of it. You need to be punished for not telling me.'

Kashibai knew Bajirao was in a jovial mood. She played along saying, 'If you are going to punish me, I cannot stop you. Tell me my punishment.'

'The punishment is ... I shall fulfil all your desires!'

'Oh my! Really? I am overwhelmed. But you don't have to do that. In this state, a woman asks for many absurd things and my mother-in-law is taking care of me. But now that you mention it, I would like one thing done.'

'Please command,' Bajirao said, bowing dramatically.

'I wish to build a temple on the banks of the Narmada. When you go on your campaign, I wish to come along.'

Bajirao's smile vanished. Then he said, 'Well, I was not

planning to go beyond the Tapi. But now that I have promised, I shall fulfil it.'

Kashibai was thrilled. She said, changing the topic, 'You need to spend some time looking at domestic matters too. Do you realize your son is grown up now?'

'I know. He is learning well at the court at Satara.'

'And what about your daughter-in-law? It has been five years since she came into our house. She will soon come of age. We have to perform the rites for the same. It is time we built a separate mahal for the couple.'

'Really? I never realized how time flies. I will get the construction started immediately.'

'I wish for one more thing. I hope you won't refuse'

'I have already promised to fulfil all your wishes. Ask.'

'I wish to visit my parents' house before we leave. It has been quite a while since I have been to Chas.'

'Sure! We still have a week before we leave. You may visit Chas in the meantime. I will send a letter to Krishnarao today itself.'

Kashibai was genuinely happy. Lying on her bed, she kept gazing at the lamp burning in a corner of the room. After a while, as the lamp burnt itself out, she too fell asleep.

Kashibai was busy with her prayers when the chief priest, Krishna Bhat, came in and said, 'I have come with my married daughter. I wanted her to take your blessings.'

Kashibai said, 'I will be in my quarters in a while. You can bring her there.'

After some time Krishna Bhat entered Kashibai's private chambers with his daughter. She was a girl of ten, shy and trying to stand straight in the nine-yard traditional sari which she wore along with a nose ring and anklets.

'Please take Baisaheb's blessings,' Krishna Bhat said to his daughter who touched Kashibai's feet.

'May you live a long married life,' Kashibai blessed her and asked, 'Which family is she married into?'

'They are the Mehendales who worked under Dabhade. Unfortunately, since the death of the Dabhades, the Brahmans there are not getting their yearly salaries. The annual donation during Shravan too has been stopped.'

'Why is that?'

'I am not sure but I know for a fact that a lot of Brahmans are suffering.'

'Have you consulted Appa regarding this?'

'He does not like his servants advising on things which are outside their purview.'

'Anyway, now that you have told me I will inform Shrimant. Let him look into it.'

Sensing that Krishna Bhat wanted to talk some more, Kashibai asked, 'Did you have anything else to say?'

'Shrimant was responsible for the death of the Chhatrapati's commander. It has created a lot of bad blood and he also carries the sin of his death.'

'Krishna Bhat!' Kashibai said, raising her voice. 'These things happen in warfare and you cannot blame the Peshwa for every death.'

'It is not about the death alone. Shrimant has been out for months at a stretch and has forsaken the Brahman traditions too.'

'Please remain within your limits before you make such accusations, Krishna Bhat. Who has given you the right to comment on the Peshwa's behaviour?'

Krishna Bhat realized that he may have transgressed and apologized saying, 'I did not mean to accuse Shrimant himself. But the blame for any misdemeanour by even one of the thousands of his troops would come on Shrimant, wouldn't it?'

'What are you suggesting we should do?'

'A dip in the holy Narmada is enough to wash off all the sins, whether committed deliberately or inadvertently. Donating money to the Brahmans there would add to Shrimant's glory.'

'Krishna Bhat, you may speak your mind.'

'I was worried it may hurt you, Baisaheb, but the fact is that all Brahmans from Paithan in the north to Tungabhadra in the south are gossiping. I cannot shut their mouths.'

Krishna Bhat's rant was not music to Kashibai's ears but she had no choice. He was the chief priest and a confidant of Radhabai's. She knew that if she refused to take action, he would go and voice his opinion to Radhabai. She said, 'I will look into it.' Then, in order to end the meeting, she said, 'And, before you leave, please go to the office and collect a sari and some sweets for your daughter. After all, she has come to meet us for the first time and should not return empty-handed.'

The priest walked out of the chambers satisfied.

Nana returned from Satara with Mahadoba Purandare and reported to Bajirao at his office. Nana said, 'Virubai has sent an important message for you. She says she sent a few reminders regarding the slaves she wanted as maids and handmaidens, but you have not taken any action yet. She has sent a strongly worded letter this time.'

Bajirao thought for a while and said, 'You have come at the right time. The annual slave bazaar is on at this moment. Please select twenty-odd maids you think would be approved by the Chhatrapati and send them to Satara.'

The next day, Nana went about inspecting the slave bazaar. The bazaar would start around Diwali and go on for a fortnight. Women, aged seven to sixty, would be on sale, with traders coming in from different parts of the country. Despite roaming around for a long time, he could not find anyone who he thought was befitting.

He called for the city kotwal and said, 'I am not able to find anyone worthwhile. Can you help?'

The kotwal said, after saluting, 'Sarkar, please leave the matter in my hands. I shall get you what you want. We have all kinds here. There are women from Gandhar who are beautiful and fair-skinned but they lose their shape after a few years. The ones from Allahabad, Lucknow and Delhi are experts in singing and dancing but are not good for housework. The ones from Karnatak are dark but have nice features and age gracefully. There are some from Rajasthan and then a few from Kamrup. The ones from the east would not appeal to the Chhatrapati as they have small eyes and noses. The ones from Konkan are not good as they are very dark. They are fit only for guard duty.'

Nana was impressed with the knowledge the kotwal had. He said, 'You seem to know a lot.'

'It is my duty, sarkar. I shall select a few and bring them for your inspection by afternoon.'

True to his word, the kotwal had arranged for an inspection that afternoon. Most of them were less than thirteen years of age. The eldest was a twenty-year-old Multani girl. Nana selected them and, after a lot of haggling, managed to procure them for twenty thousand rupias.

The maids were handed over to the servants and were housed in a separate building before being sent across to Satara.

Kashibai, on her visit to her parents' place at Chas, was having a very good time roaming the fields without any care. Her brother, Krishnarao, was a little nervous that the Peshwa's wife was walking around unescorted. But Kashibai assured him that the Peshwa would not mind. Kashibai's daughter-in-law, Gopika, too enjoyed the change.

Kashibai's childhood friends made a beeline to meet her – she was the Peshwa's wife after all. They were enamoured upon seeing her and hesitated to talk freely. Krishnarao's wife, Rakhmabai, encouraged each one of them to speak frankly.

Walking on the sandy banks of the river Bheema, Kashibai reminisced about her childhood days. After a darshan at the Someshwar temple, they returned home.

Kashibai was eager to return to Pune. She had met so many of her childhood friends and each one of them had some suggestion or complaint or the other. Someone wanted a proper source of water in their village, while someone else wanted a job. There were endless demands. She was at her wits' end wondering whether she would be able to fulfil any of them.

Kashibai sat in her palanquin after bidding farewell to all. As the palanquin moved through the thick woods, she turned to see her parents' home once again. She had had a wonderful time and was returning with lots of good memories.

The advance party for Khandesh had left and so did Kashibai's palanquin. The next day Bajirao and his men were to leave from Pune.

After finishing the work in the office, when Bajirao reached his quarters, Kunwar informed him, 'Everyone is waiting for you in the dining room for the meal.'

'Send a message that I shall not be having dinner here. I am staying at Kothrud gardens tonight and shall leave tomorrow morning from there itself.'

As Bajirao stepped out to go to Mastani's haveli, the eighth-day moon spread a lovely light across the gardens.

Mastani was waiting for Bajirao and said as he stepped in, 'I was wondering whether you would be able to come.'

Bajirao removed his turban and relaxed in the comfortable seating area saying, 'I was busy in the office, finishing some work, when I got your message. I would have come, nonetheless.'

'I was keen that I get a chance to serve you before you leave for your campaign.'

Bajirao looked around the room. Two large tanpuras and a sarangi were kept in a corner, along with a pair of ghungroos. Looking at Mastani he said, 'Why are you standing so far away? Come and sit here.'

Mastani sat near him on her knees. The dupatta slipped down to her shoulders but she did not bother to put it back on her head. Bajirao said, 'You should have seen the kind of excitement that was created because of the food I ate here.'

'Really? I wonder why. Your servants had taught me how to cook in the right manner. What mistake did I commit?'

'It is not about the fact that I came here or what you cooked. It was because of what I ate.'

'I don't understand,' she said, her mehndi-coloured fingers resting on her soft cheeks.

'I am a Brahman and we are not supposed to eat in a Musalmaan's house. On top of it, I ate what I am not evensupposed to touch.'

'Had I known this would create such a problem, I would not have served Shrimant.'

'Not Shrimant,' Bajirao said, shaking his head. 'Rau.'

Mastani blushed and said, her voice almost a whisper, 'Yes ... Rau.'

'That's better! Mastani, there are only two women who call me Rau. My Matushree, whom I worship, and you, who resides in my heart.'

'It is my privilege and good fortune if this is really true.'

'Do you doubt that?'

'No, I don't. I believe you. But it is your nature which sometimes scares me. You do things in haste and I am the one who has to face the consequences.'

'Did anything happen which makes you say that?'

'It was the day after you had dinner with me – Appa Swami's men came and threatened Jamdar. Their message was a threat couched as advice. They said: "A dancer should know whether the floor is slippery or not. Else, she may break her leg."'

Bajirao dismissed it with a wave of his hand saying, 'Let them say what they have to. No one can stop me. You know the message I left in the dining room today? That I would be spending the night here and leaving for the campaign from here itself.'

'Why do you do things to irk those in the haveli? You might as well have had dinner there and then come over.'

'It is my nature, Mastani. I cannot tolerate an enemy challenging me in the battlefield. Likewise, I get upset if someone tries to use his or her position and interfere in my personal life. If that makes them angry, so be it.'

Realizing that Bajirao was getting angry, Mastani changed the topic. 'I heard Baisaheb is going too. Is that so?'

'Yes. We will take a holy dip in the Narmada.'

'Oh, that's good. I hope Baisaheb can manage the journey, though.'

She added, 'Rau, may I request something?'

Bajirao put his finger on her soft, pink lips and said, 'I am not used to these lips making requests.'

Mastani blinked and said, 'What else can a slave do?'

'These lips are to command and not request. Tell me, Mastani.'

'I have surrendered myself at your feet. At most I can plead but never command, Rau. You know, I wish I could join you on your campaigns at times. When you are tired I would sing and dance for you hoping that it would make you forget, at least for a while, all your aches and pains.'

'Oh! We can do that any time. I am leaving tomorrow, you can accompany me if you want.'

Mastani fiddled affectionately with Bajirao's pearl necklace for a while. Then she said, shaking her head, 'Not this time. I will come some other time and, if you like my services, you will ask for them again.'

'Fine. It will be as you wish. By the way, I have something planned for you. You cannot continue staying so far away in these gardens. I am building a new mahal for Nana. I will build another one for my Mastani too.'

Mastani shook her head slowly and said, 'Rau, do you realize what people will say?'

'Let them say what they have to. To be frank, to imagine what people might say tickles me to no end.'

'It seems it is Rau's hobby to jump into the fire pit.'

Bajirao, looking at the musical instruments lying in the corner, said, 'Why don't you play something for me?'

'As you wish,' Mastani said and picked up the sarangi.

As she fiddled with the tuning, Bajirao said, 'It seems the sarangi was eager to feel your fingers on it. Play something to soothe my anguished soul. When you stay in the mahal nearby, I will be able to hear you each night.'

Bajirao was lost in pleasant dreams of the future but Mastani, on the other hand, felt she was entering a tornado which would lift her off her feet and fling her far away. Her mind was in a turmoil. She tuned the sarangi and began singing. Bajirao, closing his eyes in enjoyment, drummed his fingers on his knees in rhythm.

Mastani sang...

> *'I was scared of the dark clouds.*
> *Oh, Shyama, I was scared*
> *It rained all over...'*

After Mastani's performance, they lay down on the bed. She spoke of the dark clouds in her mind while Bajirao tried his best to allay her fears. The two, engrossed in each other, never realized when the night gave way to dawn. A lovely morning star shimmered in the sky. Mastani, scared of the future she saw for herself, made Bajirao promise many a thing. The birds in the gardens chirped as the sun rose over the eastern horizon and soon the footsteps of the soldiers were heard. Bajirao gently removed himself from Mastani's embrace and walked out of the haveli.

The province of Khandesh burned in the hot summer and the sands of the river Tapi, true to her name in Hindi meaning 'hot', added to the discomfort by radiating heat all day. Bajirao's sardars were busy collecting the rent, rather extracting it by force, from all over the province while the Nizam, having heard of the tactics used by them, was feeling restless. Bajirao's emissary stationed in the Nizam's court tried to deflect his attention from Khandesh. Bajirao's sardars, in the meantime, loaded camel after camel of loot and soon they moved southwards.

As soon as the main task of the campaign was over, Kashibai proposed the ceremony of the holy dip in the river Narmada. The day of the full moon in the month of Chaitra was selected for the ceremony. Malhar Rao Holkar, Bajirao's key sardar from the Malwa region, had come for the occasion. At Raver Khedi, where the river was shallow, they crossed over to the other side and camped in the midst of a dense jungle. The horses roamed freely, drinking water from the river.

In the other part of Hindustan, Chimaji Appa's team, headed by Shinde and Pawar, was busy collecting dues. Bajirao was at Raver Khedi would receive their news at regular intervals. He was testing the waters with the Badshah at Delhi, while he worked out a strategy to free all important Hindu pilgrimage places which were still under Mughal rule.

On a hot and sultry afternoon, Bajirao and Holkar enjoyed a swim in the cool waters of the Narmada till sunset.

After returning to the camp, Bajirao relaxed on a low seating arrangement and looked towards the partition separating the area where Kashibai sat. He asked, 'So, have you got a taste of camp life now?'

'It is so hot here! How do you manage to stay in such weather? Moreover, how do you find the energy to go out riding on campaigns? It is so strenuous.'

'It is not, actually. I am used to it since childhood. You know, I feel suffocated in the haveli at Pune. The open skies, large fields and dense forests – they are so exhilarating! A man can hardly think freely imprisoned within the four walls of the haveli.'

Malhar Rao, listening to their conversation, said, 'Shrimant should consider making Shanivar wada more comfortable in summers. We have some expert artisans from Rajasthan well versed in this field.'

'Malhar Rao, I will show you the work our artisans have done. Nana's mahal is about to get ready. In the main chamber, a thin translucent wall of flowing water creates a soothing sight while keeping the mahal cool all day.'

Kashibai said, 'That reminds me, while Nana's mahal is almost ready, I saw the construction of another mahal in progress. Whom is it for?'

Bajirao hesitated for a moment and then dodged the question saying, 'Well! Let the mahal get ready first. We can always find someone or the other to stay there.'

Turning to Malhar Rao, he said, 'Tomorrow is the day of the holy dip. I hope everything is as per plan.'

'Yes, Shrimant,' Malhar Rao said.

Kashibai said, 'There is such beautiful scenery around. Shrimant stays here often but I find there isn't a Mahadev temple here. I would be happy if Shrimant orders a small temple to be built here.'

Bajirao looked at the vast expanse of the Narmada from his tent. He said, after a while, 'I like the idea but I wonder whether we would be able to have someone posted here to look after the temple and also do the regular puja. It would otherwise become a home for wild dogs and wolves.'

Malhar Rao said, 'Shrimant, we will never allow that. We will find someone to take care of the temple.'

The next morning, the ceremony began with Krishna Bhat taking charge. People gathered at the bank expectantly, waiting for donations from the Peshwa. The ceremony went on for nearly four hours. Kashibai, walking on the sandy banks, was reminded of her father's home on the banks of the Bheema.

Malhar Rao selected a place for the new temple. A shivalinga, found in the Narmada, was placed on a tray by Kashibai and consecrated by Krishna Bhat. All rituals were carried out elaborately with the sound of the mantras resounding as the Brahmans chanted them, sitting in the open air.

While returning to their camp, Bajirao asked Kashibai, 'I hope everything was to your satisfaction.'

'Yes, I am really pleased. It has been a long time since we performed such religious rites together.'

Bajirao asked, looking at the place where they had consecrated the new deity, 'We got the temple made but what about the name? What do you have in mind?'

Kashibai said, 'We have a Someshwar temple back home, in my father's village. Let us call this Rameshwar.'

'Then Rameshwar it shall be!'

The moment Bajirao heard of the Nizam and his troops marching towards the north, they decided to move out of Khandesh and proceed towards Pune. En route, they stopped at many religious places taking care to ride slow, mindful of Kashibai's delicate health. The victorious contingent reached Pune to be welcomed by the first showers of the monsoon.

Appa too had returned just before the rains. Both Chimaji Appa and Bajirao spent the monsoon months tallying the loot. It had been a remarkably successful campaign. Radhabai took care of her daughter-in-law who was now in the advanced stage of her pregnancy.

One day, while relaxing in Appa's chambers, Bajirao said, 'I notice your health has deteriorated again. I must now order you to stay put here or move to the court at Satara till you become fit.'

'I must be a little tanned, having been out in the sun.' Appa tried to brush the topic aside.

Bajirao said, 'Don't try fooling me.'

Appa pleaded, 'I cannot stay put until the task at Konkan is over. The habshis there are creating havoc and the Portuguese too have raised their heads again. They need to be taught a lesson. I cannot sit in the office pushing papers.'

Bajirao tried his best, but Appa was adamant.

Bajirao said, 'I believe the Brahmans are not getting their donations since the death of Dabhade. Should we start that? It would make them happy.'

'If that alone would make the Brahmans happy, we should surely start it.' Appa's taunt was not lost on Bajirao so he asked, 'What else could be the reason?'

Appa did not answer directly. He said, 'I don't know. I don't keep tabs on everything that happens in Pune.'

Bajirao guessed the real reason and decided not to probe further. He said, 'Let us start the donations at least. If they are still not satisfied, we shall see.'

Both knew but they had chosen not to broach the topic. At that moment Yesu rushed in to say, 'Please pardon me for intruding without permission. Baisaheb has given birth to a boy.'

'That is wonderful news,' Appa exclaimed. 'I have another nephew now,' and saying so, he removed a ring from his finger and gifted it to Yesu.

Bajirao did not express his happiness openly. Looking at his younger brother affectionately, he said, 'Appa, for the first time I am seeing a person happy to share someone else's happiness.'

Trumpets and cannons in the city square announced the arrival of the Peshwa's newborn son. The Peshwa's personal elephant was taken out for a round, while the servants were sent to the houses of the sardars with bags of sugar, a traditional way of announcing good news.

That afternoon, Mastani sat alone near a fountain as she enjoyed watching the coloured fish swimming in the pool. She threw a fistful of grains into the water and chuckled at the fish fighting for each morsel. Wearing a rich embroidered sari and sporting a bindi in the tradition of Hindus, she looked resplendent.

Looking at her reflection in the water, she adjusted her nath, the traditional nose ring worn by Maharashtrian ladies. For a moment, the thought that Rau had not visited her since his return from the campaign crossed her mind, but the next moment, her mind comforted her saying that Rau was her's alone and the only reason for not visiting her would be the load of work that he had to finish.

At that moment, she saw Basanti running towards her shouting, 'Baiji! Baiji!'

'There is good news,' Basanti said, trying to catch her breath.

Mastani understood the reason behind her excitement when Basanti put a lump of sugar in her palm. She asked, 'Is it a boy?'

'Yes!'

'That is great news!'

'Baiji, the whole city is celebrating. Married women are performing puja at the riverbank.'

'What does one do on such occasions? I will ask the pandit who comes to teach me the Brahman customs.'

Basanti said, 'You don't need to ask him. I will tell you, send a pair of kurta-pyjama and a traditional cap for the young one.'

'Oh, is that so? I shall do that right away.'

Mastani managed to climb the steps to her haveli with difficulty. The swelling in her legs had increased and she had to hold Basanti's hand for support. On reaching upstairs, she got a box filled with Bajirao's favourite sweets and said, 'Here, Basanti! Take this to the haveli and give my regards to Shrimant.' Taking out a lovely pearl necklace from a bag, she added, 'And take this jewellery from Bundelkhand as my gift.'

Basanti turned to go when Mastani said, 'Wait! I have not given anything for Baisaheb. Let me think of something appropriate.'

Basanti said, 'How would it reach Kashibai? You know Appa Swami has given strict instructions not to allow anyone to enter her quarters. I am able to reach Shrimant's quarters but cannot step anywhere near Kashibai's.'

Mastani thought for a moment and then an idea struck her. Taking a pinch of ash from a silver tray kept nearby, she said,

'This is holy ash from the Mrityunjay temple. I will pack it in a wooden box. Give it to Shrimant saying it is for the baby and Baisaheb. He will know what to do.'

'I will do as you say,' Basanti said.

Mastani, tired of speaking, closed her eyes and dozed off. After a while, hearing noises outside, she opened her eyes to find that Bajirao's servants had arrived. Bajirao had sent her a tray of sweets in celebration of the newborn.

Mastani was delighted to receive them. She wondered whether what she saw was a dream or reality.

Everyone was joyful with the arrival of the Ganesha festival in the month of August. Kashibai, lying on her bed, was issuing orders for the festivities. She was in charge of the dance and other celebrations.

Chimaji Appa was busy in the north and would correspond regularly with Bajirao, sending updates. Then Ambaji Pant Purandare died suddenly and the Peshwa household was greatly saddened. He had been in the services of the Peshwas since Bajirao's father's time and was the seniormost member of the household. Bajirao personally met Mahadoba Purandare, Ambaji's son, and offered him his condolences.

As a mark of respect and official mourning, the trumpets and horns were silent for four days.

The office work increased considerably after the death of Ambaji Pant and both Bajirao and Appa would spend several hours, late into the night, clearing the papers.

One evening, when Bajirao returned to his quarters after work, Kunwar came in and said, 'I have good news. Baisaheb has delivered a baby boy.'

Bajirao was lost in thought and said, a little irritated, 'Are you giving me the news of the birth of Raghunath Pant now, after a month?'

'I am not talking of Raghunath Pant. I am talking of Baisaheb who stays at Kothrud gardens.'

'You mean Mastani?' Bajirao said, getting up. 'When did she deliver?'

Kunwar said, 'It has been more than a week.'

'More than a week? And I hear of it now? I have servants posted there. Were they sleeping?'

'They would come here every day but were unable to leave a message due to strict instructions from Appa to not allow them anywhere near the house. I happened to be in the gardens this morning and that's how I got the news.'

Bajirao said, 'Why did you not shout and announce the news instead of telling me in private?'

Kunwar was clearly nervous as he fished for an appropriate response. He said, 'Shrimant, the son was born to a mistress. I was worried Appa would get upset if I announced this in the office.'

Bajirao's face fell. He said, 'So what if she is a mistress? Isn't the birth of a child a happy moment for anyone, especially the mother? Isn't your mother a mistress to a Rajputana royal? Was your mother not elated to have given birth to you?'

Kunwar had not expected his birth to be brought into the picture and was clearly embarrassed. He said, without looking at Bajirao, 'Shrimant, what prestige does a mistress' son have? He is treated like dirt. Who cares whether he lives or dies?'

Bajirao stood up and walked out saying, 'Get my horse ready. I am leaving for Kothrud right now. Hurry up!'

Chanda Jamdar saw Bajirao Peshwa arriving and informed

Basanti, who rushed down the steps to receive him. She said, 'Baiji was remembering Shrimant just a while ago.'

'I am too late,' Bajirao muttered to himself as he stepped in. Basanti came in and offered a tumbler of sherbet on a tray but Bajirao ignored it and asked, 'Where is Mastani? Where is my Chiranjeev? I want to see them first.'

'I will go in and check.'

Bajirao's impatience was running high. He glanced at the tanpura and the sarangi kept on a diwan, but they gave him no solace. Rather, it irritated him that Mastani was taking so much time. At that moment, he heard a voice, 'I have a gift for you.'

Bajirao turned to see Mastani standing with a babe. Her face seemed a little drained but her eyes overflowed with joy.

Bajirao rushed forward extending his hands but Mastani moved away and said, 'Uh, uh! One should see a newborn from a little distance and not try to hold it.'

'It is my child! Let me see if he resembles you.'

Mastani said, blushing a little, 'Our little gentleman seems to have taken after his father.'

Bajirao said, in mock anger, 'I can decide that, provided I am able to see him. The way he clings to you, I cannot see anything.'

'If Shrimant was so eager to see his son's face, should he not have come earlier?' Mastani asked. Bajirao realized that she was very hurt.

He said, sitting down on the bed, 'I made a mistake but please don't torture me now.'

Mastani sat down beside Bajirao. The child, with lovely pink cheeks, a straight nose and beautiful delicate lips, was asleep. Bajirao looked at him with immense pride and then clapped once.

Kunwar, waiting outside, came in with a small pouch. Bajirao took out a gold necklace from the pouch and draped it around the child's neck. Mastani said, 'The pandit tells me that as per Hindu custom, the child should be named on the eleventh day. I am not sure if you will be here on that day. What shall I name him?'

Mastani continued without waiting for his reply, 'You remember the Janmashtami night when you came to meet me?'

'How can I forget? That image of you undressing slowly as you stood behind the gossamer screen, the lamp behind you and...'

'Stop!' Mastani said, hiding her face as she blushed. 'Is it necessary to describe it in such detail?'

'Fine. So what was it you were saying about that Janmashtami night?'

'We met for the first time, hence, I have decided to name our son Krishnasingh.'

'Oh, that's nice. I like the name.'

'It is nice,' Bajirao repeated, putting a piece of sweet in his mouth. 'But I would call him...' He stopped as he thought for a moment.

'Do you not like the name?' Mastani asked.

'I like it but, you know, my son will be like a sword – a *shamsher*. A man needs to be able to fight with a shamsher, whether in love or war. And he needs to be a *bahadur*, a daredevil. I will name him Shamsher Bahadur.'

Mastani was overwhelmed hearing Bajirao. In his presence, she felt that she dissolved into him, losing her own identity. She said, 'It is a name appropriate for Rau's son. He will remind me of love and remind Rau of war.'

Bajirao returned late at night to his quarters and issued

orders immediately. The next morning, before Appa could realize, the servants had left with boxes of jewels and expensive clothes to Kothrud gardens. The Brahman who had been teaching Mastani the Hindu customs was lavishly gifted as well.

THREE

Chanda Jamdar returned to Kothrud gardens riding a horse. Basanti rushed down the steps when she heard him and stretched out her hands to lift Shamsher off the horse. Chanda Jamdar said, 'He is truly Shrimant's son. I have been riding for two hours but he is not tired at all!'

In the hot sun, Shamsher's face had turned red and the violet satin dress enhanced his fair colour. He wore an embroidered cap and white pyjamas. The red shoes added to his charm. Kissing Shamsher on his cheeks, Basanti said, 'He is our Peshwa sarkar. You have been blessed to have given him a ride. What do you say, Shrimant?'

Shamsher smiled. Basanti rubbed her cheeks against his and walked up the stairs. Chanda handed over the reins to the syce and said, walking along with her, 'Basanti, I may be blessed but I am not going to take him for a ride into the city ever again.'

'Why, what happened?'

'I was put through a lot of trouble and insults. I don't intend to face them any more.'

He continued, 'It so happened that when we reached the town, we realized it was a day of celebrations as Matushree had just returned from her pilgrimage and she was visiting the city, meeting people. Everyone had lined up on the streets to have a glimpse of her. She got down from her palanquin near the temple and walked the rest of the way. It was an unbelievable sight with hordes of women scrambling to touch her feet. The city police chief had to make way for her to move. I too got down and touched her feet.'

'What happened then?'

'Spotting Shamsher in the crowd, she asked, "Whose child is it?" Before I could answer, someone from the crowd said, "It is Rau Swami's son."'

'What did Matushree say then?' Basanti asked eagerly.

'She asked "You mean Mastani's?" and then she turned her face away immediately. Her hand that had been stretched out to give prasad to Shamsher was withdrawn and she sat in her palanquin without looking back at us even once. I quickly put Shamsher on the horse and made my way out.'

Basanti let out a deep sigh. It had been so ever since Shamsher's birth. She had never given much credence to the gossip going around but the fact that Radhabai had shown such contempt for Shamsher hurt her deeply. She said, 'What happened next?'

'The city kotwal accosted me and reminded me of Appa Swami's orders that I was not to be seen loitering the streets of Pune and that I should return to Kothrud immediately. I quickly disappeared before he could berate me further. Baiji, I am done with taking Shamsher out for a ride to the city.'

Basanti asked, 'Now that Matushree has returned from her pilgrimage, what about Rau?'

Jamdar said, 'I heard someone saying that he was to return within a month.'

The next day, a grand meal had been organized to celebrate Radhabai's return from her pilgrimage. The Brahmans were given donations under the personal supervision of Chimaji Appa. All the prominent ladies of Pune – wives of moneylenders, sardars and top officials – came with expensive gifts to pay their respects to Radhabai. The programme went on for nearly three hours.

The Brahman tutor appointed for Mastani explained in great detail how the celebrations were carried out. Mastani said, 'I too should give something to Matushree. Will you carry it on my behalf?'

'She will not take anything which is touched by you.'

'I will not touch it. You can take it yourself.'

'I can try but I doubt if Appa Swami will allow. I need to take his permission first before offering it to Matushree,' the Brahman replied.

The Brahman was unable to meet Appa the next day. Appa had fallen ill with fever on the day of the grand lunch and had not recovered. He had been drenched to the bone in the battle at Rewas where he had personally killed Siddhisat. The habshis had finally been thrown out and the territory of Konkan, first discovered by Lord Parashurama, had been freed of foreigners and Musalmaans. Both Brahmendra Swami of Dhawadshi and the Chhatrapati at Satara had been extremely pleased with Appa's exploits and had sent letters of congratulations. But Appa was barely in a state to even read the letters.

In spite of his poor health, Appa had gone to receive Radhabai, who had been on her way back from her pilgrimage, at the village of Pabal, a distance of nearly forty miles from Pune. The journey took a further toll on his health and he was unable to ride the horse, forcing him to travel most of the distance in a palanquin. Then Appa had insisted on being one of the bearers for Radhabai's palanquin for nearly a mile despite her protests. This exertion had further deteriorated his already frail health. The next day's celebrations and the efforts he made to supervise were like the last straw. Appa collapsed and fell unconscious.

Kashibai had been to Rajputana with Bajirao and had returned to Pune a few days back. The moment she heard of Appa's poor health, she rushed to meet him. She called for Mahadoba Purandare and asked him to supervise his treatment personally.

The next morning, Kashibai asked the physician after he had checked Appa, 'How is he now?'

'I was expecting the fever to subside but it hasn't. He is sleeping fitfully. But what he speaks in his sleep is something the servants should not hear.'

'Can you elaborate? I don't understand.'

The physician said, as he put his things back in his bag, 'Appa starts babbling in his delirious state saying things like "Rau has lost his mind to the dancer. There is a limit to his free spirit. How much can I do alone?" He keeps on blabbering such things. The servants listen to his prattle. It is not good.'

Kashibai did not respond. The physician was surprised at the lack of her reaction. Then she asked, 'Did Matushree hear him babble?'

'No. Luckily, he began after she had left.'

The physician wiped the sweat off his face and said, 'Baisaheb, Appa will not listen to anyone other than you.'

'What is your advice?'

'He should not take on any hard tasks for a while. The body and the mind are both tired and need rest for at least a year.

We will continue the medication which will improve his health. You need to convince him.'

'If that helps to improve his health I would surely try but I am not sure of his mind. I have to think of some other way for it.'

The physician took his leave. The news of Appa Swami's deteriorating health had spread a pall of gloom over the haveli. Appa would often turn delirious and faint. The physicians were trying their best, while prayers and offerings to the gods continued. Appa's ill health had dampened the excitement created by Radhabai's return from her pilgrimage.

The donations to the Brahmans contined. Paramhans Baba sent holy ash and water from his temple through one of his disciples. After a week, Appa seemed to get a little better.

One day, Mahadoba Purandare came to meet Kashibai hurriedly. She treated him like a son and he had permission to walk into her quarters at any time. Kashibai's heart skipped a beat seeing Mahadoba worried. She asked, her voice quivering, 'I hope everything is fine?'

'I have an important message for you, Baisaheb. No, not regarding Appa,' Mahadoba clarified, realizing that Kashibai may be worried. 'Mastani wants to pay a visit. She has asked for permission to see Appa Swami.'

Kashibai frowned upon hearing Mastani's name. She recalled the year she had spent with Bajirao when he was in Rajasthan. She had seen him at close quarters and observed the slight but noticeable changes in his behaviour. There was a hint of formality which had crept in though he showered his love on young Raghunath and Janardhan Pant, the latter was barely a year old now. Mastani's name touched a raw nerve, but she said, hiding her emotions, 'Why does that Musalmaan woman want to meet Appa Swami?'

'She says Rau would get upset if she does not enquire about his health.'

Kashibai struggled to keep her emotions in check. She said, 'Mahadoba, my brother-in-law is not well and there are no elders around. Matushree, since her return from the pilgrimage, keeps herself busy with her puja most of the time. Please inform Mastani that she already has an eye on Shrimant and may spare the younger brother.'

Mahadoba muttered, looking down, 'I will find some excuse and send her servant back.'

He turned to go when Kashibai asked, 'Mahadoba, have you ever seen her?'

He said, 'I was told she danced during the Janmashtami festival at Satara.'

'I heard too, but that evening I was not well and had retired early.'

'I too was not able to attend as I had been given the task of managing the queen's palace, and by the time I returned the festivities were over. I hear that Shrimant has not allowed her to dance in public since then. Baisaheb, if I may, why do you ask?'

'You are like a son to me and so I can be frank. Tell me, how does she look?'

He said, 'Those who have seen her cannot stop praising her looks and compare her skin colour to that of the ketaki flower. I am told her neck is so fair and the skin so translucent that when she eats a paan, one can see the red colour inside.'

Mahadoba, realizing that he had said more than what was necessary, checked himself saying, 'Anyway, Baisaheb, she is a mere dancer and a Musalmaan. What do her looks count for?'

Kashibai did not answer. Mahadoba, seeing a faraway look in her eyes, walked away quietly without waiting for her to respond.

Chimaji Appa, feeling a little better, was permitted by the physician to take a short walk in the morning and evening, and to visit the Mrityunjay temple. The office was still out of bounds.

He reached Kothrud gardens in his palanquin one evening, with Visaji Pant Pethe in tow. They walked in the gardens for a while and then prayed at the Mrityunjay temple. After the prayers, Chimaji Appa came out and relaxed in the hall outside where a seating arrangement had been prepared for him. A priest came in and said, 'Narayan Dikshit's disciple, Shiv Bhat, has been waiting to meet you for a fortnight. He would be obliged if you can spare a few moments.'

For a while Appa was silent. Visaji Pant, standing nearby, said, 'Appa is not keeping well. I suggest we keep the meeting for some other day.'

Appa sat with his back resting against a bolster near one of the pillars of the hall. A sacred thread, which Radhabai had got from the Kalbhairav temple at Kashi, was tied to his right wrist. Fiddling with the thread, Appa said, 'Narayan Dikshit was of great help to Matushree during her pilgrimage. If his disciple has come, it is appropriate that I meet him.'

He said, turning towards the priest, 'Let him in.'

Shiv Bhat came into the hall and said, folding his hands in namaskar, 'Narayan Dikshit has sent holy Ganga water for you and some prasad from the Vishweshwar temple. I have handed it to the servants at the haveli. I had to meet you to deliver Dikshit ji's message personally.'

Narayan Dikshit was a priest who carried a reputation for his intellect at Kashi and had the blessings of Shrimant Peshwa. He had had cordial relations with the Peshwa household since the time of Balaji Vishwanath, Shrimant's father and the previous Peshwa. Appa asked, 'I hope Dikshit ji is keeping well. I am told he took a lot of trouble to keep Matushree comfortable during her visit.'

Shiv Bhat said, folding his hands in supplication, 'He is fine. He has asked me to meet you to discuss something important. If I may meet you in private, it would…'

Visaji Pant shuffled his feet, wondering whether he should leave, when Appa said, 'Visaji is not an outsider. You may speak without hesitation.'

Shiv Bhat gathered his thoughts before speaking. 'Matushree has earned a lot of goodwill with her pilgrimage and the Peshwa is trying his best to make all religious places free of Muslim rule. Yet Appa's health continues to suffer. We believe there is a reason for it.'

'Shiv Bhat ji, this is nature's way of dealing with it. I had exerted myself beyond my means for a while and now I am suffering.'

'Dikshit ji believes your ill health is due to the fact that some of Shrimant's family members do not adhere to religious protocols.'

'I am surprised to hear him say that. Matushree has performed all the rites under his supervision.'

'She did donate a lot there, but the sad part is that all the beneficiaries were Chitpavan Brahmans.'

Appa said, 'Is that so?'

'Yes! Shrimant may not believe it but despite spending lakhs, we did not receive anything worthwhile. No wonder Shrimant suffers so much.'

Visaji Pant said, before Appa could react, 'Shiv Bhat, wasn't Mahadoba Purandare with Matushree all along.'

Shiv Bhat nodded. 'Yes, he was. He is a Deshashtha Brahman, I agree, but the fact that Matushree was openly favouring the Chitpavans was something he did not dare to criticize.'

Shiv Bhat continued, 'She donated a lot here in Pune too, but once again it was the Chitpavans who got most of the benefit.'

Visaji Pant said, 'Well, the Brahmans are never satisfied however large a donation they receive.'

Appa said, turning to Shiv Bhat, 'I will see that Matushree takes care of the Deshashtha Brahmans. You may leave now.'

Shiv Bhat seemed to be in a mood to continue their discussion but the blunt way in which Appa had ended the meeting was enough for him to leave quietly. Appa said, turning to Visaji the moment Shiv Bhat left, 'The angst of the other Brahmans is quite understandable. The Peshwas are Chitpavans and I don't want anyone to feel that we are biased. I will talk to Rau about this. We don't want a mountain to be made out of a molehill.'

A servant, standing outside holding a small basket, saluted to attract Appa's attention and said, 'Mastanibai has sent this basket of fruits for you. If you permit, I will bring it in.'

'Mastani! Rau's concubine?' Appa frowned in irritation. He was silent for a while as he closed his eyes.

He said, 'Ask her not to visit me here. The Brahmans are already upset and the last thing I want is for them to complain about a Musalmaan despoiling the temple by entering it. I will meet her near the tree there once I step out,' he said, pointing at a tamarind tree in the garden.

Keeping the basket down, the servant saluted and left.

A few tamarind trees created a dense shade near the temple. Appa stood in the shade while the syce held the reins of his horse. The palanquin bearers also stood nearby waiting for their lord. Mastani came, adjusting the dupatta on her head, and saluted. Shamsher and Basanti were with her. Mastani turned to Shamsher and said, 'Beta, please salute Shrimant.'

Shamsher Bahadur saluted smartly in an elaborate mujra thrice, but Appa scarcely bothered to even glance at him. Mastani stood, her head bowed, waiting for Appa to speak. He asked, 'You wanted to meet me? What do you want?'

'I was told you are not well and was keen to visit you at the haveli. But I was denied permission.'

'I am fine now. And even if I weren't, there are enough people to worry about me. A dancer need not take so much interest in my health.'

Appa's tone was harsh. Mastani said, swallowing the insults, 'I was worried hearing about your condition. I was also worried that if I don't meet you, Rau would be upset.'

Appa had been standing with his face turned away from Mastani. Hearing Rau's name, he looked at her and shouted, his voice rising in anger, 'Did I hear you say "Rau"? My elder brother is the Peshwa of the Maratha empire. People address him as Shrimant. I cannot tolerate such disrespect. If I hear him referred to as Rau again, I will be forced to take strict action.'

He turned to Visaji Pant and said, 'These dancers have no manners. It is time they learnt how to behave. Under whose supervision are they?'

'I am not sure but I have heard that they are under the direct command of Vahini,' Visaji said, a little hesitatingly.

'Really?'

Mastani was worried hearing Kashibai's name and adjusted

her dupatta once more. She said beseechingly, 'Please pardon me. I must have uttered what was in my mind. I will ensure that I address the Peshwa as Shrimant. I wish you to take care of your health. I had come to meet you and give my regards. That is all.'

'Anything else?' Appa asked, his voice dripping with contempt.

Mastani took Shamsher's hand in hers and said, 'Chiranjeev has saluted Shrimant. I would be obliged if you bless him. I don't want anything else.'

'There is no need for my blessings,' Appa said and, without even glancing at Shamsher, jumped on to his horse and rode away.

Getting down at Shanivar wada, he handed over the reins to the syce and said, 'Visaji, I should not have been rude to Rau's son. It is not that poor fellow's fault. Please send a gift of a hundred rupias from my personal account for the boy.'

By the time Shrimant Bajirao Peshwa and his forces returned to Pune, the Maratha flag was fluttering in many parts of the country.

Bajirao had returned from Rajputana territory and the cantonment spread for miles on the outskirts of Pune. Appa was to receive Bajirao personally but Radhabai did not allow him to travel because of his delicate condition. Nana, along with key officials, went to meet Bajirao. An elephant with a silver howdah lumbered along for the royal welcome.

At the confluence of the rivers, father and son met. Bajirao declined the howdah and entered the city on horseback.

After praying at the temple, Bajirao went to meet his

mother to take her blessings. They would be meeting after two years. Ever since Radhabai had gone on her pilgrimage, the only contact between them had been through letters.

Seeing Bajirao enter the haveli, Radhabai rushed to meet him and pulling his hand affectionately, she dragged him to her quarters. They sat talking for a while. Bajirao said, looking at Appa, 'He is luckier than me. He gets to see you more often.' Pointing at Nana, he said, 'And he has grown up so much!'

Appa said, 'Now that Rau has made a special mahal for him, Nana has moved out.'

Bajirao got Appa's hint. He had heard, when in Rajputana, about Gopika's coming of age. Nana had returned to Pune hurriedly for the function. Bajirao said, avoiding Radhabai's gaze, 'So it seems I got the mahal made at the right time, isn't it?'

Radhabai did not smile. A single thought troubled her. She said, 'Rau, I visited different parts of the country and prayed at the pilgrimage spots in many places. Sadashiv Pant and I were received with great courtesy wherever we went. Yet, one thing irks me.'

'Was there any inconvenience?' Rau asked.

'No. It is not about that. The moment we crossed Bundelkhand and entered Mughal territory, I could sense that we were not in our land any more. We were at the mercy of those foreigners. It was very humiliating.'

Radhabai's words pierced Bajirao's heart. All his efforts to consolidate the Maratha empire seemed wasted. He said, 'These religious places have been under their control for five hundred years. Even Chhatrapati Shivaji Maharaj made a lot of effort, but was not able to succeed. The political situation was such that I was hoping the day you step into Varanasi, you would get the news that we have freed the territory of the

Mughals. Alas! It did not happen. All plans were in place and I was expecting Sawai Jaisingh to support me. But he backed out at the last moment.'

Nana said, 'While Rau Swami was busy making these plans, I heard that Chhatrapati Maharaj in Satara was quite unhappy.'

'Why is that so?'

'He wanted the matter to be resolved by dialogue and not by taking up arms.'

Bajirao erupted, 'We have seen the results of not taking up arms for the past five hundred years. Why should we kowtow to the Mughal Emperor? We have managed to drive away the habshis from Konkan. Now the time has come to ask the Mughals to leave this country.'

Appa knew of Bajirao's impatience with the Chhatrapati's style and said, trying to change the topic, 'Rau must be tired. I suggest you rest for a while now.'

Bajirao left soon after. Chimaji Appa and Radhabai sat talking when suddenly she asked, 'I was told that Rau has got two mansions built in the precincts of the wada. One is for Nana, but the other one – who is it for? When I enquired in the office, they said they didn't know.'

Appa did not know how to respond to his mother's direct questioning. He said, 'Rau's favourite artisans have built the mansion. I am sure there is someone he has in mind.'

Radhabai let out a deep sigh and said, 'Appa, a man's words may lie but his face reveals the truth. I have the answer now!'

Most of the sardars who had accompanied Bajirao after the campaign in the north went home after a brief stay at Pune, except for Bhivrao Rethrekar. Unlike others, he enjoyed a close rapport with the Peshwa and stayed back in Pune on Chimaji Appa's insistence. One night, Appa and Bhivrao sat chatting till late at night.

Appa said, 'Bajipant, you did a fantastic job in Bundelkhand. If not for you, Rau would have found it very difficult.'

Bajipant said, pride evident on his face, 'Things worked out well. If only certain things had happened the way we had hoped, Shrimant would have been sitting on the Mughal throne today.'

'It is because of the support of sardars like you that Shrimant Peshwa can dream big. You and your men lay down your lives but the Peshwa gets all the credit. I know the dedication with which people like Shinde, Holkar and Pilaji Jadhavrao throw themselves into the tasks assigned by Shrimant. But for you and such brave souls, what would the Peshwa achieve?'

Bajipant sat with his back resting against a bolster. A large oil painting of Bajirao hung on a wall which showed him sitting on a horse, nibbling on a cob of corn as he supervised a battle. It was a picture of casual arrogance, that of a determined and confident man who knew he could depend on his men. Pointing at the painting, Bajipant said, 'Do you see that painting there? Rau's very presence creates an energy which is inexplicable. The troops are willing to give their best. We are mere conduits for what Rau wishes to do.'

Bajipant had summarized it well. Appa knew the kind of magical effect his brother had on the sardars. He was aware that Bajipant too considered Bajirao to be his elder brother. He said, 'I suggest you camp here till the monsoon ends. We have lots of plans to make and your advice would be useful during the deliberations.'

They continued talking. Soon, the guard at the gate rang

the gong indicating midnight. Bajipant had been looking for an opportunity to speak to Appa in private. Seeing his amiable disposition, he took the chance and said, 'Appa, I want to say something but I'm a little hesitant...'

Appa said, a little surprised, 'Since when have you hesitated to speak? Please say whatever you have in mind.'

'We had done a good job in Rajasthan and could have marched on to Delhi any time but, you know...' He hesitated, not knowing how he should proceed.

'Bajipant, please continue,' Appa said.

'Shrimant was received with a lot of courtesy by the Maharajas of both Udaipur and Jaipur. But...'

'Rau insulted Sawai Jaisingh by pulling away his hookah in a crowded durbar,' Appa completed Bajipant's statement adding, 'that is what you wanted to say, isn't it?'

Appa continued, 'That is not true. These are rumours being spread to spoil our good relations with the Rajputs.'

'Appa, I was not referring to that episode. In any case, I am no one to complain even if he had behaved so. Those Rajputs, surviving on the largesse given by the Mughal Badshah and used to kowtowing before the Mughals, have no right to expect any good behaviour. What I wanted to say was something else. For reasons best known to Shrimant, I came to know that he has started enjoying wine. I was very surprised when I heard that.'

'Wine?' Appa exclaimed. 'I am sure you have heard it wrong. My sister-in-law was with him the whole time. She would have come to know of it.'

'I too did not believe when I first heard it. But the truth pierced my heart – and it hurts. I am convinced now.'

'Chhee! Bajipant! I cannot believe it. And my Vahini...'

'What could she do? Shrimant was busy all the time on

one campaign or another, literally living his life on horseback. Vahinisaheb was taking care of the two small children and was, most of the time, not with him.'

Appa said, 'I had heard of Shrimant partaking meat in the company of Malhar Rao Holkar but I ignored it. I believe my brother is a wise man and will not do wrong. It really surprises me when you say he has started drinking wine.'

Bajipant said, 'Appa, Shrimant has taken on the job of a Kshatriya. We too, despite being Brahmans, have picked up the sword but we were never tempted to drink wine or eat meat. Rau Swami's behaviour is surely extraordinary.'

Bajipant spoke with the confidence of someone who knew. Unable to accept the bitter truth, Appa said, 'I may concede for a moment that he has started drinking wine. But do you know how he got into this habit?'

'Why blame anyone but a weakness of the mind, Appa? We knew that he could not refuse the wine offered during marriage celebrations in Rajputana, lest the hosts feel offended and we ignored it thinking it was a one-off case. But it is such transgressions that make one an addict in no time. There is no doubt that he is hooked to it now. I thought it was my duty to inform you, that's all.'

Appa could not speak as a bout of coughing racked his chest. He was quiet for a while. It was late in the night and the conversation had reached a point where neither wanted to continue any further.

Dark clouds threatened to shed their weight. The wind had stopped and there was a feeling of restlessness in the air.

Bajirao was in Mastani's mansion at Kothrud gardens. Two

astrologers sat before him studying a piece of paper with deep concentration. After a while, they summarized their findings and left when Bajirao nodded his head in satisfaction.

A whiff of perfume made Bajirao turn to see Mastani enter, softly humming a song. She sat on her knees and offered a paan to Bajirao saying, 'What did the astrologers say about our Shamsher's future?'

Bajirao looked at her for a moment, enjoying the paan, and then said, 'What do you think is his future? Take a guess.'

'What can I guess? I have no idea of such things.'

'Well, the astrologers predict a life of royalty. He will grow up to be a ruler.'

'Rau must be joking. He is Mastani's son – a low-born woman's. Your joke is cruel.'

Mastani's eyes clouded up with tears. Rau, used to seeing intense passion in those eyes, was disturbed to see her cry. He said, 'I am now seeing you in a new avatar – from a passionate lover to a concerned mother! The world may laugh at you but you know what I would do, don't you?'

Mastani wiped her tears saying, 'I can understand but…'

'Now let me see that smile on your lovely lips.'

Mastani smiled. Rau continued, 'Do you know what the astrologers said when I asked them how many women will he enjoy?'

'What a question to ask! What will they think of you!'

'Why? What is wrong with that? Shamsher is my son, after all. They said, he would have the good fortune of enjoying the company of many women.'

'Really?' Mastani's smile vanished as she said, 'I don't like what you asked.'

'I have named him Shamsher! He will hold a sword, a

shamsher, in one hand, while with the other hand, he will hold a beautiful woman who befits only a brave warrior.'

Mastani said, looking into Bajirao's eyes, 'You probably wish that he follows in your footsteps.'

'How can you say that?'

Mastani did not reply. Bajirao, lifting her chin gently, said, 'I am honoured to have a beautiful woman in my arms right now!'

Mastani felt fulfilled. She lay in his arms, while the sense of protection in the embrace soothed her tormented soul.

After a while, Kunwar came in to report. Then Bajirao said, 'I need to quench my thirst.'

Kunwar got the hint and soon, two servants came in with a pair of tumblers on a silver tray. A long-necked pitcher was placed alongside.

Mastani looked at the tray and asked, 'Shall I pour some wine for you?'

Bajirao was in a playful mood. Looking into her eyes, he said, 'You are wine personified. Why do I need anything else? When I have something which is far more addictive, why do I need this?'

A shiver of excitement ran through Mastani's body. At the same time, she shuddered with fear, worried about her future and where things would lead. She said, 'I feel scared.'

'I am with you! Why should you be scared? Are you worried about what people will say?'

'They may say whatever they wish to me, but not to you.'

Bajirao said, 'Mastani and Rau are not two individuals any more. Let me remove your doubts – I will drink wine only when you offer it.'

Mastani's dupatta slipped and she hurriedly covered herself saying, 'I know you eat with me, much against the wishes of the Brahmans. Now you are going to have wine with me? Since when did you start enjoying that?'

'Since the day you danced at Satara and I saw your face when you removed your veil. That very day!'

'I never realized...' Mastani mumbled.

'How could you? Can a mirror see itself? After having you and experiencing that high, no wine can come close.'

Mastani said shyly, 'Don't praise me so much. Serving you gives me pleasure. I am not some apsara that will intoxicate you more than wine. What am I in comparison to this *madira*?'

Bajirao placed his fingers on Mastani's lips to silence her and said, 'Don't say that. Apsaras are not worthy enough to be even your handmaidens. Rau is not one to be mesmerized by any ordinary person. The day your eyes met mine, I knew you had a force which could penetrate my soul. It was clear that this Mastani was meant for Rau and no one else.'

Mastani caressed Bajirao's fingers and said, 'I was not convinced about what you had said earlier, but now I believe one can be drunk without touching a drop of wine. This intoxication is more inebriating!'

'Mastani, words alone are not going to douse this fire of passion. Look at the clouds gathering outside. Can you hear the peacocks crowing? They dance to tease the clouds to release their burden. The parched earth is satisfied when it receives the first showers. Mastani! Pour me that wine and let me be fulfilled!'

Bajirao's words lit a fire within Mastani. Her body reverberated to the sweet sound of his words. She lifted the pitcher and filled a tumbler. 'Here!'

'No! Not this way,' Bajirao said.

Mastani could feel the ardour in his words. She said, teasing him, 'And may I know what your way is?'

'You need to take a sip first. Only then can I drink it.'

'No. Never!'

'Rau is not used to being refused. He only commands.'

'Don't be so adamant. How can I touch it and ruin it with my lips!'

'Till your lips don't taste it, it is not worth having. I long for your lips to pour their sweetness into it. Now, don't make me wait!'

Mastani shook her head shyly but Bajirao got up and forced her to take a few sips. Then, with his left arm hugging her waist, he drank from the tumbler and drained it in one go. He said, looking into her eyes, 'Now I am satisfied!'

Mastani let out a deep sigh. It had started raining and a cool, pleasant breeze was blowing. Despite Bajirao's embrace, Mastani shivered with an unknown fear. Bajirao sensed her emotions and said, 'Mastani, when you are in my arms, even Death will think twice.'

He said, filling up the tumbler, 'Ask, Mastani, what do you want? Ask for it!'

Mastani did not respond. Lifting her chin gently, Bajirao repeated, 'Ask! Why are you so quiet?'

'I am in heaven when in your arms. What more can I ask for? I don't want anything.'

'You have to ask! Let me feel happy by giving.'

'If you so insist, this is my wish: whenever I feel like meeting Rau, I should not have to ask for permission and should be able to meet you without being bound by protocol, rules or decorum of any kind.'

'That's it? You ask for this after all the hesitation?'

Bajirao was drunk and his voice seemed loud.

Mastani put her slender arms around Bajirao's neck and rested her head on his shoulders. She said, 'Mastani is a mere dancer while Rau is the Peshwa. The gap between us is too large to bridge. Sometimes the yearning to meet you is uncontrollable. At such times, I wish to have the freedom to meet you wherever you are – whether in your haveli, on a campaign, resting in a camp or whether it is day or night. All I want is to be able to meet you!'

Bajirao laughed aloud, making Mastani a little nervous. He said, 'Your wish is granted, Mastani!'

Mastani gently held his hand and said, 'I know you are drunk and I am not going to take advantage of your inebriated state to ask you to grant me my wish. Please think carefully before giving me your word.'

'Think carefully? Had I been thinking I would never have had you in my life, Mastani! If I wasted time thinking, I would not be able to go on my campaigns, lead the troops while nibbling at a corncob. Only the timid waste their time thinking. I am not drunk. My word is final. Whenever, wherever and in whatever condition you wish to see me, the doors of my mahal, haveli, tent and mansion are all open for you. Does that make you happy now?'

Mastani whispered, 'I have always been happy, whether you fulfil my wish or not. Now I am in seventh heaven!'

She blushed and hid her face against his chest.

Appa, noticing Bajirao entering the office in the afternoon, quietly slipped away and went to Kashibai's quarters. He sent a message through the guard to inform Kashibai of his arrival.

Then without waiting for the guard to return, he entered her room to see her sitting with her two younger sons. She said, 'Come in! What brings you here at this time?'

Yesu came and took the two children away. Appa looked around the room which was tastefully decorated with curtains and carpets, many of them brought by traders from different countries. Despite the glamour, dark circles around Kashibai's eyes dampened the effect. Appa licked his lips nervously before saying, 'Rau has returned from his campaign in the north and is planning yet another one.'

'Oh, is that so?'

'Are you saying you don't know of it, Vahini? I thought Rau would have told you that he has set his sights on Delhi.'

'Why should he tell me?' Kashibai said, avoiding Appa's eyes. 'Who am I?'

Appa could sense the anguish in her voice. He said, 'You don't know but when Rau went to Rajasthan, you were sent with him on Matushree's express command.'

'Is that so? I always thought Rau agreed because I insisted on accompanying him.'

'That may be partly true, but Matushree had explicit instructions. Anyway, the plans for Delhi were made during the stay in Rajasthan itself.'

Kashibai let out a deep sigh. 'I will know only if he has time for me.'

'That could have been the case in Rajasthan, but has he not spoken about it after returning to Pune?'

Kashibai turned her face abruptly. Despite her best efforts, a sob escaped her lips. A distressed Appa exclaimed, 'Vahini! Why are you crying?'

Kashibai wiped her tears saying, 'Why do you want me to spell it out?'

'Vahini, I am unable to understand. Did Rau say something to hurt you?'

Kashibai could not hold back her tears. Appa's discomfort was evident as he shuffled his feet not knowing how to console his sister-in-law. He said, 'Vahini! Please be calm. I can come back later.'

Kashibai pleaded, 'Please sit down. I came to know of Shrimant's arrival only when the servants informed me.'

'What? Are you saying you are not aware that Rau has been in Pune for a week now?'

Kashibai said, 'Can you imagine the torment I go through? Getting to know from the servants that he has returned?'

'Rau never came here?' Appa muttered to himself and then asked, 'Where was he then for the past one week?'

Appa, having blurted that out, realized his mistake. It was a rhetorical question. Kashibai's silence conveyed her knowledge of the situation. Appa's heart wrenched in anguish at his sister-in-law's predicament. He said, 'Vahini, now that you have begun the topic, I want to say something.'

'Please do.'

'Vahini, I am worried that Rau's behaviour may become the talk of the town, fodder for gossip. I was keen to share my thoughts with you earlier. Bajipant told me about the way Rau had behaved in Rajasthan. He indulged in activities which I had never expected him to do, even in my dreams.'

'Indulged? What do you mean? What are you talking about?'

'I told Bajipant that he may have been mistaken. I said that Vahini was there with Rau all the time and he may have had meat when on a campaign, to give company to his sardars. He may have enjoyed the company of a dancer on an evening, but I told him that Rau would never forsake his religion and even touch a drop of wine. After all, can a diamond produced by Matushree turn out to be mere stone?'

Kashibai could not bear to hear Appa's words and tried to cover her ears with her palms. Appa asked, hoping against hope, 'Vahini, tell me it is not true!'

Kashibai's silence said it all. Appa said, 'What I heard is true then.'

His was the voice of a heartbroken man. He was in tears. Kashibai said, 'I saw it all but my lips were sealed. I was helpless. What could I do?'

The words hit Appa with a force that was difficult for him to bear. He had been indisposed for the past two months and had dived into office work without caring much for his health. Chhatrapati Maharaj had given the job of Peshwa to his elder brother and he truly believed that his job was to give him his complete support, come what may.

Appa could sense that he was disintegrating from within. His resolve, his faith, his entire belief in the system was being questioned and he feared that he may lose it. Brushing aside the negative thoughts, he said, 'Vahini, we should not give much credence to these things. It is not that a Brahman who eats meat or drinks wine will go to hell. I would ignore it as a mere transgression. You need to take charge.'

Kashibai's resolve had, in the meantime, given way. She said, her voice full of emotion, 'It would not have hurt so much if the matter had restricted itself to what you just mentioned. But…'

Appa knew what Kashibai was referring to and said, 'I know he had made a few such transgressions earlier.'

Kashibai, desperate to get her brother-in-law's support, said, 'Isn't it your job to get your brother to see what is right and what is not?'

'Vahini, I do not have the power to sit in judgement on his actions.'

'Who says so?'

'It is evident, isn't it? Vahini, the very mention of his name makes the throne at Delhi shake with fear. Do you think I can give Rau a moral lecture on propriety?'

'You too had the same opportunities when on campaigns. Did you fall for any temptations?'

'Vahini, my brother and I are like chalk and cheese. But I had hoped against hope when Bajipant told me of Rau's behaviour. I really wished that it was not true.'

He continued, letting out a deep sigh, 'I know the moral values of the Rajasthan kings. It is no wonder that they, who stay inebriated because of wine or in a stupor after consuming opium, can have a bad influence on Rau. If one is in the constant company of such men, this kind of inappropriate behaviour needs to be pardoned.'

'You don't know the kind of language Rau had used when he was drunk,' Kashibai said, her voice breaking down. 'I am ashamed to say but one day, when Kunwar escorted Shrimant to my tent, he was barely able to stand. Hie eyes were red and he struggled to reach his bed. He was about to fall when I held his hand and helped him. He said, "Mastani, I am drunk with the wine of your eyes." I wish the earth had split and swallowed me in that instant. Can you believe it, he addressed me with that concubine's name!'

'What? Rau called you Mastani? Has he lost his mind?'

'He surely has! I cannot even tell you what he said after that. I may die with shame but not repeat the words I had to hear. My entire life shattered in front of me. A wife being called by a concubine's name! What was I to do?'

Appa sat with his head bowed in shame. He did not know how to console his sister-in-law. Kashibai sobbed uncontrollably, hiding her face in her sari.

After a while, Appa left Kashibai's quarters. He said, as he turned to go, 'Vahini, you are like a mother to me and I shall surely find a way out. Please have faith. She is a mere mistress! A thousand such women can be sacrificed for the prestige of the Peshwas. We erred in ignoring this Mastani and letting her mesmerize Rau.'

Appa did not wait to act. He did not return to the office but went to his private chambers and called for the clerk. He immediately dictated a few messages and then, satisfied, turned to other matters of the office.

Bajirao had not been to Kothrud gardens that day. Some work or the other occupied him for the next three days and on the fourth day, he turned his favourite white horse towards the gardens to meet Mastani. The thought of meeting her brought a smile on his face. Kunwar, noticing that his master had plans to meet Mastani, said, 'Huzoor, it seems you are going to Kothrud gardens?'

'Yes, that is right. Why do you ask?'

'Mastani sahiba is not there any more.'

'What do you mean, not there? Where is she?'

'I am not sure of that, but I do know that they are not staying at the mansion any more.'

'What?' Bajirao spurred his horse to reach the gardens faster.

As soon as he entered the gardens, he realized that there was no activity visible and not a single soul could be seen inside the mansion. A servant came running and saluted. 'Where is Mastani?' Bajirao asked.

'They left two days back. I don't know what happened but she jumped on to the horse with Shamsher and left. The servants followed the next day with the luggage.'

'Didn't she say anything? Where did she go?'

'She only said that her stay here was done and fate had something else in store and that they would go on whichever path Allah showed. She asked me not to tell anyone about her whereabouts.'

Bajirao dismounted and whipped the servant on his back shouting, 'Tell me! Tell me, where is she?'

The servant became paranoid and screamed, 'Shrimant! Wait! Mastanibai sahiba has gone towards Pabal village. I don't know anything beyond that.' He stood with folded hands lest he was whipped again.

'That much will suffice,' Bajirao said and jumped on to his horse. Before Kunwar could react, Bajirao had spurred the horse and galloped away at full speed. Kunwar followed suit.

It was a dark, cloudy day. The wind blew hard. Bajirao, unmindful of everything, rode relentlessly, whipping the horse to spur him on. The loyal steed galloped as fast as it could and, within a few minutes, they vanished from Kunwar's sight.

They rode for nearly two hours, covering a distance of more

than forty miles. By the time they reached the outskirts of Pabal, Bajirao and his horse were drenched in sweat. Slowing down, he asked a few men standing on the road, as he gasped to recover his breath, 'Is this the village of Pabal?'

One of them replied, 'Yes. And where are you from?' The man asked casually.

'Mastani ... has she crossed this village?'

'Mastani? Who's she?'

Bajirao was in no mood to explain and his whip fell on the man's back with a crack. 'You rascal! How dare you ask such questions? Don't you know Mastani?'

The men quickly realized that they were not talking to an ordinary man. Surely this man, who showed such anger, was someone of authority. Before they could speak, a few horsemen came their way and one of them exclaimed, 'Is that not Shrimant sarkar himself?'

Bajirao asked angrily, 'And who are you now?'

The man saluted elaborately saying, 'Mastanibai is staying nearby. Please follow me, sarkar.'

They soon reached a garden and the horsemen, leading the way, pointed to a small hut in one corner of the garden saying, 'Mastanibai sahiba has been staying there since last evening. They plan to proceed on their journey tomorrow.'

Bajirao spurred his horse in eager anticipation.

Mastani sat inside the small hut, a temporary ramshackle dwelling. On hearing the horse, her maid came out to see who the stranger could be. Within moments, Bajirao reached the hut and, brushing her aside with his hand, entered through the low door.

Mastani was sitting with Shamsher on her lap and on seeing Bajirao, she stood up adjusting the dupatta on her head. She said, 'My lord? Is that you? How did you find us?'

Bajirao did not answer. Throwing the whip aside, he hugged and kissed her repeatedly. 'Mastani! My dear Mastani! What happened? Why did you leave Pune so suddenly?'

Shamsher, unable to understand anything, looked at Bajirao with a mixture of fear and curiosity, and started crying. Basanti came in quickly and took him away.

Bajirao sat down on a charpoy in the room. He was tired and drenched in sweat. Mastani used the edge of her dupatta to wipe the sweat from his face. She said, 'You rode all the way! I can't believe it!'

The words were redundant. The eyes had spoken what words could never convey. Rau said, anguish evident in his voice, 'Mastani, I would have found you even if you were a thousand miles away. But Mastani, why did you leave? Just the other day you were lost in my embrace ... and now? What is wrong with you?'

'Nothing.'

Mastani knew that her silence was not going to last for long but she wanted to delay the inevitable. She said, 'Rau is tired. I suggest you rest for a while.'

Bajirao was in no mood for small talk. He brushed aside the tumbler of milk offered by her and said, 'I am not here to rest. I want to know what happened.'

Mastani said, 'Rau should not forget that he is a Peshwa. The fact that he rushed all the way to meet a mere dancer will be the talk of the town tomorrow.'

Bajirao got up from the charpoy saying, 'If you were so worried about what people would say, what made you leave in the first place?'

Mastani continued her tactic of evasive answers. 'People in Pune will be worried. They will be searching for you. I request you to at least send a message so that they are at ease. I will tell you my story later.'

Bajirao's irritated look conveyed a lot. She continued, 'Rau, I did not leave of my own free will. I had taken a vow to live my life under your shadow but within a few hours of my promise, I had no option but to pack my bags.'

'Who is it that made you do this? Give me a name, Mastani.'

'Is that necessary? Why don't you assume that I left of my own accord? No one forced me.'

'Huh! That is impossible. Impossible! I can believe that the sun rose in the west, but I cannot believe that you would leave me and go away on your own. Tell me!'

'I was ordered, Rau.'

'Ordered? Who ordered?'

'I will tell you the name but you must promise not to react and take action against him.'

'You are forcing me to promise. Anyway, tell me now!'

'Are you sure?'

Bajirao let out a deep sigh and said, 'Yes, I promise!'

'Appa Swami.'

'What? Appa?' Despite being quite sure that no one other than Appa could have had the courage to take such an action, Bajirao was hoping against hope that it was not him. He let out a deep sigh and said, 'Mastani, I could have done nothing even if I had not given you my word. He is my younger brother, after all. I wonder why he took such a step without consulting me even once.'

'Don't worry your head about this. Appa Swami ordered and I left. I have been asked to leave the boundaries of the state as soon as possible.'

'Oh, is that so?'

Then Bajirao got up and said, 'Those were Appa's orders. I have come to take you back. Now, pack your bags and get ready to move.'

'Will you listen to me for once? Please allow me to speak.'

Bajirao nodded impatiently.

'Let me not return to Pune. Our matter has reached the haveli now and I fear for poor Shamsher. He will get crushed in the ensuing mêlée. Please don't force me to return.'

Bajirao erupted, 'I am not used to hearing no. Mine is the last word! I give you an hour's time to get ready and move.'

'I beg you! I don't want to be the reason for a misunderstanding between two brothers. Please! People will say all kinds of things.'

'Who will dare to? I will pull his tongue out, whosoever tries.'

'No one will dare, in your presence. But they will all gossip behind your back. Rau, the unspoken word is more hurtful.'

'I cannot do anything about that. I have made up my mind. If I have to fight with Death to separate us, then let it be so!'

The dark clouds threatened to rain any moment. It was getting late. Bajirao looked at the sky and said, 'It is late now. I will give you time till dawn. By the time the morning star is visible on the horizon, I want your palanquin to be on its way to Pune.'

Bajirao ordered the servants standing outside to start preparing for their move.

That night Bajirao dined with Mastani. The horsemen, who had arrived in search of the Peshwa, were hosted in the nearby village of Pabal. Having found out that the Peshwa was in the hut with Mastani, none dared to go that way. They waited at the village gate the next morning for their master to arrive.

Bajirao's anger had dissipated by the time he had his dinner.

They both talked for a long time that night. Mastani said, sitting close to Bajirao, 'Girls find the homeward journey very pleasant but when I was moving out of Pune, I found it suffocating. There is something that troubles me...'

'What is it?' Bajirao asked, hugging her.

'A woman lives with the hope that her mother's home is always a place to rest in case the world discards her. But who will wait for me?'

'Mastani, I don't understand. What are you trying to say?'

'I don't have anyone I can call my own and with whom I can cry to my heart's content. A married woman finds that solace in her parents' house.'

Mastani's voice quivered. Bajirao could understand her agony and patted her head gently saying, 'I can understand. But I want you to know that I am there for you, for everything you ever need!'

'You came all the way for a mere mortal like me – a fallen woman. Let my journey stop where I am right now. Grant me this village as my home.'

'Is that all? Consider it done! The moment I reach Pune, I will issue the orders.'

At sunrise, Mastani's palanquin moved towards Pune.

Within three days, the orders were issued. Appa's office received the papers for his signature. The villages of Kendur and Pabal had been gifted to Mastani by Shrimant Peshwa. Appa put the papers aside after scanning through them.

The preparations for the campaign to the north were in full swing with the Peshwa's emissary Venkajiram sending daily updates from the Delhi durbar. Feelers were being sent to the mansabdars in the Mughal court to test their loyalties while Bajirao updated the Chhatrapati at Satara to take his advice.

Though things seemed normal on the surface, discontent was simmering within. Appa did not react immediately despite knowing that Mastani had returned to the gardens at Kothrud. Bajirao too did not confront Appa directly for having taken action without his knowledge. The two brothers avoided the topic but the tension was palpable. It was only a matter of time till it exploded.

One day, while sitting in the office and looking into some papers, Appa said, 'I have been wanting to ask you for a while now. We got a mahal made for Nana, but who is to be the resident of the other mahal?'

Bajirao did not answer immediately. Then he said, measuring each word, 'It is for Mastani.'

'Mastani? That concubine?'

'Yes! I have made my instructions clear – she is my mistress and needs to be taken care of.'

'There are many residences one can think of for the dancer. In any case, she is quite comfortable currently at the mansion at Kothrud. If she wants, we can always give her another mahal there or, for that matter, anywhere in Pune.'

Bajirao said, 'I want her to be within the precincts of Shanivar wada.'

'May I ask why? You can always visit her whenever you wish.'

'Appa, let me make it clear – if she were to stay in the haveli, at least I will come to know when someone gives her the marching orders.'

It was a direct assault on Appa. Bajirao had, till date, never interfered in his work and had never raised a finger at his decision, but now a mere dancer had created a rift. Appa knew that his elder brother was besotted by the dancer but he had not expected him to react so strongly. With a lot of restraint he said, 'Rau, you are my elder brother and like a father to me. Not just that, you are the Peshwa of the Maratha empire. It is not right to keep a concubine in the haveli. Tongues will wag.'

'Concubine?' Bajirao said, his voice rising in anger. 'Appa, never ever use that word again. Is that understood? When I say she is a dancer, isn't that enough? Do I need to clarify more?'

'I shall be careful, now that you have clarified.'

'I don't want any further discussion on the topic.'

'Rau has decided then, I suppose.'

'About what?'

'About her staying at the haveli.'

'That is precisely the reason I got the mahal built.'

'Have you given any thought to Vahini's feelings?'

'I have decided after considering all angles. I don't need your advice,' Bajirao said. 'And,' he continued, 'please don't interfere in my personal matters henceforth.'

Appa asked, keeping the papers aside, 'Rau, do you really mean what you say?'

'Yes. Let me repeat! Don't interfere in my personal matters. You may consider it my command, if you wish. Else, you may take it as the Peshwa's diktat. Is that clear now?'

Appa nodded his head. He had never been spoken to in such a manner by his elder brother and all he could do was walk out of the room without saying a word.

Bapuji Shripat was waiting for Appa outside. Appa indicated with his hand to follow him to his quarters. Handing over a sheaf of papers to Bapuji, he said 'Take these. They are the papers to gift the villages of Kendur and Pabal to Mastani. I am the administrator on behalf of the Peshwa. Put my seal on the papers and get them processed.'

Bapuji took the papers and before he could comment, Appa said, 'I am not feeling well. Please ask the office not to disturb me.'

It was the month of Ashaadh, and the middle of the monsoons. The torrential rains had made movement almost impossible. The horses were stuck in their stables and the elephants had no need to go to the river for their bath as they were being drenched in the downpour. But the office of the Peshwa worked in full swing, preparing for the impending campaign.

Kashibai's leg pain had resurfaced. Added to it were other ailments. She was barely able to digest her food and her taste buds had become dull. She would ask for spicy dishes and then find it difficult to eat them.

Bajirao would enquire about her health once in a while. Kashibai would try to hide her pain with a smile whenever he was around.

Hearing that she had not visited the dining room for three days, Appa came in to enquire. Annapoorna was sitting with her when he entered and, on seeing him, she got up and left the room, adjusting the pallu on her head. Appa looked at her as she walked away and said, 'Vahini, I am told you have not eaten anything properly for the past three days. Is that true?'

'I don't have any appetite. I don't feel like eating anything.'

'But how can this go on? Have you taken the medicines given by the vaidyaraj?'

Pointing to a row of medicine bottles lined up on the shelf, she said, 'I am sure I will be fine soon.'

'That is what you say but look at your face! It is so pale.

Pilaji Jadhavrao has sent some tiger oil for you. I believe it will relieve your pain.'

'Send it across. No harm in trying one more remedy! You don't need to worry about me. Take care of your own health.'

'I am perfectly fine now, Vahini. In fact, Rau may leave for Delhi soon and I will be accompanying him.'

'It is in your nature to follow him like a shadow. I know you are not taking adequate care of your health. Annapoorna was telling me about it. You don't need to worry about me. Shrimant too enquires about me once in a while and his words are more soothing than the medicines our vaidyaraj gives.'

Kashibai spoke smilingly but Appa could see the pain in her eyes as she tried to hide her anguish. He said, 'Shrimant has given me strict orders.'

'Regarding what?'

'That I should not interfere in his personal matters.'

'So are you saying you are not going to? Just because he has ordered?'

'Vahini, what am I to do? I have a difficult choice – a well on one side and a valley on the other. I am concerned about you.'

'What I hear, is it true?'

'What have you heard, Vahini?'

'That Shrimant is going to let the dancer stay in the newly built mahal? Is that true?'

'Yes, it is.'

'And yet you will not interfere in his matters?'

'I am stuck. I am standing at the crossroads, Vahini.'

'Call Pilaji Jadhavrao. He has sent tiger oil, hasn't he? Ask him to send a bottle of poison for me instead!'

'Vahini!'

'I mean it! It is better that I die before I see the dancer stay in this haveli.'

Appa was shocked at Kashibai's words. His mind was in a torment. He could undertand the anguish and the torture his Vahini was going through. But Bajirao's words rang in his mind ... 'You may consider it as an elder brother's advice or the Peshwa's command; don't interfere in my personal matters.' Appa could not bear to see Kashibai suffering. He said, hoping to lift her mood, 'Vahini, one should not be so despondent. Hope is what keeps one alive. Change is the only constant in nature. Things will change – for the better.'

'I am living in hope alone. Please promise me one thing,' Kashibai said.

'You don't need to ask me to promise. Just command and it shall be done.'

'Promise me that you will not take Shrimant's words to heart. He may order you not to interfere in his personal matters but you have to look after him. You are my only hope now. If you too give up, it would be disastrous.'

'Vahini, Chimaji Appa is Rau's younger brother and like Lakshman following Ram, I am duty-bound to follow my brother. Vahini, don't let such thoughts trouble you. Take care of your health and your two young children. I am proud to say Nana is managing the job at the office very well. You are lucky that by the grace of the Lord, you have everything you wish for. Let not negative thoughts cloud your mind.'

Kashibai said, 'I will try my best and I won't let you down. Can I beg you for one thing?'

Appa said, 'Vahini! What is wrong with you? You are begging instead of ordering!'

Kashibai replied, 'Think what you may, but I want to say something! Do what it takes but don't allow this dancer to step into the haveli. If another woman steps into the haveli, I will not be able to breathe even for a moment. I entreat you! Please help me!'

'I will do my best, Vahini. Please don't torture yourself.'

'I heard one more thing about this dancer. Is that true?'

'What did you hear?'

'That Shrimant has gifted her two villages. I am told that anonymous complaints are already reaching Satara.'

Appa looked down and said, 'It is true, Vahini. I tried my best but Rau was hell-bent on his decision. Till date such a gift was given to one who showed valour in a battle or had sacrificed his life for the kingdom. It has never happened before that a mere dancer has been given such a gift.'

'So whatever I heard is true,' Kashibai said, trying to hide her disappointment but the tone of her voice gave her away.

The chief priest, Krishna Bhat, stood facing Bajirao, wearing an embroidered dhoti and a simple angavastram. He was carrying an almanac with him.

'Krishna Bhat, tell me an auspicious day for moving into the new house.'

'Give me a minute,' said Krishna Bhat and then turned the pages of the almanac. After a few calculations on his fingers, he asked instead of answering, 'By the way, Shrimant, who is entering the house?'

Bajirao was not used to being questioned. He reprimanded in a stern voice, 'Krishna Bhat, answer what you are asked. Don't ask unnecessary questions.'

Krishna Bhat was red-faced and replied hurriedly, 'There is a good day a week from now.'

'Fine.'

'It is a great day. The person who moves in will enjoy the comforts of the house for a long time.'

Bajirao smiled. He said, 'I wanted such a day. Very good.' Turning to Bapuji Shripat standing in a corner he said, 'Bapuji, I had got a mahal ready along with Nana's. Now that the priest has given us an auspicious day, let the preparations for the *grihapravesh* be made.'

Bapuji adjusted the angavastram on his shoulders and said, 'The mahal is ready to be occupied. I was only waiting for your command.'

'Fine. Mastani will move into the mahal on that day.'

'Oh! You mean, Mastani the dancer?' Bapuji asked, a little surprised.

'You heard me right. Do you have any objection?'

'No, no! I mean, who am I to object? But...' He left the sentence unfinished.

'But what?'

'Matushree may not like it.'

'That is my problem. I will tackle it. You do as you are told.'

'I shall,' said Bapuji and saluted before leaving.

Bajirao left shortly afterwards to go to Mastani's mansion at Kothrud. It had rained a little while back and there was a pleasant coolness in the air. Bajirao said, as soon as he had settled down on the large cushions, 'I have some good news for you.'

'Your presence here is in itself good news. What more do I want?'

'You remember I had promised that you could meet me whenever you wished.'

'Oh! I am surprised Rau remembers a promise he made when he was drunk.'

'I have got a mahal ready for you, Mastani.'

'Mahal? Where?'

'Within the precincts of the haveli.'

Bajirao's words left Mastani wide-eyed. She said, 'You mean within the Shanivar haveli – where the Peshwa resides?'

'You heard right. It is in my haveli and adjacent to my quarters. You will not need anybody's permission to meet me and no one can ask you to go away.'

'What would Matushree think? Has Rau thought about it?'

'What would she think? The fact that you are dear to me is known to one and all. If people don't realize this even after knowing that I personally went to Pabal to get you back, then we cannot make them understand. The chief purohit has given us a date. I want my beloved Mastani to step into her new mahal on that day.'

Mastani was overjoyed. 'What more pleasure can I get than being close to you. I would have been happy to stay in one of the huts where your maids reside. It is truly my good fortune that I am going to live in your haveli.'

Basanti came in with a pitcher of wine. Filling up a tumbler Bajirao said, 'There is one more thing.'

He continued, taking a sip of the frothy wine, 'I forgot to mention! I am going to leave for a campaign after the house-warming ceremony. I will be away for a while from my Mastani.'

Mastani said, 'You remember you had promised to take me along on your campaigns. Last time Baisahiba accompanied you. I would like to come with you this time.'

Bajirao refilled his tumbler and said, 'It is a difficult campaign. We are entering the lion's den this time. It is going to be very stressful.'

'It is not that only I would suffer. You are going to bear the hardships too.'

'I have been used to it since my childhood.'

'I will be there with you to share your troubles. I can manage, believe me.'

Bajirao was downing one drink after another. Keeping his empty tumbler down, he said, 'Mastani, these lovely lips, your doe eyes and this delicate figure – are they meant to rough it out in the open? These fingers delicately decorated with mehndi – are they for holding the reins of a horse? You should be here to soothe my soul when I return tired from the campaign.'

Mastani wrapped her arms around Bajirao's neck and said, looking into his eyes, 'I know what you are hinting at. When you don't want to agree, you start complimenting my looks and divert my attention. Won't I be able to soothe your tired soul out there?'

Bajirao was enjoying the conversation. Mastani's touch lit a fire in him. He said with his face close to her cheeks, 'If you insist, I will take you along. Be prepared for the hardships.'

Mastani said, 'Rau, the day I gave myself and my body to you, I was prepared for all kinds of hardships. So shall I consider your decision final?'

'Of course! It is final.'

'Give me your word,' Mastani said, hugging him again.

Bajirao pressed his lips on hers and then said, looking into her eyes, 'Did you get it?'

Mastani smiled. 'I need it thrice. Only then do I consider it given!'

The tradition of giving donations to the Brahmans, stopped since the death of Dabhade, was begun again. Thousands of Brahmans had assembled in the gardens adjacent to the Shanivar haveli, while Chimaji Appa gave out the dole according to the long list with him. The Brahmans seemed pleased.

Bajirao came in to take his mother's blessings. Krishna Bhat Karve sat next to her looking into a list. Radhabai said, 'Ever since I returned from Kashi, I was keen to see this ceremony. I am pleased that my wish is fulfilled now.'

Bajirao said nothing and sat down on a carpet nearby.

Radhabai continued, 'Appa had made up his mind to take care of the Brahmans during the Shravan month. Apparently, the Chhatrapati too is happy.'

Bajirao's silence was uncomfortable and Radhabai asked, 'It seems Rau is not happy?'

Bajirao said, 'The debt is increasing day by day and here we are giving away thousands of rupees to these Brahmans who do nothing but twiddle their thumbs. I don't approve of it but if all of you have decided, I am not going to object.'

Radhabai was distressed hearing Bajirao's comments. But she knew that as the Prime Minister appointed by the Maharaj, it was the Peshwa's job to look into the affairs of the state. She said, 'The debt is not something new. I agree that you need to worry about it but then each person has a role to perform, doesn't he?'

Bajirao knew that his mother would not speak out unless she had something on her mind. He looked at Krishna Bhat and the two other Brahmans sitting nearby. Blunt as always, he said, 'I don't understand the context in which Matushree is saying this. I might, if she elaborates.'

'The whole of Pune is screaming at the top of its voice. Do I understand that Rau is unable to hear that too?'

'I would be obliged if Matushree takes the trouble to explain. The people in Pune have a habit of making a mountain out of a molehill. There was a lot of criticism when Matushree went on pilgrimage. Later, when the trip turned out to be successful, the same people changed their minds. Thus, I don't care about what people say. If Matushree wants to say something, I am all ears.'

Radhabai said, 'Rau, you are worried about the growing debt but do you bother how much is being spent on your luxuries? It does not seem to affect you.'

Never had Radhabai referred to Bajirao's extravagant spending habits. Bajirao understood what she was referring to yet he restrained himself. He said in a humble tone, 'Matushree, I am not trying to defend myself. There is surely scope to improve but I don't understand the connection between the state debt and my spending. I spend my personal money on things I like. You cannot compare that with the debt which the state owes. The tradition of donating large sums to the Brahmans has been going on since the elder Maharaj's time, but I believe that when we are in a state of crisis, such things have to stop.'

Krishna Bhat interrupted, 'If the Peshwa himself says such things then what are we Brahmans supposed to do?'

'The one who wields power does not worry about these things.'

'Is Shrimant suggesting that we leave our study of the Vedas and become peasants? If that be the case, you may state it directly. If we are not treated well in this Brahman kingdom, we can surely find many others who will be willing to host us.

There are the Rajputs and the Nawab at Hyderabad amongst others, not to mention the Mughal Badshah who, I am told, donates freely. The Brahmans can take refuge there. Matushree! Please say something!'

Bajirao was not used to such impertinence. He frowned in irritation but Radhabai interrupted before he could react. She said, 'Krishna Bhat! Please do not speak when I am talking to Rau.'

She turned to Bajirao and said, 'The debt problem is not a new one. The Brahmans too are your subjects and you, as Peshwa, need to take care of their livelihood. If that means we have to spend a little more, it will only benefit the kingdom.'

Bajirao did not react noticing Radhabai's decisive tone. Not wanting an argument in the presence of the servants and other officials, he checked himself. Radhabai continued, 'Whenever we donate, the blessings accrue to the state, after all.'

Bajirao asked, 'How do you say that?'

'When you are on your campaigns all over the country, there are always instances when one may not be able to follow the Brahmanical codes. There have been instances when you have ignored the religious customs, haven't you?'

Shiv Bhat sitting next to Krishna Bhat interrupted saying, 'I have proof. There have been many such instances.'

Bajirao erupted, 'What exactly are you blabbering about?'

Krishna Bhat said defensively, 'I don't have to list the transgressions. The official mail has carried our observations many times.'

'I would like to know to what exactly our chief purohit is referring?' Bajirao challenged. Krishna Bhat had touched a raw nerve and Bajirao was not one to take the insinuation quietly.

He was further infuriated that the priest was using his mother as a shield.

Krishna Bhat said, 'I have a long list, if you wish to take a look.'

Radhabai had to step in. 'Now, leave it at that! Rau, it is always possible that one may forget certain things when on a war campaign. Your father too had made such mistakes but the moment he would return he would go for a *prayaschitta* and purify his soul.'

Krishna Bhat added, 'That is precisely what I am saying too: that the Peshwa should atone for his sins. It would allow him to hold his head high and we can proudly say that our Peshwa has washed his sins away.'

Bajirao had reached the limit of his tolerance. Krishna Bhat's words created the spark needed to light the fuse. He erupted, 'Krishna Bhat, it is fine to give moral lectures sitting here in the safe confines of Pune. Out there, our pilgrim centres continue to suffer under Mughal rule, cows are being slaughtered daily and Brahmans are being forcibly converted. I have been toiling away day and night to end this tyranny. Do you realize the kind of effort it takes? All you can do is wave the rule book at me when I share a meal with a landlord or a Maratha.'

Krishna Bhat said, 'It would be enough if Shrimant agrees that he has sinned. I am not interested in having a debate with Shrimant on what is right or wrong. Let us Brahmans decide that. A Kshatriya, with a sword in his hand, cannot comment on these things.'

Radhabai did not like Krishna Bhat's snub. She said, 'Krishna Bhat, please keep in mind that you are speaking to the Peshwa. You need to stay within your limits. If you wish to say something to the Peshwa, please tell me. I will convey your message.'

Bajirao was not used to tolerating such insults. His mind was in a turmoil for a few moments. He said, after a while, 'Now that the topic is being discussed openly, let me say this: I am willing to atone for my sins.'

'That is what we have been asking for,' Krishna Bhat said, adjusting the cap on his head.

Radhabai added, 'Me too.'

Bajirao's next comment put a twist to the solution when he said, 'But it will be done in the manner I propose.'

'There are many options: you may shave your head, drink cow urine, donate cows or a she-buffalo or gold to the Brahmans. Whatever you choose, we will get the formalities done accordingly.'

Bajirao's laugh was tinged with sarcasm. He said, 'What's the point of these useless suggestions? I will do what suits me.'

Krishna Bhat hurriedly added, 'Sure, sure! If Shrimant has something else in mind, he may please state. We shall take care of it.'

Bajirao said, 'Krishna Bhat, one should be careful before making such tall claims. You don't even know what I am talking about. You might recall that we had a new mahal built recently. I will perform my atonement there.'

'We don't have any objection. The ceremony can be performed anywhere. If you don't have the time to visit a temple, it is fine. We shall get the necessary arrangements done.'

'We need to call a special guest for the same.'

'Who do you have in mind?'

'Mastani.'

'What? That dancer?'

'Krishna Bhat, please don't cross your limits. I am not used to anyone raising his voice in my presence.'

Bajirao stood up without waiting to see Radhabai's reaction. He said, his voice stern and commanding, 'Please listen carefully! I am going to invite Mastani and if you don't like the sound of the mantras being recited there, you are free to stuff your ears with cotton wool.'

Bajirao walked away without waiting for anyone to respond.

The spark would have quickly turned into a violent conflagration had Chimaji Appa not intervened. The two brothers sat discussing the plans for Delhi estimating where Muhammad Khan Bangash would try and hold them, and the probable location on the banks of the Ganga where Vazir Kamruddin Khan was likely to hold fort. Mirbaksh Khan had shown his inclination to support the Marathas and they discussed which of his conditions they should agree to. Sawai Jaisingh was in favour of the Marathas and they had to decide how to take the most advantage of it. The deliberations continued for long. Venkajiram, their emissary in Delhi, had been sending regular updates. After a while, Chimaji Appa put down the papers on which he had been taking notes. Bringing up a topic which had been troubling him for sometime, he said, 'Rau, is it true, what I heard?'

'It is. I am going to move Mastani in soon and Krishna Bhat has already given us an auspicious date. Do you have anything to say about that, Appa?'

Appa was stunned hearing Rau's unexpectedly blunt and direct answer. He said, trying to keep his emotions at bay, 'Rau,

I have never interfered in your personal life till date. You made her your mistress, yet I never said anything. I accepted it as a social norm followed by many others.'

'Appa, I may be engrossed in my campaigns but I hope you don't presume that I don't keep an eye on the things happening here.'

'I don't get you.'

'Did you not order Mastani to leave Pune?'

Hesitatingly, Appa nodded his head.

'Yet you claim that you ignore it as a mere social more. It is only because Mastani happens to be a singer and of a different religion. It hurts me to know that she is being ill-treated. Yet, I kept quiet but now I find that my silence is being taken for my weakness. That is why I was forced to speak bluntly in the presence of Matushree though, in retrospect, I should not have.'

'Don't you feel you have crossed the line, Rau?' Appa asked.

'Yes, I agree. You must understand that when everyone tries to corner you, one's inner feelings come out naturally.'

Appa said, avoiding Rau's gaze, 'I agree that Krishna Bhat too overstepped his boundaries but you should have thought of Matushree. Do you know she did not come out of the puja room the entire day? When asked, she replied, "I went on a pilgrimage thinking it would make things better but is this what I get for all my trouble?" She was very hurt, Rau.'

'Appa, I know I could have avoided that but you know my nature. If I am challenged I cannot sit quiet and I'm tempted to react. Anyway, let bygones be bygones. What can we do now?'

Appa said, in a mildly suggestive tone, 'Can we not talk it out?'

'I am surprised that earlier you took action without discussing and now you are asking me to talk it out.'

Bajirao continued, seeing Appa quiet, 'I know her now for nearly five years. She is very dear to me and has also borne me a son. But I find that people around are plotting to kill her. Do you expect me to not do anything? Am I the only who should show restraint?'

Appa said, 'Let us forget the past for a moment, Rau. I am sure we can work out something.'

'Tell me what you have in mind, Appa.'

'Things were not bad when you had given residence to the dancer in the gardens at Kothrud. But now you talk of getting her over here.'

'And I intend to do so at the earliest.'

'May I say something?'

Bajirao nodded.

'You will be out on a campaign soon. It is quite likely that we will be out for nearly eight to ten months. I am told you are planning to take Mastani along. Is that true?'

'You heard right.'

'This is what I suggest then: why can't you delay her move? She will be with you in any case for the next many months. In the meantime, Matushree will be at ease knowing that the issue has been deferred. We can decide appropriately when you return.'

Appa was careful in his choice of words knowing that his brother would easily detect his true intent. Bajirao too recognized Appa's ploy, but keeping in mind his mother's feelings he gave his suggestion some thought. He said, 'I agree, Appa. Let us decide when we return from Delhi. Is that fine with you?'

Appa was overjoyed that he had been able to defer the unavoidable for a while. Bajirao said, changing the topic, 'Appa,

I am told your second wife has now come of age and there will be a consummation ceremony soon. And yet here you are, busy with office work.'

Bajirao noticed his brother blushing at the mention of Annapoorna. Appa stood up hurriedly, too embarrassed to continue the discussion.

'I will take your leave. It is getting late now.'

It had been a week since the consummation ceremony of Annapoorna when Nana returned from Satara. He went to meet Appa who asked, 'How are things at Satara?'

'I will talk of Satara later but first I am eager to hear about how things are here.'

'About what?'

'Kaka, I have been back for three days now but I still haven't had a chance to meet Rau in private. When I asked in the office, I was told that he is at Kothrud gardens. Tell me, Kaka, how are things here?'

Nana had come to the point without beating around the bush. Appa knew that Nana was a mature lad, despite being ten years his junior. He asked, 'What are people saying about it in Satara?'

'I could not believe what I heard but when I saw things for myself, it was hard to accept that Rau Swami is head over heels in love with a mere dancer.'

'Don't speak so condescendingly about Rau, Nana!'

'I may not, but what about society? It is better that I know the truth. What is it, Kaka?'

Appa said, 'You have heard right, Nana. I tried my best but Rau is hell-bent and will not listen to anyone.'

'Rau is spending time with the dancer and ignoring urgent matters at hand. Is it so?'

'Nana, you are too young to have experienced life yet.'

'I am told Rau is planning to take her on the campaign. Is that also true?'

'It is. But, in a way, it helps our cause.'

Nana looked askance and Appa explained. 'A minor transgression can prevent a large tragedy sometimes.'

'I am told that Rau is planning to move her into the haveli.'

'That is right. I tried my best but he is determined.'

Nana was silent for a while. He had faced a lot of embarrassment in the court at Satara, having to answer such questions. He was worried that the Chhatrapati would not like Rau's behaviour and may be prompted to take action.

A unique situation had arisen confronting both Nana and Appa and they did not know how to deal with it.

The mild autumn sun felt pleasant on the banks of the Mutha. From where Appa sat, the road towards Kothrud gardens across the river could be seen clearly. He could see a few horsemen waiting for Bajirao at the riverbank beneath the shade of the trees.

Nana said, pointing his finger in the direction of the river, 'Kaka, see!'

Bajirao and a few horsemen could be seen galloping towards the haveli. Appa said, 'Now that you have seen it with your own eyes, you know the truth.'

Nana asked, unable to face Appa, 'May I ask something? Does my Matushree know of this?'

'Women have an intuitive knowledge and they sense these things quite easily.'

'Kaka, tell me honestly – does she know?'

'Yes. But what can she do?'

'Did she say anything?'

'What can she say? All she can do is to bear it stoically.'

Nana's torment was evident. He said, 'Kaka, we cannot just sit and watch! Today's whisper will turn into a loud roar soon. I am surprised to see Rau's behaviour. On the one hand, he chalks out a plan to attack the Badshah at Delhi and, on the other, he spends his time with a dancer. How does he manage both?'

'That's my brother – a unique personality. He would have a dozen things going on in his mind yet you may not get a hint of them.'

'I can think of a way to separate them when they are on the campaign. I have a plan.'

'What do you intend to do?'

'I will see that I give company to Rau all the time. That way, he will not have time for her.'

Appa did not want to dampen Nana's enthusiasm. He said, 'You can propose to join him on the campaign and he just might agree. But be careful! Rau is not an average man. Whatever he does, whether in love or war, is extraordinary!'

After four days, Nana found an appropriate moment and expressed to Bajirao his desire to accompany him on the campaign with his cavalry. To Nana's surprise, Bajirao agreed immediately. He issued the orders: Chiranjeev's troops were to follow his main contingent at a distance of fifty miles and guard the rear. Nana's ploy to be with him had not worked for the moment!

It was the festival of Dussehra after two days. On the day of Vijayadashmi, Bajirao was to march towards Delhi from Bhamburda. The plans had received the royal consent with personal wishes from the Chhatrapati. Paramhans Baba from

Dhawadshi had sent his blessings in the form of the temple's sacred ash. In the morning, Appa, as he was about to leave for his daily darshan, came upon a group of men at the western gate of the haveli. On enquiry, he was told that they were carrying four large crates. He asked one of the men who seemed to be their leader, 'What is in these crates?'

'These are gifts from Mastanibai.'

Appa raised an enquiring eyebrow hearing Mastani's name. 'What do they contain?'

'I don't know. I was just told that they are for Shrimant. I have not seen what is inside.'

'Oh, is that so? I need to check them.'

'Mastanibai has ordered that they be deposited at Shrimant's quarters without any delay.'

'Your Baisahiba may have forgotten that we do check things at the gate. We cannot allow anything to pass without inspection.'

Appa asked the guards to open the crates when the man said, 'May I request the boxes be opened in the presence of Shrimant?'

Appa ignored his request saying, 'I don't need anybody's permission. Now, open them without delay.'

The guards opened a crate to find it filled with fruits, and other items. Appa spotted two large pitchers and asked, raising his voice, 'What is in these pitchers?'

One of the guards opened the pitchers and smelling it said, 'Sarkar, they seem to be filled with wine.'

'What? Who has the temerity to send wine here?' Appa shouted. 'Is this sent by that dancer Mastani?'

'Sir, the crates were sent by Mastanibai. We do not know what is inside.'

'Empty these pitchers into the river,' Appa ordered. 'And let the dancer know that we will not tolerate such things here ever again.'

A small crowd of servants had gathered to watch. Bajirao was on his way to the office when he noticed the crowd. The servants moved away the moment they saw Shrimant approaching. Bajirao asked in a loud voice, 'What is going on here?'

The man who had come from Kothrud said, 'We have brought some gifts from Kothrud for you, Shrimant.'

'Gifts? Then why are these people crowding here?'

'The guards were inspecting the crates.'

'Why do you need to do that?' Bajirao asked, looking at the guards.

'We wanted to ensure that we are not allowing anything which should not be allowed into the haveli.'

Bajirao noticed the pitchers of wine and said, smiling, 'If the gift is for me, I will surely accept it, whatever it may be.'

'Rau,' Appa interrupted, 'we have never allowed such things inside the haveli.'

'What do you mean "such things"? Do you know what the pitchers contain?' Bajirao said, stifling his laughter.

'Wine, of course!'

Bajirao smiled. 'If that be the case, it would have been ideal. The weather is good and it is early morning. We must taste it, shall we?'

The guard moved back, while disappointment was writ large on Appa's face. He had not expected Bajirao to make fun of him. He said, 'If that is what Rau wishes, I am not needed here and might as well proceed to the office.'

Appa was about to leave when Bajirao raised his hand indicating him to stop. He nodded at Kunwar, who filled up a tumbler from the pitcher and gave it to him. Bajirao then offered the tumbler to Appa saying, 'When your mind has preconceived notions, all logic fails. You have been wracking your mind assuming that this pitcher contains wine, but in reality it is filled with sherbet.'

'Sherbet?' Appa exclaimed with an incredulous look on his face.

'Yes. You may taste it yourself, if you don't believe me,' Bajirao said.

'No, no! Wine or sherbet, whatever it is! Rau may command as he deems fit for what we should do with these.'

Bajirao smiled and said, 'Please take them back to Kothrud gardens and tell Mastanibai that we shall enjoy the sherbet on our campaign.'

Thenceforth, crates of pitchers were seen regularly entering the Shanivar wada. Assuming that they were full of sherbet, no one bothered to inspect them.

The Maratha campaign against the Delhi Badshah began. Appa had been sent to keep a check on the Nizam, leaving the entire responsibility of the campaign on Bajirao. The huge army moved northwards. Mastani's palanquin accompanied Bajirao's contingent till they reached the banks of the Godavari. With the speed of movement increasing as they crossed the river, Mastani mounted a horse, refusing the comforts of her palanquin, to keep pace with the rest of the contingent.

Within a month, they had crossed the Narmada and camped at Raver Khedi. Shinde, Holkar and Pawar came to pay their respects to the Peshwa. The total strength of the troops had now increased to nearly a hundred thousand. The plans, already discussed in detail in Pune, were revisited before proceeding further.

The Badshah at Delhi, on receiving the news of Bajirao's march, ordered Khan Dauran, Sadat Khan, Muhammad Khan Bangash and Vazir Kamruddin to intercept the Marathas. The huge Mughal army left Delhi and the news that the two armies may clash at the Doab spread like wildfire. In the meantime, Bajirao's emissaries stationed at Delhi ensured that the Peshwa was fully aware of the Mughal strength and their plans. Bajirao nominated Malhar Rao Holkar to intercept Muhammad Bangash at the Doab while Bhimrao Rethrekar was given the task of collecting tax from the Bundelkhand region. The plan was to let Pawar and Shinde move towards Gwalior, crossing the Yamuna later, and reach Delhi from the western side. It was clear that the Marathas were now determined to lay siege to Delhi. Bajirao, having estimated the calibre of the current ruler at Delhi, was convinced that he could fulfil the dream of the elder Maharaj who had wanted the flag of Hindavi Swaraj to be unfurled at Delhi.

Bajirao wrote to all the Rajput sardars asking them for their help, appealing to their religious sentiments while threatening them with dire consequences if they refused. As expected, their emissaries came running to Raver Khedi to show their solidarity and extend their hand of friendship. They promised not to support the Mughals under any circumstances. Bajirao had won his first victory on the strength of correspondence alone. A few Rajputs were not in favour of Hindavi Swaraj, one of them being Raja Gopal Singh and his son Anirudh Singh of Bhadawar.

The message from the Mughal durbar that 'you need not be worried about the Maratha army. We are there to support you; just ensure that they do not cross the Chambal', was enough to spur Gopal Singh into action. He took it upon himself to stop the Marathas.

The moment Bajirao heard this, he decided to lead the troops himself.

As part of their strategy, Shinde, Holkar and Rethrekar were ready to move. Bajirao personally supervised the contingent as he inspected the lines, patting a sardar's back and complimenting another leader for his earlier exploits. He spent four full days meeting the troops. Each and every shiladar was known to him personally. Bajirao had ensured that all of them knew their tasks and had a clear understanding of what they were to achieve.

After they departed, the cantonment at Raver was left with just twenty thousand cavalry. The month of December brought along cold winds from across the Narmada.

Earlier, with Kashibai, Bajirao had stayed at Raver for the holy dip in the Narmada. This time the zenankhana stayed in the safe confines of the fortress at Raver, while Bajirao himself camped in the tents along with his troops.

His plan was to march on to Bhadawar. After giving detailed instructions, he reached Mastani's quarters in the fortress late in the night. The lovely fort, built on a small hillock near the banks of the Narmada, looked beautiful at night. The wide expanse of the river, as it took a leisurely turn, could be seen from the fort.

Mastani stood outside looking at the star-studded sky with a woollen shawl wrapped around her. She did not notice Bajirao standing behind her till he hugged her, putting his hands around her waist. She exclaimed, with her delicate fingers on her lips, 'Oh, is that you? I did not notice you coming.'

'On this cold night, when everyone is sleeping, I expected you to be in bed but I find you watching the stars out here.'

'How can I sleep till I see you?'

'Why?'

Mastani blurted, 'It is so cold and...' She bit her tongue and stopped, her cheeks blushing red.

'I see!' Pulling her closer, he whispered, 'I don't feel cold at all!'

Mastani gently extricated herself saying, 'Now, be careful of what you say here! This is not Kothrud where you can say whatever comes to your mind.'

'Why? What is different here?'

'You are in your cantonment, planning a campaign. What will your soldiers think of you? That they are far away from their families, while the Peshwa is enjoying his nights?'

'Do you think they would say that?'

'Yes, what else would they say?'

'Don't worry about them. What are you doing out here?'

Pointing at the temple in the distance, she said, 'I was looking at that.'

'What about it?'

'Look at the row of soldiers waiting for their turn for darshan! What temple is it?'

Bajirao glanced in the direction and said, 'Rameshwar.'

'Rameshwar? I have camped here before when en route to Bundelkhand but I had never seen it.'

'That is because it was built by Kashibai. On our last visit to Khandesh, we had stopped here for a holy dip. She liked the place so much that she insisted on building a temple there.'

Mastani said, fiddling with the buttons on Bajirao's jacket, 'It is such a lovely night and tomorrow we will leave this place. I wish I could visit the temple before we leave.'

'I don't mind, if you are game to walk in this cold night.'

Adjusting her shawl, Mastani said, 'Let us go!'

She slipped her feet into her sandals and they walked out of the fortress in the direction of the temple. Two servants, seeing them walk, rushed to help. Bajirao instructed them to run ahead and get the crowds cleared.

They walked hand in hand on a narrow mud path, dodging small stones along the way. Mastani would at times clutch Bajirao's arm in fear, upon hearing sounds from the trees nearby. He said, 'Look, I told you it is not easy to walk at night.' But Mastani, determined to have darshan, just shook her head and continued.

After a while, they reached the temple. The spire, made of silver and copper, gleamed in the moonlight. A couple of *mashaals* lit up the entrance, while a row of oil lamps could be seen burning inside.

Bajirao reached the temple first. He removed his shoes and went inside. Mastani was following him a few steps behind when the priest came out and said, 'Wait! I cannot allow you to enter. This temple is only for Hindus.'

Mastani's foot stopped in midstep. Bajirao, in the meantime, returned after a quick darshan to find Mastani still outside. He asked, 'What happened? Don't you want to see the idol?'

Hiding her disappointment, she said, 'It is much more beautiful to see from here. It is so lovely!'

Bajirao laughed saying, 'It has to be! After all, we spent such a large amount building it.'

Looking at the crowd of soldiers outside, Mastani said, 'I haven't seen such a crowd before. Is there a special occasion tonight?'

'It is a tradition that before going on a campaign, the soldiers visit a temple. This temple is called Rameshwar, after Lord Rama, who ventured to cross the ocean.'

Mastani laughed. Bajirao asked, 'Why, don't you believe me?'

'I am laughing at the naivety of your soldiers. When they have Rau as their commander, what is the need for divine intervention?'

Looking at the soldiers standing at a respectful distance, Bajirao said, 'Let us move. With us standing here, these poor fellows are hesitant to enter.'

On returning to the fortress, Bajirao removed his coat and turban and lay down to rest in Mastani's room. Adjusting the curtain on the windows, Mastani said, 'Can you believe it, I received a letter from Chiranjeev today?'

'Really? Nana wrote to you?'

'Yes. A short note to say that he had wanted to meet me in Pune but we had left by then.'

'That is really surprising,' Bajirao said, making himself comfortable on the bed. 'I wonder what he wanted to talk about.'

'Shall I reply to his letter?'

'Sure.'

'He too is on this campaign, isn't he?'

'Yes, he is managing the rear guard.'

'If Rau permits, I would like to meet him when we camp next. He had come to meet me in Pune but could not. At least we can meet in the cantonment.'

'Sure! You can do that,' Bajirao said as he snuffed out the lamps, enveloping the room in darkness.

Gopal Singh and his son were at ease at Bhadawar. They had received the Badshah's firman through Sadat Khan asking them not to allow the Peshwa to cross the Chambal and capture the fort at Ater. But Sadat Khan's troops were miles away when the Marathas attacked Ater. The father and son duo had no choice but to repulse the attack personally. The sound of gunfire and the constant shower of arrows began. The Marathas soon surrounded the fort and were pushing hard.

Bajirao sent a few of his troops into the town where they entered from three directions. Soon, fires could be seen all around, making the people run for their lives. Next, Bajirao sent his emissary to the fort giving Gopal Singh two hours to surrender and save his life.

Sadat Khan's messenger reached at the same time and urged Gopal Singh not to give in and hold on till the Mughal forces reached. Falling for Sadat Khan's promises, Anirudh Singh insulted the Maratha emissary and asked him to leave.

It was afternoon and the deadline given had ended. Bajirao and a thousand soldiers on horseback, shouting 'Har Har Mahadev', attacked the fort with renewed vigour. Within half an hour, the door gave way and the troops entered. A bloody battle ensued. The words 'Kill, kill!' could be heard repeatedly as the Marathas took charge. Soon, dead bodies were seen littered everywhere.

Anirudh Singh was captured and presented before the Peshwa who sat under the shade of a tree, his naked sword lying on the side. Sounds of terror could be heard in the distance. Seeing the Rajput king, with his hands tied behind his back, Bajirao stood up and pointed his sword at his throat. He said, 'I had never imagined that the Rajputs would be so foolish. Instead of fighting hand in hand with us against the Mughals, you are falling prey to their sweet talk. I am ashamed to see the devotees of Eklangji behave so.'

Anirudh Singh had never imagined the Marathas to be so powerful. Tears streamed down his cheeks as he pleaded, 'I ask for pardon. I failed to recognize you and your might.'

He fell down at Bajirao's feet begging for mercy.

Despite his anger, Bajirao felt pity for the young Rajput. He said, 'Put him in chains and throw him into the dungeon. We will decide his fate later.'

By evening, the fort had been taken over while the Maratha camp was set up on the banks of the Chambal a mile away.

Bajirao ensured that the Maratha troops guarded various posts in the ravines along the rivers Chambal and Kuwari. They intended to intercept the Mughals there. That night, Bajirao and his key sardars inspected all the posts giving instructions wherever necessary.

The trumpets sounded on the fort at Ater, as the Maratha flag flew high on the mast. Mastani, sitting in her camp, heard the same and prayed on her knees to Allah for Bajirao's safety. While excited at the Maratha victory, she waited anxiously for him to return.

It was evening and a reddish glow spread across the sky. A group of nearly fifty cavalry soldiers stopped near Mastani's tent. Basanti came running in and announced, 'Baisaheb, the young master has come to meet you.'

'What? Has Nana come?'

'That is right.'

'Why are you keeping him waiting? Usher him in right away.'

Nana soon came in and stood in front of Mastani. He had been riding for long and was covered in dust. His fair skin was complimented by his bright red turban. A spitting image of his father, Mastani was overwhelmed on seeing him. She had heard a lot about him in Pune but had never got a chance to meet him in person as he had been busy in Satara most of the time. Mastani observed that he had his father's large forehead, big eyes and a strong, well-built body. There was barely a hint of a moustache on his lips, yet he looked manly in all respects.

Nana was looking around and then, realizing that he was in the presence of Mastani, he bowed and said, 'I am seeing Mastani sahiba for the first time.'

'I was keen to meet you, Chiranjeev, but it appears that it was destined that we meet on a battlefield here.'

Noticing the dust on his dress, she added, 'It seems Chiranjeev has been riding for a long time.'

'That is right. I was asked to manage the rear guard and I had to travel nearly twenty miles.'

Mastani said, 'You must be tired then. Please rest for a while. I just heard that Shrimant is expected in another hour or so. We can meet once you are rested. I will try my best to do whatever possible to make you comfortable.'

Nana observed Mastani keenly. Ever since he had heard of her, he had created a mental image of her. Her mellifluous voice, her womanly figure – she was the epitome of beauty. It wasn't surprising that she had cast a spell on the Peshwa. A million thoughts rushed through Nana's mind. He barely heard Mastani, so lost in thought was he. Coming to his senses, he said, 'Huh? Did you say something? I did not hear you.'

Mastani burst out laughing. Settling down on a diwan, she said, 'It seems Chiranjeev is distracted. I said you should rest a while and then we can meet when Rau returns.'

'I shall do as you say. I will meet Rau, report to him on the tasks given, and then meet you.'

'Yes, I will wait for you,' Mastani said.

Nana bowed low before he turned to go when Mastani muttered, 'Inshallah! We shall meet again.'

It was a full moon night in the month of February when the Maratha flag fluttered in the cold wind at Ater fort. Bajirao, riding his horse, had been informing the soldiers of the victory. That night he got the message from his spies that Sadat Khan's nephew, Abul Mansur Khan Safdarjung, was trying to provide support to the king of Bhadawar. Malhar Rao Holkar's camp was five miles away from Bajirao's and he was immediately called for.

Malhar Rao reached in no time and conferred with Bajirao till the early hours of the morning. The guard informed Bajirao that Chiranjeev was waiting to meet him. Bajirao, in deep consultation with Malhar Rao, paused for a moment, frowning at the interruption. He said, without showing his irritation, 'Please ask Chiranjeev to wait for a while. I will send for him soon.'

Bajirao said, turning towards Malhar Rao, 'Except for this king at Bhadawar, all the Rajput kings are on our side. The Mughal strength is drastically reduced now. We need to tackle their sardars, Khan Dauran, Sadat Khan, Muhammad Bangash and Kamruddin, separately. Earlier, I wanted you to tackle Sadat Khan, but now his nephew is coming to help this king. You need to stop him at the Doab. The festival of colours, Holi, is a few days away. Let the Maratha soldiers play it with their blood.'

On cue, Kunwar got the tray of paan indicating the end of the meeting. Giving a paan to Malhar Rao as he stood up, Bajirao said, 'Keep in mind what I have said: don't confront the enemy directly. Take them unawares. Let us make the Mughals beg for mercy. We need to teach them a lesson. In case you need help, send an urgent message so that we can come in to support.'

For every statement of Bajirao's, Malhar Rao nodded his head saying, 'Ji, sarkar. Ji, Shrimant.'

He took his leave and then galloped away at full speed.

After a couple of hours, Bajirao received the message that Holkar's troops had crossed the Yamuna near the Doab and entered the northern territory. Then Bajirao called for Chiranjeev, who came in and touched his feet before sitting down.

Bajirao asked, 'You came unannounced. Any urgent work?'

'I have done the task as entrusted by Rau Swami. The rear guard is safe and we have been keeping constant vigil. We have blocked the way towards the Deccan at Burhanpur. At Asirgadh, we have a strong garrison which is keeping an eye on any movement. Rau need not worry about the Deccan and can proceed forward with ease.'

'Then what brings you here?'

Nana did not answer Bajirao's question directly. He said instead, 'I had not met you for a long time; hence I thought I would drop in.'

'To meet me or Mastani,' Bajirao asked bluntly.

'She had sent a letter hence I came over,' Nana said, hesitatingly.

'So did you meet her?'

'Yes, for a brief moment. She asked me to meet you first and then see her again. I was waiting for you.'

Bajirao's change of expression was a welcome relief to Nana. He relaxed and said, 'I heard of the victory the moment I came here. It is our first victory. I don't have any doubt that we will have many such victories going forward.'

Bajirao's mind was preoccupied with a thousand things and he had no time for small talk. He said, 'It is good that you came. I have a task for you.'

'Please command,' Nana said, excitedly.

'The battle has begun and the biggest hurdle, this fort at Ater, has been captured paving the way for our northward journey. But the Mughal mansabdars are not going to take it lying down. We have to be prepared for an intense and prolonged fight.'

'Please tell me what I should do and I will make myself available.'

'No, that is not necessary. Currently, Holkar and Shinde are doing a fine job. Bajipant Rethrekar too is supporting us. There is a task for you, though.'

'Please command,' Nana repeated.

'The families of our servants, maids and other staff need to be escorted to Bundelkhand. We will then be free of their responsibility and can concentrate on the battles ahead.'

Nana was overjoyed that he now had the opportunity he had been dreaming of. He had been wanting to spend time with Mastani but had not been able to yet. Now, with the orders to move everyone to Bundelkhand, the chance had presented itself. He said, without showing his eagerness, 'I shall do as you say, but I would be pleased if I could get an opportunity to show my valour with a sword in hand.'

'I can understand your eagerness, Nana, but there will be many such occasions ahead. Remember, life is not about using your sword in the battlefield alone but in all battles of life.'

Nana was about to speak but kept quiet. The father knew what the son was thinking, but he did not elaborate. Bajirao said, 'It is getting late now. Make arrangements to move the families to Bundelkhand. On our return, they can join us.'

Nana said, 'I shall do as ordered. I will send some of the soldiers from my contingent to Bundelkhand to escort the families.'

Bajirao said, 'We need not use the cavalry for such small jobs.'

Nana said, 'But we have Mastanibai and her support staff too. Should we not have soldiers for their protection?'

Bajirao remarked, 'I have given orders for the families of the staff to be shifted. It does not include Mastani.'

'Then shall I arrange to send her to the Deccan?'

'No! She will remain where I am,' and saying so Bajirao stood up. Nana immediately followed suit and after saluting hurriedly, left the tent.

That evening, the families of the staff left for Bundelkhand. The only people who stayed back were Mastani, Basanti and Kunwar.

Bajirao had managed to collect nearly twenty lakh rupias worth of revenue of which fifteen lakhs was in cash and the rest in kind. Most of the collections were sent across to the Deccan. Meanwhile, in the Doab, Malhar Rao Holkar was creating havoc raiding territories and establishing the Maratha supremacy. He had captured Shikohabad and the fort keeper there was forced to cough up a sum of two lakh rupias. The Maratha flag flew on the fort that evening. Holkar's troops had reached Jaleshwar when they heard of a probable confrontation with Safdarjung. Holkar was keen to avoid a direct conflict but realizing that Safdarjung was retreating, he sent a contingent of fifteen hundred cavalry to chase him.

For someone like Malhar Rao, a battle veteran, this was a classic blunder. Safdarjung retreated to join forces with Sadat Khan and Malhar Rao realized, albeit late, that he would have to pay a heavy price for his error of judgement. Bajirao had repeatedly told him not to take on the enemy in a direct confrontation but he had erred.

Shrimant Peshwa was sent an urgent message. Bajirao read the message and was surprised that a seasoned warrior like Malhar Rao had slipped. Each moment was crucial and Bajirao decided to send his troops for support.

At that moment another urgent message came in. There was no time to read the letter as at the same time Bajirao heard a huge commotion and troops were seen galloping towards the fort of Ater. Malhar Rao's troops had managed to cross the Yamuna and escape with their lives.

That evening Malhar Rao presented himself at Bajirao's tent and stood with his head bowed. Bajirao rushed to embrace him and said patting his back, 'Malhar Rao, why are you upset? This is a battle and mistakes can happen. I am there to support you. Don't be so despondent.'

Malhar Rao said, 'I ignored your advice and had to pay a heavy price.'

Bajirao held Malhar Rao's hand and, making him sit down, said, 'Now, take these thoughts out of your mind. In a large campaign like ours, one should not dwell on such minor mishaps.'

Bajirao asked his other sardars to join them for a meeting. That night, they conferred for a long time discussing their next steps.

The Marathas had established their supremacy in no uncertain terms. The loot they had managed to amass was significant. Thanks to the Peshwa's diplomacy, the Mughals had lost all their so-called supporters. The habshis had been vanquished in Konkan, though the English and the Portuguese were making some noise in Mumbai and Vasai, respectively. Gaekwad had managed Gujarat, while Chimaji Appa had taken control of the Malwa region. There was only one path open for the Mughals to solicit support. And that was the Khyber Pass. The Maratha spies were spread far and wide in the pass. There did not seem to be any immediate support that would be available to the Mughals. Bajirao, as he conferred with his sardars, took stock of the situation. It was a new moon the next day. The new year would begin then and Bajirao felt it was necessary to take decisive action soon.

Letters and messages were going back and forth between the Mughal Badshah and the Peshwa. The spies ensured that they gave timely information to Bajirao. He got the news that the Mughals were spreading rumours of having routed Malhar Rao Holkar and how the troops had drowned in the Yamuna. They also spread word that Bajirao had crossed the Narmada and was on his way to the Deccan. The Mughal sardars, eager to please the Badshah, talked of how they would soon ensure that the green flag, with the symbol of the moon and stars, would soon be seen fluttering across the south right up to Thanjavur. The troops at Delhi were busy celebrating their success. Dancers and singers crowded the cantonments as the soldiers looked for entertainment. Sadat Khan and Muhammad Khan Bangash joined Khan Dauran at Mathura and they took out a procession celebrating their success. The festivities continued for three days. Meanwhile, the Marathas were nowhere to be seen.

After two days, Bajirao and his men moved out of their camp at Kotila. Bajirao warned Mastani before leaving, 'Henceforth, the going will be tough and a test of your endurance. You said you would match me step for step. Now is the time to prove it.'

Mastani had put on a soldier's uniform and mounted her horse without saying a word.

At nightfall, the Maratha troops increased their speed and crossed the Yamuna to move northwards. All plans had been made in advance: each unit had clear instructions on where to proceed, when and how much time to take to reach the destination.

It had been four hours since leaving Kotila but Bajirao had not pulled his reins to stop. The eastern sky was becoming brighter and Bajirao spurred his horse to move faster.

Meanwhile in Mathura, the Mughals were busy celebrating on the streets accompanied by fireworks. The Marathas could see the sky light up from a distance as Bajirao turned his troops to the left of Fatehpur Sikri. None of the Mughals realized that a contingent of fifty thousand Maratha soldiers had passed through that night, crossing the area between Fatehpur Sikri and Deeg, a narrow gap of less than forty miles. As the Marathas crossed the villages in the night, the villagers simply assumed that the noise of the moving troops must be that of the Mughal soldiers riding through. None thought it necessary to alert the Mughal mansabdars. The second day too passed similarly with Bajirao halting for a mere two hours for rest.

At a halt, Bajirao conferred with his spies who had news from Sadat Khan's camp as well as from Delhi. The Badshah had honoured Sadat Khan for having driven the Peshwa away. The Mughals, in short, were blissfully unaware of the march of the Marathas.

The Mughals continued to think that the Peshwa and his army had crossed the Narmada and were on their way to Pune. The irony was that just a few miles away, Bajirao and his fifty thousand men were galloping rapidly to reach Delhi. The men had covered a distance which would have normally taken days in a very short time.

On the day before Ram Navami, the Maratha troops descended on the southern part of Delhi like a swarm of locusts. A huge celebration was on at the temple of Kalkadevi. The Mughal mansabdars were caught unguarded and the Marathas managed to collect a loot which included more than fifty elephants. Lakhs in cash were looted from the streets around the temple. That night, they camped near the southern entrance of the city. By midnight, the news of the loot reached the Badshah, but he turned a deaf ear assuming that the common public had a habit of exaggerating such things. He laughed when someone suggested that the Peshwa himself had arrived and was supervising the loot. The Badshah simply assumed that the temple goers, under the spell of opium on the occasion of Ram Navmi, were blabbering.

The Badshah was in for a surprise the next morning when he was told that the city was swarming with Maratha troops, looting whatever they could lay their hands on. The Badshah had just returned from his prayers at the Jama Masjid. His entire army had been despatched earlier to tackle the Marathas. Assuming that the messenger was simply making a mountain out of a molehill, he reprimanded him. After all, the Badshah believed, when Sadat Khan and Kamruddin were chasing the Marathas away, there was no way they could be in the city of Delhi. It must be some dacoits or shoplifters whom the people were assuming to be the Marathas, the Badshah concluded and walked off to his private quarters for his morning meal. The Marathas, in the meantime, managed to capture the royal elephants and horses which had been despatched to participate in the Ram Navami celebrations. The Peshwa sent his emissary with a message for the Badshah.

Bajirao stood in his camp, his hands behind his back, as he looked at the capital city of the Mughals. Delhi! Indraprastha! How many memories it evoked! Hundreds of years of subjugation and torture! Death, torture, atrocities! There had been no end to Mughal tyranny. Since the time of the elder Maharaj, it had been the dream of the Marathas to capture this seat of Mughal power. It was this Sultanate which had betrayed the trust reposed by the elder Maharaj.

Now the city was in the clutches of the Marathas. All he had to do was squeeze his fist to suffocate the Sultanate and take his revenge. Within minutes, all the arrogance of the Diwan-e-Khas and the Peacock Throne would be reduced to dust. Bajirao's eyes emitted a burning desire for revenge. He spat on the ground with disgust and turned around upon hearing footsteps. It was Malhar Rao Holkar. The spark was waiting to erupt. Bajirao ordered, 'Burn this cursed city! Malhar Rao, take your revenge! Burn everything you can lay your hands on.'

But the Maratha sardars like Holkar, Pilaji Jadhavrao and others were men of experience and steeped in politics. They knew they were playing with fire. Instead of establishing their supremacy by burning the city, they believed they were better off walking away with the loot. But they knew that Bajirao's anger was a reaction to the hundreds of years of Mughal tyranny which deserved such a revengeful punishment. Malhar Rao said, 'This is not the time to take revenge, Shrimant!'

Bajirao erupted, 'Really? Then when is a good time? It

is these Mughals who butchered two thousand of my men at Jaleshwar. Each of my men is worth a hundred thousand Mughals. Malhar Rao, that day you returned defeated, but I patted your back and did not let your spirits down. And now, as we stand at the threshold of the city, we have them by the neck. We have a golden chance to snub them. Let us show them their place!'

Malhar Rao persisted. 'Shrimant, if we burn the city down, we would have broken all ties with the empire. I request you to show some patience.'

'Patience, my foot! Is this the same Malhar Rao who ran away from Jaleshwar or is it the brave Holkar who taught the Mughals a lesson in Malwa?'

Pilaji Jadhavrao, standing nearby, interrupted. 'Shrimant, Malhar Rao is right. It is time to exhibit some restraint.'

'Let the sardars do that. The Peshwa will lead his men himself into the city. I am sure our shiladars will reciprocate my sentiments. You can sit and discuss politics in the meantime.'

Pilaji was taken aback. He had known him since his childhood. It was Pilaji who had taught Bajirao to handle the sword. Balaji Vishwanath's son had grown up under his mentorship. Now the Peshwa, with the power of his sword and the faith of thousands of his loyal men, was ready to finish off the Mughal power once and for all. The only person who could dare to oppose him and speak his mind was Pilaji Kaka.

Pilaji threw his sword on the ground and placing his turban at Bajirao's feet said, 'Shrimant, I am placing my prestige at your feet. It has been a tradition since the elder Nanasaheb's time. Please allow us to enter the city first. You can watch the carnage from here.'

Bajirao gently helped Pilaji stand up and embraced him

saying, 'Pilaji Kaka! I may be a Peshwa for the others but not for you. Please stand up. Can I forget the fact that I owe my life to you? Please speak your mind. I am all ears.'

'I request you to agree with Holkar's wish.'

'Should I run away after seeing two thousand of my men butchered by these devils?'

'You may punish Holkar for that but don't allow your political relations to be marred forever,' Malhar Rao said, his voice full of anguish.

Malhar Rao burned with the guilt of the single defeat he had had to face. It was the only time he had faced such ignominy. Bajirao had consoled him in Ater but his wounded pride still hurt. He had won countless battles in Malwa and Rajputana, fighting shoulder to shoulder with Chimaji Appa. Every part of his body had been battle scarred. Images of the past fifteen years of struggle raced through his mind.

He said, finding the Peshwa silent, 'Shrimant, I am obliged that you consoled me and lifted my spirits then. I would like to redeem my guilt now.'

'What do you mean?'

'If Shrimant believes that I failed in my duties, I request you to behead your loyal servant right away. I am all yours!'

For a moment, Bajirao was nonplussed. He could not believe what he had just heard. He said, 'Malhar Rao, this sword is for beheading enemies and not friends!'

Seeing that Bajirao had mellowed a bit, Malhar Rao ventured, 'Our emissary has gone to meet the Badshah. Let us wait for him to return. In the meantime, Bajipant Rethrekar and others are tackling Sadat Khan. Once we know the outcome, we can go for a final blow.'

Bajirao agreed to Malhar Rao's suggestions and did not

allow the troops to enter the city. At the same time, he ordered that they plunder and loot outside the walls of the city. The burning fires were visible from the Badshah's court.

That evening the Badshah's emissaries presented themselves to the Peshwa, accompanied by Sawai Jaisingh's emissary, Raja Bakhatmal. They pleaded with the Peshwa to save the city from being plundered and agreed with the terms and conditions put forth by Bajirao. That night, after deliberations with his sardars, Bajirao sent a list of his demands to the Badshah. The Mughal Emperor was to send, at the earliest, a sum of one crore rupias and merge six of the Subahs into the Maratha empire. The deadline given was till morning with a strong warning that if the Badshah failed to agree to the demands, the Peshwa would let his troops loose on the city.

By now, the entire city was reeling under the vice-like grip of the Marathas. Everyone wanted to run out of the city, but they were stranded knowing that each exit was being guarded by the Marathas. Shrimant Peshwa, aware that his troops were itching for action, decided to move them a little away to the banks of the Talkatora lake. He waited patiently for the Mughal Badshah to respond.

It was the third day since the Marathas had laid siege to Delhi. But the Mughal pride was too strong. The Badshah consulted his advisers. Then instead of accepting the demands, the Badshah sent his city police chief, Mir Hasan Khan Koka, and the cavalry in charge, Amir Muzaffar Khan, with a few ordinary officials for a reconnaissance tour of the city. They had barely reached Rakabgunj when Bajirao got news of their movement and sent Malhar Rao Holkar, Ranoji Shinde and Tukoji Pawar to intercept them.

It took little time for the Marathas to butcher Mughal pride.

The Mughal officials ran for their lives, rushing back to the safe confines of their respective havelis. Malhar Rao Holkar took his revenge, killing and beheading most of the thousand soldiers. That evening, the Maratha sardars requested the Peshwa to demand that the Badshah himself be brought in person with his hands tied behind his back to meet him. But Malhar Rao Holkar thought differently. He advised that while the Marathas had reached Delhi and laid siege to it, the Mughal commanders Sadat Khan and Kamruddin Khan were on their way back to Delhi and that it was wise not to spend more time in the city. He suggested that they should start retreating as soon as possible. He said, 'Shrimant, there is no point in insulting the Mughals any more. They have been shown their place. What can be more insulting for the Mughal pride than the fact that their Badshah, Salamat, is hiding in the zenankhana? Let us not waste our time here any more.'

Shrimant Peshwa and his men turned southwards and marched back. By the time they reached Pune, it was June.

Ever since the formal creation of Hindavi Swaraj, when Shivaji Maharaj had been coronated, no one had had the courage to march into the city of Delhi and make mincemeat of the Mughal sardars. Bajirao's feat had left everyone in Hindustan stunned. Chhatrapati Shahu Maharaj and Paramhans Baba sent personal letters of congratulations praising Bajirao.

The streets of Pune were lined with thousands of people who had come to cheer the returning army. The citizens, eager to show their gratitude, welcomed them with a shower of flowers. The Peshwa, sitting atop a silver howdah, entered the city to the sound of trumpets. It took nearly an hour for the procession to reach Shanivar wada from the main chowk, a distance of just a few hundred metres. After darshan at the Ganesha temple in the city, Bajirao entered the haveli.

Radhabai welcomed him first, putting a tilak on his forehead. She said, looking at Appa, 'I am blessed to have borne such a valiant son. I cannot forget the day his father had gone to the court at Delhi with a proposal for Hindavi Swaraj. He had had to fight his way out of the city, and had barely managed to save his life. Rau has today avenged the insults his father had suffered.'

Radhabai could not stop praising her son. Realizing that she had not yet invited her daughter-in-law, she said, 'You don't sit and listen to oldies like me. Get Kashibai to welcome her husband and ask her to ward off the evil before he enters the haveli.'

Bajirao reached Kashibai's chambers. Kashibai stood at the door holding a traditional tray in her hand to welcome her husband. She wore an embroidered green silk sari. Bajirao removed his sandals and walked up the steps to the door. Kashibai put a tilak on his forehead and then performed the aarti as she moved the tray with the oil lamps around his face.

Bajirao stepped into her room and sat down on a diwan, arranged aesthetically with soft bolsters and pillows. Kashibai came in with a tumbler of saffron-flavoured milk. She said, handing the tumbler, 'You must be tired. Have a glass of milk.'

Kashibai was seeing Bajirao after nearly nine months. He had been received with pomp and ceremony throughout the city. He said, teasing Kashibai, 'The whole city erupted to receive me, but I must say, the response here is quite lukewarm.'

Kashibai asked nervously, 'Did I miss something? Why is Swami upset?'

'I am being ordered to have a tumbler of milk kept on the tray here.'

'Chhee, chhee! Who can order you?' Kashibai said.

'It may have slipped your mind that my hands are tired, having held the sword for months together.'

Kashibai, unable to understand Bajirao's comment, said, 'If Shrimant were not to speak in riddles, it would be easier for me to understand.'

Bajirao smiled. 'I wish that you serve me yourself.'

Kashibai blushed and when she stretched out her hand, Bajirao deliberately brushed his fingers against hers. She realized that he was in a playful mood and her cheeks blushed pink. She did not dare to look up. Bajirao said, keeping the tumbler down after taking a sip, 'Do I see tears in your eyes? What has happened?'

'Can't there be tears of happiness?'

The sky outside had been overcast with dark clouds since morning. There had been a sudden shower a while ago. Kashibai was in a similar state. Bajirao's words awakened a deep-rooted fear and the mask of happiness which she had been trying to put on gave way baring her true feelings. She could not stop the flow of tears.

Bajirao took her hand in his. 'What is this? Why don't you say what you feel?'

The tears flowed freely now. Kashibai wiped her tears but they refused to stop. Bajirao said, 'The whole city is celebrating today but here, in my mahal, I find you sad. Will you not say something?'

'When you left nine months ago, you did not even meet me before leaving. I was praying for your health and safety each day, waiting with bated breath for every news of you. But, you did not send even one letter in all these months.'

Bajirao could feel her shivering as he held her hand. He patted her arm gently and let out a deep sigh. 'I am sure Chiranjeev and Appa were corresponding regularly.'

'Yes, they were. And, for that matter, Bajipant Rethrekar and Holkar too sent their news. Shinde, Avji Kavde, Pilaji Jadhavrao wrote but I was waiting for a letter from my Swami! My eyes were eager to read a few lines written by you, but alas, it was not to happen. These thoughts were racing through my mind when I welcomed you.'

Bajirao felt guilty hearing Kashibai's words. He realized he had been on a high for the past eight or nine months – a high created by victory and romance! In the potent combination of the two, he had not bothered to think of anything else. He had never realized it would lead to such consequences.

'I realize I made a mistake. But if you don't, then who else will pardon me, Kashi?'

Kashibai turned to face Bajirao, surprised. In all their twenty-two years of marriage, he had never addressed her as 'Kashi'. It was the most pleasant sound she had heard and each part of her body reverberated to that. She asked 'What did you just say?'

Bajirao said, 'Kashi, Bajirao has never asked for forgiveness, but today I stand before you guilty and ask for pardon. Kashi, you have pardoned me for all my sins before. Won't you pardon me now?'

Kashibai was overwhelmed seeing Bajirao pleading before her. All her anger vanished. She picked up the tumbler of milk and giving it to Bajirao said, 'Please finish this. Let us enjoy this day to the fullest and please forget whatever I said. I have no complaints now.'

It was late in the afternoon. Basanti was on the terrace of the mansion at Kothrud gardens. Shading her forehead with her palm, she looked in the direction of the city and then came down. She had been doing this every fifteen minutes for the past two hours. This time she came down running and said, trying to catch her breath, 'Baiji, Shrimant is on his way!'

Mastani ran towards the door. Soon, they could see Bajirao and Kunwar riding at full speed towards the mansion. They dismounted at the bottom of the steps. Bajirao climbed up the steps and said to her, 'It seems you were expecting me!'

'Rau has returned after a successful campaign and the whole city is celebrating the victory. I heard you got a hero's welcome in the haveli. I was not expecting you to remember this lowly servant of yours, hence I was not worried.'

'Oh, is that so?' Bajirao taunted, before taking her into his arms as his lips locked hers. They sat down on a comfortable seating arrangement on the floor. Mastani prepared a paan as Bajirao reclined against a bolster.

Bajirao, admiring Mastani, said, 'God has given me more than I expected.'

Mastani blushed. 'While having one's meal, one should be able to discern between the dessert and the main course.'

'I know that and have decided what dessert I want to enjoy. I have made up my mind now; I want to hear your sweet voice whenever I wish to.'

'Rau is the Peshwa of the Maratha empire and should think of the consequences of whatever he decides.'

'I don't have a habit of beating around the bush, Mastani. I say what I feel. I don't hide things. I saw you, got swept away by your heavenly beauty and fell in love. I made you mine and now I don't want you to be far away from me. That is why I have decided that I will shift you to the mahal I had constructed for you in my haveli. I have come to take you there.'

'Really?'

'I mean it. You have to come. Now!'

Mastani had been waiting for this precious moment for the past one and a half years. She knew that the bonds of love were not one-sided. Her respect and admiration for Rau had turned into love and she could not bear his absence for even a moment. She had heard of the mahal being constructed for her, but somehow had not been able to imagine the moment when she would actually move there. Bajirao's words now were music to her ears and her heart sang in happiness, but the words that came out of her mouth were different.

She said, 'I am a Musalmaan woman and a lowly dancer. Has Rau thought of the consequences of bringing me into his Brahman household?'

'I don't need to take permission from anyone for what I want to do. I should have asked you to move there long back.'

Mastani clapped once and Basanti came in with a tray laden with delicacies. Shamsher followed Basanti, wearing an embroidered cap and silk kurta and pyjamas. He was nearly three years old now.

Bajirao looked at the young boy with admiration. The black spot of kohl on his cheek, as a mark to ward off evil, added to his charm. Mastani patted his cheeks affectionately saying, 'Will you not give salaam to your Abbajaan?'

Basanti, standing in a corner, said a little loudly, 'Baiji, hasn't the Panditji told you not to use these words.'

Mastani, taken aback by Basanti's reprimand, recovered in a moment and said, 'I had forgotten. Beta Shamsher, won't you do namaskar to your father?'

Bajirao picked up Shamsher and put him on his lap. Giving him a cashew nut, he asked, 'I am seeing you after a long time. Did you forget me?'

'I did not see Rau Swami but Masaheb talked about you every day.'

Bajirao kissed his cheeks a few times. 'Would you like to stay in the haveli?'

'Yes, I would. But can I get Chanda Jamdar along to play with?'

'Chhee! We don't play with servants. You will have Raghunath and Janardhan Pant to play with. What do you say?'

Shamsher merely nodded his head.

Bajirao spent another hour at the mansion.

It was late in the night when Mastani's palanquin moved towards Shanivar wada.

At the north gate, the palanquin stopped. Four servants and a few clerks from Bajirao's office were present to receive them. Bajirao was informed of her arrival as soon as her palanquin reached her mahal.

FOUR

There were victories all over. The contingent at Vasai had finally managed to end the firangi domination on the western coast. The arrival of Nadir Shah had sounded a death knell for the Mughal empire and, for the first time, the Mughals appealed to the Marathas for help. Bajirao sent his men up to the Narmada in response but, by the time they reached the banks of the river, they were told that Nadir Shah had retreated to Lahore. The Nizam of Bhopal managed to extend his rule by crafting a treaty of friendship. The Marathas had literally no enemies now across all of Hindustan.

With the peaceful reign in the subcontinent in the background, Bajirao reached Satara along with Mastani to pay his respects to the Chhatrapati.

The next day, Shrimant Peshwa was invited to the durbar. The whole town of Satara, the seat of the Maratha empire, was out on the streets to have a glimpse of the Peshwa.

The durbar was in full attendance with all the senior officials and ministers present.

Trumpets and horns announced the arrival of the Chhatrapati who followed the staff bearer and the mace bearers. Those in the durbar bent low in mujra and waited for the Chhatrapati to take his seat before taking theirs. Addressing the durbar, the Chhatrapati said, 'It was twenty years ago that I had bestowed the responsibility of Peshwa on a young inexperienced man, much against the wishes of many of my senior ministers and advisers. Today that man has proved his mettle by getting the Mughal empire to its knees and removing the threat of the firangis from Hindustan. My grandfather's dream of Hindavi Swaraj has been fulfilled by him. I am deeply satisfied. The battle cry of Shrimant Bajirao Peshwa has reached its zenith today. It is my pleasure to honour him.'

The Chhatrapati paused for a moment to look at those present. As expected, not all seemed excited. The minister responsible for foreign affairs stood up and said, 'There is no doubt the Peshwa's exploits have expanded the borders of the empire. But in the process, we must remember that he has also managed to create a lot of enemies, Maharaj.'

The Chhatrapati was not happy hearing the minister's comment and said, 'It is obvious that if we run an empire, we would have to face enemies too. After all, you all have your jobs only because we have such problems.'

Bajirao stood up and said, 'If Maharaj permits, I would like to say a few words.'

'Please go ahead. I would love to hear your views.'

'I heard the minister refer to our enemies and I agree with him. The difference is I do not go and meet them.'

'I don't understand what you are hinting at.'

'I have been told by my enemies that there are certain eminent members of the durbar who are in regular touch with them. Greed for money and power can make one do anything. Now that our enemy cannot lure our men, we are safe.'

The assembly was stunned into silence. It was a direct attack on some of those present in the durbar. Bajirao's blunt stance had ensured that no one would speak against him. The minister desperately tried to continue his argument saying, 'If the Peshwa doubts anyone, he may please inform the Chhatrapati. I am sure Maharaj will take the necessary steps.'

The Maharaj was upset that the atmosphere of celebration, the purpose for which the durbar had been called, was being vitiated with accusations and counter-accusations. He said, 'This is not the time to discuss all this. We are assembled here to felicitate Bajirao and his brother, Chimaji Appa, for having freed all of Hindustan from the clutches of the Mughal empire. Isn't that so?'

He looked at the minister who was forced to say, 'Yes, it is, Maharaj.'

'Then let us begin the ceremony.'

On cue, a servant came in carrying a silver tray with royal clothes, a diamond necklace and five pearls, each the size of a marble. Bajirao accepted by touching the tray reverently to his forehead. His manservant, standing nearby, took the tray away.

Addressing the durbar, Chhatrapati Shahu said, 'I hope the durbar is convinced that the belief I had reposed in the Peshwa has been fully justified. Bajirao has worked diligently and with utmost sincerity. We have felicitated him as per protocol but I wish to do more. I command that the Peshwa ask for whatever he wishes and it shall be granted. Let the durbar be a witness to it.'

Another senior minister stood up and said, 'This is not the protocol followed in the durbar.'

'Why do you say that?'

'The elder Maharaj had set some rules which we follow. It is not as per protocol to make such an open-ended offer.'

Shahu Maharaj replied bluntly, 'I will ask for your advice when I need it. I don't need to follow protocol when I am dealing with Shrimant Peshwa.'

Turning to Bajirao, he said, 'Ask! Please ask without any hesitation.'

Bajirao stood up and bending once in mujra said, 'This servant of yours does not deserve the kind of honour I have received. I don't want anything else.'

'I know you will not ask, yet I am repeating what I said: ask what you want and it shall be granted.'

The durbar was silent. Everyone waited with bated breath to hear what Bajirao would ask for. Bajirao went to the servant standing behind the throne holding the Chhatrapati's sandals. Taking the sandals in his hands, he said, 'It will be my honour if these sandals remain with me and that I continue to be your loyal servant. I wish the Maharaj blesses me that I continue to be of help and that I can offer my services with the same devotion and commitment.'

There was an audible gasp as the durbar breathed in relief. Many had expected Bajirao to ask for something impossible. The Chhatrapati smiled and said, 'Is that all? Let me ask you something then.'

'Please command,' Bajirao replied.

'I intend to go for shikar near the Jarandi hills. I have heard of you making the Mughals bite dust. I would like to see how you do the same to a tiger!'

'It would be my pleasure,' a beaming Bajirao said.

The durbar was dismissed.

As soon as Bajirao left the main durbar hall, a khoja from the zenankhana came running and said, 'Virubai Ranisahiba wishes to see Shrimant.'

As he walked up the steps leading to the queens' quarters and entered the large hall, he heard the words, 'Was the Peshwa planning to leave without meeting me?'

'I would have met Rani sahiba earlier, but the events were such that there was no time. I was planning to meet Rani sahiba once I was a little free.'

'I hope the durbar honoured you to your satisfaction.'

'The Maharaj has personally honoured me. What more can I wish for.'

'I wish to call your wife to the royal palace and honour her too.'

'But...' Bajirao began when he was interrupted.

'I will not listen to any excuses. Please send your wife to the palace. I would like to honour her suitably.'

For a moment, Bajirao was silent. He was in a dilemma. He could not tell the queen that it was Mastani who was accompanying him, and not Kashibai. He said, 'Is there such a need? We have received much more than we expected.'

'Let me be the judge of that,' Virubai persisted.

Bajirao stood up and took his leave. Virubai had put him in a spot and he had to find a way to avoid the embarrassment.

Bajirao and the Maharaj returned to Satara after their hunting expedition, spending nearly a week in the forest.

Bajirao discovered that he was faced with a difficult situation on his return. On Virubai's insistence, Bajirao had sent Mastani to present herself to both the queens. Realizing that the lady who had arrived in the palanquin was a mistress and not the Peshwa's wife, the queens were enraged and had made their displeasure evident. As expected, they refused to meet her and asked the palanquin bearers to return. The matter was already a subject of gossip in the royal palace.

At the same time, two of Bajirao's moneylenders, Joshi and Angal, were in Satara. They came to meet Bajirao and broached the topic as soon as they settled down. Bajirao, already irritated with the gossip going around, was further annoyed finding the same being discussed by the two.

Waving his hand in the air, with the diamonds on his rings glinting in the light of the lamps, Angal commented, 'I feel you should not have resorted to this.'

'Resorted to what?' Bajirao asked, his temper rising.

'It was Shrimant's wife who had been invited to the royal palace. If she was not present, you could have excused yourself stating your inability to fulfil their wish rather than sending a mistress in her place. It is quite natural for the queens to get upset.'

Bajirao erupted, 'I don't understand the reason for getting so upset. Others may consider Mastani as my mistress, but to me she is no less than a wife.'

The moneylenders had come to meet Bajirao on the insistence of Shahu Maharaj. They said, 'Shrimant, how can one consider a mistress a wife?'

'Why? What does she lack?'

'We cannot comment on her abilities, but society at large considers someone a wife only when there is a legal marriage as per religious protocol and when the waters from the Ganga, Saraswati, Yamuna and Sindhu are sprinkled to sanctify the union. You cannot simply start calling someone your wife!'

Bajirao, listening patiently till then, was enraged on hearing the reference to religious rites. He said, 'What an irony that you talk of the rivers which were under Mughal rule till I, putting my life at stake, rode across them on my horse. I don't need your lectures about the greatness of these rivers. If sprinkling the waters of these rivers can sanctify a relationship then words spoken by me, whose actions have released these rivers from their bonds of slavery, should also suffice. I have tolerated a lot of insults but the time has come to stop this. Yes, Mastani is a dancer and a singer. But I have given her the same status as that of a wife. I am not going to allow anyone to insult her by quoting religious rites.'

The moneylenders were taken aback hearing Bajirao's stinging retort. His face was red with anger and they thought it wise not to incense him further. Angal, despite his reservations, tried using a different tactic. 'Shrimant, you have been personally felicitated by the Maharaj for having defeated the Delhi Badshah as well as the firangis in Konkan. We wish that such a small incident should not be the reason for the Maharaj to get upset.'

'What do you mean by a small incident? Insulting Mastani is not a small thing. And you need not act as a mediator to resolve these issues. If I was felicitated it was because of my exploits, and they were well deserving of a grand reception. But that does not give anyone the liberty to insult Mastani. Please convey my regards to Shahu Maharaj and inform him that the Peshwa is leaving for Pune tomorrow morning. We don't believe in staying even for a day more in a place where Mastani gets insulted.'

Joshi tried, 'But Shrimant...'

Bajirao snapped, cutting him short. 'Enough! I don't want to hear a word more. It's decided. When the sun rises tomorrow morning, Bajirao Peshwa's horse would have crossed the borders of Satara. Now please leave. You are dismissed.'

Bajirao reached Pune without any notice. But before his arrival, the news of how Bajirao had sent Mastani to meet the queen and the way her palanquin was asked to return was the talk of the town. It was gossip which got more attention than the felicitation which Bajirao received at the court of Shahu Maharaj.

The month of June had begun and the first showers had drenched Pune when the news of Chimaji Appa's return to Pune after a victorious campaign at Vasai came in. The city and its residents forgot gossipmongering for a while as they busied themselves in welcoming their hero. The Marathas had been waging a war against the Portuguese for nearly five years and had lost more than twenty-two thousand men. Chimaji Appa's decisive victory gladdened everyone's heart. The whole city went to the sangam of the Mula and Mutha rivers to receive Appa.

Bajirao rode on his horse along with Chiranjeev Nanasaheb to welcome his brother. Appa arrived with his troops while the elephants and horses, acquired as loot in the battle, formed a separate contingent. He had carried with him huge bells from the churches, a reminder and souvenir of the battle won against the Portuguese. The church bells, reminiscent of Portuguese domination for nearly two centuries, had been silenced forever.

Trumpets and horns announced the arrival of the victorious warriors. Bajirao was surprised that Appa was not on horseback but in a palanquin. As soon as the bearers put the palanquin on the ground, one of the scribes stepped forward and said, 'Appa was not feeling well, hence he chose to sit in the palanquin.'

Bajirao gently pulled the curtains aside to find Appa sitting with his eyes closed. He seemed frail, resting against a pillow. He opened his eyes with an effort and said, a weak smile on his lips, 'Why did you take the trouble to receive me here? I was on my way in any case.'

Bajirao squeezed Appa's hand affectionately. 'Appa, the kind of victory you have won deserves a welcome where if all men were to lie down on the ground to make a path for you, it would not be enough! But Appa, the victory comes at the cost of your health! That is not right.'

'It is just the usual cough and cold, nothing to worry about,' Appa waved his hand, trying to dismiss the issue.

Bajirao patted Appa's hand as he looked at his brother's frail body. Appa's eyes had sunk deep in their sockets. His face looked wan and his breathing was uneven and shallow. Without saying anything, Bajirao stood up and ordered the men to carry the palanquin to the haveli immediately.

The palanquin entered the city preceded by a lot of fanfare as the citizens welcomed their heroes. After a traditional welcome at the gates of the haveli, they finally entered the wada.

For nearly eight days, the only topic of discussion on everyone's lips was of the victory Appa had managed to get for the Marathas. The huge bells were hung in the courtyard of the haveli for everyone to look at. Later, they were shifted to the temples at Theur, Jejuri and Nashik. One of the bells was gifted to Krishnarao Chaskar, another was demanded by Kashibai, while Joshi was handed one to be hung in the Someshwar temple at Chas.

After a week, Appa's health seemed to be improving. One day, Nana visited him and after some small talk said, 'Kaka, Rau Swami's behaviour is getting increasingly uninhibited. I am sure you would have heard of what happened in Satara?'

Appa said, 'I did. I am at a loss to figure out how to make him get over this habit of his.'

'Kaka, if you give up, what will we do? All my efforts to remain in the Chhatrapati's good books were reduced to dust with that one episode of Rau's. He does not bother to think of the kind of damage his actions result in.'

Appa let out a deep sigh saying, 'I don't know what is in store for us. On the one hand, the trumpets celebrate my victory at Vasai and, on the other, we are put to shame by Rau's behaviour. I wonder how many such Vasais we have to win to compensate for what Rau does. Nana, we cannot win every battle and we have to accept that we are going to lose some.'

Seeing Appa lose hope, Nana wondered what he should do next. He was in a dilemma. He could not sit and watch helplessly yet he did not know what he could do!

He said, 'Ever since my mother has heard of the incident at Satara, she has not stopped crying. Rau did not bother to think of how his actions would hurt her.'

Appa said, 'There is a saying in Sanskrit – *Kamaturanam na bhayam na lajja* – meaning that an individual beside himself with lust has neither fear nor a sense of shame. I had never imagined that I would actually see a live demonstration of the phrase in my own house!'

Nana was rattled. He said, 'Kaka, please don't utter such words. If you give up, I will lose all hope. It is only you who can convince Rau Swami. Please find an opportune moment at the earliest and speak to him.'

Appa nodded. 'I had been hoping that Rau would realize on his own, but now I will have to intervene as he probably does not realize the damage he is causing to himself and to others.'

For a long time, Appa and his nephew were silent. Appa's happiness at the conquest he had achieved tasted like mud when he thought of his brother's behaviour. Bajirao, on the other hand, was in his own world with victory kissing his feet. The whole of Hindustan was scared to utter his name and, in such a condition, it was impossible for anyone to point fingers at him, least of all his brother.

Appa said after some time, 'I will surely talk to Rau. But I suggest you try and speak to Mastani too.'

Nana asked, 'Why do you say that?'

'I am told you both know each other well now.'

'Well, it is true that I met her once when on the campaign to Delhi. Now that she is staying at the wada, I did meet her a few times in the garden. But what exactly do you want me to speak to her about?'

'Give her whatever she wants in lieu of leaving Rau. Find out what she desires. Meanwhile, I shall try to dissuade Rau and keep him away from her.'

Nana could not understand what Appa meant when he asked him to agree to whatever she desired. He wondered whether Appa knew more than what he had revealed.

Two days later, Appa and Bajirao sat conferring alone, discussing various topics. Appa could not mask his desperation and blurted out, 'Rau, the victory which we have achieved is being marred by a single blot.'

'What are you referring to?' Bajirao asked, knowing very well what Appa was alluding to.

'Mastani.'

'What about her?'

'Rau, despite objection from each one of us, you have had your way in getting her into the haveli. You know how much that has hurt everyone.'

'I know.'

'Yet it surprises me that you don't want to leave her.'

'Are you suggesting I sacrifice her?'

'Would you?'

'The day my heart stops beating in my chest I would have sacrificed her!'

It was late in the night. The lamps burning in the hall flickered with a sudden gust of wind. Appa said, 'Rau, please don't speak ill at this late hour.'

'What can be a bigger ill omen than the talk of discarding Mastani,' Bajirao said, keeping his cool. He did not show any rancour as he said, 'Appa what surprises me is that you celebrate when I make the Nizam come to his knees or when the Delhi Badshah is shown his place. The entire state rejoices in my victories and everyone, from Rajarshi Maharaj to the common solider, is out on the streets celebrating. Yet when I indulge in a private pleasure, something which soothes my soul, you take objection to it.'

'Rau Swami is interpreting it wrongly,' Appa tried.

'Wrongly? May I understand what you mean?'

'No one would have an iota of objection if you were to indulge in personal enjoyment elsewhere, but despite vociferous objections from Matushree, Vahinisaheb and your sons, you got a mahal made for Mastani right here in the haveli. An intrusion from someone like her has despoiled the purity of the haveli. This place has become a living hell, Rau! Don't you give any weightage to our emotions and values?'

'I had kept her away from all of you as I respected your sentiments, but now she is a part of me – someone who I cannot live without!'

Appa erupted, 'I don't understand, Rau! The tradition of a dancer or a singer being kept as a mistress or a concubine is generations old. But your ways are different! You don't seem to differentiate between an inner wear from what is worn for occasions.'

Bajirao was surprised to hear Appa speak so bluntly. He had never seen him so agitated. Bajirao knew his brother – he may have a weak constitution, but his will was strong. He said, without raising his voice, 'It is irrelevant how many mistresses others have had. There is one and only one for Bajirao.'

'I don't get you,' Appa said.

'It is not easy being Bajirao. Others may have had mistresses but they are not Bajirao.'

'I don't know what you are saying. I am neither Bajirao nor do I have a mistress.'

'Appa, let me clarify. I am in love with Mastani and it is a fact that she will continue to stay with me. How should I demonstrate that before you can believe me?'

Appa could sense a desperation in Bajirao's voice. He was silent for a while before he said, 'Rau, would you at least do one thing for me?'

'Tell me,' Bajirao said, nodding his head.

'If you wish that I live for a little longer, would you…'

'Appa! What kind of comment is this? Would I not want you to live for long?'

'Then promise me one thing! Will you promise not to visit Mastani during this holy period of four months till October?'

Bajirao was silent and avoided meeting Appa's questioning gaze. Seeing him silent, Appa asked, 'Does your silence mean you don't agree? Can Rau not do this for his brother?'

Bajirao let out a deep sigh and said, 'I have been doing things for others. I have never asked others to do anything for me. Appa, tell me clearly: what is it that you really want?'

'I want you to leave Mastani forever, Rau!'

'That is impossible!'

'At least, to satisfy the conservative Brahman community of Pune, ask Mastani to not meet you for these four months?'

Bajirao relented and said, 'Well, if you so insist, I give you my word. I shall not meet her till the holy period is over. Does that satisfy you?'

Appa had managed a small yet important victory. He said, 'Yes, it does – for the time being!'

Kashibai's leg pain, despite relentless efforts by the physicians and trying all kinds of remedies including tying sacred threads from various temples, had not eased. Yet, she never missed her morning prayers at the tulsi plant for it gave her immense mental peace.

She was busy with her prayers when she noticed that the chief priest, Krishna Bhat, was absent. This had not happened before. She asked Yesu, 'I don't see Krishna Bhat today. Where is he?'

Yesu returned after a while and said, 'I searched but he is nowhere to be found.'

Kashibai went to her quarters and changed into her regular clothes. As she put on her jewellery, she looked at Yesu standing near her, fidgeting a little. She asked, 'Do you want to say something?'

'I am not sure how to put it, Baisaheb,' Yesu said hesitatingly. 'I think I know the reason for Krishna Bhat's absence.'

'And that is...?'

'I am told,' Yesu began, aware that she was treading on eggshells, 'that Krishna Bhat has vowed never to enter the haveli till it is purified. Do you understand what I am referring to?'

'Yes, I do,' Kashibai said, letting out a deep sigh. Suddenly the jewellery she was adorning herself with seemed to have lost its sheen. She said, putting a necklace back into its box, 'Yesu, would you do one thing for me?'

'Yes, Baisaheb.'

'Can you arrange for me to meet Mastani?'

'What are you saying, Baisaheb? Why would you want to meet a mere courtesan?'

'She may have been one, but I want to see the face of the woman who has besotted Shrimant to the extent that he does not see anything else in this world.'

'Chhee, chhee! I cannot ask her to meet you. If Shrimant hears of this, I will be doomed.'

'Fine then. Will you ask Nana to come to me?'

Soon Nanasaheb entered Kashibai's quarters. She said, as he sat down, 'Nana, I want your help.'

He looked at her questioningly while she continued, 'Nana, I would like to see Mastani once.'

'Mastani?'

'Yes. I would like to meet her.'

Nana was silent for a while. He said, without looking at his mother, 'It is impossible, Matushree.'

'Why do you say that?'

'Well, her mahal opens into Rau's quarters. No one else can go in there.'

He continued after pausing for a while, 'I have an idea though. Soon there will be the celebrations for Janmashtami. I am told she dances only during these celebrations. Rau Swami has promised Appa that he will not visit Mastani for these four months of Chaturmas. I will take you to her mahal on Janmashtami. But Matushree, may I warn you that you are unnecessarily stressing yourself. Can you not avoid this?'

'Nana, you are far too young to understand this yet,' Kashibai said. 'It is not easy to fathom a woman's mind. For twenty years, I have stayed with my swami like his shadow. I never realized when and how someone else occupied his heart and started ruling it. I know that she has ensnared him with her beauty and I am curious to see the river which has flooded his heart. I would like to see her for myself.'

'Matushree, how does it help you?'

'It is not about that, Nana! I may have lost the battle, but at least I will know who defeated me! That is all I wish.'

'I will try my best, Matushree. After all, whether we win or lose is in the hands of the Lord.'

There was only one door to enter Mastani's quarters and that was through Bajirao's private chambers. No one other than the Peshwa was allowed to use that door. The other door, on the outside periphery, was towards the riverbank and was guarded.

Anyone trying to enter through that gate would have to face the guards first.

In the morning, when the doors leading to the Peshwa's quarters were opened, two young boys entered her mahal. Mastani had been sitting in the garden with Shamsher, enjoying the cool breeze coming through the fountains. The two young boys were the Peshwa's younger sons – Raghunath Pant, five years old, and his younger brother, Janardhan Pant.

Wearing a simple white kurta and a pair of silk pyjamas, Raghunath, holding his brother's hand, looked at Mastani as she walked in, having been informed by Basanti of their arrival. Mastani asked, surprised to see them there, 'How did you come in? Where are the servants?'

'We got in without their knowledge. Else, they would not have allowed us.'

Mastani asked, 'And what if they come to know?'

'Who would come to know?'

'Your father!'

'Oh! He would just ask us not to do it again.'

Mastani smiled and asked, 'Then what are you here for?'

'We were told there is a hall of mirrors here and we wanted to see that.'

'I will show you. By the way, do you know him?' she asked, pointing at Shamsher.

Raghunath shook his head. Mastani said, 'He is your brother.'

'No! Our elder brother is Nana Swami.'

Mastani laughed saying, 'That is true. But he too is your brother.'

'I have never heard of him,' Raghunath said, his hand on his waist. 'What is his name?'

'I am Shamsher Bahadur,' Shamsher answered without waiting for Mastani.

'I see! You are Mastani's son,' Raghunath replied.

'Please speak with courtesy,' Shamsher shouted.

Mastani intervened saying, 'Don't get upset, Shamsher. They are your brothers. Won't you show them around?'

'Let them first address you as Mastani Masahiba.'

'Oh!' Raghunath said, raising his eyebrows questioningly, 'is she Mastani Masahiba?'

Shamsher smiled. He said, 'Yes. Now, let me show you around. Do you see the hall there? It has fountains on all sides and is very cool even during the hot months.'

After they had a tour of the mahal, they sat down on comfortable carpets in the main hall. Janardhan said, picking up a piece of sweetmeat from the tray which Basanti offered, 'Wah! Your mahal is really nice. It is better than ours, in fact.'

Mastani looked at him lovingly and said, 'You liked it, it seems!'

'Yes! We will come here every day to play.'

'What about the guards?'

'We can manage to slip in without their knowledge.'

They were busy chatting when Nana entered and asked, 'So what are you eating here?'

Raghunath dropped the piece of sweetmeat he was eating and stood up, wiping his hands on his pyjamas saying, 'Nothing! We were not eating anything.'

'Now don't lie to me. Is that an example for you to set for your younger brother here? Tell me the truth.'

Raghunath shook his head and persisted, 'No! I didn't eat anything.'

'Show me your hands!'

'I was just taking a look,' Raghunath tried desperately.

Mastani intervened, 'Nana, what is wrong if the children eat sweets?'

'What do you mean? It would be a topic of discussion in the entire haveli.'

'It is just a piece of sweet. It is not meat,' Mastani said.

'I agree. But you can't stop people from saying all kinds of things.'

'Let them! I will send the children back now. If Rau objects, I will handle it.'

Basanti took the two away. Nana sat down on a swing and gave it a slight push. The silver bells hung on the chains tinkled softly. Mastani looked at Nana who seemed a little nervous. She said, 'Nana, you don't visit me these days. Are you upset about anything?'

'No, no! There is no reason for me to be upset.'

'Then why is it that I haven't seen you for so long?'

'I have been quite occupied with all the work at the office.'

'What brings you here today?'

'Nothing, really. I just remembered that it will be the day of Janmashtami soon.'

'I know. Rau does not allow me to dance any more but on that day, at least, I can.'

'But no one other than Rau watches you, isn't it? Will he allow me?'

'You need to ask your father. I will be happy if you can come.'

Nana fidgeted, looking around for a while. He did not know how to broach the topic. He said, 'My Matushree wants to meet you.'

Mastani said, 'It is my honour if Kashibai sahiba wants to

meet me. I had admired the temple she had built on the banks of the Narmada. But I have been shunned by the people here. Would I get permission to visit her quarters?'

Nana said, 'That may be difficult.'

'Then how do I meet her? She will not come here and I cannot go there!'

'She can see you during the Janmashtami celebrations.'

'That is a good idea,' Mastani said. 'I will be glad if she comes. Please convey my regards to her and let her rest assured that the place will be made ready by the Brahmans. A wall separates the two of us. We are so close, yet so far!'

'Please let Shrimant know of it,' Mastani added.

'That may not be required. Shrimant may not come here for some time now.'

'Why do you say that?' Mastani asked, surprised at Nana's comment.

'I don't know the reason, but I am told so.'

Mastani's face fell and her eyes were teary. She said, 'I have been observing you since you came in, Nana. You know something, yet you don't want to tell me. Now you are saying that Rau won't visit me here. I don't know why you are torturing me so.'

Nana left without replying.

It was quite obvious that the path would clear itself.

In an emotional moment, Bajirao had given his word to Appa that he would not visit Mastani for four months, but by the end of four days, he was desperate. He had, in the last three days, gone to the door a few times and returned, eager to see Mastani yet troubled by the promise he had made to his brother.

The clerk from his personal staff presented some papers which had the details of the celebrations planned for the Janmashtami festival. Seeing that, Bajirao ordered, 'Please ensure that Mastani's dance is planned as part of the celebrations.'

The clerk was surprised hearing Bajirao's orders, but did not have the courage to question. Bajirao felt good that he had found a way to see her.

On the day of Janmashtami, all preparations were done as per the plan. A vetiver screen was set up behind which Kashibai sat. Her leg pain had been troubling her again and she wondered whether she would be able to sit for two hours to watch the performance. But the sheer desire to see Mastani's face, at least once, made her bear the pain. The bhajans were over and soon Mastani arrived, her anklets tinkling as she walked down the hall. Her presence lit up the place.

Mastani bent thrice in a low mujra. She glanced in the direction of the screen casually and touched her palm to her forehead in salaam. Then, turning to the idol of Lord Krishna, she began her dance.

The performance lasted for more than two hours. Kashibai, watching Mastani and her radiant beauty from behind the screen, felt a pang of jealousy stab her heart. Sitting there alone, she felt suffocated and yearned for fresh air.

Mastani's dance had mesmerized everyone. Her graceful turns, her svelte figure, her elegance and her charm were stunning.

At the end of the performance, she saluted once before standing in a corner. Bajirao stood up and walked away without saying a word, followed by Nana. Eager to speak to Kashibai, Mastani rushed to the screen. Pushing it aside, she said, 'I hope Baisahiba liked...'

There was no one behind the screen. A few pods of cardamom lay on the cushions. Mastani's radiant face turned pale. She turned towards the hall in a pensive mood and sat down at the feet of Krishna's idol.

It was past midnight but sleep eluded Bajirao. He turned on his side, hearing the gong strike the hour. He had not slept a wink. It had been eight days since his meeting with Appa. He had not seen Mastani for eight days now, nor had he spoken to her. Their eyes had met, but their lips were parched.

It was raining outside. Despite it being late August, the monsoon had not ended. Getting up from his bed, Bajirao wrapped a shawl around himself. He glanced at the long-necked pitcher kept in a corner and, after a moment, filled a tumbler, gulping down the wine in one go. The guard outside, hearing the sound of his movement, came in and asked, 'If Shrimant wishes to have something, I may get it.'

Bajirao waved his hand dismissively. He walked around his room lost in thought and, without realizing, reached the door leading to Mastani's quarters. A thin silk curtain hung on the door. Pushing the curtain aside, he opened the door and stepped into her mahal.

In the dead silence of the night, the creaking door sounded harsh. Bajirao, barefoot and without his turban, walked in the darkness to reach the courtyard leading to the private quarters.

Subrao Jethi, the personal attendant of Mastani, stood guard at the courtyard. He stood up hurriedly hearing the noise and picked up a burning mashaal. Surprised to find the Peshwa, he saluted quickly before asking, 'Shall I inform Mastanibai sahiba?'

'Is she awake?' Bajirao asked.

'Ji.'

'How do you know that?'

'She asked me a few times to bring you here, but I was worried as Shrimant had strictly informed me that he was not to be disturbed.'

'Where is she?' Bajirao asked and then, without waiting for him to answer, said, 'No, wait! I will go in myself.'

Subrao stood in Bajirao's way, shivering but trying his best to hold Bajirao back. Bajirao asked, 'What is the matter, Subrao?'

He said, 'She has been crying her heart out ever since the dance got over. Let me inform her so that she may have the time to make up her face before she receives you.'

Brushing Subrao aside with his hand, Bajirao rushed into her chambers. Mastani was sitting on her bed sobbing softly, still in her dance costume.

Bajirao put his hand lightly on her shoulder. Surprised, she turned to look at him and then without saying a word she hugged him tightly, her sobs increasing in their intensity. Caressing her back affectionately, Bajirao asked, 'Mastani, what is the matter?'

'You ask "what is the matter"? It has been eight days since I have seen you! Today I saw you but you did not speak a word. Rau, I don't want to live like this!' Mastani said in between sobs.

'Don't say such words, Mastani. If there is someone who is truly disgusted with this world, it is Rau.'

Mastani, wiping her tears with the back of her hand, asked, 'Why, what has happened?'

'I have become a headache for everyone around, Mastani.'

'You are everything for me, Rau. Don't say that!'

'Am I supposed to live on this hope?'

'What do you want me to do, Rau? Why is Baisahiba angry with me?'

Bajirao was unaware of Kashibai's reaction and said, 'I have no idea. Why should she be angry with you?'

'I was told that she would be watching me dance. I had hoped to impress her and then speak my heart out to her. But, alas! When I pushed the curtains aside, I was disappointed to find that she had left. She had not bothered to say a word to me. Why does she hate me so much, Rau?'

Mastani's tears flowed freely. Bajirao hugged her and said, 'You are mistaken, Mastani. She is not keeping well these days; you know that. I am quite sure that she could not sit for long and hence had to leave.'

Mastani was silent for a while. She said, 'Rau, you won't understand the language of women. She may not have spoken, but I could read in her eyes the hatred she nurses against me. I have not heard a single word of love or affection here in the last seven–eight years.'

'What are you accusing me of, Mastani?'

'No, I am not talking about you. I am alive only because of you. But Matushree hates me and Appa had asked me to leave Pune forever. The other day, the queens at Satara insulted me and turned me back. Now, Kashibai sahiba comes to see me dance and goes away without saying a word. What am I to deduce from all this, other than sheer hatred! Yes, they all just hate me!'

'Mastani, you have made up your mind. Have you thought about Rau?'

'There is not a single moment in my life when I don't think of you.'

'Then you realize how irrelevant we are for the people you just mentioned, don't you?'

'Yes, I know that; and that is what hurts me, Rau! Maybe, the day I met you at Kothrud gardens was not an auspicious one. Rau, I am taking you away from your near and dear ones. The thought haunts me that I am the one creating the rift. I sometimes wonder what exactly have I given you – is it just my body? You can have many more desirable bodies at the snap of a finger. Rau's is a name well regarded all over Hindustan, yet your family is willing to desert you. Rau, I gave you my heart but not to give you more troubles.'

Mastani's sobs were uncontrollable now. Bajirao held her hand. Then he gently brushed aside her hair from her face and said, 'What is the point in recalling the past? There is always divine intervention when two people meet and fall in love. I strongly believe in it. These eight days felt like eight years to me. You are so much a part of me, Mastani!'

'I was told that Appa had asked you to give him your word. Is that so?'

'Yes!' Bajirao said. 'I fail to understand them. On the one hand, they make me a hero and on the other, they behave like animals the moment they hear your name. I don't understand it.'

Suddenly, Mastani stood up and Bajirao asked, 'What is it?'

Getting up, she brought a pitcher and a pair of tumblers from the next room. Bajirao said, pointing to the pitcher, 'This is better! The wine will give me company all my life.'

Bajirao let out a deep sigh and said, 'You know, Mastani! Till the time I remain drunk, I forget all my pains and troubles. I get deep solace, but the moment I am out of it, they all come screaming back to make my life hell. Fill up my tumbler, Mastani! Let me get drunk.'

Mastani handed him a tumbler filled with wine. Bajirao touched it to her lips before sipping from it. He gulped down a few drinks and soon was inebriated.

It was almost dawn. The rains had stopped a while back.

'Mastani!' Bajirao called.

'What is it, Rau?'

'Come near me!'

Mastani lost herself in Bajirao's embrace. He said, 'My arms have protected you till now, never allowing any evil to touch you. But I have enough sense left in me to know that the future may be different.'

Bajirao's voice trembled. Mastani realized that his hands too were shaking. She said, pressing his palms gently, 'Rau, stay here with me and forget everything else in the world.'

Bajirao said, 'That is what I did so far, Mastani, but it seems the world is not willing to forgive or forget.'

He continued, his voice rising steadily, 'What a pity, Mastani, that Bajirao, who commands a million-plus army, is unable to take his son, Shamsher, openly into the courtyard of his own haveli holding his hand. Nowadays, there is talk of Raghunath Pant's thread ceremony and possible marriage alliances for Sadashiv Pant, but no one seems to be bothered that Rau has another son and he too has grown up. What about his thread ceremony? To avoid such embarrassing questions, Matushree avoids me these days. Appa too finds his health as an excuse to stay as far away as possible. Yes, I admit that Nana gives me company and does not run away. Mastani, I am willing to bear many things but I cannot accept the fact that my own son is treated like a maid's child and has to hide himself from the sight of others. Is that what my prestige commands? Is that what my glory boils down to? My inability to have my own son walk with his shoulders straight, facing the world with pride? Mastani, I wonder what attracted you to this unfortunate Bajirao? Could you not find anyone else? It would have been better for you to have stayed with a shiladar! At the very least, your dignity would not have been compromised.'

Bajirao continued to speak, his voice sounding loud in the predawn silence.

She said, cupping his mouth with her hand, 'Don't say such things, Rau! If you truly love me, just do one thing for me.'

'What do you want me to do?'

'Get me a little poison. I want to escape from this world.'

'Poison?' Bajirao said, his voice rising again. 'Mastani, the kind of ill wishes we get each day are more poisonous than what you can find anywhere! And yet we are alive. Mastani, I don't know why fate is playing this cruel game with you and me. I may be Shrimant Peshwa, but am I not a human being first? Am I not entitled to my emotions? But all I get to hear is the accusation that a Brahman Peshwa has fallen in the bad company of a dancer. They believe that you are the cause of all their troubles. The very people who hail me as Shrimant Peshwa would not hesitate for even a moment to crush me. I could have faced them as Bajirao if not as Peshwa, but I feel I am chained all over. It is only you with whom I can speak my heart out!'

It was getting light. The guards and servants could be heard now.

Mastani said, 'Rau, it will be sunrise soon. You have given your word to Appa. Please don't come back here again and break your promise.'

Bajirao kissed her forehead lovingly and said, 'That will not be possible, Mastani! I may promise anything, but this separation is impossible! Think what you may, but I am not going to stay in my mahal any more. I want to be in your mahal day and night, and if heaven falls because of that then so be it!'

For two days, Bajirao stayed in Mastani's quarters, neither attending office nor showing his face in his haveli. He spent a few hours in the office on the third day before returning to Mastani's mahal.

Appa was deeply hurt when the news of Bajirao's move spread. He had been promised by Rau that he would take care for the next four months and not step into Mastani's mahal. Radhabai too was unable to accept the fact that her elder son was spending all his time with a mere dancer and getting drunk on wine. She felt helpless. Kashibai, on the other hand, already troubled with her leg pain, was bedridden. The only ones who continued to work diligently were Nana and Mahadoba Purandare.

One day, Radhabai held a meeting with her daughters, Bhiubai Baramatkar and Anubai Ghorpade Ichalkaranjikar, in her quarters. Radhabai had also called Appa, Nana and Mahadoba Purandare for the discussion. It was evident that the topic for the same would be Rau. Bhiubai said, 'I had suspected Rau's inclination for such things the day he had sent that Bhikaji to our house.'

Appa and Nana were quiet. Appa was battling his cough and was trying to suppress a fresh bout when Anubai snubbed her sister saying, 'Bhiubai, repeating what the world knows does not show any wisdom.'

'Then what is wise, if I may ask?' Bhiubai asked, her

anger erupting. 'I know Rau is dear to you. You would quite obviously endorse all his indulgences.'

Radhabai, not liking the war of words between the sisters, stepped in. 'Now, will you both stop fighting. We are here to solve a problem, let us put our minds to it. Appa, Anu and Bhiu are here. Abaji Naik is our elder son-in-law's father but he refuses to enter our haveli. When asked, he sent a message saying "We shall not step into a haveli which has been despoiled." Our other son-in-law, Ichalkaranjikar's family has not yet openly protested but I am sure soon they too will. You need to find a way out, Appa.'

Appa was about to speak when another bout of coughing racked his body. Anubai said, 'Appa, I hope you are taking your medicines regularly?'

Appa let out a deep sigh and said, 'Yes, I am; whatever medicines can do, they will. Rest is left to fate!'

Anubai smiled. 'Come on! Don't be so despondent. If my brother had left everything to fate, he would not be the hero of Vasai, chasing away those Portuguese. Isn't that so, Matushree?'

'Anu, what are you blabbering about? It is time to think of the matter at hand.'

'I am not blabbering, but I do wonder why we are breaking our heads over such a trivial matter.'

'Is it a trivial matter, Anutai?' Nana asked.

'What else? Has no one before not kept a dancer as a mistress?'

'Things may be happening elsewhere but if the sanctity of this haveli, the residence of the Peshwa, is threatened, we need to be worried, Anutai! Now it is left in the hands of the Lord to find a way out for us.'

'Why invoke the Lord for it? I will find a way out.'

'What do you mean?'

'I will speak to Rau myself. I have been told that none of us have bothered to speak to him to understand his point of view. All you have done is to point fingers and label him a criminal. I have known him since his childhood. He is a free-spirited man and a romantic. He loves the finer things of life but you all are suffocating him. I will speak to him and see if we can find a way out.'

'He who does not listen to society will listen to you it seems,' Bhiubai taunted.

Appa did not comment but continued to hear his sisters sparring with each other. Radhabai said, 'If Anubai wants to try, let her.'

Nana said, 'Anutai, Rau is in Mastani's quarters all the time. It is not going to be easy for you to meet him.'

Radhabai suddenly said, 'I had asked our family priest to give a suitable date for Raghunath's thread ceremony. I thought I would also find a date for Sadashiv Pant's wedding but, to my surprise, the priest put his hands on his ears and said that no one from Pune was willing to do any such service for the haveli. He added that the Pune Brahmans have boycotted the Peshwa family.'

Appa erupted, 'What do the Brahmans think of themselves? Who are they to boycott the Peshwa?'

Radhabai said, 'Appa, anger will not solve the problem. We need to use wisdom instead of force. I had suggested Onkarji's daughter for Raghunath Pant. Do you know Onkarji's reply?'

She continued, 'He said, "The father has a Musalmaan mistress. Who knows, the next generation might keep four concubines at home. It is better that we push our daughter into a well and let her drown rather than give her to such a family."'

Saying so, Radhabai dabbed her eyes with the edge of her pallu. No one till date had dared to insult the Peshwa and now it was all happening because of the way Rau was conducting himself. She said, 'Appa, look at my fate! I have to hear all this in the last years of my life. How I wish I too had left this world when my swami died. But I did not jump into the sati fire thinking that I should be there to bring up my children. I won't be surprised if, thanks to my eldest son's acts, people spit on our face.'

No one knew how to counter Radhabai's point. They had never expected such a stinging reply from Onkarji. He would not have dared to write such a note had he not had the support of the entire city of Pune. Else, insulting the Peshwa's mother was unthinkable. Radhabai had no choice but to bear it stoically.

For a long time, Nana and Appa conferred with Radhabai. After they left Radhabai's quarters, Appa nodded to Nana to follow him. The two talked well into the night in Appa's quarters.

Soon after Janmashtami, Kashibai was bedridden. Though her leg pain had reduced considerably, she had lost her appetite and had become weak. The news of her illness spread all over prompting the Nizam to send his personal physician, Bharmana, to attend to her. His medicines gave partial relief but did not cure her completely.

Bajirao did not comment much but kept a close eye on things. He visited Kashibai one evening. On seeing him enter,

Kashibai sat up on the bed. Her face was pale and the eyes had lost their shine. Husband and wife were meeting after a long time. Bajirao was depressed seeing Kashibai's weakness. He said, sitting on the bed beside her, 'I hope the medicine given by the Nizam's physician has brought you some relief.'

'Swami can see for himself whether the medicines have made a difference or not.' Bajirao could sense the hurt with which Kashibai uttered the words. He said, 'One should not be so adamant. If you take the medicines regularly, your health is bound to improve.'

Bajirao took Kashibai's frail hand in his and said, rubbing it affectionately, 'I feel bad that I am not able to help you other than provide for the medicines.'

Kashibai did not respond. For a moment, she glanced at the table where a row of medicine bottles were kept. Bajirao said, pointing at one of the bottles, 'Does it not contain the medicine which Bharmana vaidya has given?'

Kashibai nodded her head. Bajirao poured the medicine into a small bowl and brought it near her lips. Kashibai shook her head vigorously saying, 'No, please!'

'Don't you want your health to improve?'

'I am taking the medicines.'

'Why not allow me to? I would feel good.'

'No, please don't!'

'Why do you say that?'

'I have been ordered by Matushree not to partake of anything given by you.'

'Matushree? Did she say that?'

Kashibai had tears in her eyes. She said, 'I have been told that you have despoiled yourself by touching the food served by the Musalmaan dancer.'

Keeping the bowl aside, Bajirao asked, 'Do you believe in all this?'

'It is not about belief. I believe what I see.'

'What have you seen?'

'What is left to see now? I have lost all zeal to fight. How I wish the Lord would take me away!'

'You are referring to Mastani, aren't you, when you say that you have seen it with your own eyes?'

'Yes.'

'Is she really bad?'

'Do you want everyone to praise her just because she is dear to you?'

Kashibai's voice took on an edge. It was the first time she had openly challenged her husband. Bajirao was genuinely concerned. He said, 'Kashi! I know Matushree, my brother, the Maharaj himself – all of them believe whatever others say. Are you too going to do that?'

'I believe what you are doing is not right.'

'Am I doing things which I should not?'

'Yes. What can be worse than having a Musalmaan mistress in the haveli? You spend all your time with her. The Brahmans are upset. I have to listen to their grumblings all the time. Is this what I get for serving my husband with utmost loyalty for twenty years?'

Kashibai's tears flowed freely. Bajirao said, 'You are not well. Such anger will only make your health worse.'

'What's the point of being healthy? My husband left me when I was healthy.'

'Kashi, may I ask you something?'

'You don't have to take permission to do so.'

'Kashi, you have a right to get upset. You know I am in love with Mastani. I can't explain how and why this happened. But you are a woman. If you don't understand another woman, who would?'

Hearing this, Kashibai lost all her restraint. She said, 'What surprises me is your inability to understand the heart of a woman who has stayed with you for twenty years. What is it that I lacked, that made you get a mistress into our house? I have given you three lovely sons. I served Matushree with devotion and followed whatever she asked me to do. I never disobeyed Shrimant's wishes even once. I treat your younger brother like my own. And yet, what do I get? In my father's house…'

At the mention of her father's house, a sob escaped her lips. She said, wiping her tears, 'My body shivers at the thought of what the people back home will be saying. My mother sent me messages thrice regarding her wish to come and see me, and each time I had to write back requesting her to not come. I am ashamed to show my face to her. How I used to roam in my father's village with pride! Three years back, when you were on the campaign to Rajasthan, I had gone to my village. The number of people who had come to pay their respects! Many women had come to tell their stories, some expecting help, some to simply share their woes. I cannot even think of showing my black face there now. Is this what I deserve? Is this what I get? For what crime of mine? Would Swami care to tell?'

In the silence of the room, the words sounded like bullets which pierced Bajirao's heart. He stood with his head bowed. Drained and tired, Kashibai too fell silent.

After a while, Bajirao looked at Kashibai and said, his voice choking, 'Kashi, you have enriched my life for the past twenty years. You never gave me even one chance to complain about anything. I know you obeyed each command of my mother's and looked after my brother as your own. You are truly the jewel in the crown. But you must remember that I have seen the world much more than you, coming in contact with innumerable people every day. I realize that there is hardly any difference between good and bad, right and wrong! Mastani was introduced to me as a dancer and a singer but soon, subconsciously and without any effort from either side, the bonds of love strengthened, tying us forever. By the time I came to my senses, she was an intrinsic part of me. At times, when I am with myself, I do feel that I may be doing things wrongly, but the attraction overpowers me. I am suffocated by my own thoughts and I don't know how to get out of them. I am blamed by everyone but somehow I had this belief that my Kashi would understand me, would not consider me to be wrong. But no! You too blame me, Kashi. Can you not pardon me?'

Saying so, Bajirao put Kashibai's hand on his forehead.

For a few moments, Kashibai stared at Bajirao. She had never dared to look into his eyes ever since she had been married. He was her lord, her everything. But today, she was seeing a very different Bajirao, a common man who was begging for forgiveness. In her heart, he was the idol she prayed to each day but here was an ordinary mortal! An intense desire to preserve the image she cherished filled her. She said, 'What is this? I have never seen you so distraught. What kind of language is this? I will bear whatever I have to. You do what you feel is right. I have been with you for twenty years. Am I going to leave you now?'

Bajirao simply looked at Kashibai. He had nothing more to say.

It had become impossible to meet Bajirao in the haveli. Anubai had sent messages but they were unable to fix a meeting for her. Bajirao would go to Mastani's mahal the moment he finished his office work. It was as if he had nothing to do with the rest of the haveli. His world revolved around Mastani and Shamsher Bahadur.

But Anubai was not one to give up so easily. Determined to enter Mastani's quarters, her palanquin landed at the door leading in from the riverfront. The guard quickly sent in a message that the Peshwa's sister, Anubai Ghorpade, was requesting an audience. Anubai was ushered in immediately. As she walked in through the corridors, she could see that the mahal was heavily guarded, with armed guards at each step. She was waiting on a large verandah when Bajirao came and said, 'What brings my dear sister here?'

'What else could I do? The servants are scared to pass on my messages to you. I have to come to the door myself if I have to meet you, isn't it?' Anubai's voice did not carry any ill-feeling as she laughed merrily describing her own frustration at trying to meet Bajirao.

Bajirao joined in her laughter. She was his favourite sister and she could take liberties with him. As Anubai settled herself on the diwan, Bajirao asked, 'So, what is it that you wanted to speak to me about?'

At that moment, Shamsher Bahadur came in running. He stopped on seeing an unfamiliar person in the room and stared at Anubai. Bajirao held his hand saying, 'This is your aunt. Please do namaskar.'

'Oh! Is he that son of yours?' Anubai asked.

'What do you mean by "that son"?'

'Mastani's son, I mean.'

'That is right. We have to get his thread ceremony performed now.'

'Sacred thread ceremony?' Anubai asked, putting her finger to her lips in amazement.

'Why? What is so surprising about it? We will get it done at the same time that we do Raghunath Pant's. Appa's son's marriage is being planned as well. Once all these are done, I can leave for my campaign in peace.'

'Rau, I came here to speak to you about a few things.'

'About Shamsher's thread ceremony?'

'Yes, it does not seem possible, Rau.'

'Why do you say that?'

'The Pune Brahmans have boycotted the Peshwa household. None of the ceremonies are being carried out and we are not even able to get anyone to do the daily puja.'

Bajirao had heard this before. He said, 'All due to my staying in Mastani's mahal, is it?'

'That is right, Rau. Can you not listen to others for once, for a little while?'

'Impossible! Anu, you know me. I don't follow someone else's commands. If anyone challenges me, my response is to accept it.'

Anubai knew her brother's nature, yet was surprised to see the adamance and his blunt admission of the situation. She said, trying to change the topic, 'Your son looks a lot like Nana when he was of this age, doesn't he?'

'Anyway, forget about things here, Anu. Tell me about yourself. How is the horse I gifted you last time?'

'Oh, I enjoy going on long rides. I was teasing my husband the other day that I should be on horseback accompanying him on his campaigns.'

'That suits Mastani, not you.'

'You know Matushree has not smiled for months. Should you not do something about it, Rau?'

Since Anu was Bajirao's favourite sister, he tolerated her more than anyone else. He listened to her without getting upset. He said, 'You and I have been discussing what one should or should not do, but do you realize, you haven't done one thing yet?'

'And that is…?'

'You haven't met Mastani yet!'

Anubai sat upright and said, 'How true! Please call her immediately. I am eager to see her.'

Bajirao clapped once and after a while, Mastani stepped in.

Wearing a richly embroidered sari, the dark maroon colour further accentuating her fair skin, she looked in every sense a royal Maharashtrian lady. Anubai noticed her beautiful chandrahaar necklace and thick silver anklets, and she could not help but admire her lovely figure. The dot of kumkum on her forehead completed the attire.

She bent thrice in the traditional Maharashtrian way. Her pearl bangles tinkled softly as she put her hands together in namaskar. Anubai, mesmerized with her beauty, said, 'Please sit down.'

Mastani did not sit but stood shyly in a corner. Bajirao, having realized the impact of Mastani's appearance on his sister, smiled knowingly. He said, 'Anubai, this is Mastani, the Musalmaan lady we were talking of!'

Bajirao's reference to her being a Musalmaan was a deliberate taunt, which Anubai noticed. She said, 'Enough of that now! You need not go on about it. No one seeing her in such an attire would believe that she is anyone but a royal lady born into a traditional Brahman household. Who would say that she is a dancer?'

'Who else but everyone in this haveli?'

'Rau, I don't need to be told what others say. I too was prejudiced, the way the others are. She may have been born in a Musalmaan household, but she suits you undoubtedly.'

'And to think of you having come here to advise me to leave her, Anubai!'

Mastani, standing till then with her head bowed, said, 'Baisaheb, please punish me if I have wronged. Is it a crime to love someone more than anything else?'

Anubai was surprised to hear a direct question from Mastani. She was impressed at her boldness to proclaim her love without hesitation. She said, 'You made a mistake, Mastani.'

'How is that?'

'You made a mistake of being born in a Musalmaan household. You should have come into this house as a daughter-in-law!'

'Fate is not in our hands, Baisaheb!' Mastani sighed and left, folding her hands in namaskar once again.

Bajirao said, as Mastani exited, 'So, what do you have to say now? You have known me since childhood. Having met Mastani and my son, do you still suggest that I leave her?'

Anubai did not answer immediately, but sighed deeply instead. After a while, she said, 'You know, Rau...'

'What?'

'Had I been a man, I would never have left such a woman!' Anubai admitted.

Having nothing else to say, Anubai sat for a little while and then left.

The festival of Ganesha Chaturthi arrived but no one

seemed excited. The boycott called by the Brahmans continued. Emboldened by the support at large, they assembled at public houses and openly voiced their dissent against the Peshwa's behaviour. The repercussions of the same were felt in Shanivar wada adding to Radhabai's and Appa's torment. Nana felt like a caged animal. A campaign against the Nizam's son, Nasirgunj, was being discussed bringing respite with the change of topic to occupy the minds of everyone. Bajirao would attend the discussions once in a while. Despite the work at hand, a pall of gloom hung over the haveli.

One afternoon, Bajirao went to his private quarters instead of Mastani's mahal as he normally did for his siesta. He was about to lie down on his bed when Kunwar came in and said, 'Subrao Jethi and Chanda Jamdar had an urgent request to meet you.'

'Send them in,' Bajirao said, wondering what the urgency could be.

They came in and said, without preamble, 'We heard that there will be a raid on Mastani's mahal tonight.'

'Raid?' Bajirao asked. 'Who could think of raiding her quarters?'

'We are not sure, but we got to hear of a plan to raid her mahal tonight. The idea seems to be to finish her off.'

'I see!' Bajirao said. 'You may go now.'

That evening Bajirao went to Mastani's mahal and stayed for dinner, as he normally did. Subrao guarded the courtyard outside Mastani's room, a sword tied at his waist. The main door was being guarded heavily. Bajirao personally inspected the guards before retiring for the night.

Bajirao was alert. He believed that anything was possible, but it hurt him to know that such an attack was being planned despite the attackers knowing that he was likely to be present. The desperation to remove Mastani seemed to have crossed its limit. Bajirao turned to see Mastani sleeping peacefully, one hand of hers across his chest.

It was past midnight as the guard struck the gong announcing the hour. Bajirao gently removed Mastani's hand from his chest and paced the floor. His alert ears picked up a scraping sound and he stealthily walked out of the room.

The lamp burning in the verandah outside threw a pale yellow light around. Bajirao noticed that Subrao stood guard, pacing the verandah slowly.

Suddenly, there was a loud clamour indicating a fight at the door. Bajirao coolly walked towards the gate without a weapon in his hand. The moment he reached the door, the matter was clear. One of the guards was on the ground, blood flowing from his chest. The rest of them had been tied to the pillars in the courtyard. One of the attackers came forward, his naked sword dripping with blood and exclaimed, seeing Bajirao, 'Sarkar, is that you?'

Bajirao shouted, slapping his face hard. 'Yes, it is me! Shrimant Bajirao Peshwa, but who are you? And how dare you enter this place and attack?'

'We have been ordered to do this.'

'Who ordered you?'

'I don't have the permission to tell his name.'

At that moment, a whistle blew somewhere outside and the attackers ran out of the gate, vanishing into the inky darkness of the night.

For a long time, Bajirao stood staring into the dark night. Subrao, in the meantime, had untied the guards. He said, 'Shrimant, I shall chase them.'

Bajirao raised his hand saying, 'No, let it be! They will not dare to come again.'

Without saying anything further, he walked back to Mastani's room.

The next day, Bajirao called for his confidant, Bhiku Raut. Bhiku commanded a unit of tall, dark and strong men, all of the Mehtar caste. Bajirao asked him to select twenty such men with their horses to guard Mastani's mahal.

Despite the upcoming festival of Diwali, the haveli continued to wear a forlorn look. The atmosphere was spoilt with suspicion and distrust, while the servants gossiped amongst themselves.

One afternoon, as Bajirao was busy looking into papers at the office, he heard some scuffles at the door.

Four guards were dragging Krishna Bhat, tied in chains, to the Peshwa's office. Krishna Bhat shouted, 'You idiots! How dare you touch me with your despoiled hands, you scum! You will be severely punished for this.'

Bajirao raised his hands to stop the guards and asked, 'What is the matter?'

'We have caught the person behind the attackers, sarkar.'

Bajirao looked at Krishna Bhat in surprise and said, 'Was that you?'

When Krishna Bhat did not answer, Bajirao repeated, 'Krishna Bhat, is this true – you were the one behind the attack?'

'I am a Brahman and I don't indulge in such heinous crimes.'

Bajirao was losing his patience with the play of words. He said, raising his voice, 'I am not saying you did this, but you masterminded the whole plan, didn't you?'

'When the Peshwa crosses all limits, stays with a Musalmaan

all day, drunk, and is not aware of whether it is day or night, the chief priest is forced to take steps to remedy the situation.'

Bajirao's nostrils flared in anger. He said, 'Please directly answer what you are questioned about.'

'Yes! I ordered the attackers. It was unfortunate that we could not reach Mastani.'

'Oh, really? What temerity!' Looking at the guard standing nearby, he said, 'Get my whip from the stables!'

'Shrimant may think twice before taking any such step. The entire city of Pune supports me. If people come to know that the Peswha has assaulted the chief priest, you alone will be answerable for what will follow.'

In the meantime, the servant had returned with a whip. Bajirao, his hand raised in anger, was about to whip Krishna Bhat when he heard, 'What is going on? What is this, Bajirao? Are you planning to whip poor Krishna Bhat?'

'Poor, my foot! If you know what he has done, you will not spare him at all.'

'What has he done?'

'He sent his men to Mastani's mahal with the intention of finishing her off. This Brahman, who claims to read the Vedas all day, did not flinch once before ordering a murder.'

'Is that true?' Radhabai asked, a little surprised. 'Why would he do so?'

'Please ask him.'

'Matushree,' Krishna Bhat said, 'I would suggest you ask your son who is keeping a Musalmaan as a mistress.'

'Oh, so it is about that!' Radhabai exclaimed and then turning towards Bajirao said, 'Rau, such behaviour is quite likely to evoke strong sentiments. It is not surprising that someone took up the cause on behalf of the entire Brahman community.'

Bajirao's hand, raised to whip the offender, came down slowly as he realized the implication of his mother's comments. His tone changed as he said, 'I get it now ... I was sure that Krishna Bhat alone would never have dared to do such a thing. I know on whose assurances he was carrying out the act. Matushree, rather than sending a servant of yours, it would have been better if you had pronounced whatever punishment you wished me to undergo.'

'Rau,' Radhabai said, 'it has been the norm that the guilty be punished. I suggest you accept your guilt and then bear whatever punishment the Brahmans decide for you. That way you will be free of your sins.'

'What crime have I committed, Matushree?'

'Rau, are you still out of your mind?'

Radhabai had raised her voice. It was late in the afternoon and the scribes, sitting in the office, were keenly listening to mother and son. Bajirao, who was the Peshwa and whose word was the law, was being questioned like an ordinary criminal.

Bajirao had never answered his mother back but being insulted in front of the servants was too much for him to bear. He thundered, 'Matushree, I respect you as my mother but that has its place when I visit you in your quarters. I suggest you keep in mind that this is the office of the Peshwa and that I, as Peshwa, decide what can be said here. If someone dares to transgress, I will not be responsible if I am forced to punish the offender.'

Radhabai could not believe her ears. It was as if a bolt of lightning had struck her. She was seeing her son in a new light today. She had seen him as an adamant but innocent child, a war hero preparing to leave for a battle, or as a Peshwa sitting in court, taking harsh and bold decisions, but never had she imagined that the same son would today reprimand and warn his own mother. Her throat went dry and not a word escaped her lips. A slight tremor passed through her body. Mahadoba Purandare, standing close by, held her hand as she walked away with his support.

The festival of Diwali arrived and while Shanivar wada glimmered in the light of the lamps, there was no sign of happiness on anyone's face. It was as if someone had died. On the day of Naraka Chaturdashi, the morning bath ceremony took place as per schedule. The servant, sent to call the Peshwa for the ritual, was informed that Bajirao had taken his bath in Mastani's quarters.

That afternoon, Radhabai sent a message through Kunwar stating, 'Rau may please continue to stay in Mastani's quarters. The daughter-in-law will not be doing the traditional aarti on the day of Padwa.'

Unsure of whether Kunwar would pass on the message verbatim, she ensured that three different messengers reached Bajirao. Chimaji Appa, ignoring his own health, was trying to rack his brains on solving this problem. He would pour his heart out to Nana. The two of them – nephew and uncle – would confer for hours trying to find a way out. But the knot seemed to be getting tighter and more complicated.

Not a single Brahman entered the Peshwa household on the day of Lakshmi puja. Finally, Appa was able to convince Shiv Bhat to perform the puja, luring him with a large donation.

On the day of Pratipada, Bajirao decorated Mastani's mahal. A mild fragrance of *kesar* filled the air. Mastani served Bajirao herself when he sat down for his meal. That evening, she performed the traditional aarti, as Bajirao sat on a low wooden stool watching her holding the tray with the lamps. Mastani, wearing a dark green silk sari, looked like a traditional Maharashtrian royal beauty. Her long tresses were embellished with flowers. A big bindi on her forehead, dangling pearl earrings, pearl necklace, bangles on her wrist – all made her look arresting. The waistband, loosely tied, accentuated her slim yet sensual figure. Bajirao exclaimed, 'Wah! Even the apsaras in heaven would look ordinary in comparison.'

Mastani said, 'Forget the apsaras, tell me whether Rau likes it or not.'

'I shall let you know that later.'

'Why, if I may ask, later?'

'There is a time and place for everything,' Bajirao said, flirting with her.

Shamsher, sitting nearby, asked, seeing his mother with a tray in her hand for the traditional aarti, 'When will you do this to me?'

'Today, the wife performs the aarti for the husband, my son,' Bajirao explained. 'You are not married yet.'

'Then get me married,' Shamsher said.

Bajirao laughed. 'We will, but what is the rush? First, we have to get your sacred thread ceremony done and then we can think of marriage.'

Mastani asked, 'Is it true that none of the Brahmans are willing to perform the puja?'

Mastani's question dampened the festive spirit. Bajirao felt as if the oil lamps had been snuffed out, plunging the room into darkness. He said, 'Why should you be worried? I shall organize the ceremonies.'

Bajirao nodded to Basanti standing nearby, who realizing

they wanted to be left alone, took Shamsher out into the garden.

Turning to Mastani, Bajirao said, 'What would you like to ask me for? Ask!'

Mastani smiled saying, 'If you have anything left, you may give it to me.'

Bajirao laughed out loud. 'I have given you whatever I had, yet I feel it is not enough.'

'Rau has given me a place in his heart, what more can I ask for?'

After a while, Bajirao said, 'Today is the day of Pratipada. I would like to give you everything of mine.'

Taking off his navagraha ring, Bajirao kept it on the tray which Mastani was holding. He said, letting out a deep sigh, 'Mastani, this is all I have. I give this to you today. Now, Bajirao is completely and truly yours.'

Mastani was at a loss for words. The stones in the ring glinted in the light of the lamps. She asked, 'What is this?'

'It is the ring which Kashi had given me as a token of her love.'

'You are handing over that ring to me – to Mastani?'

'Yes! This ring was the final link between me and my wife. I have ended that now!'

'That is not possible. You have legally married Kashibai, with all religious honours. Relationships don't end just because one says so.'

'You don't know, Mastani. Kashibai has closed the doors of her mahal on my face. Now you are my Kashi.'

A shiver of delight passed through Mastani's body. She was aware of the way Kashibai had insulted her on Janmashtami. Yet, she had always maintained her protocol and never said a word against her. On this auspicious day, Bajirao, fed up with Kashi, had accorded Mastani the status of his wife. She was aware that it opened up an extremely dangerous future for her, however tempting. She said, 'Rau, the steps leading to a temple can never become the sanctum sanctorum. Let me be what I am. I don't need anything else.'

Picking up the ring, Bajirao said, 'Mastani! Mastani! Not everyone can be as wise as you are. I wish to bridge the gap which keeps us apart. I can't bear this separation any more. When will this torment end?'

'Such words don't suit Shrimant Bajirao Peshwa. After all, your status...'

'Enough! I am tired of hearing these words. They hold no meaning for me now. If I had had my way, I would have been at the peak of my happiness and not in the deep valleys of sorrow. I get the Delhi durbar to my knees, but have to fight the irascible and arrogant Brahmans in Pune. I captured all of Hindustan, yet I'm not able to make the Chhatrapati happy. I wiped away the enemies from Konkan, but created more of them in the durbar at Satara itself! Anyway, forget the politics. I have handed this ring to you – from now on, you are everything to me!'

The news of events in Pune and Satara had a habit of circulating all over like wildfire. The way Mastani was insulted in Satara, the boycott of the Brahman community, Bajirao's moving into Mastani's quarters – all of these were being discussed across Hindustan. Malhar Rao Holkar at Malwa, Ranoji Shinde at Gwalior, Pilaji at Rajasthan – they also heard and were concerned.

They were Bajirao's bosom friends and without waiting further, they decided to see for themselves. They all landed at Pune and met Appa Swami. For three days, they conferred among each other and finally decided that it was best to confront and confer with Bajirao himself.

The decision to meet was easily taken but the actual meeting seemed difficult. Despite sending messages to Mastani's quarters, there was no response. Finally, Bajirao agreed to meet them for an hour late in the night.

The three of them sat in the hall leading to Mastani's mahal as they waited expectantly for the door to open. As soon as Bajirao entered, the sardars stood up with their palms touching their foreheads in mujra.

Bajirao waved his hand casually and asked them to sit. Bajirao, wearing a simple embroidered dhoti and a silk kurta, stared vacantly at his sardars. It did not take more than a casual glance for Malhar Rao Holkar to realize that Bajirao was intoxicated. He had spent many an evening with him, during campaigns, sharing a pitcher of wine. There had been nights when they had laughed and shared jokes, with their arms around each other, the bonds of friendship eliminating the difference of master and servant. This was the same Bajirao who would spend countless hours and sleepless nights till he had personally attended to all the wounded. Malhar Rao could not forget the image of Bajirao standing with a naked sword in his hand, avenging the treachery of the Dabhades. 'How many memories!' mused Malhar Rao. 'Had anyone bothered to ask what caste or religion these memories belonged to? No one had lost their sleep asking questions like who did he sleep with or what did the Peshwa eat then?'

But the Bajirao standing in the hall was a different one.

Gone was the daunting look which terrified the enemies. Neither was the affectionate hand visible, which had solaced countless wounded in battle. All Malhar Rao could visualize was one hand of Bajirao's holding the dancer's waist and the other one balancing a tumbler of wine. The intoxicated eyes were fixed on Malhar Rao with a strange arrogance.

Malhar Rao said, 'Shrimant, we have come to meet you.'

'I can see that,' Bajirao snapped.

'We were busy consolidating the empire, but when we heard of the events in Pune, we thought we would come and meet you.'

'What empire are you talking of?'

'The Maratha empire, of course! What else, Shrimant?'

'Oh! You mean your empire.'

'Ours? It is everyone's.'

'Maybe! But not mine, for sure.'

'Shrimant, why do you say that? We have all sacrificed to come to this stage.'

'That might be the case. The empire belongs to the Peshwa, not Bajirao. In fact, he is entitled to nothing. Isn't that the case, Ranoji Baba?'

Ranoji sat with his knees folded. He said, rubbing his palms nervously, 'Shrimant, when Ranoji plunged himself into battle, he did not care to ask whether it was the Peshwa or Bajirao who gave the orders. When Jankoji had put his son at the feet of Shrimant, he had said just one thing: "Come what may, but never leave these feet." That was the order my father had given me and I have been loyal to his words to this date. I have served at your feet, Shrimant! I am but an ordinary shiladar who speaks the language of the heart.'

For a moment Bajirao's eyes sparked with emotion. He said, 'Then what are you doing here in Pune – wasting time?'

Ranoji said, 'Shrimant, please don't ignore us. We came all the way when we heard of certain things and were worried about you.'

'What things, Ranoji? That the Brahmans have disowned us? The elephant walks on, Ranoji, let the dogs bark as much as they wish to!'

'Who is talking of the Brahmans, Shrimant? But Appa, Matushree and Chhatrapati Maharaj himself are all hurt. Should we not be worried?' Ranoji appealed.

'You don't have to be worried, Ranoji. If this is what you wanted to talk about, rest assured that I am not concerned. My decision is final.'

Malhar Rao interrupted, 'Shrimant, are we not being adamant about a minor issue?'

'It may be for others, Malhar Rao! But to me, it is a matter of life and death.'

'All they want is that you leave Mastani for a while. Stay away till things settle down. Let time be the healer.'

'Bajirao has not learnt to retreat, Malhar Rao!' Bajirao thundered.

'It is not retreat, Shrimant. This is just being politically right.'

Bajirao said, his voice taking on an edge, 'Malhar Rao, I never expected you to give me such advice. Mastani is alive because she is under my protection. Despite me being with her, there was an attempt to finish her off. Keep in mind that our fates are interlinked from now on. Whatever happens will happen to both of us. I cannot leave an innocent woman in the hands of wolves who are baying for her blood. It is better that I leave this world. That would be far better!'

Pilaji Jadhav sat listening quietly. Sporting a large tilak, a rudraksh necklace and a small curved dagger at his waist, he observed Bajirao while others spoke. His white whiskers quivered with emotion as he taunted, 'Shabbash! Had the elder Nanasaheb been alive, he would have been proud of his son. I feel my teachings in the jungles of Pandavgarh have not gone waste!'

The words were unexpected. Pilaji Jadhav was much older than him, almost a father figure. Bajirao recalled how as a child, when he was being taught the art of handling a sword, Pilaji would say 'Shabbash!' and pat his back whenever he had executed a difficult manoeuvre. Bajirao said, 'Pilaji Kaka, I am glad at least you understand me. Everyone else is clamouring for me to leave Mastani.'

'I too am saying the same,' Pilaji said in a grave voice. 'Shrimant, at times one is forced to listen to others. I suggest Shrimant leave Mastani alone for a while.'

'It is impossible!'

Bajirao had shouted the words without realizing it. For a moment, he had been encouraged by Pilaji's words assuming that he had his support. In his anger, he snubbed him saying, 'Pilaji Kaka, if you too are repeating what others are saying, I am sorry to say I will have to end this conversation now. I will consider it my mistake to have assumed that grey hair was a sign of maturity.'

Malhar Rao was hurt seeing Bajirao insult the elderly sardar. He said, 'Shrimant, Pilaji is like your father. I request you to not snub him.'

Pilaji Rao's voice boomed as he said, 'Bajirao! Listen to me. Don't challenge fate deliberately.'

Ranoji and Malhar Rao were taken aback at Pilaji addressing the Peshwa by his first name. Ranoji was about to stand up when Bajirao said, 'Pilaji Kaka, I am not challenging my fate. I know the end. It is true that you taught me to use the sword, but probably did not teach me to fight. I am willing to take up the challenge. Till date, the protocol of accepting a difficult task was the honour and prerogative of my sardars. I am, today, taking up a challenge, that's all!'

There was silence in the hall. No one had expected the Peshwa to openly take up arms against everyone. They were deeply hurt that their best efforts had had no effect on the Peshwa. In fact, on the contrary, his vanity had now been challenged. Malhar Rao tried again. 'Shrimant, we give you our word: we will not allow anyone to come near Mastani and shall protect her with all our might. Please trust us.'

'Malhar Rao, her life was threatened despite me being in the same mahal. People dared to enter the quarters in my presence and I cannot even imagine her fate if I were to leave her alone. No, that is not possible!'

Pilaji's mind was in turmoil. He had known the Peshwa since he was a boy. Vishwasrao had been his childhood name. Pilaji had often carried young Vishwasrao on his shoulders. His heart was not willing to accept Bajirao's logic. Taking out his dagger and placing it at Bajirao's feet, he said, 'Vishwasrao, Baji! Till date, you have made us proud. We have done whatever you have asked us to do. If our loyalty is going to be rewarded in the manner in which you say, it is better that this old man dies right here. At least I can hope to reach heaven by dying at your feet.'

'Kaka! What are you saying? Please get up!' Bajirao said, pulling his feet back hurriedly. But Pilaji was not one to give up easily. He continued to cling to Bajirao's feet and said, 'Visubhau, I will not leave you till you give me your word.'

'But, Kaka...'

'I don't want to hear anything more,' Pilaji said, tears flowing down his cheeks. 'Why should you be worried when we are promising you Mastani's safety? No one can dare to touch her. Don't you believe us? Appa Swami, Matushree, the Chhatrapati – they are all your well-wishers and will realize sooner than later that they have been too harsh on you. That day, they themselves will bring Mastani with honour to your quarters. This is my word! Please listen to me. I beg you.'

'No, Kaka, this is not possible.'

'Then pick up the dagger and let me die at the hands of my master. What else can I wish for? This old man has shed his blood for the empire, but now he will have the good fortune to shed his blood for his master. I have always said that my head lies at your feet. Cut if off and let it be at your feet now!'

Pilaji Rao started banging his head on Bajirao's feet. His tears flowed freely. Bajirao, unable to bear it any more, gently pulled up Pilaji Rao and hugged him. He said, his voice choked with emotion, 'Kaka, if at all someone has to cut his head off, let it be me. I accept your appeal, Kaka! I am giving a part of my heart to you. I leave the rest to my fate.'

'Do you mean what you say, Bajirao?' Pilaji asked.

'I mean it, Kaka. I say it with all my heart.'

Pilaji's tears continued to flow but his lips parted in a wide smile. He did not say anything further.

That night, Bajirao left Pune on horseback even before sunrise. The horse galloped towards Patas.

Mastani, in her deep and contented sleep, was dreaming of

what she had told Rau that evening: 'I will not allow you to be away from my sight even for a moment.'

Despite the boycott being followed by all the Brahmans, Shiv Bhat had gone ahead and performed the puja at the Shanivar wada. He had had to pay with his life as he was stoned to death by an incensed mob. Appa Swami immediately ordered the city kotwal to catch the perpetrators but the order was ignored. Nana put guards outside Mastani's mahal ensuring that she would not be able to follow Bajirao to Patas. The mahal was being guarded from inside by Bhiku Raut and his men from the sweeper caste, while Nana's men kept vigil outside. Nana's men were placed right up to the courtyard just inside the main gate. Mastani was trapped inside her own house.

Mastani sent word for a meeting with Nana. After delaying for two days, Nana finally came to meet her on the third day. The lamps lit at Diwali were still burning and the mahal looked resplendent but Mastani was sans any jewellery. All she wore was sindoor in her hair, a mangalsutra and a few simple glass bangles. She was praying at the tulsi plant when Nana walked in. Sitting next to him on a small carpet, she said, 'Rau has gone away but I wonder why you are upset with me, Nana. It has been eight days, but you never came in to enquire about me.'

Nana was enamoured. Mastani looked as beautiful as before despite any make-up or jewellery. In fact, the simple attire further enhanced her features. Rau was far away and Nana knew that Mastani was now fully under his control making him confident that she would agree to whatever he wanted. He said, 'I never imagined that you would look so arresting even in such simple attire. No wonder Rau is madly in love with you.'

Mastani looked sharply at Nana. She realized that Nana was trying to flirt with her. It was something she had not expected. A shiver ran through her body as Nana continued, 'You called for me. Did you want to discuss regarding the guards we have put outside?'

'That is right,' Mastani said, looking at him hesitatingly. 'Nana, you have always been fond of me. I wonder what made you take such a harsh step. Please tell me where I have erred for you to take such measures.'

'I am ensuring that nothing unexpected happens.'

'Don't you believe me? Don't you trust me?'

Mastani pleaded, giving Nana a chance to interpret her words to suit his convenience. He said, 'I had tried to meet you earlier too, but I could never find you alone. Now we can be truly alone, the guards outside ensuring that no one disturbs us. We can do whatever we feel like, no one will know.'

Mastani was deeply hurt hearing him. She said, 'Nana, I promise you I will not step out of the mahal without your permission, but please don't insult me by putting your guards outside.'

'How does that insult you? I don't understand.'

'Nana, people think I am a witch, someone who has mesmerized Rau with magical powers. That is why, they say, you have appointed the guards to prevent me from fleeing. If keeping me and Rau apart makes you happy, I give you my word – I will never meet him again. But don't doubt me, please. I am already suffering in the absence of Rau. Don't trouble me further.'

Nana stood up saying, 'Do I have your word? Please promise

me.' He put out his hand. Mastani looked at him for a moment and then put her palm on his. Nana squeezed it gently saying, 'You have held my hand and given me your word. Don't forget that.'

Mastani said, taking her hand away, 'I hope you will take the guards away.'

'The guards inside will not be required. The guards outside will continue.'

'That is fine. I am happy to hear that. Please give me leave now. Khuda hafiz!'

Nana, sitting on the carpet, admired her figure as she walked away towards her inner quarters.

The four-storeyed stable at Patas was the temporary residence of the Peshwa. He had been there for four days now but the restlessness had not reduced.

Baburao Phadnavis managed to get some office work done by the Peshwa. The campaign against Nasirgunj was being planned. The two brothers were to leave for the Godavari soon to intercept Nasirgunj's troops. But Bajirao was not able to put his mind to the job at hand. He merely skimmed through the papers, his mind elsewhere.

The day would somehow pass but nights were a torture for Bajirao. He would pace the hall restlessly. He had left Pune in a huff, knowing that his family members hated her. But he was worried for her health and safety. He was hoping that the sardars would be true to their word and ensure that no harm came to her. Unable to bear the separation any more, he called for Kunwar. He said, 'Please get my horse ready. I need to return to Pune right now.'

'Sarkar, it is not possible.'

'What? Why do you say that?' Bajirao shouted.

'The roads to Pune are cut off, sarkar. It is, I am told, to ensure that you are unable to return to Pune.'

'What do you mean? Who has cut them off?'

'I don't know, Swami. I just got the news from the servants here.'

'What temerity! No one was able to stop Bajirao when he marched on to Delhi. It seems whoever has done this does not care for his life! Get my horse ready and get two men with mashaals. Let the message be sent in advance – Bajirao Peshwa is returning to Pune. If anyone tries to stop him, he will have to face Bajirao's sword.'

Kunwar was about to reply but Bajirao's face was red with anger. He decided otherwise and left to implement the orders.

Soon, the syce brought in Bajirao's favourite horse. The two men holding the torches were already on horseback. Bajirao took his sword in his hand and spurred the horse in the direction of Pune.

As soon as they reached the canal at the border of Patas, they could see a group of men guarding the road. Bajirao shouted, raising his sword in the air, 'Move!'

Bajirao's challenge had no effect on the men. There were around fifty of them. They had not moved an inch and Bajirao had to rein in his horse to stop. He said, screaming in anger, 'The Peshwa is returning to Pune. Now, get out of my way!'

No one moved. In the light of the mashaals, Bajirao looked at the men. They had swords tied at their waist but none had unsheathed them. They stood with their heads bowed. No one dared to take out their weapon to challenge their master.

Bajirao looked at their leader and exclaimed, 'Is that Amrutrao Dhayber?'

'Yes, Swami. It is me.'

'And you dare to stand here, obstructing me?'

'I have been ordered to block all roads leading to Pune.'

Bajirao looked at the men standing with Amrutrao. He recognized Dhodopant Potnis, Janoji Dhamdhere, Tulaji Shitole, Subhaji Shelar – all standing like ordinary soldiers, but were, in fact, Bajirao's top sardars. He shouted once more, 'Get out of my way. Now!'

'It is not possible,' Dhamdhere replied.

'Then be prepared for the outcome. Once Bajirao raises his sword, it comes down only after beheading someone.'

No one moved despite the direct threat. Dhondopant stood as before, his spine straight, facing his master. He said, 'Shrimant, this body has borne the attacks of our enemies and has shed blood for my master. I have seen many naked swords threatening to take my life. The only one I had not seen was your shamsher. If this is what my fate decrees, then so be it! Please behead me, Swami. Let me be the first one to bear it. But don't ask me to move aside.'

The rest of the men too stood still, facing their Peshwa boldly. They were Bajirao's childhood friends, men who had fought with him shoulder to shoulder in many battles. Bajirao had grown up with them. He could clearly see the pain and the angst on their faces as they stood defiantly trying to block their master's way. Subhaji Shelar said, 'Swami, the road to Pune may be blocked but all other roads are open. The road northwards is where we have to intercept Nasirgunj. We are willing to lay down our lives for Swami's victory there. This is the first time Swami has raised his sword against us. It will be the last time. Give us a chance to show our loyalty. Lead us into a campaign and see how we lay down our lives for you. After that, you may go wherever you wish.'

Bajirao was in a strange dilemma. He had faced many complex situations before but never had it happened that his own men, with swords at their waist, were willing to boldly face their Peshwa for a cause they believed in and yet were not willing to take up arms. Unconsciously, he sheathed his sword and turned his horse in the direction of Patas. On reaching his haveli, he threw the sword on the diwan and said, 'Kunwar, get me my pitcher of wine. Let me see if I can see her eyes in the dark liquid.'

Gopika prepared a paan and offered it to Nana. It was a full moon night and Nana could see the lights of the distant Omkareshwar temple through the bushes. Wearing a long kurta with churidar pyjamas, Nana stepped out of his mahal and walked towards Mastani's twirling his moustache in eager anticipation.

He reached the gate and informed the guard, but did not wait for his return. Instead, he walked up the steps leading to Mastani's private quarters.

Mastani sat near an idol of Lord Krishna, praying. Surprised to see Nana at that late hour, she said, 'Nana, what a coincidence! I was just thinking about you.'

Nana smiled. 'When two minds meet, it is not necessary to communicate.'

Nana stood in the verandah. Mastani said, 'Why are you standing outside? Come in.'

The room was filled with the fragrance of dhoop and incense sticks. Surprised at the way the Krishna idol was decorated, he said, 'I did not know you pray to Lord Krishna.'

'Why not?'

Nana said, attracted by the way Mastani's eyebrows danced as she spoke, 'I mean, you are a Musalmaan. It surprised me to see you pray with such devotion.'

'Nana, there are unexpected events which change a person's life forever.'

'I have experienced such ... unexpected events that you talk of.'

Mastani's smile was enchanting. Nana felt it was a moment he had been waiting for. He said, holding her hand, 'You remember you had given me your word holding my hand?'

'Yes, I do.' Mastani nodded.

Caressing her hands, Nana said, 'Your hands are so beautiful!'

In an instant, Mastani realized what Nana was leading to. It was a bolt from the blue. She said, controlling her emotions, 'Your hands remind me of Shamsher. After all, a mother knows how gentle the touch of a son's hand can be.'

Nana recoiled in horror as if he had touched a snake. He said, stepping back, 'What do you mean?'

'Do I need to explain what a son is, Nana? Seeing you, my motherly love makes me want to feed you, to make you sit and chat for a while. Come, sit down here,' she said, pointing to a low seating arrangement.

Nana had beads of sweat on his forehead. His legs trembled and he sat down lest he fall. Mastani watched Nana's reaction and said, a gentle smile on her lips, 'Nana, I can read your thoughts. You did not realize it, but your face spoke volumes.'

Nana said, unable to face her, 'I am sorry, I made a mistake. Please pardon me.'

Mastani said, her voice sans any anger, 'Nana, one should think before stepping into fire. You are my son and it is a mother's duty to advise her son. Your father is already accused of doing things which a Brahman should not be doing – thanks to me. Now, unknowingly – yes, I mean unknowingly – you were going to commit a sin far more heinous. I know a little bit about religion, and incest would be the worst kind of sin, which is unpardonable.'

Nana had no courage to look at Mastani. He repeated, 'Matushree, I made a mistake. Please pardon me.'

Mastani continued, 'Nana, such a mistake can ruin one's life forever. Do you realize how your father would react were he to know of this? He would commit another crime of killing his own son.'

Nana was a changed person. Unable to hold his emotions any longer, he stood up and then fell at Mastani's feet. Hugging her feet, he cried, 'Matushree, please say that you have pardoned me. I beg you, please don't punish me.'

Mastani's eyes were moist. She held his shoulders and lifted him up. She hugged him saying, 'Nana, what else can a mother do other than pardon her son? Each part of my body cries out for you. You and Shamsher are no different for me. Please wipe those tears away.'

Nana tried wiping his tears but they continued to flow. He said, 'Matushree, it was only you who could have saved me. I am blessed.'

Mastani patted his back affectionately and said, 'Nana, many great men have fallen for such crimes. You are still so young! I know your immature mind decided to play a game. You were under the impression that Rau would hate me if he were to find out that I was enamoured by you. It is a pity that you have not realized that Rau and I are not two individuals any more. The bodies may be separated by force but our minds have merged into one. Had Rau seen you embracing me, he still would not have believed his own eyes for his faith in me transcends what his eyes would see!'

All Nana could do was to mutely follow Mastani as she made him sit on the diwan while serving him sweets.

Appa's palanquin stopped near his quarters at Shanivar wada. He was returning from his usual morning darshan when Mahadoba Purandare came in running and shouted, 'Shrimant! There has been a catastrophe!'

A shiver ran down his spine thinking of the many possibilities. He asked, 'What has happened?'

'We have been snubbed, Swami. Mastani has escaped from her haveli and run away.'

'When did this happen?'

'Last night.'

'On a full moon night? Were our guards sleeping?'

They both rushed to Mastani's mahal. Appa was stepping into her quarters for the first time. The guards stood with their heads bowed, worried about the kind of punishment they were likely to get. Appa stepped in and, for a moment, threw a surprised glance at the idol of Krishna. The flowers decorating the idol were fresh and had not dried. He stepped out of the mahal after peeping into the other rooms and enquired, 'Where is Nana?'

'I checked this morning and was told that he left for Kothrud gardens at dawn.'

Appa noticed a rope hanging from the boundary walls of the haveli, on the side which faced the river. He remarked, 'I am surprised that the dancer, who I am told is quite petite, has managed to scale a seven-foot wall.'

Appa was impressed at the way Mastani had escaped and said, 'Well, I am more surprised at why she was not born in a Brahman household. We would have happily got her married to Rau and been relieved of all this trouble.'

The news of Mastani's escape soon reached the bazaars and was the topic of discussion all around. The Brahmans now had another reason to gossip.

Appa sat conferring with Mahadoba Purandare in his chambers. He did not need the services of an astrologer to know Mastani's whereabouts. He was sure that having reached Patas, she would be in the arms of Bajirao by now. The question was 'what next?'

Mahadoba cleared his throat nervously and said, 'If you may ... I would like to suggest something.'

'Please go on,' Appa said.

'We have tried everything possible to keep Mastani and Rau apart, but it seems fate does not support us. Now the only option I see before us is to eliminate Mastani forever. That is the only way to get Rau back on track.'

Appa said, 'Mahadoba, I don't have the authority to issue such orders.'

'Who else has the authority, Shrimant?'

'Chhatrapati Swami. He is the only one who can decide. Please send him a chronology of the events till now. If he orders, we will take the next step.'

Mahadoba nodded his head.

The stable Patas had been converted into a temporary royal palace. A fortnight with Mastani seemed like heaven. The cold winter seemed enjoyable with the pleasant warm rays of the sun bathing the gardens the whole day. Bajirao and Mastani spent happy days together.

Pitchers of wine were being consumed, day and night. The mind and body were numb, indifferent to the happenings of the world around. All they knew was the union of two bodies and souls – Mastani and Bajirao, Bajirao and Mastani – fused into one. The lingering kisses, the unending embraces and the sweet words – it was romance at its peak, unbridled, unfettered and unaffected by reality.

Finally one night, Bajirao said, 'I feel you should return, Mastani. This dream world has to end.'

Kissing him gently on his lips, Mastani said, 'Where shall I return to?'

'To Pune, to the haveli.'

'I have managed to escape from that very place. You want me to go back there?'

Bajirao could feel a slight tremor in Mastani's body. He said, 'Yes, I do. I want you to go back there. It is your place.'

'No,' Mastani said hugging Bajirao tightly. 'I don't want to leave you. I would like to die in these arms.'

Bajirao caressed her affectionately saying, 'Dreams do not last forever, Mastani. We have to face reality sooner than later. Let us face the world together.'

'Rau, can you imagine what my state will be if I were to return to the haveli?'

'I cannot,' Bajirao uttered.

'Yet, you want me to return. Why?'

'I am bound by my promise. I don't want people to point fingers at me saying that I helped you escape.'

'Why bother about what people say? Have they bothered about us?'

'Not all questions can be answered, Mastani. Was it difficult for me to kill the sardars who were blocking my way? Could I not have stayed in the haveli defying the wishes of Matushree, Appa and others? But man is bound by some obligations, if not all. Your presence converts this ordinary house into heaven. But the night ends giving way to the day; similarly our togetherness has to end giving way to separation.'

Mastani hugged Bajirao in response. He continued, 'Mastani, it is time to leave.'

'Rau, what will I do when you are out on your campaign?'

'Don't worry. My men will take care of you.'

'It is impossible to think of being alone.'

She sobbed with her head on his chest. 'Rau, I have suffered a lot. It is not possible to explain the kind of torture I have gone through. If only you knew, you would not ask me to return.'

'Mastani, I am aware. Nothing is hidden from me. I know a mother will always forgive her son.'

Surprised at Bajirao's comment, Mastani looked up to face him. She said, 'Oh! That means ... that means, you know...'

Tears rolled down her cheeks as she was unable to complete her statement.

'Yes, I know. Yet I ask you to return. You belong there.'

'Why are you punishing me?' Mastani asked, in between her sobs.

'So that we can remain together forever.'

'Remain together – by staying apart?'

'My mother will pardon me soon enough. My brother too will understand. Then we don't need to meet in secret. They will send you to me the way a father sends his daughter in marriage. They may not do it wholeheartedly, but surely with their heads bowed in shame. Mastani, I want you to believe in the power of this embrace. I shall return soon – the moment the campaign is over. I will be camping on the banks of the Narmada. There we need not be bound by the norms of the Deccan. My mother and brother will send you there. Wait for that day! The meeting of Bajirao and Mastani will take place regally there.'

Mastani wiped her tears. She felt a little better. She looked at Bajirao trying to capture in her heart his face the way she was seeing him now. She said, 'I will do whatever you say. If that means I have to die, so be it.'

Then, losing her composure again, she fell into his arms shouting, 'Rau, Rau!'

It was dawn. Mastani stood up. The palanquin bearers were ready. Mahadoba Purandare had come personally to escort the palanquin. Mastani adjusted the dupatta around her head as she walked down the steps, accompanied by Bajirao. As soon as she sat down in the palanquin, she looked up at Bajirao. He asked, 'Anything else, Mastani?'

She whispered, 'Inshallah, we will meet soon!'

Mastani touched her palm to her forehead in aadaab as the bearers lifted the palanquin. The curtain was drawn and the bearers moved briskly towards Pune.

That afternoon Bajirao's men, led by Shinde and Holkar, moved towards the Godavari. Soon, Appa's men joined the main army and together they continued their journey northwards. The Nizam's son, Nasirgunj, waited for the Marathas at Ahmednagar. It was a battle for which preparations had gone on for months. The two armies clashed and, as expected, the Marathas overpowered the Nizam's army within days. Nasirgunj was captured and presented before the Peshwa. After a treaty at Paithan on the banks of the Godavari, the Nizam's son was able to return alive. He had to give in a lot to save his life.

The next day a messenger arrived from Pune with an urgent message for the Peshwa. Bajirao read the message and was shattered. He had been campaigning for three months single-mindedly and that one message tore his heart apart.

In the meantime, letters of congratulations were pouring in from the Chhatrapati and Paramhans Baba. Appa entered Bajirao's tent to give him the good news, but his face told a different story. He said, trying to smile, 'Rau's victory has been well received by the court at Satara.'

'But the news of my defeat has reached the banks of the Godavari.'

Bajirao's voice betrayed his emotions. It was clear he was deeply hurt. Appa asked, 'Have you received some bad news?'

Appa knew everything but had not expected that the events in Pune would be conveyed to the Peshwa with such alacrity. Bajirao flung the letter towards Appa saying, 'Read it for yourself!'

Appa glanced at the letter quickly and said, trying to put on a brave face, 'What can poor Nana do?'

'It is not his fault. It is my fate!' Bajirao taunted. 'I was born on an inauspicious day, Appa.'

'Rau, standing here on the banks of the holy Godavari, why do you speak such ill words. Today, everyone is celebrating your success.'

'So does that give anyone the right to arrest Mastani and put her in the haveli near Parvati?'

'Rau, I was helpless. What could I do?'

'Helpless? Appa, you were helpless? You are the one controlling everything and yet you use these words? It surprises me.'

'Mastani had managed to escape once despite the haveli being heavily guarded and hence Nana, with my advice, has put her under guard at the haveli in Parvati gardens.'

Bajirao had a crooked smile when he said, 'Appa, when man loses his sense of right and wrong, he loses his balance.'

'Are you saying I have lost my balance?'

'Yes, I am! My brother, whose very name is enough to make the enemies shiver, is saying he is afraid of a mere dancer? She managed to escape once and in response you have put her under heavy guard, is it? Appa, how much faith I had when I sent her back from Patas! I was hoping that you all would show a little bit of humanity. But my hopes have been shattered! The entire Maratha power is working to ensure that a harmless soul can remain under captivity. I never realized you would have to take recourse to using all forces to keep a hapless woman under your control. Appa, I know you deliberately carried out the sacred thread ceremony of my younger son and the marriage ceremony of the elder one, in my absence. I know many such events have taken place without my presence. The act of imprisoning her seems deliberate and with a vengeance against me. She is being treated like a criminal! Where else can I find such a superb example of brotherly love!'

Bajirao's taunts were not lost on Appa who said, 'Rau, I know you have been hurt but the world knows how much you have bothered about my feelings.'

Bajirao was enraged. He said, 'Did you even bother to find out what place Mastani holds in your brother's heart? We are not two but have fused into one. You have destroyed my faith in you now. I know you find me at fault. I believe Matushree too may feel that I am a blot on the Peshwa family but isn't there anything called pardon? I pardon hundreds of state prisoners and those who commit crimes against the Maratha throne. Isn't the Peshwa too entitled to some humanitarian considerations? Had I wished, couldn't I have had Mastani by my side in a matter of minutes? But I did not exercise my will beyond a point. You can take away everything except one's fate. And if fate so determines, things will happen the way they have to. Today is Krishna Panchami, the festival of colours. I will burn in my memories. I don't need anyone with me. I am going away across the Narmada where I can be with myself, away from others. Appa, please return to Pune.'

Appa said, a little worried, 'Rau, your health is not okay. On top of it, there is the pressure of the campaign. If you permit, I will return to Pune right away, release Mastani from her captivity and send her to you. I pray you to look after your health. Don't be so adamant!'

'Enough!' Bajirao shouted. 'I don't need to beg for my peace. Whatever I have got has been on my own strength. I am not going to plead with you to release Mastani. I had built Shanivar wada with a lot of passion but it seems fate has other plans for me. I am going to spend the rest of my life outside Pune. You, my son and Matushree can enjoy the wada. Please convey my regards to Matushree. Please tell her Rau always believed mothers have infinite compassion and an ability to forgive, but this is where I erred. I now realize all mothers are not the same. Appa, leave now! Let me be with myself!'

After two days, the cantonment moved. Chimaji Appa tried to meet Bajirao a couple of times but was unsuccessful. Dejected, he turned towards Pune while Bajirao marched northwards. The treaty with Nasirgunj had given the Marathas control over the parganas of Handa and Khargone. Bajirao wanted to reach the Narmada to take charge of the newly acquired territories. They reached Khandwa travelling through Burhanpur and Asirgarh. By the time they reached Raver Khedi, winter had ended and the warmth of the summer was perceptible.

Bajirao camped on the northern banks of the Narmada. He suffered from fever intermittently and, despite the objections from the scribes and other sardars, he would involve himself in office work and not take enough rest. The sardars, doing their rounds of the territories of Itwa, Badwahi and other such towns, would report their tax collections regularly.

Bajirao liked visiting a wooded area on the riverbank each afternoon for a siesta. He would read the letters arriving from the Deccan there. Each evening, wrapped in a shawl, he would return to his camp after a visit to the Rameshwar temple. Despite the heat, he shivered due to a mild fever. Kunwar, ever-alert, served at his master's feet, day and night.

He asked once, unable to control his feelings, 'Swami, I wish you would listen to me once.'

Bajirao's eyes were red with fever. He said, after a while, 'What is it, Kunwar?'

'You have not eaten a morsel in the last two days. Nor have you taken the medicines given by the vaidyaraj. How long can this go on?'

Kunwar was massaging Bajirao's legs. Bajirao moved his legs away saying, 'What else is left for me? Now things have to end!'

Kunwar hugged his feet and said, 'I cannot bear to hear such things, Swami! Please don't be so despondent. If this servant of yours has erred, please let him know.'

Bajirao smiled wryly. 'I have been doing things to please others – my family, my men and my sardars. But no one bothered to know what I wanted. If you insist, I will eat a little. Come, lay the plates. Let us eat together.'

Kunwar was overjoyed as he stood up, wiping his tears.

He laid the plates for the meal. Bajirao somehow managed to eat a little. After a lot of cajoling, he took the medicines too. Kunwar knew his master was merely indulging his wishes and no more. After a while, Kunwar helped Bajirao lie down on the bed, put the blanket over his feet and stepped out of the tent.

The next day, having sweated profusely through the night, Bajirao felt better. He called for the sardars and said, 'Tomorrow is Akshay Tritiya. We shall have our durbar on the banks of the river and honour our sardars there. But the privilege of honouring would be given to the shiladars. After all, they have fought with me shoulder to shoulder in all the campaigns.'

That evening, Bajirao received a message from Appa that Mastani had been released from her house arrest at Parvati gardens. Instead of a smile, Bajirao seemed even more pensive after that.

The durbar was in full flow but Bajirao could not sit for long. His fever had intensified again and he had to return to his tent. The men were slowly losing their confidence in his health and were dejected. A letter was sent to Pune.

In his delirium, he would shout and scream at his sardars. No one knew when he would pick up anything lying nearby and throw it at the person. Most of the sardars started avoiding the meetings. Bajirao's health deteriorated steadily.

It was a hot afternoon and, despite ardent pleas from his sardars, Bajirao jumped into the waters of the Narmada to cool himself. Janoji Dhamdhere and Tuloji Shitole dived in after him to ensure his safety.

Bajirao stayed in the water for nearly half an hour. His fever had abated but he shivered constantly. While others were sweating due to the heat, Bajirao's teeth chattered as he could not bear the cold. He was wrapped in a blanket and the palanquin bearers took him to his tent. After a while, he asked, 'How is Mastani?'

No one knew how to answer him and looked down.

'Oh, I see!' Bajirao said, and remained silent.

Bajirao's men sat around his bed. After a while, he seemed better. The sun had gone down and it was a little cooler. His fever had returned and soon he became unconscious. The men tried their best to do whatever it took – whether taking recourse to the Brahmans, giving ample donations, making fervent prayers at the temple or anything else. The Brahmans, assembled at the Rameshwar temple, chanted the Mrityunjay mantra continuously. Now with medicines showing no effect, the last resort was to fall at the feet of the Lord. Bajirao would talk incoherently in his sleep. Only Kunwar and the vaidyaraj were allowed inside the tent. The others – scribes, sardars and such – stood outside, feeling helpless and shattered.

A messenger arrived soon with the news that Kashibai was on her way with Janardhan Pant. Bajirao, in his semi-unconscious state, had no clue of her imminent arrival.

On the day of Ekadashi, Kashibai's palanquin finally reached Raver Khedi. She stepped out of the palanquin, holding Janardhan Pant's hand. As she entered Bajirao's tent, she was not sure of what she was expecting to see.

It had been six months since she had seen her husband.

Kashibai was shocked beyond belief on seeing Bajirao's face. The eyes had sunk deep into their sockets. The face, which normally glowed with confidence, had lost its colour. Kashibai stared at him for a few moments before she burst into tears. She asked, touching his feet, 'What have you done to yourself? What is it, Swami?'

Bajirao opened his eyes with a lot of effort. There was no one else in the tent. They were alone – the two of them, except for Kunwar who stood in a corner with his head bowed. Bajirao could barely keep his eyes open. He mumbled, 'Is that you, Mastani? You have come, is it? I knew! I was sure they would send you to me. See!'

Kashibai turned away unable to face him. She knew Bajirao was delirious. Kunwar gently stepped towards Bajirao and whispered, 'Swami, Kashibai sahiba has come from Pune. It is Matushree Kashibai!'

Bajirao barely heard him and replied, 'Yes, I know. I know Mastani would visit Rau. Mastani, why are you standing so far away? Come near me! Come into my arms. Normally you hug me the moment you see me. Why are you so far away today?'

Bajirao's voice was choked with emotion. He was quiet for a while. Kashibai, wiping her tears, stepped up to him and asked, holding his hand in hers, 'Kunwar, how long has he had this fever?'

'For eight days now.'

'And has there been any respite?'

'Not really. Despite our request to not jump in, he insisted on having a bath in the river which aggravated the fever.'

'What were you doing? Did you not stop him?'

Kunwar just stood with his head bowed in response. Kashibai gently massaged Bajirao's hand. She wanted to speak to him. He opened his eyes after a while and said, 'Mastani, I am feeling good. Your touch has always doused the fires of my body and soul. You know, Mastani, you have finally reached your husband's place. The doors of this haveli will remain open forever.'

Kashibai, unable to bear it any longer, stood up. She said, looking at Bajirao, 'Please don't exert yourself. You will be fine soon. Please lie down.'

Without trying to hold her tears back, she stepped out of the tent sobbing. Her tent had been set up next to Bajirao's. Kunwar followed her into her tent. She sat on the bed sobbing when he said, 'Baisaheb ... Baisaheb, please calm yourself.'

Wiping her tears, Kashibai said, 'I am fine, Kunwar. I trust the Lord will take care.'

Kunwar could not resist and said, 'I know ... till yesterday he was chanting your name all the time. I don't know why...'

Kashibai could not believe her ears. She said, putting her hand on his shoulder, 'Are you telling me the truth? Kunwar, is that true? Did he really ask for me?'

Kunwar said, in tears, 'You will not believe me, Baisaheb? I am at his bedside, day and night. He was remembering you the whole of yesterday.'

'What was he saying, Kunwar?'

Kunwar replied, 'He was saying, "Kashi has been with me for twenty years but has never hurt me. But one day, she shut the doors of her quarters on my face. She, the doors of whose heart and mahal, were always open for me, told me bluntly that I was not welcome any more! I had never imagined that even in my wildest dreams..." Baisaheb, he spoke a lot ... I don't know what to say!'

Kashibai was overwhelmed with emotion. She said, shaking his shoulders, 'Kunwar, I hope you are telling the truth! Or are you saying this just to please me?'

Kunwar fell at Kashibai's feet and said, 'I touch your feet and tell the truth, Baisaheb! He was asking for you the whole day. He said something and then fell asleep.'

'What was it? What did he say?'

'I could not understand everything as he was delirious but I could make out a few words. He said, "Kashi, I was not able to understand your devotion. You gave everything to me, Kashi! I never hated you but loved you always. Kashi, I may have behaved in whatever way, but one thing is for sure, your place in heaven is secure."'

Kunwar could not continue as his voice was choked with sobs.

It was late in the night. Kashibai sat at Bajirao's bedside. In the silence of the night, the sound of the Brahmans chanting the Mrityunjay mantra could be heard.

It was soon daybreak and the chattering of the birds woke up Bajirao. He was drenched in sweat and he looked fresh, as if he had woken up from a deep sleep. He said, looking at Kashibai, 'Mastani, I had managed to keep Death away but now there is no more resistance. I have fulfilled my promise, Mastani! Can you hear the voices outside, Mastani?'

Kashibai said, wiping her tears, 'It is dawn and it is the birds in the woods outside.'

'Oh, is that so?' Bajirao asked. 'It is the voice of the trumpets and horns, Mastani! They are your people. You know, they are bringing you to my place with full honours. You know how a newly-wed is escorted to her husband's place! Can you hear the trumpets and the shehnai?'

All Kashibai could do was turn her face away.

'Are you feeling shy, Mastani? I can understand! After all, you have come here as a newly-wedded bride. Hear the noise? They are all saying their goodbyes, as they bid you adieu. My Matushree, my brother, sons, everyone – they have all come to see you off. And why those tears? Oh, I know now! It is because Kashi is not there in the crowd, isn't it?'

Kashibai could not stop her sobs. Bajirao took her hand and said, 'Now, wipe those tears away, Mastani. Kashi ... Mastani ... they are both one and same to me. I believe they are no different ... Mastani ... Kashi ... Mastani.'

Suddenly, the hand holding Kashibai's went limp. Kashibai threw a surprised glance at Bajirao. His eyes were closed but a faint smile of contentment lingered on his lips. Within a moment, the truth dawned on Kashibai and she screamed, 'Swami! Swami! My Swami has left me!'

Saying so, she flung herself on his chest.

As if on cue, at that precise moment, the chanting of the Mrityunjay mantra stopped.